AF652477

प्रतिमानाटकम्

PRATIMĀNĀṬAKAM

श्रीः

महाकविभासप्रणीतं

प्रतिमानाटकम्

PRATIMĀNĀṬAKAM

OF

BHĀSA

Edited with a short Sanskrit Commentary, English Translation and Critical Notes by

M.R. KALE

MOTILAL BANARSIDASS PUBLISHERS
PRIVATE LIMITED • DELHI

First Edition: Bombay, 1930
Reprint: Delhi, 1977, 1983, 1991, 1995, 1998

ISBN: 81-208-0852-5

Also available at:

MOTILAL BANARSIDASS

41 U.A. Bungalow Road, Jawahar Nagar, Delhi 110 007
8, Mahalaxmi Chamber, Warden Road, Mumbai 400 026
120 Royapettah High Road, Mylapore, Chennai 600 004
Sanas Plaza, Subhash Nagar, Pune 411 002
16 St. Mark's Road, Bangalore 560 001
8 Camac Street, Calcutta 700 017
Ashok Rajpath, Patna 800 004
Chowk, Varanasi 221 001

PRINTED IN INDIA
BY JAINENDRA PRAKASH JAIN AT SHRI JAINENDRA PRESS,
A-45 NARAINA, PHASE I, NEW DELHI 110 028
AND PUBLISHED BY NARENDRA PRAKASH JAIN FOR
MOTILAL BANARSIDASS PUBLISHERS PRIVATE LIMITED,
BUNGALOW ROAD, DELHI 110 007

PREFACE

This edition of the Pratimā follows the same lines as those of the other plays edited by me.* It is based on the printed editions of the play, especially those of the late learned T. G. Shāstri and the late Prof. S. M. Paranjpe. I had a mind to bring out an edition of the play in 1927 and with that view had collected almost all the passages bearing on the incidents of the play from the Ayodhya and Araṇya kāṇḍas of the Rāmāyaṇa, and also had written part of the Sanskrit Com.; but as there was no prospect of the edition being ready in time, further work was stopped. In preparing this edition I have consulted Prof. Devadhars' ed. also in addition to the two mentioned above. I am indebted especially to Prof. Paranjpe's scholarly edition for some quotations and hints. In it he has displayed singular literary acumen. The English translation that it should be useful to the students ought to be close and neither indifferent nor loose. Again the notes ought to be to the point and must be neither too scanty nor unnecessarily prolix. This aim I have kept in view in preparing the present edition. I am however aware of the imperfections of this edition also. There are some obscure passages in the text and in spite of the learned commentary of the late M. M. G. Shastri the meaning of these remains uncertain though an attempt is made to interpret them in this edition. I acknowledge my grateful thanks to M. M. G. Śāstri and to Professors Paranjpe and Devadhar for the help derived from their editions. My thanks are due to Dr. Sukthankar, Mr. B. R. Hiwargaonkar and other Scholars, whose articles on Bhāsa were of great help in writing the

---

* The special features of these editions are--

A short Sanskrit commentary where an ancient commentary is not available. The Sanskrit rendering of the Prakrit passages given as part of the text for the convenience of students; an Introduction containing a brief outline of the Sanskrit drama, information about the Poet, criticism on the play, Characters of the principal dramatis personae etc.

introduction. My thanks are also due to my friend Mr. L. S. Bhandare B. A. S. T. C. to whom, owing to my continued ill health this year also, I had to leave the work of writing especially the critical remarks and the characters of the chief persons in the play. My thanks are due to D. V. Mulgaonkar Esq., the managing Proprietor of the firm of Messrs Gopal Narayen & Co., Book Sellers & Publishers, but for whose patronage the book would not have seen light this year.

M. R. KALE

BOMBAY,
March 1930.

PREFATORY NOTE TO THE PRESENT EDITION

This Second edition is reprint of the first edition.

Pages referred to the other works of the author in notes are pages of editions published after 1960.

December 1977.
25-B, Goodwill Bldg.
Mahim, Bombay-16/DD.

V.M. Kale

INTRODUCTION.

THE SANSKRIT DRAMA.[1]

We shall begin with a brief outline of the general structure and arrangement of the Sanskrit Drama, as developed by the later writers on dramaturgy.[2] Poetry in Sanskrit, from its inherent nature, as apart from its intrinsic merit, is divided into two kinds—दृश्य 'what is capable of being seen or exhibited' and श्रव्य 'what can only be heard or chanted. The drama falls under the first division. 'Rúpaka' is the general term in Sanskrit for all dramatic compositions, which also comprises a subordinate class called *Uparu'paka.* The Rúpaka,[3] which has Rasa or sentiment for its substratum, is divided into ten classes, *viz.* नाटकं सप्रकरणं भाणः प्रहसनं डिमः। व्यायोगसमवकारौ वीथ्यङ्केहामृगा इति ॥. Of the Uparúpakas or Minor Dramas there are eighteen varities, the most important of which are *Nâṭikás*, such as the Ratnâvalî, Viddhaśâlabhañjikâ, &c, *Troṭakas*, such as the Vikramorvaśiya, &c.

Having thus disposed of the divisions into which the whole of the scenic art is capable of falling, we turn to the principle of division among the *Rûpakas* themselves, which is threefold[4]—(1) वस्तु or the Plot of the play: (2) नेता or the

---

1 This Section is the same as that prefixed to my ed. of the Ratnávalî with some changes and omissions.

2 The information given here has been mainly culled from the Daśarûpaka.

3 अवस्थानुकृतिर्नाट्यं रूपं दृश्यतयोच्यते । रूपकं तत्समावेशाद्दशधैव रसाश्रयम् ॥ D.-R. रूप्यतेऽभिनयैर्यत्र वस्तु तद्रूपकं विदुः । नाटकाद्यैर्दशाविधम्. *Nâṭya* is another and perhaps a wider term for the drama or the dramatic art, and is so called because it represents the different situations in (the scenes presented by) life. The sage Bharata is the founder of the science of music and dramaturgy and his work is styled the *Nâṭya Sâstra.* *Nâṭya* is also called *Rûpa* inasmuch as it has *dṛisyatá* or the capability of being seen, and *Rupaka* inasmuch as its subject-matter is represented by actors assuming particular characters.

4 वस्तु नेता रसस्तेषां भेदकः ।.

Hero; and (3) रस or the Sentiment. These three are the essential constituents, nay, the very life-blood, of every dramatic piece. Each of these we shall succinctly deal with in its order.

---

1 VASTU OR THE PLOT.

Vastu is primarily of two kinds: आधिकारिक or 'principal and प्रासंगिक or 'accessory.' The Principal is that which relates to the chief characters or the persons concerned with the essential interest of the piece, and pervades the whole arrangement. The Accessory is that which appears in furtherance of the main topic, and is concerned with characters other than the Hero and the Heroine. This latter is of two kinds, *viz Patâkâ* and *Prakarî*. *Patâkâ* or 'banner' is an episode by which the progress of the plot is illustrated, furthered or hindered (so as to give additional interest to it). It is of considerable length and sometimes extends to the very end of a play. The *Prakarî* is also an episodical incident—of limited duration and minor importance—one in which the principal characters take no part. Besides these two, there are three other elements requisite for the development of the plot. These are बीज or the seed, बिन्दु or the drop, and कार्य or the final issue. *Bija*[1] is the circumstance leading to the ultimate end briefly stated, which, as the plot develops, bears multifarious results and which is, as it were, the seed of the plot. *Bindu*[2] is what cements a break in the plot caused by the introduction of some other incident. *Kârya* is the final object of the plot, which being attained the whole is finished. These five are technically called Arthaprakṛitis (अर्थप्रकृतयः).

The *Vastu,* which is thus divided into five classes, may again be divided into three classes according to the source of its derivation. It may be borrowed from history or tradition, or it may be fictitious, or mixed, *i. e.*, partly drawn from history and partly the creation of the poet's fancy. A *Nâṭaka* belongs to the first class, a *Prakaraṇa* to the second.

As regards its development a dramatic plot has five stages or conditions called *Avasthâs*. They are (1) आरम्भ beginning

---

1 स्वल्पोद्दिष्टस्तु तद्धेतुर्बीजं विस्तार्यनेकधा ।

2 अवान्तरार्थविच्छेदे बिन्दुरच्छेदकारणम् ।

or setting on foot of the enterprise, (2) यत्न effort, (3) प्राप्त्याशा prospect of success, (4) नियताप्ति certain attainment through the removal of obstacles, and (5) फलागम obtainment of the desired object. While these five stages are in progress, there must be some links to connect them with the principal and subordinate parts of the main action (the episodes and incidents). These are called the *Samdhis* or junctures. They are five in number, answering to the five *Arthaprakritis*, each of which they join with its corresponding stage, *viz.*, मुख (Protasis or the opening juncture), प्रतिमुख (Epitasis), गर्भ (catastasis), अवमर्श (Peripateia), and निर्वहण (Catastrophe), also called उपसंहृति or उपसंहार). Thus *Mukhasaṃdhi* is the combination of the Bîja and Ârambha, *i. e.*, wherein the seed is sown, so to speak, with all its *Rasas*. In the *Pratimukha* there is the means (*yatna*) to the chief end, as originally implied by the Bîja in the Mukha which herein sprouts up. In the *Garbha* there is attainment and non-attainment of the desired end, implying a further sprouting up of the orginal Bîja. There are impediments, but the main plot gains ground under resistance. The *Avamarshasaṃdhi* is that in which the seed attains a more luxuriant growth than in the *Garbha*, being accompanied by *Niyatâpti* of the end, but whose final result is postponed further off by fresh impediments of various sorts, as in the Śákuntala the King's forgetting Śak. 'ter marriage owing to Durvásas' curse. The *Nirvahana* or consummation is the harmonious combination of all the aforesaid parts leading to the final catastrophe.

The subject-matter, whether historical, fictitious, or mixed, is, from its inherent nature, capable of a twofold division. It is divided into (1) सूच्य—deserving to be suggested or implied only, as being of a dry and otherwise unfit character; and (2) दृश्यश्रव्य-fit to be represented and heard as being highly sentimental and pleasing. The suggestions or implications are made in five ways—विष्कम्भचूलिकाङ्कास्याङ्कावतारप्रवेशकैः। of these Bhása has made use of प्रवेशक and विष्कम्भक, for which see notes.

The subject-matter is further divided into three kinds—सर्वश्राव्यं or प्रकाशं, अश्राव्यं or स्वगतं and नियतश्राव्यम्. The last is of two kinds, जनान्तिक and अपवारितक or अपवार्य. Independent of these divisions there is one called आकाशभाषित (आकाशे) or speech from the void.

2 NETA OR THE HERO.

The Hero is required to be modest, decorous, comely, munificent, civil, of sweet address, eloquent, sprung from a noble family, &c.[1] Heroes are mentioned as of four kinds, *viz.*, **धीरोदात्त, धीरललित, धीरशान्त** and **धीरोद्धत**. **धीरोदात्त**[2] or the hero of sublime qualities is one who is magnanimous, patient, not given to boasting, self possessed, of firm resolve, whose high-spirit is concealed and who is true to his engagements, as Ráma. '*Dhiralalita*,' or Hero who is graceful and firm, is defined as निश्चिन्तो मृदुरनिशं कलापरो धीरललितः स्यात्। (Sáh. D. III. 23) *i. e.*, one who is free from cares, ever gentle and always given to the arts, like Vatsarâja We are not concerned with the other two classes of Heroes here. Each of these Heroes may be of one or other of four sorts. He may be, **दक्षिण** or 'gallant,' *i. e.*, equally devoted to many women, though principally attached to one; or **शठ** 'sly' *i. e.*, one who being attached to one lady, covertly acts in a way unpleasant to her; or he may be **धृष्ट** 'bold,' openly making his professions to another, and not ashamed even when reproached; or lastly he may be **अनुकूल** 'favourable,' devoted to one Heroine only. The धीरोदात्त Hero has eight manly qualities—शोभा, विलास, माधुर्य, गाम्भीर्य, धैर्य, तेजस्, लालित्य and **औदार्य**.

The Náyikâ or the Heroine who must be possessed of qualities similar to those of the Hero is of three kinds.[3] She may be the wife of the hero (स्वीया), as Sîta in the Pratimâ or the Uttar.; or one belonging to another (अन्या or परकीया), or a common woman (सामान्या or साधारणस्त्री) as Vasantasenā in the Mrich. Further details are not given here as not being required for the present play.

---

3 RASA OR SENTIMENT.

Rasa is that lasting impression of feeling produced to his everwhelming delight in a man of poetic susceptibility by

---

1. नेता विनीतो मधुरस्त्यागी दक्षः प्रियंवदः। रक्तलोकः शुचिर्वाग्मी रूढवंशः स्थिरो युवा ॥ बुद्ध्युत्साहस्मृतिप्रज्ञाकलामानसमन्वितः। शूरो दृढश्च तेजस्वी शास्त्रचक्षुश्च धार्मिकः ॥ भेदैश्चतुर्धा ललितशान्तोदात्तोद्धतैरयम् ॥

2. महासत्त्वोऽतिगंभीरः क्षमावानविकत्थनः। स्थिरो निगूढाहंकारो धीरोदात्तो दृढव्रतः ॥ D. R.

3. स्वान्या साधारणस्त्रीति तद्गुणा नायिका त्रिधा।

the proper action of the *Vibhávas,* and *Anubhávas*, as well as the *Sâttvika*-bhâvas and the *Vyabhichâribhávas*,.[1] Bhava (भाव) or 'feeling' is the complete pervasion of the heart by any emotion, whether of pleasure or of pain, arising from the object under sight. Vibháva (विभाव) or an Excitant is that which being perceived nourishes the main sentiment. It is divided into (1) *Âlambana*, that which is, as it were, the support or substratum of the Rasa—the person or thing with reference to whom or which a sentiment arises—such as the Hero or the Heroine, and (2) *Uddípana* or what excites or enhances (adds to the development of) the sentiment, such as the moon, the beauties of the vernal season, &c ; beauty, decorations, &c. of the principal characters, in the case of शृङ्गार. *Ânubháva* or an Ensuant is the outward manifestation of the internal feeling through the eyes, face &c. The Sâttvika or natural *bhâvas* are a subdivision of *Anuabâva*, and are mentioned as eight in number—स्तम्भप्रलयरोमाञ्चाः स्वेदो वैवर्ण्यवेपथू । अश्रुवैस्वर्यमित्यष्टौ । The *Vyabhichâris* or the Accessories are those *bhâvas* which are not strictly confined to any *Rasa*, but appearing and disappearing like waves in the ocean, they serve as feeders to the prevailing sentiment and strengthen it in different ways. *Stháyibháva* (स्थायिभाव) or the Permanent Sentiment[2] of a composition is one—the ocean melting all salt into water—which, not being interrupted by any sentiment contrary or akin to its nature occurring at intervals, converts all of them into its own nature.' Now a *Rasa* would prove contrary to another if the आश्रय or substratum of both were the same. But as अङ्गी (principal) and अङ्ग (subordinate) a रस may be mixed with one or more of others.

There are eight Sthâyibhâvas, रति, हास, शोक, क्रोध, उत्साह भय, जुगुप्सा, and विस्मय on which are based respectively the sentiments—शृङ्गार the Erotic, हास्य the Comic, करुण the Pathetic, रौद्र the Furious, वीर the Heroic, भयानक the Terrible, बीभत्स the Loathsome, and अद्भुत the Marvellous. There is a ninth sentiment, that of शान्त the Quietistic, having शम or tranquillity for its Sthâyibhâva. But it is not suited to dramatic purposes

---

1. विभावैरनुभावैश्च सात्त्विकैर्व्यभिचारिभिः । आनीयमानः स्वाद्यत्वं स्थायी भावो रसः स्मृतः ॥ सुखदुःखादिकैर्भावैर्भावस्तद्भावभावनम् । ज्ञायमानतया तत्र विभावो भावपोषकृत् ॥ आलम्बनोद्दीपनत्वप्रभेदेन स च द्विधा । अनुभावो विकारस्तु भावसंसूचनात्मकः ॥

2. विरुद्धैरविरुद्धैर्वा भावैर्विच्छिद्यते न यः । आत्मभावं नयत्यन्यान्स स्थायी लवणाकरः ॥.

and rarely occurs as a main sentiment in a drama. Of these eight sentiments शृङ्गार and हास्य, वीर and अद्भुत, बीभत्स and भयानक, and रौद्र and करुण are akin to each other as they proceed from the same condition of the mind.

---

4 THE GENERAL CONDUCT OF THE NÂTAKA.

Every dramatic piece opens with a Prelude or Prologue (प्रस्तावना) which is itself introduced by what is called the *Nândi*. This *Nândî* according to some must suggest the gist of the whole plot. The Sûtradhâra may sometimes retire after the recital of the Nândî, in which case another actor, called स्थापक (for he *establishes* as it were the topic of the play), takes his place. In the Prelude, which may begin with a brief allusion to the poet's literary attainments, his genealogy, &c., the Sûtradhâra or the Sthâpaka suggests the subject in the form of the Bîja, or by a simple beginning, or by naming the character about to enter, as in the Śákuntala. He must please the audience with sweet songs descriptive of some season and couched in the Bhârátî Vṛitti. The प्रस्तावना is of two kinds—(1) प्ररोचना as in the Ratn., and (2) आमुख, in which the Sûtradhâra holds conversation with the actress or his assistants, bearing on the subject to be introduced. This latter is of three kinds, of which one is प्रयोगातिशय. When the entry of a character is directly indicated by the Sûtradhárâ, saying 'Here he enters,' that is Prayogâtiśaya.

The Prelude being over, the piece is commenced, being hereafter arranged and exhibited in the manner indicated in the three foregoing Sections. The whole matter should be well determined and divided into Acts and Scenes. A Nâṭaka may consist of from five to ten acts. The Hero should be of the Dhîrodátta class. The Sentiment should be शृङ्गार or वीर (or sometimes करुण), others being introduced as conducive to its development. Nothing should be introduced into the play, which either misbeseems the Hero or is discordant with the main sentiment. An Act must not be tiresomely long, should be full of *Rasa* and introduced by *Vishkhambhaka*, &c, according to necessity. Its close is marked by the exit of all characters Such incidents as journeys, m cres, wars &c., should not be represented in a play; they ay only be indicated. The death of the Hero must never be exhibited. This accounts for the somewhat monotonous character of Sanskrit plays, and the absence of tragedies in Sanskrit.[1] The play should end, as it began, with a Benediction or prayer, called the Bharatavâkya, which is generally repeated by the principal personage, not in his dramatic character but as a member of the dramatic party (भरत), and contains an expresion of their wishes for general prosperity and happiness. The unity of interest or action must be maintained throughout.

As regards the language to be used in a piece, the Hero and the higher characters speak in classical Sanskrit while females and the minor characters speak in the different Prákrit dialects.

The student will see from the foregoing sketch that the characteristic peculiarities of the Indian Drama are mainly three—(1) Its peculiar structure; (2) the absence of the distinction between Comedy and Tragedy; and (3) the diversity of language to be spoken by the characters. The above-mentioned general characteristics of a Nâtaka belong with certain modifications to the other divisions of the Rûpaka as well.

BHĀSA'S PLAYS.

By the discovery of thirteen dramas about the year 1909–10, by the late Mm. Ganapati Shástri of Trivendrum, it seemed that the lost treasure of the plays of the famous dramatist Bhása was recovered and Bhása ceased to be a mere name. The names of these thirteen plays are :—(1) मध्यमव्यायोग (2) पञ्चरात्र (3) दूतवाक्य (4) दूतघटोत्कच (5) कर्णभार (6) ऊरुभङ्ग (7) प्रतिमा (8) अभिषेक (9) बालचरित

1 Wilson observes—They (the Hindu plays) never offer a calamitous conclusion, which, as Johnson remarks, was enough to constitute Tragedy in Shakespeare's days; and although they propose to excite all the emotions of the human breast, terror and pity included, they never effect this object by leaving a painful impression upon the mind of the spectator. The Hindus in fact have no Tradegy............The absence of tragic catastrophe in the Hindu dramas is not merely an unconscious omission; such a catastrophe is prohibited by a positive rule. The conduct of what may be termed the classical drama of the Hindus is exemplary and dignified. Nor is its moral purport neglected; and one of their writers declares, in an illustration familiar to ancient and modern poetry, that the chief end of the Theatre is to disguise, by the insidious sweet, the unpalatable, but salutary bitter, of the cup.

(10) प्रतिज्ञायौगन्धरायण (11) स्वप्नवासवदत्त (12) अविमारक and (13) चारुदत्त. The first six of these are based on the Mahâbhârata, प्रतिमा and अभिषेक on the Rámâyaṇa, बालचरित on Harivanṃsha, प्रतिज्ञायौगन्धरायण and स्वप्नवासवदत्त are based on the stories of Vatsarája and Vāsavadattā, which were current in the poet's time. They could not have been based on the Bṛhatkathá of Gunádhya, as Bhása was much anterior to him. The sources of अविमारक and चारुदत्त cannot be definitely traced. Unfortunately, in none of the manuscripts the name of the writer of these plays is mentioned. Mr. Ganapati Śástri, however, after having subjected these dramas to a critical examination came to the conclusion that all the thirteen dramas were written by one author and that author was Bhâsa of great fame, so highly praised by Kálidása and other poets. This Bhāsa theory propounded by Ganapati Shástri and supported by scholars like Mr. S. M. Parànjape Hiwargaokar, Keith, Thomas, has been strongly contested by eminent scholars like Mr. P. V. Káne, Rangácharya Raddy, Bhattanáth Shastri, Dr. Barnett and Messrs. Krishna Pisharodi and Rama Pisharodi. Between these two extremes stand Dr. Sukthankar and Prof. Winternitz, who accept the Bhāsa theory with reserve, as in their opinion the evidence so far adduced is not quite conclusive

Most of these scholars agree that all the thirteen plays are written by one and the same author. The grounds on which the common authorship of the plays has been established may be briefly stated thus:—

(1) All these plays begin with the stage-direction नान्द्यन्ते ततः प्रविशति सूत्रधारः, whereas the classical dramas begin with the नान्दी (followed by नान्द्यन्ते सूत्रधारः).

(2) In these plays the word स्थापना is invariably used for the prologue, whereas in the classical dramas the word प्रस्तावना is used.

(3) In none of these plays the name of the dramatist is mentioned, whereas in the classical plays the name of the dramatist and his family history are given.

(4) In most of these dramas the names of the chief Dramatis Personae are mentioned in the opening verse. This is technically called मुद्रालंकार.

(5) The भरतवाक्यs of the plays are almost the same. 'इमामपि महीं कृत्स्नां राजसिंहः प्रशास्तु नः । is repeated with a slight variation in many plays.

(6) Striking similarity in the language and style of the plays. The use of the same imagery, the repetition of the same peculiar words, expressions, sentences, stanzas and quadrants of verses.

(7) In these plays grammatical solecisms or archaisms (आर्षप्रयोगs) are very common.

(8) In most of these plays a dramatic device called पताका-स्थान (*i. e.* a sort of dramatic irony) is used.

The principal arguments which Ganapati Shastri has advanced to support his Bhāsa theory may be briefly stated thus :—

(1) The technique of all these plays, such as the commencement made by the सूत्रधार, the non-mention of the poet in the introductory part of the dramas &c. shows that the poet lived in times before the practice of beginning with the नान्दी and the mentioning of the poet's name came into vogue.

(2) The numerous grammatical archaisms (आर्षप्रयोगs) in disregard of Pánini's rules show that the author of these plays must have lived long before Pánini.

(3) The disregard that is shown to certain rules found in the *Nátyas'ástra* in these plays, shows that their author was an ancient poet.

(4) These plays are characterised by an intensity of *Rasa* and by a marvellously exquisite flow of language and an all round grace of poetical elegance common only to the archaic compositions of the sages like *Válmiki, Vyása.* This shows that the author of these plays was an archaic poet of renown and lived in times when Sanskrit was a spoken language.

(5) Tradition ascribes the authorship of the *Svapnavasavadatta*, one of these thirteeen plays, to Bhása. Therefore the author of the Svap. and the other closely similar plays must be Bhása himself, who has been extolled by Kálidasa and Bāna.

(6) Kálidása has borrowed some expressions and ideas from some of these plays. A poet like Kálidása would imitate only a great poet like Bhása, whom he has highly praised and placed at the head of the ancient poets of great renown.

These arguments with the exception of 1 and 5 are not very sound.

(2) The assertion that Bhása is prior to Páṇini cannot be correct. The grammarian connot be later than 500 B. C. While Bhása who is certainly later than Udayana, the hero of the Svapnavásavadatta, must be placed after 450 B. C. The archaisms in Bhása may, however, be due to Pàn's. grammar not having been so universally recognised in the short interval that separated the two as it was in after times.

(3) Bhása cannot be regarded as anterior to Bharata, the author of the Nátyaśástra. For Kálidâsa in his Vikramorvaśîya * clearly regards Bharata, of hoary antiquity, as a divine sage—a muni who could have a free access to the assembly of the gods, while he speaks of Bhāsa only as a poet who was his predecessor.

4. The Śástri argues from the simplicity and archaisms in the plays that they were written at a time when Sanskrit was a living language. But if Bhása lived after 450 B. C, as shown above, then certainly he lived at a time when Sans. had ceased to be a spoken language (except it may be in the case of the Pandits). For even Buddha thought it necessary to preach in the Pali language, as Sanskrit could not be understood by the masses.

6. The Śástri argues that Kálidása has consciously borrowed several ideas and expressions from his illustrious predecessor. We cannot allow this to go unchallenged. For Bhása himself may be shown to be indebted to the two epics for many of the ideas and expressions found in his plays. We concede so far that Kálidàsa might have read Bhàsa's plays and unconsciously worked up some of his ideas in his plays. But it is certainly hazardous to assume that a poet of first rate genius like Kálidasa should seek to rise to eminnce by borrowing a few ideas and picking up a few things from his predecessor, however great he may be. Again, it is not unalloyed praise that Kálidása has bestowed on Bhása, as Bána and some others have done. For after referring to Bhâsa, Saumilla and others (as of wide renown) he says—

पुराणमित्येव न साधु सर्वं न चापि काव्यं नवमित्यवद्यम् ।
सन्तः परीक्ष्यान्यतरद्भजन्ते मूढः परप्रत्ययनेयबुद्धिः ॥

Here evidently Kálidàsa calls those people fools who judge of the excellence of a Kávya merely because it is old; and he

---

* मुनिना भरतेन यः प्रयोगो भवतीष्वष्टरसाश्रयो नियुक्तः । ललिताभिनयं तमद्यभर्ता मरुतां द्रष्टुमनाः सलोकपालः ॥ II. 18.

requests those who are competent to judge for themselves to deliver their verdict on the score of merit. Obviously, therefore, Káli. endeavours here to vindicate his superior claim to greatness as a poet and dramatist.

We do not propose here to deal with the arguments that have been adduced in favour of or against the authenticity of these plays. That we have done in our introduction to the Svapnavásavadatta. We must, however, admit the following facts:—

1 From the references to Bhása directly by his name by Kálidàsa, Bāṅa and others and from the quotations by poets like Dandin, it is clear that there was a poet Bhása by name, who enjoyed great reputation as a dramatist for many centuries.

2 From the two references to Svapnavàsavadatta ; by Abhinavagupta, *viz.* कचित्क्रीडा यथा स्वप्नवासवदत्तायां &c. and संचितपक्ष्मकपाटं &c. (see pp. 17, 20 Introd. to Svapna) it is evident that the play known to him was at least partially different from the Svap. of the Triv. series and that it was in all probability a larger work comprising more Acts and scenes than it. Again Śáradátanaya when pointing out, in his भावप्रकाश, the stages of the action of the Svap. (see Introd. p. 18.) says that Udayana formed a conjecture on seeing the *tilaka* mark on the face of Padmávatí about the existence of Vásavadatta; and as such a scene is quite out of place in the play, the conclusion follows that the Svap. before him was also a larger work.

Hence it seems and also from the omission in it of the Śloka पादाक्रान्तानि पुष्पाणि (Intro. p. 19) that the Svap. in its present form is an abridged edition of the original Svap. of Bhása and not the genuine work in its entirety. And what is true of the Svap. may be true of the other plays also.

All this leads us to believe that the present plays, while preserving the language and ideas of the original works may more or less be adaptations made for the convenience of the stage by the Chakkyars or, the hereditary actors of Malabar as held by Messrs A. K. Pishárodi and K R. Pishárodi. The principal arguments on which the Pishárodis base their theory are—That there was a large demand for dramas suitable for the reformed Kerala stage, that dramas were compiled to meet this demand, that there is a tradition that such compilations were made in ancient times and that select acts from some of these thirteen plays were staged by the Chakkyars. But where is the evidence to prove that the Trivandrum group of plays are compilations made by the Chakkyars? The above arguments prove nothing regarding the thirteen plays except that select acts from some of them were staged by the Chakkyars.

After a careful examination of the evidence adduced and the arguments set forth by the protagonists and opponents of the Bhāsa theory, we maintain that the evidence in favour of the Bhāsa theory is much stronger and we are led to the conclusion that the author of the Sv. group of plays, even as they are, is the ancient poet Bhása of great fame in Sanskrit literature

THE DATE OF BHA'SA.

The date of Bhàsa, like that of many other Sanskrit writers is very difficult to determine for want of sufficient data and of reliable chronology to draw our conclusion from. It is not possible to accurately fix the date of Bhása. All that we can do with the help of the scanty materials at our disposal is to fix approximately the limits of the period during which the poet must have flourished. That Bhása is an ancient poet, much anterior to Kálidása, is a fact established beyond doubt by the very reference to him by that poet in the prologue of the Málavikágnimitra. The internal evidence of his style which is absolutely free from the artificiality of the Kávya literature, the presence of a number of archaic forms and uncouth constructions in his works, the old-world atmosphere in which his characters move-all these point to his great antiquity. And we have shown in our introduction to Svap. (see pp. XXII, XXIII) that he can reasonably be placed between 450—370 B. C.; and in this view Prof. Paranjpe also concurs.

This may be clear from this play also. For in the Vth Act Bhása makes Rávaṇa speak of an Arthaśastra by Bṛhaspatî. So he does not seem to be aware of the existence of Chânakya's Arthaśastra, which he would have certainly referred to, had he lived after Chánakya. The Mahábhárata (Śanti p. 59) tells us that Bṛhaspati was a writer on Arthaśástra, who epitomised the original Dandanīti composed by Brahma. Kautilya too acknowledges Brihaspati as his predecessor as a writer on Arthaśástra. It follows, therefore, that Chaṇa.'s Artha. was not in existence in Bhása's time. So it may be concluded that Bhása could not have been later them 370 B. C.

BHASA'S MERITS AS A DRAMATIST.

Bhása was certainly a talented dramatist judging from the number and variety of his dramas. The principal characteristics of his plays that strike the reader most are their simplicity in construction, naturalness in style, and realism in description as well as the dramatic qualities of vigour, life and action and sharpness of characterisation. The plot of each drama is unfolded in a few effective situations that follow each other in their natural sequence and that are calculated to bring out the sentiment in hand. The style is simple, clear and sweet.* It is free from all artificiality and rhetorical devices naticeable in the later Sanskrit dramas The words are simple and apt. Long compounds and elaborate figures of speech so common in the later Sánskrit literature are conspicuous by their absence. The compounds used by Bhàsa consist at the most of six or seven words and these too are rarely used. Sometimes we come across an artificial style with the use of alliteration and Yamakas.† The figures that commonly embellish his style are the Upamâ and Utpreksha. Far-fetched conceits are never indulged in. In spite of its simplicity, Bhasa's style is sometimes obscure. Sentences are sometimes elliptical and it is difficult to get at their meaning unless we supply the ellipsis. Sometimes the connection between sentences is left by the poet to be found out by their reader. It is his compressed style that makes some part of Bhása's writing obscure; and the reader in order to clear up the obscurities must have recourse to a comparison with his originals, the Ràmayana and the Mahabharata as well as his own works. Another feature of Bhāsa's style that contributes to its obscurity is his use of

---

*(1) गुणानां वा विशालानां सत्काराणां च नित्यशः ।
कर्तारः सुलभा लोके विज्ञातारस्तु दुर्लभाः ॥ (Sv. Act IV. 9).

(2) काष्ठादग्निर्जायते मथ्यमानाद् भूमिस्तोयं खन्यमाना ददाति ।
सोत्साहानां नास्त्यसाध्यं नराणां मार्गारब्धाः सर्वयत्नाः फलन्ति ॥
(Praty. Act 1-18).

(3) शिक्षा क्षयं गच्छति कालपर्ययात् सुबद्धमूला निपतन्ति पादपाः
जलं जलस्थाना गतं च शुष्यति हुतंच दत्तंच तथैव तिष्ठति ॥
(Karnabhara Sl. 19)

(4) कथं लम्बसटः सिंहो मृगेण विनिपात्यते ।
गजो वा सुमहान् मत्तः सृगालेन निहन्यते ॥ (Abh. Act. III-19

† (1) रघुकुलप्रदीपस्य सर्वलोकनयनाभिरामस्य रामस्य च सुविपुलमहाग्रीवस्य सुग्रीवस्य च &c (Abhisheka).

forms of words and expressions that became obsolete in the later Sanskrit literature. The archaic or ungrammatical forms and constructions clearly show that the style of Bhāsa was greatly influenced by the style of the Epics. Bhása no doubt drew his inspiration from the Epics and the dominating influence of the Epics is clearly seen everywhere in his dramas. Along with many beautiful expressions and ideas of the Epics, along with their naturalness and simplicity of diction, Bhasa seems to have unconsciously adopted even the solecisms from his great originals.

Bhāsa's descriptions are simple, natural and straightforward. He aims more at producing cumulative effect by grouping together striking details than finishing his pictures with a few suggestive strokes. His descriptions, beautiful and realistic as they are, are never touched with the glow of imagination, and are never lifted into the sphere of the sublime like those of Kálidasa and Bhavabhûti.

Bhása's characters are sharply distinguished or individualised. Every character is strongly marked with its own individuality, and made to help the development of the plot, each in its way. The predominance of male characters and the martial spirit exhibited by most of them is a notable feature of Bhāsa's dramas. The dramas clearly reflect the spirit of an heroic age.

One of the striking features of Bhāsa's dramas is the use of a dramatic device called पताकास्थान in order to excite astonishment. In the *Pratijnanataka* (Act, II), Mahasena, father of Vāsavadattā and his queen are speaking about the merits of the several suitors of Vāsavadattā. The King then asks his queen, "Which of these, do you think, is worthy of our daughter"? Presently a chamberlain enters and says, 'Vatsaraja.' He brings the joyful tidings of Vatsarȧja's capture and being unable to contain himself with joy bursts out "Vatsaraja.' Similarly in the Abhisheka (Act V), when Ravaṇa taunts Sîtá and says to

---

(2) निहतपतितगजतुरगनररुधिरकलिलभूमिप्रदेशस्य विक्षिप्तवर्म चर्मातपत्रचामरतोमरशरकुन्त &c. (Urubhanga P. 90).

(3) सम्प्राप्ता हरिवरबाहुसम्प्रगुप्ता.
किष्किन्धा तव नृप बाहुसम्प्रगुप्ता । (Abhisheka I–7).

(4) शून्यः प्राप्तो यदि रथो भग्नो मम मनोरथः ।
नून दशरथं नेतुं कालेन प्रेषितो रथः ॥ (Pratima. II–11).

her, "When that wretch of a mortal together with his brother Lakshmaṇa is killed by Indrajit, by whom wilt thou be set free"? A Rākṣasa enters and says, "By Ràma."

Lastly a word about the influence of Bhása on the later Sanskrit literature. The influence of Bhása is seen in very few instances in the dramas of Kalidasa. About his ref rence to Bhâsa* in his introduction to the Málavikágnimitra we have said our say elsewhere (see *supra* p). But we must admit that sometimes the coincidence of the descriptions of the same scenes and events is so striking that we cannot but feel that Kálidasa drew his inspiration from Bhāsa†. Mr. Ganapati Śástri's remark, 'That the dramatic excellence of Bhása has been a model for Kálidasa could well be established from the fact that the Śàkuntala is mostly adorned with the ideas and expressions peculiar to Bhāsa" must be taken in the light of an over-enthusiastic admirer of Bhása. And even what Kálidasa has borrowed bears the unmistakable stamp of his individuality and conclusively proves the immense superiority of the premier poet of India over his illustrious predecessor.

The Play

The Pratima is based on the principal incidents of Rámá's life as told in the Ayodhayâkand and the Aranyakánda of the Ráma., with the additional incident of his return to Ayodhyá after Sitá's rescue and his coronation as the king of the earth. The other Ràma play, Abhisheka, derives its materials mainly from the Kishkindhá, Sundara and Yuddhakándas of the Rámayaṇa. The poet has also introduced several innovations of his own in the development of the plot. It is thus a play based partly on historical matter and partly on the poet's creative faculty. It is named Pratima owing to the Statue or Pratima of Daśaratha, which Bharata saw in the statue-house and being informed of his father's death and the exile

* प्रथितयशसां भाससौमिल्लकविपुत्रादीनां प्रबन्धानतिक्रम्य वर्तमानकवेः कालिदासस्य क्रियायां कथं परिषदो बहुमानः ।

† Of the description of अशोकवन in the *Abhisheka* with Kanva's address to the creepers in the fourth act of the Śákuntala and the descriptions of the earth as it appears to Meghanáda descending down from above in the *Avimaraka* and to Dushyanta coming down from heaven to Hemakuta in the Shakuntala.

of his brother, Ráma with Sitá and Lakshmaṇa, he made up his mind straight to go to the forest where his brother was, rejecting the proposal of his coronation made by Vasishtha, Vámadeva and the citizens. It thus helps the development of the plot in some way. The poet, however, is not very happy in inventing this scene. For Bharata on reaching the edifice does not know what house it was, whether it was a temple of some deity. On entering it Bharata comes to know that it is the house containing the statues of the kings of the Ikshváku race. But when was the house built? Certainly not when Bharata left for his maternal uncle's country; for in that case he would have known about it. Again why did it contain the statues of four kings only, if the Ikshvákus were to be commemorated? How also could the tatue of Dasaratha come to be there within fifteen days of his death, when his obsequies even were not performed? But this difficulty might be obviated by the supposition that Daśaratha built the statue-house after Bharata had gone to his maternal uncle's house and also had got his statue made ready to be set up there as soon as his death would occur. But still the Pratima is not the turning point of the play, so that it could have been named after it, as the clay cart is, as the ornaments of gold given by Vasantasena to Chandala's son to make a gold play-cart in place of the clay-cart, which plays an important part in the further development of the plot of the Mṛchchakatika. It has no connection with the plot. Bharata could have as well gone to the forest after having learned in Ayodhyá about his brother's exile in the forest.

TIME ANALYSIS AND DURATION OF THE ACTION.

The action of the play covers a period of 14 years. The time of action of the 1st Act is the morning of the 10th day of the bright half of the month of Chaitra on which the coronation of Ráma, was to take place as is clear from Vasishthá's words— प्रातस्त्वामभिषेकाहि यौवराज्ये नराधिपः । Ayod. V. 10. and इति प्रत्यर्चितान्राजा ब्राह्मणानिदमब्रवीत् । चैत्र श्रीमानयं मासः पुण्यः पुष्पितकाननः ॥ Ayod. III. 3, 4. and अद्य चन्द्रोऽभ्युपगमत्पुष्यात्पूर्वं पुनर्वसुम् । श्वः पुष्पयोगं नियतं वक्ष्यन्ते दैवचिन्तकाः ॥ श्वसत्वाहमभिषेक्ष्यामि यौवराज्ये परंतप । Ayod. VI. 21, 22. Ráma left Ayodhayá for the forest on the same day. चैत्रे पुष्यनक्षत्रेऽयो ध्यातो वनं प्रति रामस्य प्रस्थानमिति

स्वप्नमयोध्याकान्डो । चैत्रे पुष्यश्च शुक्लपक्षे एव । तत्रापि नवम्यादि दिनत्रये एवेति स्पष्टमेव ज्योतिषादौ । तत्र नवमी रिक्तात्वादभिषेका योग्या । दशम्येव तु पूर्णत्वाद्योग्या । एवंच चैत्र शुक्ल दशम्यां प्रस्थानम् । com. on Sund. 108. 34.

Act II. An interval of five days separates the second Act from the first, the action of which begins on the sixth day. For the Rámá, states that Das'aratha died at about the hour of midnight on the sixth day from the departure of Râma to the forest. तुदीनं कथयन् नराधिपः प्रियस्य पुत्रस्य विवासनातुरः । गतेर्धरात्रे भृशदुःखपीडितस्तदा जहौ प्राणमुदारदर्शनः ।—Ayod. ch. 64. 78 स राजा रजनीं षष्टीं रामे प्रव्राजिते वनम् । अर्धरात्रे दशरथः सोऽस्मरद् दुष्कृतं कृतम ॥—Ayod. 63. 4. Act III. The events of the third Act begin about fifteen days after those of the second. For Bharata returned to Ayodhyà after his father's death on the 1st or the 2nd of the bright half of Vaisákha—the day on which the constellation कृत्तिका was to end and Rohiní to set in. See note कृत्तिका विषयः p. 37. And it was about noon when Bharata arrived at the Statue-house. Devakulika, the keeper of the house, was just then taking his meal after having finished his morning duties. See p. 38. So the action of the 3rd Act begins at about mid-day of the first or second of the bright half of Vaisákha.

Time Analysis-Act IV. An interval of about two days must have passed between the events of the third and those of the fourth Acts. For Bharata declares his intention at the close of the last Act to start to see Ráma without entering Ayodhyá. And it is clear from the conversation between the two maids of Kaikeyî in the introductary part of the present Act.—हला नन्दिनिके अद्य कौसल्यापुरोगैः सर्वैरन्तःपुरैः &c. and नन्दिनिका's reply—प्रकृतिभिरानीतमभिषेकं विसृज्य रामतपोवनं गतः कुमारः that Bharata left for Ràmás तपोवनं on the very day of his arrival on the border of Ayodhyá. And the conversation must have taken place in the evening of that day when Bharata had already left. Now Ráma was residing at that time on the Chitrākuta mountain and the journey to it from Ayodhyâ required about two days. Bharata therefore must have reached Ramá's penance-grove after a couple of days from the day he started for it. So the events of the fourth Act take place on the 3rd day of the bright half of Vaiśàkha.

Act V.—A period of about thirteen years must be allowed to pass between the events of the previous Act and those of this For while Ráma is sitting with Sîtá in the beginning of this act discussing the question about the way in which to perform the annual Śraddha of his father falling on the next day, Rávaṇa arrives there in the disguise of a guest and succeeds in carrying off Sîta. And we know from the Ramá. that the abduction of Sîtá took place in the thirteenth year of Rámá's exile to the forest, and on the eighth day of the Mágha or Phalguna of that year. See notes p. 48, note on श्वः The events of this Act therefore take place on this day.

Act VI. The विष्कम्भक of the sixth Act follows close upon the kidnapping of Sîta by Rávaṅa. The events of the main Act, however, take place some four months after those of the preceding Act. For Sumantra, who was deputed by Bharata to go to Janasthana and learn the tidings of the welfare of his brother Ràma and others, comes back disappointed and tells Bhárata that Ráma was not in Janasthana, but his wife being carried off by Ràvaṅa had gone to the Rishyamukha mountain and there he had reinstated Sugriva who had been deprived of his kingdom and wife by Válī, on his throne. And when Ráma went to dwell on the mountain प्रस्रवण after having crowned Sugrîva King in Kishkindhá it was the time of the advent of the rainy reason. *cf.* अभिषिक्ते तु सुग्रीवे प्रविष्टे वानरे गुहाम् । आजगाम सह भ्रात्रा रामः प्रस्रवणं गिरिम् ॥ and the words of Lakshmaṅa addressed to Ráma grieved at the separation of his beloved wife—शरत्कालं प्रतीक्षस्व प्रावृट् कालोयामागतः । Kish. K. ch. 27, 1, 39; and Ráma's address to Lakshmaṅa— स तदा वालिनं हत्वा सुग्रीवमभिषिच्य च । वसन्माल्यवतः पृष्ठे रामो लक्ष्मणमब्रवीत् ॥ अयं स कालः संप्राप्तः समयोद्य जलागमः । Kish. K. ch. 28, 1, 2. So it was the end of Jyeshtha or the beginning of A'shádha, and Sîtá was carried away by Rávaṅa on the 8th of the dark half of Magha or Falguna. A period of about four months, therefore, intervenes between the two Acts.

Act VII. The seventh Act describes the return of Ramá to Ayodhyá after the rescue of Sîtá and the destruction of Rāvaṅa and his subsequent coronation. And as Bharata had desired Ráma to come immediately after the completion of the fourteenth year of his exile, he came to the hermitage of Bharadwaja on the 5th day of the dark half of Chaitra. पूर्णे चतुर्दशे वर्षे पञ्चम्यां लक्ष्मणाग्रजः। भारद्वाजाश्रमं प्राप्य ववन्दे नियतो मुनिम् ॥ Yudh K. 124. 1. So there is an interval of about nine months between the 6th and the 7th Acts. And as the poet makes Ráma say—अद्यैव यास्यामि पुरीमयोध्यां Śl. 14, the action lasts for a day only.

TECHNICAL REMARKS.

There cannot be many technical remarks as such. As the play was written when the drama was in its initial stage and the hard and fast canons of Dramaturgy were not elaborated and crystallised into their present set form, the technique of the drama is not observed, the sandhis are not properly distinguished and instead of the gradual development of the plot, the final catastrophe is reached with rapid strides. The attainment of sovereignty by Ráma is the final object to be achieved (कार्य). The Bija is cast when the Chamberlain says—महाराजो दशरथ आज्ञापयति·शीघ्रं भर्तृदारकस्य रामस्य राज्यप्रभावसंयोगकारका अभिषेकसंभारा आनीयन्तामिति । And here the Mukha Saṃdhi begins but as Rámá's coronation is obstructed at once in the first Act the Bîja is not allowed to strike root but remains dormant. We have also Patáká in the first Act, which runs to the end of the play. Bharata is its hero. He is friendly to Râma, the principal hero, as the Patákánáyaka ought to be. The Pratimukha sandhi also begins in the first Act as the Bîja is referred to again by the Kanchukin and Lakshmaṅa We have Garbha Sandhi in the third Act where the Bîja that was दृष्टनष्ट takes root, being watered as it were by the refusal of Bharata to accept the kingdom and his desire to hand over the same to Ráma. The fourth Act contains the Avamarsha Sandhi inasmuch as Bharata offers the kingdom to Ráma, but the attainment of the object is yet postponed by Ráma's determination to carry out his father's command and not to return to Ayodhyá till the completion of the period of his exile. In the 7th Act we have the Nibarhana Sandhi when all obstacles to Ráma's attainment of the kingdom are removed and he is crowned in Ayodhyá.

The above analysis of the plot will show that the denouement is faulty. Not to speak of Kâli. and Bhava. the poet does not show in it that constructive skill, which is shown by Harsha and other poets of the second class The play is like a patch-work of several incidents not leading gradually to the development of the plot The second and the fifth Acts may be removed without interfering with the action of the play. The sixth Act has some connection with the plot, as it prepares Kaikeyi's mind to be favourably disposed towards Ráma'a coronation. Ráma, the hero of the play, is of the Dhirodatta class particularly represented as धर्मवीर.

The poet has not developed any Rasa, which may be called the principal sentiment of the play. We have Karuna in the second and the third Acts and a shade of Adbhuta in the 5th.

THE PRINCIPAL CHARACTERS IN THE PLAY.

RAMA

The character of Rama, the hero of the play, is not properly developed. When he sees Sita clad in bark-garments he expresses his desire to put on one of the bark-garments himself. This detracts from his dignity as the hero of the play. Again he refuses to see his father before he departs for the forest, delivering himself of a sentiment which does not do credit to his filial piety (गतेष्वस्मासु राजा नः शिरःस्थानानि पश्यतु—Act. I 36). Then again his credulity in believing Ravana when he tells him that deer with golden flanks live in the Himalaya mountain, is ridiculous. But some of his noble qualities are well depicted by the poet. When his coronation was suddenly stopped, Rama remained as calm and composed as ever. Not only that, but he felt relieved as though a heavy burden was lifted off his mind. (विरम्यतामिदानीं पुत्रेति स्वयं राज्ञा विसर्जितस्यापनीतभारोच्छ्वसितमिव मे मनः। दिष्ट्या स एवास्मि रामः महाराज एव महाराजः।) When the Chamberlain speaks to him about the grave misfortune that was brought about by Kaikeyi, Rama defends her in a manner worthy of his high-mindedness "The King will not now retire to the forest and I shall continue to be the same child obedient to father's commands; while my brothers will not be defrauded of their pleasures." (वनगमननिवृत्तिः...भ्रातरो मे—Act I–14). When again the Chamberlain speaks bitterly of the selfishness of Kaikeyi in demanding that her son Bharata be installed, Rama argues in the same noble strain:—"If she demands the kingdom now for her son which was already promised her as bride's money, then certainly she is free from any avarice; rather we shall be guilty of it if we seek to deprive our brother of it," (शुल्के विपणितं राज्यं......भ्रातृराज्यापहारिणम्-I–15). When Lakshmana, in his uncontrollable anger, finds fault with Rama for his tender—heartedness and incites him to take up his bow, Rama tries to pacify him thus, "Whether Bharata becomes King or I become King, it is just the same to you. If you are proud of your archery, do protect him who will be king." (भरतो वा भवेद् राजा...परिपालयताम्।—Act I-20). He cheerfully puts on bark garments and says that by means of them he will acquire such religious merit as was never attained by other Kings (मङ्गलार्थै...नोपपादितम्—Act I–24). Rama's readiness to obey his father, his self-abnegation, his magnanimity and his love for his brothers are well depicted in the play.

SITA

Bhāsa is more successful in depicting the character of Sita. Her simplicity, the sweetness of her disposition, her devotion to her husband, her deep reverence for her father-in-law, her cheerful submission to her lot, are delineated with skilful touches. When Rama tells her how his coronation was stopped and how he was not a king, she does not at all feel sorry, but she is glad that her father-in-law is still king—(प्रियं मे । महाराज एव महाराजः आर्यपुत्र एवार्यपुत्रः ।) When Lakshmaṇa appears in all the fury of his anger to incite Rama to take up his bow, Sita in her simplicity and tenderness of heart says to her husband, "Noble my lord, at a time when one ought to weep, Saumitri has taken up his bow. (आर्यपुत्र, रोदितव्ये काले सौमित्रिणा धनुर्गृहीतम् ।). When Rama dissuades her from accompanying him and sharing his exile, she answers all his arguments in a manner worthy of a pure, holy, devoted wife. In whatever Sita says or does she exhibits those tender, beautiful and noble qualities, which are the glory of womanhood.

BHARATA

The character of Bharata is undoubledly drawn with great skill by the poet. Matchless are his love, reverence and loyalty towards his brother Rama. He is overpowered with anger and shame when he learns that it was his mother who had sent Rama into exile, had caused the death of his father and plunged the whole of Ayodhyā into deep grief. When Sumantra asks him to fall at the feet of his mother, Kaikeyi, he disowns her as his mother, saying, "You are not worthy to be in the company of my two mothers like a small river betwixt the Ganges and the Jumna." (मम मातृश्च......प्रवेशिता ॥ Act III–16). "I shall establish a new doctrine in the world that even a mother should be disowned if she is treacherous to her husband. (लोकोऽपूर्वं......मातात्यमाता ॥– Act I–18). He refuses to be crowned and at once starts for the forest where Rama has gone to dwell. He could not stay in Ayodhyā, because Ayodhyā without Rama was no Ayodhyā at all. (नायोध्या तं विनायोध्या सायोध्या यत्र राघवः ॥ Act III–24). Bharata is determined to dwell in the forest with Rama and serve him but he is at last persuaded to go back and rule over the kingdom. He agrees to do so on condition that he is to protect the kingdom only as a deposit, which is to be returned to Rama at the end of fourteen years. He takes the sandals of Rama in order that he may be their representative till Rama has fulfilled his vow. Bharata's self-sacrifice and his touching devotion to his brother are depicted with delicate skill by the dramatist.

LAKSHMANA.

Lakshmana's character is also well portrayed in the play. He is filled with great indignation against Kaikeyi, for depriving Rama of his kingdom and sending him into exile for fourteen years. He is so overpowered by anger that he is resolved to rid the world of womankind. He tries to incite Rama to take up the bow (क्रमप्राप्ते हृते........ निर्मनस्विता—Act I-19). Lakshmana's love for Rama is as sincere as it is deep. When Rama puts on bark-garments in order to be ready to go to the forest, Lakshmana begs of him to let him wear bark-garments so that he may accompany him to the forest (नियोगाद्भूषणान् माल्यात् ....मत्सरी–Act I–26). When Sita at the bidding of Rama tries to dissuade him from accompanying them he replies that she alone will not be able to serve the feet of Rama. Hers will be the right foot and his the left (गुरोर्मे......भविष्यति (Act I–27). Lakshmana's touching appeal produces its desired effect and he accompanies Rama and Sita and lives with them in the forest. He is as steadfast as he is joyful in serving his brother.

KAIKEYI

In painting the character of Kaikeyi, the poet has deviated from the original as it is depicted in the Rāmāyana. Bhāsa represents her as acting from pure motives in sending Rama into exile for fourteen years. It was not out of greed for the kingdom that she insisted on the king's sending Rama into exile but out of painful necessity caused by the curse which lay upon the King. Somehow the curse of the great sage was to operate and the king was destined to die of sorrow for his son. She therefore chose that the curse should operate in a manner that would at least avert the misfortune of the death of Rama. Besides her plan was known to and approved of by great sages like Vasishta, Vamadeva and others. The poet thus wants to show that Kaikeyi was not after all a wicked, selfish woman. But the poet's defence of Kaikeyi's conduct though ingenious is weak.

THE PLOT OF THE PLAY.

King Dasharatha, feeling very old and weak, thinks of installing Rama, his eldest son, on the throne and retiring to a forest. All preparations for the coronation are made and while the ceremony is being performed, it is suddenly stopped on account of Kaikeyi, who demanded from the king that Rama should be sent into exile, as a fulfilment of a promise made to her on a previous occasion. Rama is very glad that he is not burdened with the responsibilities of ruling over a kingdom and that his father is still king. Sita also is very happy that her father-in-law is still king. Rama cheerfully puts on bark-garments and is ready to go to the forest. Sita maintains her right of sharing her husband's life as his सहधर्मचारिणी. Lakshmana importnnes Rama to let him accompany them, since he must serve Rama wherever he goes. Thus all the three go to the forest and dwell there.

In the meanwhile the king is deeply grieved at the departure Rama. Separation from Rama is unbearable to him and in course of time he grows distracted and mad with grief and at last dies of a broken-heart.

Bharata, who was living with his maternal uncle in Nandigram, comes to Ayodhya after twelve years. Before he enters the city he thinks of resting himself on the outskirts. He sees a building which he thinks to be a temple and enters it with the intention of taking a rest there. When he bows to he statues in that building, he is informed by the keeper of the statue-house that the statues are of the Iksvâkus, the famous kings of Ayodhyâ. When Bharata sees the statue of his father Dasharatha, he asks the keeper of the statue-house if the statues of the living are made. On being told that the statues are made only of the dead, Bharata faints. Bharata thus learns of his father's death and the keeper of the statue-house further informs him how his mother put a stop to Rama's coronation, and how Rama with Sita and Lakshmana went to the forest. In the meanwhile the three queens, Kausalyā, Sumitrā and Kaikeyi with Sumantra, the minister, come to the statue-house. Bharata bows to Kausalyā and Sumitrā but disowns his mother, Kaikeyi and refuses to bow to her. He rejects the proposal of the coronation that is made by Vasishta, Vāmadeva and the people and straightway goes to the forest where Rama with Sita and Lakshmana has gone.

Bharata's meeting with Rama in the forest is very pathetic. He entreats Rama to let him live with him in the forest, for Rama's name is sufficient to protect the kingdom. But Rama explains to him how he came to the forest in obedience to the behest of his father and how he must fulfil the vow and how necessary it is that Bharata should go back and protect the kingdom. Bharata at last agrees to go back and rule the kingdom, provided Rama gives him his sandals and allows him to rule as their representative and receives back the kingdom as a deposit returned to the owner, at the end of the period.

About thirteen years after the meeting of Rama and Bharata in the forest, Rama is discussing with Sita as to the best way of performing the annual Srāddha of his father falling on the next day. In the meanwhile Ravana arrives there in the guise of a guest. He declares himself to be a Brahmin well-versed in the Vedas, the Mánavíya Dharmashàstra, the Arthashastra of Brihaspati, the Nyáyashastra of Medhâtithi, and the Shrádhakalpa of Práchetas. Rama, struck with the Brahmin's reference to his proficiency in Shrādhakalpa asks him by what special offering he should gratify his manes. Ravaṇa tells him that antelopes, called 'काञ्चनपार्श्वा' dwelling in the Himalayas are the best offerings. Gratified by these offerings the manes casting off old age, ascend to heaven. Rama at once resolves to go to the Himalaya mountain to catch hold of these antelopes. In the meanwhile Ravana by his magic power produces an antelope with golden flanks and Rama seeing it pursues it and goes far into the depths of the forest after it. Sita is now left alone there, as Lakshmana had gone to receive the Kulapati. Ravana seizing the opportunity carries off Sita in triumph.

Shortly after the abduction of Sita by Ravana, Sumantra, the minister, is sent by Bharata to the forest to bring tidings about Rama, Lakshmana and Sita. Sumantra comes back in deep sorrow, bringing the sad news that Rama was not in Janasthana, that Sita was carried off by Ravana and both Rama and Lakshmana had gone to the Rishyamuka mountain and there reinstated Sugriva, the king of monkeys, who had been deprived of his kingdom and wife by his brother, Vali. Bharata being deeply grieved by the news of Sita's abduction, goes to his mother Kaikeyi and severely reproaches her for being responsible for the abduction of Sita. Kaikeyi explains to Bharata how the king lay under the curse of a great sage and how she was justified in sending Rama into exile on account of the curse. Bharata is satisfied with the explanation of her conduct. He then makes preparations to march against Ravana and thus help his brother.

In the meanwhile Rama with a host of monkeys attacks Ravana, kills him, sets his brother Bibhishana on the throne and comes back with Sita to Janasthana. There Bharata arrives with a large army. The meeting of all the three mothers and the four brothers takes place in the forest of Janasthana. The fourteen years of Rama's exile are now over and Bharata asks Rama to assume the burden of the kingdom. Vasishta, Vamadeva and the people come there to perform the coronation of Rama. The coronation takes place amidst universal rejoicings and Rama receives messages of congratulation from Bibishana, Sugriva, Nila, Jambavat and others. Ravaná's Pushpaka car comes, at the mere wish of Rama, and all sit in the car and go to Ayodhyá.

DRAMATIS PERSONAE

MALES.

सूत्रधार.—The Stage-manager.

राजा.—Dasharatha, king of Ayodhyā.

राम.—The Hero—The Eldest son of Dasharatha.

लक्ष्मण.—Brother of Rama and son of Sumitrā.

भरत.—Brother of Rama and son of Kaikeyi.

शत्रुघ्न.—Brother of Rama and son of Sumitra.

सुमन्त्र.—Minister of Dasharatha.

रावण.—King of Lankā and ememy of Rama.

काञ्चुकीय.—Chamberlain.

सूत.—Charioteer of Bharata.

देवकुलिक.—The keeper of the Statue-house.

सुधाकार.—A whitewasher.

वृद्धतापसौ.—Two old ascetics who observe and describe the fight between Ravana and Jatayu.

तापस.—An ascetic.

नन्दिलक.—An attendant of the ascetic.

भट.—An officer.

FEMALES.

नटी.—The Stage-manager's wife.

सीता.—The Heroine—Wife of Rama.

कौसल्या.—Mother of Rama.

सुमित्रा.—Mother of Lakshmana.

कैकेयी.—Mother of Bharata.

अवदातिका.—A female friend of सीता

चेटी.—A female attendant of सीता.

प्रतिहारी.—A female door-keeper.

विजया.
नन्दिनिका. } Female attendants of कैकेयी.

तापसी.—A female ascetic.

॥ श्रीः ॥

प्रतिमानाटकम्

(नान्द्यन्ते ततः प्रविशति सूत्रधारः ।)

सूत्रधारः—

सीताभवः पातु सुमन्त्रतुष्टः सुग्रीवरामः सहलक्ष्मणश्च ।
यो रावणार्यप्रतिमश्च देव्या बिभीषणात्मा भरतोऽनुसर्गम् ॥ १ ॥

य आप्तकामोप्यनवाप्तकामैर्भक्त्योपसन्नः प्रददाति कामम् ।
भवार्तिहारी शरणं प्रपन्नो रामाय तस्मै नम ईश्वराय ॥
प्रतिमानाटकस्यास्य दुर्बोधस्य क्वचित्क्वचित् ।
गणेशानुग्रहाट्टीकां रचयामि तु शक्तितः ॥
यदत्रस्खलितं किञ्चिदज्ञानाद्वा प्रमादतः ।
अथवा बुद्धिवैकल्यात्तत्क्षाम्यन्तु बुधा मम ॥

अथ महाकविस्तत्रभवान्प्रतिभासम्पन्नो भासः प्रतिमाख्यं नाटकं चिकीर्षुरभीष्टनिष्प्रत्यूहसिद्ध्यर्थं परिपन्थीभूतविघ्ननिरासार्थं मङ्गलं सूत्रधारमुखेन रचयितुं तत्प्रवेशं तावदाह **नान्द्यन्त** इति । नान्दीपदनिरुक्तिस्तु—नन्दयतीति नन्दः । पचाद्यच् । नन्द एव नान्दः । प्रज्ञादित्वादण् । ततः टिड्ढाणञ् इति ङीष् । स्तुत्यर्थे नदिधातौ वा समृद्ध्यर्थेथवा पुनः । पृषोदरादिपाठेन नान्दीसाधनमीरितम् ॥ इत्यपि क्वचित् । नाट्यप्रदीपेपि नन्दन्ति काव्यानि कवीन्द्रवर्गाः कुशीलवाः पारिषदाश्च सन्तः । यस्मादलं सज्जनसिन्धुहंसी तस्मादियं सा कथितेह नान्दी ॥ इति । अत्र नान्दीपदेन पूर्वाङ्ग उक्तः । तदुक्तं यन्नाट्यवस्तुनः पूर्वं रङ्गविघ्नोपशान्तये । कुशीलवाः प्रकुर्वन्ति पूर्वरङ्गः स उच्यते ॥ प्रत्याहारादिकान्यङ्गान्यस्य भूयांसि यद्यपि । तथाप्यवश्यं कर्तव्या नान्दी विघ्नोपशान्तये॥ इति । भावप्रकाशिकायामपि सभापतिः सभासभ्या गायका वादका अपि । नटी नटश्च मोदन्ते यत्रान्योन्यानुरञ्जनात् । अतो रङ्ग इति ज्ञेयः पूर्वं यत्स प्रकल्पते । तस्मादयं पूर्वरङ्ग इति विद्वद्भिरुच्यते ॥ इति । इयं च कर्तव्या पूर्वरङ्गसूत्रधारेण । तस्या अन्ते तस्यां कृतायाम् । **तत** इति । नान्दीसमापनानन्तरमेवेति क्रियान्तरवारणार्थं तत इति पदम् । **सूत्रधार** इति । सूत्रं धारयतीति सूत्रधारः । नाट्यस्य यदनुष्ठानं तत्सूत्रं स्यात्सबीजकम् । रङ्गदैवतपूजाकृत्सूत्रधार उदीरितः । इति तल्लक्षणम् । संगीतसर्वस्वे च—वर्तनीयतया सूत्रं प्रथमं येन सूच्यते । रङ्गभूमिं समाक्रम्य सूत्रधारः स उच्यते ॥ इति । अथ आशीर्नमक्रियावस्तुनिर्देशो वापि तन्मुखम् । इति वचनादाशीर्वचनयुक्तं श्लोकं पठन् कथावस्त्वप्युपक्षिपति । **सीताभव** इति । यः देव्या रावणार्यप्रतिमः बिभीषणात्मा च स सीताभवः सुमन्त्रतुष्टः सहलक्ष्मणः भरतः च सुग्रीवरामः अनुसर्ग पातु । नः युष्मान्सामाजिकान् वेति शेषः । देव्या सहितः इति वा योजना । अस्यामबिभीषणा-

(नेपथ्याभिमुखमवलोक्य ।)

आर्ये इतस्तावत् ।

(प्रविश्य)

नटी—आर्य इयमस्मि । (अय्य इअह्मि ।)

सूत्रधारः—आर्ये इममेवेदानीं शरत्कालमधिकृत्य गीयतां तावत् ।

नटी—आर्य तथा । अय्य तह । (गायति ।)

सूत्रधारः—अस्मिन् हि काले

चरति पुलिनेषु हंसी काशांशुकवासिनी सुसंहृष्टा ।

त्मेति पदच्छेदः । सीतायाः भवः क्षेमः लक्षणया तद्धेतुः । यद्वा भवः भद्राप्तिः । भवो भद्राप्तिसत्तयोः इत्यजयः । सीताया भवः यस्मात् । यद्वा सीताभवः अस्यास्तीति सीताभवः । 'अर्श आदिभ्योच्' इत्यच् । सुमन्त्रेण शोभनेन मन्त्रेण तदाख्येन पितुः सारथिना वा तुष्टः प्रीतः । सह सहः सध्र्यङ् वा लक्ष्मणो यस्य स सहलक्ष्मणः । यः देव्या हेतुभूतया तस्या हरणात् रावणस्यारिः च तादृशोऽप्रतिमवीरस्य हननादप्रतिमोऽतुलश्च । बिभीषणः शत्रूणां भयावहः आत्मा यस्य । भरतः भरः भरणम् । पुंसि संज्ञायां घः प्रायेण इति घः । अप् वा । भरं तनोति इति भरतः । जगतो रक्षणकृत् । अत्र शाकुन्तलं—पुनर्यास्यत्याख्यां भरत इति लोकस्य भरणात् । इति । सर्गे सर्गे जन्मनि जन्मनि अनुसर्गम् । गणपतिशास्त्रिणः बिभीषणात्माभरतः इत्येकं पदं पठित्वा बिभीषणे तन्नाम्नि रावणभ्रातरि आत्माभे आत्मसमदुःखसुखे आत्ममित्रे रतः अनुरक्तः । भवतीति शेषः । इति व्याख्यान्ति । किंतु क्लिष्टमिदम् । अत्र कविना श्लेषेण सीता सुमन्त्र सुग्रीव लक्ष्मण रावण बिभीषण भरतानां नाटकीयानां पात्राणां नामनिर्देशः कृतः। तथा चाप्रतिम इति पदस्थप्रतिमाशब्देन स्वनाटकस्य नाम तथा च रामविवसनजन्यं दशरथस्य मरणं रावणारि इति पदेन रावणवधं च सूचयता मनाक्काव्यार्थसूचनमपि कृतम् । अतो मुद्राख्योलङ्कारोयम् । तदुक्तं सूच्यार्थसूचनं मुद्रा प्रकृतार्थपरैः पदैः । इति । उपजातिश्छन्दः । तल्लक्षणम् । स्यादिन्द्रवज्रा यदि तौ जगौग उपेन्द्रवज्रा जतजास्ततो गौ । अनन्तरोदीरितलक्ष्मभाजौ पादौ यदीयावुपजातयस्ताः ॥ इति ॥ १ ॥ **नेपथ्येति** नेपथ्यं रङ्गभूमिस्तदभिमुखमवलोक्येति कविवचनम् । नटेन तु अवलोकनमेव कृतं तदनुवादोयम् । एवमन्यत्रापि बोध्यम् । नेपथ्यं स्याज्जवनिका रङ्गभूमिः प्रसाधनम् । इत्यजयः। आर्ये इति भार्यां प्रति सम्बुद्धिः । पत्नी चार्येति संभाष्या इति भरतः । इतस्तावत्प्रथममिहागम्यतामित्यर्थः । गीयतामिति । सामाजिकानां श्रुतिप्रसादनायेत्यर्थः । **चरतीति** । काशानि काशकुसुमानि अंशुकमिव यस्य तत्काशांशुकं नदीतीरं तत्र वसतीति काशांशुकवासिनी । शरदि काशानां विकसनात् । तदुक्तं कालिदासेनापि शरत्समयवर्णने काशांशुका विकचपद्ममनोज्ञवक्त्रा इति । काशांशुः काशकुसुमप्रभा कवासिनी जलवासिनी चेति गणपतिशास्त्रिणः । यद्वा अंशुकं लक्षणया

(नेपथ्ये ।)

आर्य आर्य । (अय्य अय्य ।)

(आकर्ण्य)

सूत्रधारः—भवतु विज्ञातम् ।

मुदिता नरेन्द्रभवने त्वरिता प्रतिहाररक्षीव ॥ २ ॥

(निष्क्रान्तौ ।)

स्थापना ।

(प्रविश्य)

प्रतिहारी—आर्य क इह काञ्चुकीयानां सन्निहितः । (अय्य को इह कञ्चुईआणं सण्णिहिदो ।)

पक्षौ । हंसास्तु श्वेतगरुतः इत्यमरः । इदमुपमानेपि योज्यम् । काशमिव शुभ्रं दीप्तिमच्चांशुकं वस्ते इति । सुसंहृष्टा हंसी पुलिनेषु सैकतेषु चरति । इत्यर्धोक्ते नेपथ्ये आर्य-आर्येति संभ्रमवचनं श्रुत्वा तत्र दत्तकर्णः सूत्रधार आह भवतु त्वद्गीतविच्छेदकारि संभ्रमवचनमस्तु । विज्ञातं कस्येदं वाक्यमिति मया ज्ञातमित्यर्थः । अथ प्रस्तावनाङ्गप्रयोगातिशयमुपक्षिपति । **मुदितेति** मुदिता प्रीता त्वरिता स्वनियोगानुष्ठाने कृतत्वरा प्रतिहाररक्षी प्रतिहारं द्वारं रक्षतीति । कर्मण्यण् । स्त्रियां ङीप् । द्वाराधिकृता दासी नरेन्द्रभवने दशरथनृपस्य प्रासादे इव यथा चरति तथेति पूर्वेण सम्बन्धः । अनुष्टुप्छन्दः ॥ २ ॥ एवं प्रतिहारीप्रवेशे सूचिते नटीसूत्रधारयोर्निष्क्रममाह निष्क्रान्ताविति । **स्थापनेति** । कथावस्तुवंशस्य स्थापनात्स्थापना । इयमेव आमुखं प्रस्तावनेति च नाम्ना कालिदासाद्यर्वाक्तनकविकृतनाटकेषु व्यवह्रियते । भासकृतनाटकेषु चेयं स्थापनेति संज्ञयैवोपलभ्यते दर्शयति चास्य कवेः प्राचीनत्वम् । प्रस्तावनालक्षणं—सूत्रधारो नटीं ब्रूते मार्षं वापि विदूषकम् । स्वकार्यं प्रस्तुताक्षेपि चित्रोक्त्या यत्तदामुखम् । प्रस्तावना वा इति । एषामन्यतमेनार्थं पात्रं वाक्षिप्य सूत्रकृत् । प्रस्तावनान्ते निर्गच्छेत्ततो वस्तु प्रपञ्चयेत् ॥ इति । अस्याः पञ्च भेदा उक्ता साहित्यदर्पणे । यथा—उद्घात्यकः कथोद्घातः प्रयोगातिशयस्तथा । प्रवर्तकावलगिते पञ्च प्रस्तावनाभिदाः । अत्र च—यदि प्रयोग एकस्मिन्प्रयोगोऽन्यः प्रयुज्यते । तेन पात्रप्रवेशश्चेत्प्रयोगातिशयस्तदा ॥ इत्युक्तेः अत्र सूत्रधारेण पात्रप्रवेशात्प्रयोगातिशयः । प्रतिमासंज्ञमिदं नाटकम् । रामस्य वनगमनादूर्ध्वं संस्थितस्य दशरथस्य प्रतिमागृहे प्रतिमादर्शनाद्रामप्रत्यानयनार्थं तं च राज्यस्वीकारार्थं याचितुं वनं गन्तुं भरतेन निश्चयः कृतः । अतः प्रतिमाप्रधानत्वादस्य नाटकस्य तथा व्यपदेशः । प्रतिमा एव अभेदोपचारात्तथा । अत्र प्रतिममिति स्यान्मृच्छकटिकमितिवत् । अस्येतिवृत्तं मिश्रं रामायणाश्रयं कविकल्पितं च । संनिहितः सन्निधौ स्थितः । **काञ्चु-**

(प्रविश्य)

काञ्चुकीयः—भवति अयमस्मि । किं क्रियताम् ।

प्रतिहारी—आर्य महाराजो देवासुरसङ्ग्रामेष्वप्रतिहतमहारथो दशरथ आज्ञापयति–शीघ्रं भर्तृदारकस्य रामस्य राज्यप्रभावसंयोगकारका अभिषेकसंभारा आनीयन्तामिति । (अय्य महाराओ देवासुरसङ्गामेसु अप्पडिहदमहारहो दसरहो आणवेदि–सिग्घं भट्टिदारअस्स रामस्स रज्जप्पहावसञ्जोअकारआ अहिसेअसम्भारा आणीअन्तु त्ति ।)

काञ्चुकीयः—भवति यदाज्ञप्तं महाराजेन तत् सर्वं सङ्कल्पितम् । पश्य

छत्रं सव्यजनं सनन्दिपटहं भद्रासनं कल्पितं
न्यस्ता हेममयाः सदर्भकुसुमास्तीर्थाम्बुपूर्णा घटाः ।

कीयः—कञ्चुकी । अत्र छण् कथंचित्साध्यः । एतल्लक्षणं मातृगुप्ताचार्यैरुक्तम्–ये नित्यं सत्त्वसम्पन्नाः कामदोषविवर्जिताः । ज्ञानविज्ञानकुशलाः काञ्चुकीयास्तु ते स्मृताः ॥ इति । अन्यच्च–अन्तःपुरचरो वृद्धो विप्रो गुणगणान्वितः । सर्वकार्यार्थकुशलः कञ्चुकीत्यभिधीयते ॥ इति । **अप्रतिहतेति** । अप्रतिहतः अनिवर्ती महारथो रथश्रेष्ठो यस्य । यद्वा अप्रतिहतश्चासो महारथो योधविशेषः च । अस्य लक्षणं–एको दश सहस्राणि योधयेद्यस्तु धन्विनाम् । शस्त्रशास्त्रप्रवीणश्च स महारथ उच्यते ॥ इति । राज्यप्रभावसंयोगकारकाः राज्यप्रभावो राज्यप्राप्त्युत्पन्नं प्रभुत्वं तत्सम्बन्धसम्पादकाः । अभिषेकस्य संभारा उपकरणानि छत्रचामरादीनि । अत्र नायकस्य रामस्यान्तिमराज्यप्राप्तिरूपस्य फलस्य बीजोपन्यासः कृतः । तदुक्तं–अल्पमात्रं समुद्दिष्टं बहुधा यत्प्रसर्पति । फलावसानं यच्चैव बीजं तदभिधीयते ॥ इति । सङ्कल्पितं सम्यक् सम्पूर्णतया कल्पितमुपस्थापितम् । तदेव दर्शयति **छत्रमिति** । छत्रं धवलातपत्रं सव्यजनं व्यजनेन सहितं सव्यजनं सचामरं चेत्यर्थः । रामायणे चामरस्य पृथङ्निर्देशात् । नन्द आनन्दोऽस्यास्तीति नन्दी उत्सवकालः तदर्थः पटह आनकः तेन सहितम् । भद्रं च तदासनं च भद्रासनं मण्यादियुक्तं नृपासनम् । हेम्नो विकारा हेममयाः । सौवर्णाः । विकारार्थे मयट् । दर्भाः कुशाः कुसुमानि च तैः सहितं तीर्थाम्बु गङ्गादीनां जलं तेन पूर्णाः । घटाः कुम्भाः । शतमिति शेषः । शतं च शातकुम्भानां कुम्भानामग्निवर्चसाम् । इति रामायणवचनात् । पुष्यरथः क्रीडार्थो रथविशेषः न सांयुगीनः । याने चक्रिणि युद्धार्थे शताङ्गः स्यन्दनो रथः । असौ पुष्यरथश्चक्रयाने न समराय यत् ॥ इत्यमरः । पुष्यः नक्षत्रविशेषः सुखकरः । स इव रथः । यात्रोत्सवादौ सुखेन भ्रमणार्थो रथः । पुष्परथ इति पाठे कुसुमाकारत्वात्पुष्पमिव रथः इति विग्रहः । पुरे भवाः पौराः ।

युक्तः पुष्यरथश्च मन्त्रिसहिताः पौराः समभ्यागताः
सर्वस्यास्य हि मङ्गलं स भगवान् वेद्यां वसिष्ठः स्थितः ॥३॥

प्रतिहारी—यद्येवं शोभनं कृतम् । (जइ एव्वं सोहणं किदं ।)

काञ्चुकीयः—हन्त भोः ।

इदानीं भूमिपालेन कृतकृत्याः कृताः प्रजाः ।
रामाभिधानं मेदिन्यां शशाङ्कमभिषिञ्चता ॥ ४ ॥

प्रतिहारी—त्वरतां त्वरतामिदानीमार्यः । (तुवरदु तुवरदु दाणिं अय्यो ।)

काञ्चुकीयः—भवति इदं त्वर्यते । (निष्क्रान्तः ।)

प्रतिहारी— (परिक्रम्यावलोक्य ।) आर्य संभवक संभवक गच्छ । त्वमपि महाराजवचनेनार्यपुरोहितं यथोपचारेण त्वरय । (अन्यतो गत्वा ।) सारसिके सारसिके सङ्गीतशालां गत्वा नाटकीयानां विज्ञापय—कालसंवादिना नाटकेन सज्जा भवतेति । यावदहमपि सर्वं कृतमिति महाराजाय निवेदयामि । (अय्य संभवअ संभवअ गच्छ तुवं पि महाराअवअणेण अय्यपुरोहिदं जहोपआरेण तुवारेहि । सारसिए सारसिए सङ्गीदसाळं गच्छिअ णाडईआणं विण्णवेहि—काळसंवादिणा णाडएण सज्जा होह त्ति । जाव अहं वि सव्वं किदं त्ति महाराअस्स णिवेदेमि ।) (निष्क्रान्ता ।)

(ततः प्रविशत्यवदातिका वल्कलं गृहीत्वा ।)

अवदातिका—अहो अत्याहितम् । परिहासेनापीमं वल्कलमुप-

तत्र भव इत्यण् । मङ्गलं मङ्गलहेतुः । अनुष्ठापकत्वात् । शार्दूलविक्रीडितं वृत्तम् । सूर्याश्वैर्यदि मः सजौ सततगाः शार्दूलविक्रीडितम् । इति लक्षणम् ॥ ३ ॥ **इदानीमिति** । भूमिपालेन दशरथेन । कृतकृत्या धन्याः । रामः अभिधानमाख्या यस्य तं शशाङ्कं चन्द्रं तद्वत्सकलजगदाह्लादकत्वात् । अभिषिञ्चता अभिषेकपूर्वं राज्यं प्रतिपादयता । भूमिपालेन प्रजाः कृतकृत्याः कृता इति योजना । अनेनौत्सुक्यप्रदर्शनादारम्भोयम् । तदुक्तम् औत्सुक्यमात्रमारम्भः फललाभायभयसे । तेन इत आरभ्य मुखसन्धिः । संभवक इत्यपरकञ्चुकिनो नाम । आर्येत्यभिधानात् । महाराजवचनेन महाराजनिर्देशात् । यथोपचारेण यथार्होपचारपूर्वम् । सङ्गीतशाला नाट्यशाला । नाटकीयानां नटानाम् । वृद्धाच्छ इति छः । तस्य आयनेयी-इतीयादेशः । कालसंवादिना राज्याभिषेककालोचितेन । सज्जाः प्रयोगोद्यताः । यावन्निवेदयामि निवेदयिष्यामि । यावत्पुरानिपातयोर्लट् । इति भविष्यति लट् । अहो इति । अत्याहितं महाभीतिः । मया महदकार्यं कृतमिति यावत् । कैकेय्या करिष्यमाणरामराज्याभिषेको-

नयन्त्या ममैतावद् भयमासीत् किं पुनर्लोभेन परधनं हरतः। हसितुमिवेच्छामि। न खल्वेकाकिन्या हसितव्यम्। (अहो अच्चाहिदं। परिहासेण वि इमं वक्कलं उवणअन्तीए मम एत्तिअं भअं आसी किं पुण लोभेण परधणं हरन्तस्स हसिदुं विअ इच्छामि। ण खु एआइणीए हसिदव्वं।)

(ततः प्रविशति सीता सपरिवारा।)

सीता—हञ्जे अवदातिका परिशङ्कितवर्णेव दृश्यते। किन्नु खल्विवैतत्। (हञ्जे ओदादिआ परिसङ्किदवण्णा विअ दिस्सइ। किंणु हु विअ एदं।)

चेटी—भट्टिनि सुलभापराधः परिजनो नाम। अपराद्धा भविष्यति। (भट्टिणि सुलहावराहो परिअणो णाम। अवरज्झा भविस्सदि।)

सीता—नहि नहि हसितुमिवेच्छति। (णहि णहि हसिदुं विअ इच्छदि।)

अवदातिका—(उपसृत्य।) जयतु भट्टिनी। भट्टिनि न खल्वहमपराद्धा। (जेदु भट्टिणि। भट्टिणी ण खु अहं अवरज्झा।)

सीता—का त्वां पृच्छति। अवदातिके किमेतद् वामहस्तपरिगृहीतम्। (का तुमं पुच्छदि। ओदादिए किं एदं वामहत्थपरिग्गहिदं।)

अवदातिका—भट्टिनि इदं वल्कलम्। (भट्टिणि इदं वक्कळं।)

सीता—वल्कलं कस्मादानीतम्। (वक्कळं किस्स आणीदं।)

अवदातिका—शृणोतु भट्टिनी। नेपथ्यपालिन्यार्यरेवा निर्वृत्तरङ्गप्रयोजनमशोकवृक्षस्यैकं किसलयमस्माभिर्याचितासीत्। न च तया दत्तम्। ततोऽहत्यपराध इतीदं गृहीतम्। (सुणादु भट्टिणी। णेवच्छपालिणी अय्यरेवा

पघातस्य सूचनार्थमिदम्। परिहासेन नर्महेतोः। परधनं हरतः अनेन सति तदर्हे रामे भरतार्थं राज्यप्रार्थना महदकार्यमिति सूचितम्। हसितुं परिहासं कर्तुम्। **हञ्जे**—हञ्जे इति चेटीं प्रत्यामन्त्रणम्। हण्डे हञ्जे हलाह्वानं नीचां चेटीं सखीं प्रति। इत्यमरः। परिशङ्किताया भीताया इव वर्ण आकारो यस्याः सा तथाभूता। **भट्टिनी**—भट्टः राजा। सोऽस्त्यस्याः पतित्वेनेति भट्टिनी। राज्ञी कृताभिषेकायामितरासु तु भट्टिनी इत्यमरः। सुलभापराधः सुलभोपराधो यस्य। स्वल्पेपि कारणेऽपराधी स्थाप्यते इत्यर्थः। अतो भयशङ्केत्यर्थः। नामेति प्राकाश्ये। त्वां पृच्छति अपराधिनीं गणयतीत्यर्थः। **नेपथ्यपालिनी**—नेपथ्यमत्र संगीतशालास्था प्रसाधनभूमिः वेषोपकरणानि वा। तदुक्तं भरतेन-रामादिव्यञ्जको वेषो नटे नेपथ्यमिष्यते। इति। तस्य रक्षिका। आर्या चासौ रेवा च। निर्वृत्तं रङ्गप्रयोजनमस्य। रङ्गोपयुक्तशेषमित्यर्थः। किसलयं पल्लवः। तेन किसलयाप्रदानेन। अपराधः तत्कृतः अर्हति

णिव्वुत्तरङ्गप्पओअणं असोअरुक्खस्स एक्कं किसलअं अह्मेहि जाइदा आसि । ण अ ताए दिण्णं । तदो अरिहदि अवराहो त्ति इदं गहिदं ।)

सीता—पापकं कृतम् । गच्छ निर्यातय । (पावअं किदं । गच्छ णिय्यादेहि ।)

अवदातिका—भट्टिनि परिहासनिमित्तं खलु मयैतदानीतम् । (भट्टिणि परिहासणिमित्तं खु मए एदं आणीदं ।)

सीता—उन्मत्तिके एवं दोषो वर्धते । गच्छ निर्यातय निर्यातय । (उम्मात्तिए एवं दोसो वड्ढइ । गच्छ णिय्यादेहिं णिय्यादेहि ।)

अवदातिका—यद् भट्टिन्याज्ञापयति । जं भट्टिणी आणवेदि ।) (प्रस्थातुमिच्छति ।)

सीता—हला एहि तावत् । (हला एहि दाव ।)

अवदातिका—भट्टिनि इयमस्मि । (भट्टिणि इआम्हि ।)

सीता—हला किन्नु खलु ममापि तावच् शोभते । (हळा किंणु हु मम वि दाव सोहदि ।)

अवदातिका—भट्टिनि सर्वशोभनीयं सुरूपं नाम । अलङ्करोतु भट्टिनी । (भट्टिणि सव्वसोहणीअं सुरूवं णाम । अळङ्करोदु भट्टिणी ।)

सीता—आनय तावत् । (गृहीत्वालंकृत्य ।) हला पश्य किमिदानीं शोभते । (आणेहि दाव । हळा पेक्ख किं दाणिं सोहदि ।)

अवदातिका—तव खलु शोभते नाम । सौवर्णिकामिव वल्कलं संवृत्तम् । (तव खु सोहदि णाम । सोवण्णिअं विअ वक्कळं संवुत्तं ।)

सीता—हञ्जे त्वं किञ्चिन्न भणसि । (हञ्जे तुवं किंचि ण भणासि ।)

चेटी—नास्ति वाचा प्रयोजनम् । इमानि प्रहृषितानि तनूरुहाणि

वल्कलहरणमिति शेषः । निर्यातय तस्या हस्तं प्रापय । परिहासनिमित्तमतो न मयि दोष इत्यर्थः । उन्मत्तिके भ्रान्तचित्ते । किंचिद्विचार्य परिहसितुकामा सीतापि प्रस्थानोन्मुखीं तां निषिध्याह हला किन्विति । शोभते शोभनीयं भवेत् । **सर्वशोभनीयं**—सर्वेण वस्तुना सुन्दरेणासुन्दरेण वा शोभते इत्यर्थः । उक्तं च कालिदासेनाप्यभिज्ञानशाकुन्तले किमिव हि मधुराणां मण्डनं नाकृतीनाम् । इति । नामेति प्राकाश्ये । निश्चितार्थे वा । सौवर्णिकं सुवर्णमयम् । त्वया परिहितं तव देहप्रभया लब्धोत्कर्षं सम्पन्नमिति भावः । **नास्तीति**—वाचा प्रयोजनं नास्ति कथनं नावश्यकमित्यर्थः । यतः । प्रहृषितानि उद्गतानि तन्वां रोहन्तीति तनूरुहाणि रोमाणि ।

मन्त्रयन्ते । (णत्थि णाआए पओअणं । इमे परिसिदा तणुरुहा मन्तेन्ति ।) (पुलकं दर्शयति ।)

सीता—हञ्जे आदर्शं तावदानय । (हञ्जे आदंसअं दाव आणेहि ।)

चेटी—यद् भट्टिन्याज्ञापयति । (निष्क्रम्य प्रविश्य ।) भट्टिनि अयमादर्शः । (जं भट्टिणी आणवेदि । भट्टिणि अअं आदंसओ ।)

सीता—(चेटीमुखं विलोक्य ।) तिष्ठतु तावदादर्शः । त्वं किमपि वक्तुकामेव । (चिट्ठदु दाव आदंसओ । तुवं किं विं वत्तुकामा विअ ।)

चेटी—भट्टिनि एवं मया श्रुतम् । आर्यबालाकिः कञ्चुकी भणति अभिषेकोऽभिषेक इति । (भट्टिणि एवं मए सुदं । अय्यबाळाई कञ्चुई भणादि-अहिसेओ अहिसेओ त्ति ।)

सीता—कोऽपि भर्ता राज्ये भविष्यति । (को वि भट्टा रज्जे भविस्सदि ।)

(प्रविश्यापरा)

चेटी—भट्टिनि प्रियाख्यानिकं प्रियाख्यानिकम् । (भट्टिणि पिअक्खाणिअं पिअक्खाणिअं ।)

सीता—किं किं प्रतीष्य मन्त्रयसे । (किं किं पडिच्छिअ मन्तेसि ।)

चेटी—भर्तृदारकः किलाभिषिच्यते । (भट्टिदारओ किल अहिसिञ्चीअदि ।)

सीता—अपि तातः कुशली । (अवि तादो कुसळी ।)

चेटी—महाराजेनैवाभिषिच्यते । (महाराएण एव्व अहिसिञ्चीअदि ।)

सीता—यद्येवं द्वितीयं मे प्रियं श्रुतम् । विशालतरमुत्सङ्गं कुरु । (जइ एव्वं दुदीअं मे पिअं सुदं । विसाळदरं उच्छङ्गं करेहि ।)

मूलविभुजादिभ्य इति कः । रोमाञ्चस्यानन्दप्रभवत्वात् । भट्टिण्या वल्कलपरिधानोत्पन्नशोभातिशयजन्य एव ममानन्द इत्यलं वाचा कथनेनेति भावः । आदर्शो दर्पणम् । **वक्तुकामा**-वक्तुं कामो यस्याः सा तथोक्ता । तुं काममनसोरपि इति मकारलोपः । एवं यथा भट्टिण्याह तथा । वक्तुकामैवास्मीति भावः । अभिषेक इति द्विरुक्तिरानन्दोत्थं संभ्रमं द्योतयति । **कोपि भर्तेति** । दशरथे जीवति रामस्य राज्याभिषेकमनपेक्षमाणायास्तटस्थाया इवोक्तिरियम् । **प्रियाख्यानिकं** प्रियस्याख्यानमस्मिन्नस्तीति । किं प्रतीष्य कां वार्तां लब्ध्वा । भर्तृदारको ज्येष्ठत्वाद्रामः । पितरि जीवति कथमभिषेक इति दशरथस्य सरुजत्वं शङ्कते अपीति । तातः दशरथः । **द्वितीयं प्रियं** श्वशुरस्य कुशलित्वम् । विशालतरमतिविस्तृतम् । प्रियश्रावणार्हपारितोषिकग्रहणार्थमिति भावः ।

चेटी—भट्टिनि तथा । भट्टिणि तह । (तथा करोति ।)

सीता—(आभरणान्यवमुच्य ददाति ।)

चेटी—भट्टिनि पटहशब्द इव । (भट्टिणि पटहसद्दो विअ ।)

सीता—स एव । (सो एव्व ।)

चेटी—एकपदे अवघट्टिततूष्णीकः पटहशब्दः संवृत्तः । (एकपदे ओघट्टिअतुह्णीओ पटहसद्दो संवुत्तो ।)

सीता—को नु खलूद्घातोऽभिषेकस्य । अथवा बहुवृत्तान्तानि राजकुलानि नाम । (कोणु खु उग्घादो अहिसेअस्स । अहवा बहुवुत्तन्ताणि राअउलाणि णाम ।)

चेटी—भट्टिनि एवं मया श्रुतं—भर्तृदारकमभिषिच्य महाराजो वनं गमिष्यतीति । (भट्टिणि एवं मए सुदं—भट्टिदारअं अहिसिंचिअ महाराओ वणं गमिस्सदि त्ति ।)

सीता—यद्येवं न तदभिषेकोदकं मुखोदकं नाम । (जइ एव्वं ण सो अहिसेओदओ मुहोदअं णाम ।)

(ततः प्रविशति रामः ।)

रामः—हन्त भोः ।

आरब्धे पटहे स्थिते गुरुजने भद्रासने लङ्घिते
स्कन्धोच्चारणनम्यमानवदनप्रच्योतितोये घटे ।
राज्ञाहूय विसर्जिते मयि जनो धैर्येण मे विस्मितः
स्वः पुत्रः कुरुते पितुर्यदि वचः कस्तत्र भो विस्मयः ॥ ५ ॥

पटहशब्द इव पटहशब्दसदृशः । एवेति शङ्कावारणार्थम् । अवघट्टिततूष्णीकः अवघट्टितस्ताडनोत्पन्नस्तूष्णीको विरतश्च । उद्घातो विघ्नः । बहुवृत्तान्तानि बहवः नानाविधा वृत्तान्ता व्यतिकरा येषु तानि । निश्चितं कार्यं कदाचिदुपस्थितकार्यान्तरेणान्यथा क्रियते इत्याशयः । मुखोदकं पितृवियोगदुःखोत्पन्नाश्रुप्रमाजनार्थमिति भावः । हन्तेति हर्षे । **आरब्धे** इति । पटहे पटहवादने आरब्धे । गुरुजने स्थिते मङ्गलदर्शनार्थम् । भद्रासने सिंहासने लङ्घिते मयारूढे । घटे स्कन्धोच्चारणं स्कन्धस्योपरि नयनं तेन तस्मिन्कृते नम्यमानं यद् घटस्य वदनं तस्मात्प्रश्च्योतति इति प्रश्च्योति गलनप्रवृत्तं तोयं जलं यस्य तथाभूते । राज्ञा दशरथेनाहूय मयि विसर्जिते भद्रासनादुत्तीर्य वनगमनायादिष्टे इत्यर्थः । जनः मम धैर्येण विस्मितः । अभूदिति शेषः । यदि स्वः पुत्रः पितुः वचः कुरुते तर्हि तत्र आज्ञानुष्ठाने कः विस्मयः । न कश्चिदित्यर्थः । भो इति जनामन्त्रणार्थम् । अर्थान्तरन्यासालंकारः । शार्दूल-

विरंम्यतामिदानीं पुत्रेति स्वयं राज्ञा विसर्जितस्यापनीतभारोच्छ्वसितमिव मे मनः। दिष्ट्या स एवास्मि रामः महाराज एव महाराजः। यावदिदानीं मैथिलीं पश्यामि।

अवदातिका—भट्टिनि भर्तृदारकः खल्वागच्छति। नापनीतं वल्कलम्। (भट्टिणि भट्टिदारओ खु आअच्छइ। णावणीदं वक्कळं।)

रामः—मैथिलि किमास्यते।

सीता—हं आर्यपुत्रः। जयत्वार्यपुत्रः। (हं अय्यउत्तो। जेदु अय्यउत्तो।)

रामः—मैथिलि आस्यताम्। (उपविशति।)

सीता—यद् आर्यपुत्र आज्ञापयति। (जं अय्यउत्तो आणवेदि।) (उपविशति।)

अवदातिका—भट्टिनि स एव भर्तृदारकस्य वेषः। अलीकमिवैतद् भवेत्। (भट्टिणि सो एव्व भट्टिदारअस्स वेसो। अळिअं विअ एदं भवे।)

सीता—तादृशो जनोऽलीकं न मन्त्रयते। अथवा बहुवृत्तान्तानि राजकुलानि नाम। (तादिसो जणो अळिअं ण मन्तेदि। अहवा बहुवुत्तन्ताणि राअउळाणि णाम।)

रामः—मैथिलि किमिदं कथ्यते।

सीता—न खलु किञ्चित्। इयं दारिका भणति—अभिषेकोऽभिषेक इति। (ण खु किञ्चि। इअं दारिआ भणादि—अहिसेओ अहिसेओत्ति।)

रामः—अवगच्छामि ते कौतूहलम्। अस्त्यभिषेकः। श्रूयताम्।

विक्रीडितं वृत्तम्। लक्षणमुक्तम्॥ ५॥ विरम्यतामभिषेकमङ्गलादुत्तिष्ठेत्यर्थः। अपनीतः भारः राज्यभारः यस्य तदत एव उच्छ्वसितं सुखितम्। तदेव विशदीकरोति **दिष्ट्येति**। दिष्ट्या इति हर्षे। स एव यथाभिषेकात्पूर्वम्। रामः केवलरामशब्दशब्दितः न तु महाराजो राम इति। महाराजः—कैकेय्या प्रार्थितं भरताभिषेकमजानत इयमुक्तिः। स वेषः योऽभिषेकात्पूर्वं धारितः। अलीकमसत्यम्। भर्तृदारकोऽभिषिच्यते इति यच्छ्रुतं तत्। तादृशो जनः मान्याः काञ्चुकीयाः। मैथिलि–मिथिला नाम विदेहानां राजधानी। तस्या अधिपो वैदेहः तस्यापत्यं स्त्री वैदेही तत्सम्बुद्धिः। कौतूहलमभिषेकवृत्तान्तश्रवणविषयम्। अमा सह भवः अमात्यः। अमेहक्कसितसित्रेभ्य एव इति वार्त्तिकम् पा. ४.२.१०४)

---

१ विश्रम्य०

अद्यास्मि महाराजेनोपाध्यायामात्यप्रकृतिजनसमक्षमेकप्रकारसंक्षिप्तं कोसलराज्यं कृत्वा बाल्याभ्यस्तमङ्कमारोप्य मातृगोत्रं स्निग्धमाभाष्य पुत्र राम प्रतिगृह्यतां राज्यमित्युक्तः ।

सीता—तदानीमार्यपुत्रेण किं भणितम् । (तदाणीं अय्यउत्तेण किं भणिदं ।)

रामः—मैथिलि त्वं तावत् किं तर्कयसि ।

सीता—तर्कयाम्यार्यपुत्रेणाभणित्वा किञ्चिद् दीर्घं निःश्वस्य महाराजस्य पादमूलयोः पतितमिति । (तक्केमि अय्यउत्तेण अभणिअ किञ्चि दिग्घं णिस्ससिअ महाराअस्स पादमूलेसु पडिअं त्ति ।)

रामः—सुष्ठु तर्कितम् । अल्पं तुल्यशीलानि द्वन्द्वानि सृज्यन्ते । तत्र हि पादयोरस्मि पतितः ।

समं बाष्पेण पतता तस्योपरि ममाप्यधः ।
पितुर्मे क्लेदितौ पादौ ममापि क्लेदितं शिरः ॥ ६ ॥

सीता—ततस्ततः । (तदो तदो ।)

रामः—ततोऽप्रतिगृह्यमाणेष्वनुनयेषु आसन्नजरादोषैः स्वैः प्राणैरस्मि शापितः ।

अमात्या मन्त्रिणः । प्रकृष्टं कुर्वन्ति राज्यमिति प्रकृतयः सुहृदादयः । जनाः पौराः तेषां समक्षम् । एकप्रकोरण संक्षिप्तं संहतम् । कोसलानामुत्तरकोसलदेशस्य राज्यं कौसलराज्यम् । बाल्याभ्यस्तं शैशवादारभ्य परिचितम् । मातृगोत्रं कौसल्यावंशम् । स्निग्धं स्नेहपूर्वम् । अत्र रामायणम्—ज्येष्ठायामसि मे पत्न्यां सदृश्यां सदृशः सुतः । उत्पन्नस्त्वं गुणज्येष्ठो मम रामात्मजः प्रियः ॥ इति । सुष्ठु सम्यक् तर्कितमूहितम् । तव तर्को यथार्थ इति यावत् । अल्पं स्तोकं कदाचिदित्यर्थः न तु बाहुल्येन सर्वदा सर्वत्र च । तुल्यं परस्परानुरूपं शीलं स्वभावो येषां तानि । द्वंद्वानि मिथुनानि यथा आवयोरिति सूचितम् । **सममिति** । समं युगपत् मम शिरस उपरि पतता तस्य मम पितुः अधः अधः प्रदेशे अर्थात् पितुः पादयोः पतता मम च बाष्पेणाश्रुजलेन मम शिरः क्लेदितं मे पितुः पादौ च क्लेदितौ । इति व्यत्यासेनान्वयः । अतः प्रक्रमभङ्गदोषः । अतः 'क्लेदितं मे शिरः पादौ क्लेदितौ च पितुर्मम ।' इति पठनीयम् । अनुष्टुप्छन्दः ॥ ६ ॥ ततो मम राज्यस्वीकारार्थं पित्रा कृतेषु अनुनयेषु मया अप्रतिगृह्यमाणेष्वनङ्गीक्रियमाणेषु । सर्वथा राज्यस्वीकारपराङ्मुखं मां दृष्ट्वेत्यर्थः । आसन्नो जरादोषो येषां तैः प्राणैरहं शापितः । त्वं राज्यं न प्रतिपद्यसे चेज्जराजीर्णा मे प्राणाः सौकर्येणैव यास्यन्तीत्युक्तेन मया गृहीतस्त-

सीता—ततस्ततः। (तदो तदो।)

रामः—ततस्तदानीं

शत्रुघ्नलक्ष्मणगृहीतघटेऽभिषेके
छत्रे स्वयं नृपतिना रुदता गृहीते।
सम्भ्रान्तया किमपि मन्थरया च कर्णे
राज्ञः शनैरभिहितं च न चास्मि राजा॥

सीता—प्रियं मे। महाराज एव महाराजः आर्यपुत्र एवार्यपुत्रः। (पिअं मे। महाराओ एव्व महाराओ अय्यउत्तो एव्व अय्यउत्तो।)

रामः—मैथिलि किमर्थं विमुक्तालङ्कारासि।

सीता—न खलु तावदाबध्नामि। (ण खु दाव आवज्झामि।)

रामः—न खलु। प्रत्यग्रावतारितैर्भूषणैर्भवितव्यम्। तथाहि—

कर्णौ त्वरापहृतभूषणभुग्नपाशौ
संस्रंसिताभरणगौरतलौ च हस्तौ।

दनुनय इति भावः। तदानीं मम राज्याभिषेककाले। **शत्रुघ्नेति**। शत्रून् हन्तीति शत्रुघ्नः यः लक्ष्मणः तेन गृहीतः घटः यस्मिन् तथोक्ते अभिषेके प्रस्तुते इति शेषः। शत्रुघ्नलक्ष्मणाभ्यां गृहीत इति व्याख्यानं रामायणासंवादि शत्रुघ्नस्य तत्रासंनिधानात्। तदुक्तं रामायणे-गच्छता मातुलकुलं भरतेन तदानघ। शत्रुघ्नो नित्यशत्रुघ्नो नीतः प्रीतिपुरस्कृतः॥ (अयोध्या कां १.१) इति। तथापि एतदेव कवेरभिमतमिति भाति। तृतीयाङ्के किं शत्रुघ्नो मामुपगतः इति भरतकृतप्रश्नात्। रुदता आनन्दाश्रूणि मुञ्चता नृपतिना दशरथेन स्वयं छत्रे गृहीते सति। सम्भ्रान्तया त्वरायातया मन्थरया तदाख्यया कैकेयीदास्या राज्ञः कर्णे शनैः किमप्यभिहितं कथितं च अहं च राजा नास्मि च निवृत्ताभिषेकोऽभवं च। द्वौ चकारौ क्रियायौगपद्यं द्योतयतः। वसन्ततिलका वृत्तम्। उक्ता वसन्ततिलका तभजा जगौ गः। इति तल्लक्षणम्॥ ७॥ आर्यपुत्र एव न तु सर्वत्र प्रभविष्णुर्महाराज इत्यर्थः। इयं प्रियं मे इत्यादि सीतोक्तिः १० पृष्ठगतरामवचनसंवादादल्पं तुल्यशीलानीत्यादिरामवचनं समर्थयति। आबध्नामि धारयामि। अतो न विमुक्तिशङ्का कार्येत्यर्थः। तस्या वचनमाक्षिपन्नाह न खलु नैतत्सम्यगुक्तम्। यतः प्रत्यग्रं संप्रति अचिरकालादेवावतारितैः अतः तत्पूर्वमाबद्धैः। **कर्णौ इति**। त्वरया अपहृतानि अपनीतानि भूषणानि ययोस्तौ त्वरापहृतभूषणौ। अत एव भुग्नः वक्रतामापन्नः पाशः अधःप्रान्तभागो ययोस्तौ तथोक्तौ। त्वरापहृतभूषणैर्भुग्नपाशाविति वा। कर्णपाशयोर्भुग्नत्वं तद्गतभूषणानामचिरापहरणं सूचयतीत्यर्थः। तथा च हस्तौ संस्रंसितानि बलात्स्वस्थानात्प्रच्यावितानि यानि आभरणानि कटकादीनि तैः गौरं तलं ययोस्तादृशौ। अनेन हस्ततलयोरतिमार्दव

एतानि चाभरणभारनतानि गात्रे
स्थानानि नैव समतामुपयान्ति तावत् ॥ ८ ॥

सीता—पारयत्यार्यपुत्रोऽलीकमपि सत्यमिव मन्त्रयितुम् । (पारेदि अय्यउत्तो अलिअं पि सच्चं विअ मन्तेदुं ।)

रामः—तेन हि अलङ्क्रियताम् । अहमादर्शं धारयिष्ये । (तथा कृत्वा निर्वर्ण्य ।)

आदर्शे वल्कलानीव किमेते सूर्यरश्मयः ।
हसितेन परिज्ञातं क्रीडेयं नियमस्पृहा ॥ ९ ॥

अवदातिके किमेतत् ।

अवदातिका—भर्तः किन्नु खलु शोभते न शोभते इति कौतूहलेनाबद्धानि । (भट्टा किण्णुहु सोहदि ण सोहदि त्ति कोदूहळेण आबज्झा ।)

रामः—मैथिलि किमिदम् । इक्ष्वाकूणां वृद्धालङ्कारस्त्वया धार्यते । अस्त्यस्माकं प्रीतिः । आनय ।

सीता—मा खलु मा खल्वार्यपुत्रोऽमङ्गलं भणतु । (माखु माखु अय्यउत्तो अमङ्गळं भणादु ।)

रामः—मैथिलि किमर्थं वारयसि ।

सीता—उज्झिताभिषेकस्यार्यपुत्रस्यामङ्गलमिव मे प्रतिभाति । (उज्झिदाहिसेअस्स अय्यउत्तस्स अमङ्गळं विअ मे पडिहादि ।)

मुक्तम् । गात्रे तव देहे च एतानि आभरणभारेण नतानि निम्नतां गतानि स्थानानि समतां स्वोचितस्थितिं नैवोपयान्ति तावत् । अतोत्यल्पकालात्प्रागेव त्वयाभरणान्यवतारितानीति स्पष्टमायातीति भावः । वसन्ततिलकं वृत्तम् । लक्षणमुक्तम् ॥८॥ अलीकमतात्विकमर्थम् । का कथा तात्विकेऽर्थे इत्यभिप्रायः । इति ग० शा० । निर्वर्ण्य सीताया आदर्शे दृष्टं प्रतिबिम्बं निध्याय । **आदर्शे इति** । आदर्शे वल्कलानि इव भान्ति । एते सूर्यरश्मयः किमिति हसितेन परिज्ञातम् । इयं क्रीडा परिहासः किं नियमस्पृहा तपश्चरणेच्छा वा ॥ अनुष्टुप् छन्दः ॥ ९ ॥ इक्ष्वाकूणां इक्ष्वाकुर्नाम वैवस्वतमनोः पुत्रः अयोध्यावासिरघुकुलस्य मूलपुरुषः । इक्ष्वाकोः गोत्रापत्यानि पुमांसः इक्ष्वाकवः तेषाम् । वृद्धालङ्कार वार्धक्येलंकारभूतानि वल्कलानि इत्यर्थः । अस्माकं प्रीतिः धारणे कौतुकमिति यावत् । अमङ्गलं भणतु इति यदुक्तं तदेव विशदयति राज्याभिषेके विघ्निते इयं वल्कलधारणेच्छा उज्झिताभिषेकस्येति

रामः—

मा स्वयं मन्युमुत्पाद्य परिहासे विशेषतः ।
शरीरार्धेन मे पूर्वमाबद्धा हि यदा त्वया ॥ १० ॥

(नेपथ्ये)

हा हा महाराजः ।

सीता—आर्यपुत्र किमेतत् । (अय्यउत्त किं एदं ।)

रामः—(आकर्ण्य ।)

नारीणां पुरुषाणां च निर्मर्यादो यदा ध्वनिः ।
सुव्यक्तं प्रभवामीति मूले दैवेन ताडितम् ॥ ११ ॥

तूर्णं ज्ञायतां शब्दः ।

(प्रविश्य)

काञ्चुकीयः—परित्रायतां परित्रायतां कुमारः ।

रामः—आर्य कः परित्रातव्यः ।

काञ्चुकीयः—महाराजः ।

रामः—महाराज इति । आर्य ननु वक्तव्यमेकशरीरसंक्षिप्ता पृथिवी रक्षितव्येति । अथ कुत उत्पन्नोयं दोषः ।

अशुभं सूचयतीति भावः । **मा स्वयमिति** । विशेषतः परिहासे परिहासार्थं वल्कलेषु याचितेषु । स्वयं मन्युं शोकं शोकाशङ्कामिति यावत् । मा उत्पाद्य मा उत्पादय कुरु । मा अलमर्थे । मास्म मालं च वारणे । इत्यमरः । तथापि क्त्वान्तेन प्रतिषेधार्थमाशब्दप्रयोगोऽपाणिनीयः । यद्वा विशेषत इत्युत्तरार्धेन योजयितव्यम् । हि यदा विशेषतः विशेषेण मम शरीरार्धेन पत्नीत्वेन शरीरार्धभूतया त्वया एते वल्कला इति शेषः आबद्धा धारिताः । वल्कलशब्दोत्र पुंसि द्रष्टव्यः । वल्कं वल्कलमस्त्रियाम् । इत्यमरः । अनुष्टुप् छन्दः ॥ १० ॥ हा हेति द्विरुक्तिः कष्टतरावस्थां द्योतयति । **नारीणामिति** । यदा यतो नारीणां पुरुषाणां च निर्मर्यादः सीमामतिक्रान्तः अत्युच्च इति यावत् । अयं ध्वनिः शब्दः ततः सुव्यक्तं स्पष्टं दैवेन मूले सर्वप्रधाने महाराजे । न तु शाखायां । स्कन्धे वा । ताडितं प्रहृतम् । मूले नाशिते सर्वनाशः स्यादिति । कस्मादिदमित्याह प्रभवामि इति । सर्वत्राप्रतिहतं मम सामर्थ्यमतो यन्मे रुचितं तत्कर्तुं शक्नोमीति । अन्यथैतादृशस्य निर्मर्यादस्य ध्वनेः नान्यत्किंचित्कारणं संभवतीति भावः ॥ ११ ॥ तूर्णं शीघ्रम् । शब्दः शब्दकारणमिति यावत् । महाराजः परित्रातव्य इति श्रुत्वा यः सर्वपृथिव्याः परिरक्षणे समर्थः तस्य परित्राणं कथं याच्यते इति विस्मयं दर्शयन्नाह—ननु वक्तव्येति । एकस्मिन् शरीरे महाराजरूपे संक्षिप्ता संक्षिप्य स्थिता ।

काञ्चुकीयः—स्वजनात्।

रामः—स्वजनादिति। हन्त नास्ति प्रतीकारः।

शरीरेऽरिः प्रहरति हृदये स्वजनस्तथा।
कस्य स्वजनशब्दो मे लज्जामुत्पादयिष्यति॥ १२॥

काञ्चुकीयः—तत्रभवत्याः कैकेय्याः।

रामः—किमम्बायाः। तेन हि उदर्केण गुणेनात्र भवितव्यम्।

काञ्चुकीयः—कथमिव।

रामः—श्रूयताम्।

यस्याः शक्रसमो भर्ता मया पुत्रवती च या।
फले कस्मिन् स्पृहा तस्या येनाकार्यं करिष्यति॥ १३॥

काञ्चुकीयः—कुमार अलमुपहतासु स्त्रीबुद्धिषु स्वमार्जवमुपनिक्षेप्तुम्। तस्या एव खलु वचनाद् भवदभिषेको निवृत्तः।

रामः—आर्य गुणाः खल्वत्र।

दोषः आपत्तिः। स्वजनादात्मीयाज्जनात्। स्वजनादिति ब्रूषे चेत्। हन्तेति खेदे। नास्ति प्रतीकारः—परकीयो हि दोषमुत्पादयन् वधेन वा प्रतिबन्धेन वा प्रतिकर्तुं शक्यः। स्वजनस्तु न तथेत्यप्रतिकारार्हैयमापदुपस्थितेति भावः। **शरीर** इति। अरिः शरीरे प्रहरति प्रहारं करोति। तथा स्वजनः हृदये प्रहरति। शरीरप्रहारः सोढुं शक्यः। हृदयप्रहारस्तु दुःसहः शोकायैव भवतीति भावः। अत एव एतादृशः प्रहारः स्वजनात्स्याच्चेत् लज्जाकर एव भवेदित्याह कस्येति। कस्य केन धृतः अयं स्वजन इति शब्दो मे लज्जामुत्पादयिष्यति आवहेत्। कस्य स्वजनस्यैवं लज्जाकरं चेष्टितं तत्कथयेति भावः॥ १२॥ तत्रभवत्याः पूज्यायाः। तेन हि अयं दोषः कैकेय्युत्पन्नश्चेत्। उदर्केण उत्तरफलेन गुणेन गुणावहेन भवितव्यम्। अयं सांप्रतं दोषत्वेन भासमानोपि परिणामे गुणायैव कल्पेत इत्यर्थः। **यस्या** इति। यस्याः कैकेय्याः भर्ता शक्रसमः शक्रेण इन्द्रेण तुल्यः। स्वर्गीयमपीप्सितं साधयितुं समर्थः किं मानुषसाध्यमिति भावः। या च मया पुत्रवती। मां पुत्रत्वेन पश्यति। यस्या आज्ञापालनेऽहं सदैव तत्पर इति यावत्। अतस्तस्याः कस्मिन् फले साध्येऽर्थे स्पृहा भवेत्। कस्मै फलाय स्पृहयेद्येन अकार्यं निन्दितं कर्म करिष्यति। नैतन्मम मतिपथमवतरति॥ १३॥ उपहतासु कुटिलतादिदोषदुष्टासु स्त्रीबुद्धिषु स्त्रियां मतिषु स्वमात्मन आर्जवं बुद्धिसारल्यं उपक्षेप्तुमलं मारोपय। अलमिति निषेधेऽव्ययम्। तद्योगे तुमुन्प्रत्ययोऽपाणिनीयः। अलंखल्वोरित्यादिना क्त्वाप्रत्ययस्यैव विहितत्वात्। यदुक्तं तदुपपादयति **तस्या एव** इति। गुणाः खल्वत्र बहुगुणं तस्या आचरणमिदम्। के ते गुणा इत्याह

काञ्चुकीयः—कथमिव ।

रामः—श्रूयताम् ।

वनगमननिवृत्तिः पार्थिवस्यैव ताव-
न्मम पितृपरवत्ता बालभावः स एव ।
नवनृपतिविमर्शे नास्ति शङ्का प्रजाना-
मथ च न परिभोगैर्वञ्चिता भ्रातरो मे ॥ १४ ॥

काञ्चुकीयः—अथ च तयानाहूतोपसृतया भरतोऽभिषिच्यतां राज्य इत्युक्तम् । अत्राप्यलोभः ।

रामः—आर्य भवान् खल्वस्मत्पक्षपातादेव नार्थमवेक्षते । कुतः

शुल्के विपणितं राज्यं पुत्रार्थे यदि याच्यते ।
तस्या लोभोऽत्र नास्माकं भ्रातृराज्यापहारिणाम् ॥ १५ ॥

काञ्चुकीयः—अथ—

रामः—अतः परं न मातुः परिवादं श्रोतुमिच्छामि । महाराजस्य वृत्तान्तस्तावदभिधीयताम् ।

काञ्चुकीयः—ततस्तदानीं ।

वनगमनमिति । तावत्प्रथमं पार्थिवस्य नृपतेरेव वनगमनान्निश्चितादरण्यगमनान्निवृत्तिः विरामः । अन्यथा क्लेशपूर्णं वनगमनमकरिष्यदेव । गुणान्तरमाह । मम पितृपरवत्ता पितृवशत्वं न त्वनभिलषणीयं सर्वप्रभुत्वं यथाभिषिक्तस्य स्यात् । स एव बालभावः अहं पितृसान्निध्याद्यथापूर्वं बाल एवास्मीत्यर्थः । अयं तृतीयो गुणः । अपरोपि । नवनृपतेः विमर्शे परीक्षणे । अयं न्यायप्रवृत्तो भवेन्नवेति विचारे । यद्वा विमर्शः नृपतिकर्तृकः । नूतननृपस्य राज्यतन्त्रचिन्तने । प्रजानां शङ्का नास्ति । पञ्चमं गुणमाह । अथ चापि च मे मम भ्रातरः परिभोगैः न वञ्चिताः । यथापूर्वं विषयपरिभोगे स्वतन्त्रा एव । अतस्तया मयि उपकृतमेवेति भावः । मालिनी वृत्तम् । ननमयययुतेयं मालिनी भोगिलोकैः । इति लक्षणात् ॥ १४ ॥ अस्त्वेवं तत्कृत्यं गुणवत् । किंतु तया भरतस्य राज्याभिषेकोपि याचितः । अत्र कं गुणं भवान्पश्यतीति प्रश्नार्थमाह—**अथ चेति** । अनाहूताचासौ उपसृता च । स्वयमागत्य प्रार्थितवती । तत्किं न राज्यलोभात् । अथवा अयमपि अलोभगुणः वेति सोपालम्भं पृच्छति । पक्षे पातः पक्षपातस्तस्मात् । अर्थं वास्तवमर्थम् । **शुल्क** इति । शुल्कं विवाहकाले यत्कन्यार्थं वरादिष्यते तत् । शुल्के शुल्कत्वेन विपणितं देयत्वेन प्रतिश्रुतं तद्राज्यं पुत्रार्थे यदि याच्यते अत्र तस्या लोभः भ्रातृ राज्यापहारिणामस्माकं ममेत्यर्थः न लोभः किमिति प्रश्नकाकुः । परिवादं निन्दाम् । ततः तस्याः प्रार्थनाश्रवणानन्तरं तदानीं

शोकादवचनाद् राज्ञा हस्तेनैव विसर्जितः ।
किमप्यभिमतं मन्ये मोहं च नृपतिर्गतः ॥ १६ ॥

रामः—कथं मोहमुपगतः ।

(नेपथ्ये ।)

कथं कथं मोहमुपगत इति ।

यदि न सहसे राज्ञो मोहं धनुः स्पृश मा दया

रामः—(आकर्ण्य पुरतो विलोक्य ।)

अक्षोभ्यः क्षोभितः केन लक्ष्मणो धैर्यसागरः ।
येन रुष्टेन पश्यामि शताकीर्णमिवाग्रतः ॥ १७ ॥

(ततः प्रविशति धनुर्बाणपाणिर्लक्ष्मणः ।)

लक्ष्मणः—(सक्रोधम् ।) कथं कथं मोहमुपगत इति ।

यदि न सहसे राज्ञो मोहं धनुः स्पृश मा दया
स्वजननिभृतः सर्वोऽप्येवं मृदुः परिभूयते ।
अथ न रुचितं मुञ्च त्वं मामहं कृतनिश्चयो
युवतिरहितं लोकं कर्तुं यतश्छलिता वयम् ॥ १८ ॥

शोकादिति । शोकात्कैकेयीवचनोत्पन्नाद् अवचनात् किमप्यनुक्त्वा राज्ञा हस्तेन हस्तसंज्ञयैव विसर्जितः प्रेषितः । अहमितिशेषः । एतत्कुर्वतः तस्य किमप्यभिमतमिष्टमासीदितिमन्ये । नृपतिर्मोहं गतश्च । यद्वा नृपतिर्मोहं गतश्च । एतत् किमप्यभिमतं किंचिदिष्टं मन्ये । मोहावस्थायां शोकावेदनात् । इति योज्यम् ॥ १६ ॥ कथं मोहमुपगतस्तातद्दृढधीरस्वभावोपीत्याशयः । **अक्षोभ्यः** क्षोभयितुं शक्यः क्षोभ्यः न क्षोभ्यः अक्षोभ्यः धैर्यसागरः लक्ष्मणः केन क्षोभितः । येन रुष्टेन अग्रतः स्थितेन शताकीर्णं नराणां शतेनाकीर्णं व्याप्तमिव पुरः प्रदेशमिति शेषः पश्यामि । एकोपि क्रुद्धो गर्जन् लक्ष्मणो जनशतमिवाभातीत्यर्थः ॥ १७ ॥ धनुर्बाणश्च पाणौ यस्य । **कथमिति** । कथं ' कथं मोहमुपगतः ' इति केवलं पृच्छसीत्यर्थः । **यदि नेति** । यदि राज्ञः मोहं न सहसे पितुर्मोहः प्रतिकारार्ह इति मन्यसे चेदित्यर्थः । धनुः स्पृश । धनुर्गृहीत्वापकारप्रतिकारं कुरु इत्यर्थः । दया मास्तु । यद्वा दयामिति पठनीयम् । सर्वोपि स्वजननिभृतः स्वजने निभृतः विनीतः । स्वजनकृतं सर्वं सहमानः इत्यर्थः । मृदु अतीक्ष्णः । अमर्षशून्य इति यावत् । एवं परिभूयते तिरस्क्रियते । अथेतिपक्षान्तरे । न रुचितं प्रतिकारकरणं तेऽनभिमतं यदि । त्वं मां मुञ्च । अनुजानीहीत्यर्थः । किमर्थमिदमिति चेदहं लोकं युवतिरहितं कर्तुं कृतनिश्चयोस्मि । कुतोयं युवतिजने प्रद्वेष इति चेत् । यतः यस्मात्कारणात् । वयं छलिताः वञ्चिताः यौवनसम्पन्नया कैकेय्या नृपं वशीकृत्य राज्यात्प्रच्याविताः । यौवनकृतोयं दोषः । तस्माद्युवतिजातिरेव सकलोच्छेदमर्हतीति भावः । हरिणी वृत्तम् । न समरसला गः षड्वेदैर्हयैर्हरिणी मता । इति

सीता—आर्यपुत्र रोदितव्ये काले सौमित्रिणा धनुर्गृहीतम् । अपूर्वः खल्वस्यायासः । (अय्यउत्त रोदिदव्वे काले सोमित्तिणा धणू गहीदं । अपुव्वो खु से आआसो ।)

रामः—सुमित्रामातः किमिदम् ।

लक्ष्मणः—कथं कथं किमिदं नाम ।

> **क्रमप्राप्ते हृते राज्ये भुवि शोच्यासने नृपे ।**
> **इदानीमपि सन्देहः किं क्षमा निर्मनस्विता ॥ १९ ॥**

रामः—सुमित्रामातः अस्मद्राज्यभ्रंशो भवत उद्योगं जनयति । आः अपण्डितः खलु भवान् ।

> **भरतो वा भवेद् राजा वयं वा ननु तत् समम् ।**
> **यदि तेऽस्ति धनुःश्लाघा स राजा परिपाल्यताम् ॥ २० ॥**

लक्ष्मणः—न शक्नोमि रोषं धारयितुम् । भवतु भवतु । गच्छामस्तावत् । (प्रस्थितः ।)

रामः ।

> **त्रैलोक्यं दग्धुकामेव ललाटपुटसंस्थिता ।**
> **भ्रुकुटिर्लक्ष्मणस्यैषा नियतीव व्यवस्थिता ॥ २१ ॥**

लक्षणम् ॥ १८ ॥ रोदितव्ये महाराजस्य मोहप्राप्त्या रोदनार्हे । 'रुदन्त्यस्मिन्निति रोदितव्यः । बाहुलकादधिकरणे कृत्यप्रत्ययः । तथाभूते काले' इति ग. शा० । अपूर्वः आश्चर्यकरः । अस्य पितुरवस्थामगणयित्वा युवतिरहितं लोकं कर्तुमुद्यतस्यास्य । आयास खेदः । सुमित्रामातः सुमित्रा माता यस्य तस्य सम्बुद्धिः । अत्र मातृनामनिर्देशेन त्वयापि सुमित्रेण भाव्यं न तु अपकारपरेणेति ध्वनितम् । किमिदं कोयमकारणे संरम्भ इत्यर्थः । **क्रमप्राप्त** इति । क्रमेण पितुरनन्तरं ज्येष्ठपुत्रेण राज्यं प्राप्तव्यमिति क्रमेण प्राप्ते राज्ये हृते । नृपे भुवि न तु सिंहासने शोच्यमासनमवस्थानं यस्य तादृशे सति । इदानीमेवंगतावस्थायामपि सन्देहः प्रतिक्रियां प्रत्यनिश्चयः तव किं क्षमा तितिक्षा उत निर्मनस्विता अभिमानशून्यता । नैतद्वीरस्य योग्यमिति भावः ॥ १९ ॥ उद्योगं व्यवसायं जनयति प्रतिकारकर्मणि प्रवर्तयति । आः इति कोपे । अपण्डितः विचारशून्यः । **भरत** इति । भरतो राजा भवेत् वयं भवामो वा ननु तत्समं तुल्यमेव । भरते मयि च तव विशेषाभावात् । यदि ते तव धनुःश्लाघा कुशलो धनुर्धरोहमिति अभिमानोस्ति तर्हि स राजा भरतः परिपाल्यताम् । नवो रक्षणार्ह इति कृत्वेति शेषः ॥ २० ॥ धारयितुं निरोद्धुम् । भवतु भवतु त्वदुक्तं योग्यमयोग्यं वा यथा तथास्तु । **त्रैलोक्य**मिति । त्रयो लोकास्त्रैलोक्यम् । चातुर्वर्ण्यादित्वात्स्वार्थे ष्यञ् । दग्धुं

सुमित्रामातः इतस्तावत् ।

लक्ष्मणः—आर्य अयमस्मि ।

रामः—भवतः स्थैर्यमुत्पादयता मयैवमभिहितम् । उच्यतामिदानीम् ।

ताते धनुर्नमयि सत्यमवेक्षमाणे
मुञ्चानि मातरि शरं स्वधनं हरन्त्याम् ।
दोषेषु बाह्यमनुजं भरतं हनानि
किं रोषणाय रुचिरं त्रिषु पातकेषु ॥ २२ ॥

लक्ष्मणः—(सबाष्पम् ।) हा धिक् । अस्मान् अविज्ञायोपालभसे ।

यत्कृते महति क्लेशे राज्ये मे न मनोरथः ।
वर्षाणि किल वस्तव्यं चतुर्दश वने त्वया ॥ २३ ॥

कामो यस्याः सा दग्धुकामा इव । दहनोन्मुखीवेत्यर्थः । ललाटपुटे संस्थिता । नियतिरपि तथा । एषा लक्ष्मणस्य भ्रुकुटिः । भ्रुकुटिबन्ध इति यावत् । नियती विधिः इव । अत्र नियतिशब्दस्य कृदन्तत्वात् कृदिकारादक्तिनः इति ङीप् । वस्तुतो नियातिशब्दो ह्रस्वेकारान्त एवोपलभ्यते । व्यवस्थिता समाहिता । वियतीवेति पाठो न मनोरमः । स्थैर्यमुत्पादयितुं वस्तुयाथार्थ्यदर्शनेन चित्तक्षोभनिवारणात् स्थिरतामापादयितुमित्यर्थः । **तात** इति । सत्यं स्वसत्यसंधतामवेक्षमाणे पालयति तावे धनुर्नमयि (–यै–यानि) किं धनुर्नमयित्वा तातं प्रहराणि किमित्यर्थः । धनुर्नमतु इति पाठान्तरम् । किन्त्वस्मिन्प्रक्रमभङ्गदोषः । स्वधनं प्रतिश्रुतं राज्यं हरन्त्यां मातरि कैकेय्यां शरान्मुञ्चानि किम् । दोषेषु बाह्यं दोषैरलिप्तम् । अनुजं भरतं हनानि किम् । एतेषु त्रिषु पातकेषु रोषणाय क्रोधाय किं रुचिरम् । तव किमभिमतमित्यर्थः । अत्र प्रथमपङ्क्तौ ताते धनुर्न मयि इति पाठः । तस्यायमर्थः । मयि मत्सम्बन्धेन सत्यमवेक्षमाणे ताते धनुः न प्रयोज्यमिति शेषः । तातस्तु धनुः प्रहारं नार्हत्येव । किंत्वस्मिन्नर्थे पातकाभावादयं पाठो हेयः त्रिषु पातकेषु इति चतुर्थचरणोक्तपातकत्रयाभावात् । वसन्ततिलका वृत्तम् ॥ २२ ॥ अस्मानविज्ञाय ममाशयं सम्यगगृहीत्वा । उपालभसे जुगुप्ससे । **यत्कृत** इति । यत्कृते येन कारणेन कृते महति क्लेशे सति मम हृदये वर्तमाने मे राज्ये स्पृहा न तत्कारणं त्वया न ज्ञातमिति शेषः । किं तदित्यपेक्षायामाह । चतुर्दश वर्षाणि त्वया वने वस्तव्यं किल । भरतस्य राज्यप्राप्त्या केवलयाऽसंतुष्टा सा भवतो वनवासमपि प्रार्थितवतीत्यतो मे मनसः संतापो जात इत्यभिप्रायः । 'यत्कृते येनार्थेन कृते महति क्लेशे चिन्त्यमाने इति शेषः मे इ० । तमर्थमविज्ञायेति पूर्वेण वाक्येन सम्बन्धः । स इत्थंभूतोर्थः किं स्वरूप इत्याकाङ्क्षायां चतुर्दशेत्यादि । इति गणपतिशास्त्रिणः ॥ २३ ॥

---

१ नमतु, न मयि

रामः—अत्र मोहमुपगतस्तत्रभवान्। हन्त निवेदितमप्रभुत्वम्। मैथिलि

मङ्गलार्थेऽनया दत्तान् वल्कलांस्तावदानय।
करोम्यन्यैर्नृपैर्धर्मं नैवाप्तं नोपपादितम् ॥ २४ ॥

सीता—गृह्णात्वार्यपुत्रः। (गह्णदु अय्यउत्तो।)

रामः—मीथैलि किं व्यवसितम्।

सीता—ननु सहधर्मचारिणी खल्वहम्। (णं सहधम्मआरिणी क्खु अहं।)

रामः—मयैकाकिना किल गन्तव्यम्।

सीता—अतो नुखल्वनुगच्छामि। (अदो णुखु अणुगच्छामि)

रामः—वने खलु वस्तव्यम्।

सीता—तत् खलु मे प्रासादः। (तं खु मे पासादो।)

रामः—श्वश्रूश्वशुरशुश्रूषापि च ते निर्वर्तयितव्या।

सीता—एतामुद्दिश्य देवतानां प्रणामः क्रियते। (णं उद्दिसिअ देवदाणं पणामो करीअदि)

रामः—लक्ष्मण वार्यतामियम्।

लक्ष्मणः—आर्य नोत्सहे श्लाघनीये काले वारयितुमत्रभवतीम्। कुतः

अनुचरति शशाङ्कं राहुदोषेऽपि तारा
पतति च वनवृक्षे याति भूमिं लता च।

अत्रेति। अत्र मच्चतुर्दशवनवासश्रवणेनेत्यर्थः। तत्रभवान् तातः। हन्तेति खेदे। अप्रभुत्वं मोहमुपगच्छता मनःखेदनियमनेऽसामर्थ्यम्। **मङ्गलार्थ** इति। अनया अवदातिकया दत्तान् वल्कलान् मङ्गलार्थे वनगमनरूपमङ्गलकर्मानुष्ठानार्थम्। आनय तावत्। तानि परिधाय अन्यैः नृपैः नैवाप्तं बाल्ये इति शेषः। नोपपादितं नानुष्ठितं धर्मं पित्राज्ञापालनरूपं करोमि वनगमनेनाचरिष्यामि ॥ २४ ॥ व्यवसितं कर्तुमध्यवसितम्। सहधर्मचारिणीति सह पत्या धर्मं चरतीति सहधर्मचारिणी। अतः यं धर्मं त्वं चरसि तत्र मम साहचर्यमुपपन्नमेव। अतस्त्वया सह वनमागमिष्यामीति मनसि कृत्वा पत्नीति वक्तव्ये सहधर्मचारिणीत्युक्तवती। अतः असहायो गच्छसीति तव साहाय्यार्थम्। निर्वर्तयितव्या वधूधर्मतः कर्तव्या। यथा मया सहागमनं सहधर्मचारितया। देवतानां प्रणामः क्रियते देवतानां प्रसादात्तयोः कुशलं स्यादिति भावः। श्लाघनीये सीताया भवतोनुगमनाध्यवसायादिति भावः। **अनुचरतीति**। राहुदोषे राहुकृतग्रसनरूपदोषे आपद्यपि। तारा शशाङ्कमनुसरति। वनवृक्षे गजादिना भग्ने भूमिं याति मह्यां पतति लता तदाश्रया वल्ली पतति च। पङ्क-

त्यजति न च करेणुः पङ्कलग्नं गजेन्द्रं
व्रजतु चरतु धर्मं भर्तृनाथा हि नार्यः ॥ २५ ॥

(प्रविश्य)

चेटी—जयतु भट्टिनी । नेपथ्यपालिन्यार्यरेवा प्रणम्य विज्ञापयति—अवदातिकया सङ्गीतशालाया आच्छिद्य वल्कला आनीताः । इमेऽपरा अननुभूता वल्कलाः । निर्वर्त्यतां तावत् किल प्रयोजनमिति । (जेदु भट्टिणी । णेवच्छपालिणी अय्यरेवा पणमिअ विण्णवेदि आदोदिआए सङ्गीदसालादो आच्छिन्दिअ वक्कला आणीदा । इमा अवरा अणणुहूदा वक्कला । णिव्वत्तीअदु दाव किल पओअणं त्ति ।)

रामः—भद्रे आनय सन्तुष्टैषा । वयमर्थिनः ।

चेटी—गृह्णातु भर्ता । (गह्णदु भट्टा ।) (तथा कृत्वा निष्क्रान्ता ।)

(रामो गृहीत्वा परिधत्ते ।)

लक्ष्मणः—प्रसीदत्वार्यः ।

निर्योगाद् भूषणान्माल्यात् सर्वेभ्योऽर्धं प्रदाय मे ।
चीरमेकाकिना बद्धं चीरे खल्वसि मत्सरी ॥ २६ ॥

रामः—मैथिलि वार्यतामयम् ।

सीता—सौमित्रे निवर्त्यतां किल । (सोमित्ते णिवत्तिअदु किळ ।)

लक्ष्मणः—आर्ये ।

लग्नं पङ्कमग्नं गजेन्द्रं करेणुः हस्तिनी तत्सहचरी न त्यजति । एवमस्य धर्मस्य सर्वैः प्रतिपन्नत्वादस्या वारणं न युक्तमित्यर्थः । अतः इयं वनं व्रजतु धर्मं चरतु च । उक्तमर्थं सामान्येन समर्थयति । हि यतो नार्यो भर्तृनाथाः भर्ता नाथः सर्वत्र विषये प्रभुः यासां तादृश्यः । भर्तृपरतन्त्रा इत्यर्थः ॥ २५ ॥ आच्छिद्य बलादपनीय । अननुभूता अपरिहिताः । नवा इत्यर्थः । निवर्त्यतां प्रयोजनम् । अवदातिकया नीतानि वल्कलानि न प्रत्यानीतानि । अतो भट्टिन्याः कदाचिदधिकैः प्रयोजनं भवेदित्यनुमिमानाया उक्तिरियम् । वयमर्थिनः मम प्रयोजनमेतैरित्यर्थः । **निर्योगादिति** । निर्योगात् 'वस्त्रकञ्चुकादेराच्छादनात् ।' इति ग० शा० । भूषणात् जातौ एकवचनम् । अलङ्कारेभ्य इत्यर्थः । माल्यात्स्रगादेः । एवं सर्वेभ्यो भोग्यवस्तुभ्यो मे मह्यमर्धं दत्वा चीरं वल्कलानि एकाकिना बद्धं बद्धानि । चीरे मत्सरी असि खलु । खलु जिज्ञासायां कथं ते मत्सरः इत्यर्थः । यद्वा विषादे । अतो मे विषाद इत्यर्थः । अतश्चीरार्धमपि मह्यं प्रयच्छ येन त्वया सह वनमागमिष्यामीति भावः ॥ २६ ॥ तस्याभिप्रायं ज्ञात्वाह वार्यतामिति ।

गुरोर्मे पादशुश्रूषां त्वमेका कर्तुमिच्छसि ।
तवैव दक्षिणः पादो मम सव्यो भविष्यति ॥ २७ ॥

सीता—दयतां खल्वार्यपुत्रः । संतप्यते सौमित्रिः । (दीअदु खु अय्यउत्तो । सन्तप्पदि सोमित्ती ।)

रामः—सौमित्रे श्रूयताम् । वल्कलानि नाम

तपःसङ्ग्रामकवचं नियमद्विरदाङ्कुशः ।
खलीनमिन्द्रियाश्वानां गृह्यतां धर्मसारथिः ॥ २८ ॥

लक्ष्मणः—अनुगृहीतोऽस्मि । (गृहीत्वा परिधत्ते ।)

रामः—श्रुतवृत्तान्तैः पौरैः सन्निरुद्धो राजमार्गः । उत्सार्यतामुत्सार्यतां तावत् ।

लक्ष्मणः—आर्य अहमग्रतो यास्यामि । उत्सार्यतामुत्सार्यताम् ।

रामः—मैथिलि अपनीयतामवगुण्ठनम् ।

सीता—यदार्यपुत्र आज्ञापयति । (जं अय्यउत्तो आणवेदि ।) (अपनयति ।)

रामः—भो भोः पौराः शृण्वन्तु शृण्वन्तु भवन्तः ।

स्वैरं हि पश्यन्तु कलत्रमेतद् बाष्पाकुलाक्षैर्वदनैर्भवन्तः ।
निर्दोषदृश्या हि भवन्ति नार्यो यज्ञे विवाहे व्यसने वने च ॥ २९ ॥

गुरोरिति । मे मम गुरोः वनं गतस्य पादशुश्रूषां चरणसेवां त्वमेका कर्तुमिच्छसि । इति प्रश्नकाकुः । नैतद्युक्तमित्याह—तवैव शुश्रूषार्थं दक्षिणः पादः मम सव्यो भविष्यति ॥ २७ ॥ सन्तप्यते पीड्यते । **तपःसंग्रामेति** । तप एव संग्रामो युद्धं तस्मिन् कवचम् । नियमो व्रतं स एव द्विरदस्तस्य तन्नियमनार्थः अङ्कुशः सृणिः । इन्द्रियाण्येवाश्वास्तेषां खलीनं तन्निग्रहसाधनम् । धर्मस्य सारथिः । एवं भूतमिदं गृह्यताम् ॥ २८ ॥ अथ प्रस्थातुकामो रामः पुरतो जनाकुलमार्गं दृष्ट्वाह श्रुतवृत्तान्तैरिति । उत्सार्यतां जनसंमर्द इति शेषः । अवगुण्ठनं शिरोवेष्टनवस्त्रम् । सीतां दृष्ट्वा तद्दर्शनकांक्षिणः पौरा निवर्तेरन्निति मत्वाह भो भोः पौरा इत्यादि । **स्वैरमिति** । बाष्पाकुले अक्षिणी येषां तैः वदनैः उपलक्षिताः । सीतार्थं जातपीडा इति यावत् । भवन्तः एतद्वनगमनोन्मुखं कलत्रं मम भार्या सीतां स्वैरं स्वेच्छानुसारतः पश्यन्तु । ननु परकलत्रं कथं निरीक्षणीयमित्यत्राह निर्दोषदृश्या इति । नार्यः यज्ञे यज्ञकर्मणि विवाहे विवाहविधौ । व्यसने आपद्ग्रस्ता इत्यर्थः । वने स्थिताः च निर्दोषदृश्या दोषं विना

(प्रविश्य)

काञ्चुकीयः—कुमार न खलु न खलु गन्तव्यम् । एष हि महाराजः

श्रुत्वा ते वनगमनं वधूसहायं
सौभ्रात्रव्यवसितलक्ष्मणानुयात्रम् ।
उत्थाय क्षितितलरेणुरूषिताङ्गः
कान्तारद्विरद इवोपयाति जीर्णः ॥ ३० ॥

लक्ष्मणः—आर्य ।

चीरमात्रोत्तरीयाणां किं दृश्यं वनवासिनाम् ।

रामः—

गतेष्वस्मासु राजा नः शिरःस्थानानि पश्यतु ॥ ३१ ॥

(इति निष्क्रान्ताः सर्वे ।)

प्रथमोऽङ्कः ।

द्रष्टुं योग्या भवन्ति । उपजातिश्छन्दः ॥ २९ ॥ **श्रुत्वेति** । वधूः सहायोयास्मिंस्तद्व-धूसहायम् । शोभनस्य भ्रातुर्भावः सौभ्रात्रं भ्रातृप्रेम । तेन व्यवसितः कृतोद्योगः । लक्ष्मणस्तस्य अनुयात्राऽनुगमनं यस्मिन् । व्यवसितेति अनुयात्राविशेषणं वा । तथा भूतं ते वनगमनं श्रुत्वा जीर्णो वृद्धः । महाराजः उत्थाय क्षितितले यो रेणुस्तेन रुषितं लिप्तमङ्गं यस्य तथाभूतः । कान्तारद्विपो वन्यगजः । सोपि क्षितितलरेणुधूसराङ्गो भवति । इवोपयाति । प्रहर्षिणीवृत्तम् । तल्लक्षणम्—त्र्याशाभिर्मनजरगाः प्रहर्षिणीयम् । इति ॥ ३० ॥ **चीरेति** । चीरमात्रं न तु दुकूलादिकं शोभाकरम् । उत्तरीयं येषां तेषामस्माकं किं दृश्यं दर्शनीयं दर्शनेन को लाभ इत्यर्थः । अङ्कं समापयितुमिच्छन्कविराह राममुखेन । राज्ञो शोककारणपरिजिहीर्षया गच्छामः । अस्मासु गतेषु राजा नः शिरःस्थानानि प्रधान-निवासस्थानानि पश्यतु । निष्क्रान्ताः सर्वे इति अङ्कसमाप्तिं सूचयति । तदुक्तं दशरूपके एकाहचरितैकार्थमित्थमासन्ननायकम् । पात्रैस्त्रिचतुरैरङ्कं तेषामन्तेस्य निर्गमः ॥ इति ॥ अङ्कलक्षणमादिभरते—अङ्क इति रूढिशब्दो भावैश्च रसैश्च रोहयत्यर्थान् । नाना-विधानयुक्तो यस्मात्तस्माद्भवेदङ्कः ॥ यत्रार्थस्य समाप्तिर्यत्र च बीजस्य भवति संहारः । किंचिदवलग्नबिन्दुः सोङ्क इति सदावगन्तव्यः ॥ ये नायका निगदितास्तेषां प्रत्यक्षचरित-संयुक्तः । नानावस्थान्तरितः कार्यस्त्वङ्को यथार्थरसः ॥ इति प्रतिमाटीकायां प्रथमोङ्कः ॥

अथ द्वितीयोऽङ्कः ।

(ततः प्रविशति काञ्चुकीयः ।)

काञ्चुकीयः—भो भोः प्रतिहारव्यापृताः । स्वेषु स्वेषु स्थानेष्वप्रमत्ता भवन्तु भवन्तः ।

(प्रविश्य)

प्रतिहारी—आर्य किमेतत् । (अय्य किं एदं ।)

काञ्चुकीयः—एष हि महाराजः सत्यवचनरक्षणपरं राममरण्यं गच्छन्तमुपावर्तयितुमशक्तः पुत्रविरहशोकाग्निना दग्धहृदय उन्मत्त इव बहु प्रलपन् समुद्रगृहके शयानः

मेरुश्चलन्निव युगक्षयसन्निकर्षे
शोषं व्रजन्निव महोदधिरप्रमेयः ।
सूर्यः पतन्निव च मण्डलमात्रलक्ष्यः
शोकाद् भृशं शिथिलदेहमतिर्नरेन्द्रः ॥ १ ॥

प्रतिहारी—हा हा एवंगतो महाराजः । (हा हा एव्वंगओ महाराओ ।)

काञ्चुकीयः—भवति गच्छ ।

प्रतिहारी—आर्य तथा । (अय्य तह ।) (निष्कान्ता ।)

काञ्चुकीयः—(सर्वतो विलोक्य ।) अहो तु खलु रामनिर्गमनदिनादारभ्य शून्यैवेयमयोध्या संलक्ष्यते । कुतः

पूर्वाङ्कसूचिता पुत्रवियोगशोकजन्या दशरथस्यावस्थाऽस्मिन्सर्गे उपनिबद्धा । अथ तस्या वर्णनेन दशरथप्रवेशं सूचयितुं काञ्चुकीयस्य तावत्प्रवेशमाह ततः प्रविशतीति । प्रतिहारव्यापृताः द्वाररक्षिणः । अप्रमत्ताः सावधानाः । उपावर्तयितुं निवर्तयितुम् । समुद्रगृहके मुद्राभिः सहितं गृहं समुद्रगृहं नाम प्रासादारामे निदाघोष्मनिवारणार्थे जलोद्गारयत्रसनाथं क्रीडागृहम् । समुद्रगृहमित्युक्तं जलयन्त्रनिकेतनम् । इति हारावली । **मेरुरिति** । युगस्यान्तः युगान्तस्तस्य संनिकर्षे संनिधाने आसन्ने प्रलये चलन् मेरुः स्वर्णगिरिरिव । अप्रमेयः प्रमातुमियत्तया परिच्छेत्तुमशक्यः महोदधिः शोषं व्रजन् इव । मण्डलमात्रेण लक्ष्यः तेजःसंहारादित्यर्थः । पतन् सूर्य **इव शोकात्** भृशमत्यन्तं शिथिलो देहो मतिश्च यस्य तादृशः वर्तते इति शेषः । वसन्ततिलका वृत्तम् ॥ १ ॥

नागेन्द्रा यवसाभिलाषविमुखाः सास्रेक्षणा वाजिनो
हेषाशून्यमुखाः सवृद्धवनिताबालाश्च पौरा जनाः ।
त्यक्ताहारकथाः सुदीनवदनाः क्रन्दन्त उच्चैर्दिशा
रामो याति यया सदारसहजस्तामेव पश्यन्त्यमी ॥ २ ॥

यावदहमपि महाराजस्य समीपवर्ती भविष्यामि । (परिक्रम्यावलोक्य ।) अये अयं महाराजो महादेव्या सुमित्रया च सुदुःसहमपि पुत्रविरहसमुद्भवं शोकं निगृह्यात्मानमेव संस्थापयन्तीभ्यामन्वास्यमानस्तिष्ठति । कष्टा खल्ववस्था वर्तते । एष एष महाराजः

पतत्युथाय चोत्थाय हा हेत्युच्चैर्लपन् मुहुः ।
दिशं पश्यति तामेव यया यातो रघूद्वहः ॥ ३ ॥

(निष्क्रान्तः ।)

मिश्र विष्कम्भकः ।

(ततः प्रविशति यथानिर्दिष्टो राजा देव्यौ च ।)

राजा—

हा वत्स राम जगतां नयनाभिराम
हा वत्स लक्ष्मण सलक्षणसर्वगात्र ।

नागेन्द्रा इति । अमी नागेद्राः यवसाभिलाषात्तृणग्रासेच्छाया विमुखाः । वाजिनः अश्वाः अस्रैः सहिते सास्रे अक्षिणी येषां ते सास्रेक्षणाः साश्रुनयनाः । हेषाऽश्वशब्दस्तया शून्यं मुखं येषां तादृशाश्च । त्यक्ता आहारकथा यैस्ते त्यक्ताहारकथाः सुदीनवदनाः उच्चैः क्रन्दन्तः सवृद्धवनिताबालाः पौरा जनाश्च यया दिशा दारैः सहजेन च सहितः सदारसहजः रामः याति तामेव पश्यन्ति । शार्दूलवि० वृत्तम् ॥ २ ॥ महादेव्या कौसल्यया । संस्थापयन्तीभ्यां समाश्वासयन्तीभ्याम् । **पततीति** उत्थायोत्थाय मुहुर्हा हा इत्युच्चैर्लपन् पतति । स्पष्टमन्यत् ॥३॥ मिश्रविष्कम्भक इति । वृत्तवर्तिष्यमाणानां कथांशानां निदर्शकः । संक्षिप्तार्थस्तु विष्कम्भो मध्यपात्रप्रयोजितः । एकानेककृतः शुद्धः संकीर्णो नीचमध्यमैः ॥ इति दशरूपकम् । हा **वत्सेति** । नयनयोः अभिरामः रमणीयः नयनाभिरामः तत्सम्बुद्धिः । लक्षणैः सहितानि सलक्षणानि सर्वाणि गात्राणि यस्य स

---

१ अयं श्लोक एवमन्यथा पठ्यते—

हा राम लोकग्रहणाभिराम हा लक्ष्मण भ्रातृषु लक्ष्मिभूत ।
हा साध्वि वैदेहि कुलप्रदीपे हा कीर्तिरेषां गमनात्प्रनष्टा ॥

हा साध्वि मैथिलि पतिस्थितचित्तवृत्ते
हा हा गताः किल वनं बत मे तनूजाः ॥ ४ ॥

चित्रमिदं भोः यद् भ्रातृस्नेहात् पितरि विमुक्तस्नेहमपि तावल्लक्ष्मणं द्रष्टुमिच्छामि । वधु वैदेहि

रामेणापि परित्यक्तो लक्ष्मणेन च गर्हितः ।
अयशोभाजनं लोके परित्यक्तस्त्वयाप्यहम् ॥ ५ ॥

पुत्र राम वत्स लक्ष्मण वधु वैदेहि प्रयच्छत मे प्रतिवचनं पुत्रकाः । शून्यमिदं भोः । न मे कश्चित् प्रतिवचनं प्रयच्छति । कौसल्यामातः क्वासि ।

सत्यसन्ध जितक्रोध विमत्सर जगत्प्रिय ।
गुरुशुश्रूषणे युक्त प्रतिवाक्यं प्रयच्छ मे ॥ ६ ॥

हा क्वासौ सर्वजनहृदयनयनाभिरामो रामः । क्वासौ मयि गुर्वनुवृत्तिः । क्वासौ शोकार्तेष्वनुकम्पा । क्वासौ तृणवदगणितराज्यैश्वर्यः । पुत्र राम वृद्धं पितरं मां परित्यज्य किमसम्बद्धेन धर्मेण ते कृत्यम् । हा धिक् । कष्टं भोः

सूर्य इव गतो रामः सूर्यं दिवस इव लक्ष्मणोऽनुगतः ।
सूर्यदिवसावसाने छायेव न दृश्यते सीता ॥ ७ ॥

(ऊर्ध्वमवलोक्य ।) भोः कृतान्तहतक

अनपत्या वयं रामः पुत्रोऽन्यस्य महीपतेः ।
वने व्याघ्री च कैकेयी त्वया किं न कृतं त्रयम् ॥ ←

सलक्षणसर्वगात्रः । पत्यौ स्थिता चित्तवृत्तिर्यस्याः सा पतिस्थितचित्तवृत्तिः । तस्या सम्बोधनम् । वसन्ततिलकं वृत्तम् ॥४॥ **रामेणापीति** । रामेणापि तादृशपितृभक्तिशालिनापीति अपेरर्थः । गर्हितः निन्दितः मत्परित्यागादिति यावत् । त्वयापि परित्यक्तोऽहं लोके अयशोभाजनं दुष्कीर्तिपात्रं जातः ॥ ५ ॥ पुत्रकाः कः अनुकम्पार्थे । **सत्यसन्ध** इति । सत्यसन्ध सत्या संधा प्रतिज्ञा यस्य तस्य सम्बुद्धिः । स्पष्टमन्यत् ॥ ६ ॥ गुर्वी चासौ अनुरक्तिः । तृणवदगणितं राज्यैश्वर्यं येन सः । असम्बद्धेन त्वया सम्बन्धरहितेन परकीयेणेत्यर्थः । **सूर्य इव** इति । रामः सूर्य इव गतः । सूर्यं दिवस इव लक्ष्मणो राममनुगतः । सूर्यदिवसयोः अवसाने अन्तर्धाने छाया इव सीता न दृश्यते । उपमालंकारः । आर्या छन्दः । तल्लक्षणं—यस्याः प्रथमे पादे द्वादश मात्रास्तथा तृतीयेपि । अष्टादश द्वितीये चतुर्थके पञ्चदश सार्या ॥ ७ ॥ वयं नास्ति अपत्यं येषां ते अनपत्याः कृताः । रामः अन्यस्य महीपतेः पुत्रः कृतः । मां परित्यज्य गमनात् । कैकेयी च वने व्याघ्रीव कृता । त्वया इदं त्रयं किं न कृतम् । पर्यायोक्त-

कौसल्या—(सरुदितम्।) अलमिदानीं महाराजोऽतिमात्रं सन्तप्य परवशमात्मानं कर्तुम्। ननु सा तौ च कुमारौ महाराजस्य समयावसाने प्रेक्षितव्या भविष्यन्ति। (अलं दाणि महाराओ अदिमत्तं सन्तप्पिअ परवसं अत्ताणं कादुं। णं सा ते अ कुमारा महाराअस्स समआवसाणे पेक्खिदव्वा भविस्सन्ति।

राजा—का त्वं भोः।

कौसल्या—अस्निग्धपुत्रप्रसविनी खल्वहम्। (असिणिद्धपुत्तप्पसविणी खु अहं।)

राजा—किं किं सर्वजनहृदयनयनाभिरामस्य रामस्य जननी त्वमसि कौसल्या।

कौसल्या—महाराज सैव मन्दभागिनी खल्वहम्। (महाराअ सा एव मन्दभाइणी खु अहं।)

राजा—कौसल्ये सारवती खल्वसि। त्वया हि[२] खलु रामो गर्भे धृतः।

अहं हि दुःखमत्यन्तमसह्यं ज्वलनोपमम्।
नैव सोढुं न संहर्तुं शक्नोमि मुषितेन्द्रियः॥ ९॥

(सुमित्रां विलोक्य) इयमपरा का।

कौसल्या—महाराज वत्सलक्ष्मण—(महाराअ वच्छलक्खण) (इत्यर्धोक्ते।)

राजा—(सहसोत्थाय) क्वासौ क्वासौ लक्ष्मणः। न दृश्यते। भोः कष्टम्।

मलङ्कारः॥ ८॥ अलमात्मानं परवशं पराधीनं कर्तुम्। शोकवशं गत्वात्मानं पराधीनं मा कुरु इत्यर्थः। समयावसाने समयः चतुर्दश वर्षाणि यावद्वने स्थातव्यमित्येवंरूपः। तस्यावसाने अन्ते। अस्निग्धं पुत्रं प्रसूते असौ। अस्निग्धः पितुरनुनयमप्रतिपद्य वनगमनात्स्नेहाभाववान्। कौसल्योक्तममृष्यन्नाह सर्वजनहृदयेति। तादृशस्य जननी न त्वस्निग्धपुत्रस्य। सारवती सत्वसम्पन्ना शोकभारसहनात्। भारधारणक्षमा च। अहं हि इति। अहं हि खलु मुषितेन्द्रियः मुषितानि नष्टसामर्थ्यानि इन्द्रियाणि यस्य तादृशः सन् अत्यन्तमसह्यं ज्वलनस्य उपमा यस्य ज्वलनेन सदृशं वा ज्वलनोपमं दुःखं सोढुं संहर्तुं निग्रहीतुं वा न शक्नोमि॥ ९॥ सहसा वत्स लक्ष्मण इत्यर्धोक्त-

---

१ अदिमत्तं सोहस्स अत्ताणं दातुम्। इ. पा. २ तु.

(देव्यौ ससंभ्रममुत्थाय राजानमवलम्बेते ।)

कौसल्या—महाराज वत्सलक्ष्मणस्य जननी सुमित्रेति वक्तुं मयोपक्रान्तम् । (महाराअ वच्छळक्खणस्स जणणी सुमित्तत्ति वत्तुं मए उवक्कन्दं ।)

राजा—अयि सुमित्रे

तवैव पुत्रः सत्पुत्रो येन नक्तन्दिवं वने ।
रामो रघुकुलश्रेष्ठश्छाययेवानुगम्यते ॥ १० ॥

(प्रविश्य)

काञ्चुकीयः—जयतु महाराजः । एष खलु तत्रभवान् सुमन्त्रः प्राप्तः ।

राजा—(सहसोत्थाय सहर्षम् ।) अपि रामेण ।

काञ्चुकीयः—न खलु । रथेन ।

राजा—कथं कथं रथेन केवलेन । (इति मूर्छितः पतति ।)

देव्यौ—महाराज समाश्वसिहि समाश्वसिहि । (महाराअ समस्ससिहि समस्ससिहि ।) (गात्राणि परामृशतः ।)

काञ्चुकीयः—भोः कष्टम् । ईदृग्विधाः पुरुषविशेषा ईदृशीमापदं प्राप्नुवन्तीति विधिरनतिक्रमणीयः । महाराज समाश्वसिहि समाश्वसिहि ।

राजा—(किञ्चित् समाश्वस्य ।) बालाके सुमन्त्र एक एव ननु प्राप्तः ।

काञ्चुकीयः—महाराज अथ किम् ।

राजा—कष्टं भोः

शून्यः प्राप्तो यदि रथो भग्नो मम मनोरथः ।
नूनं दशरथं नेतुं कालेन प्रेषितो रथः ॥ ११ ॥

तेन हि शीघ्रं प्रवेश्यताम् ।

शब्दश्रवणानन्तरमेव । उपक्रान्तं प्रस्तुतमासीत् । **तवैवेति** । सत्पुत्रः । तत्र हेतुमाह येनेति । नक्तं च दिवा च नक्तंदिवम् । अचतुरविचतुरेत्यादिना सिद्धम् । रघुकुलश्रेष्ठः रामः छाययेव । कदाप्यपरिहानात् । अनुगम्यते ॥ १० ॥ रामेण सहेति शेषः । रथेन केवलेन रामरहितेनेत्यर्थः । ईदृशी विधा येषां ते ईदृक्विधाः । पुरुषविशेषा पुरुषश्रेष्ठाः । बालाके—बालाकिरिति काञ्चुकीयस्य नाम । **शून्य इति** । शून्यः रामादिरहितः । मनोरथः शोकाकुलं मां ज्ञात्वा कदाचिद्राम आगच्छेदित्येवं रूपः । नूनमिति मे

काञ्चुकीयः—यदाज्ञापयति महाराजः । (निष्क्रान्तः ।)

राजा—

धन्याः खलु वने वातास्तटाकपरिवर्तिनः ।
विचरन्तं वने रामं ये स्पृशन्ति यथासुखम् ॥ १२ ॥

(ततः प्रविशति सुमन्त्रः ।)

सुमन्त्रः—(सर्वतो विलोक्य सशोकम् ।)

एते भृत्याः स्वानि कर्माणि हित्वा
स्नेहाद् रामे जातबाष्पाकुलाक्षाः ।
चिन्तादीनाः शोकसंदग्धदेहा
विक्रोशन्तं पार्थिवं गर्हयन्ति ॥ १३ ॥

(उपेत्य ।) जयतु महाराजः ।

राजा—भ्रातः सुमन्त्र ।

क्व मे ज्येष्ठो रामः—

नहि नहि युक्तमभिहितं मया ।

क्व ते ज्येष्ठो रामः प्रियसुत सुतः सा क्व दुहिता
विदेहानां भर्तुर्निरतिशयभक्तिर्गुरुजने ।
क्व वा सौमित्रिर्मां हतपितृकमासन्नमरणं
किमप्याहुः किं ते सकलजनशोकार्णवकरम् ॥ १४ ॥

मृत्युरुपस्थित इत्यर्थः ॥ ११ ॥ **धन्या इति** । इमे वाताः । तटाकपरिवाहिनः तटाकः सपद्मजलाशयः तत्प्रान्तवाहिनः । एतेन तेषां सौगन्ध्यं शीतलत्वं च ध्वनितम् । कस्माद्धन्या इत्याह ये यथासुखं रामं स्पृशन्ति ॥ १२ ॥ एते इति । रामे स्नेहात् जातेन बाष्पेण आकुले अक्षिणी येषां ते जातबाष्पाकुलाक्षाः । चिन्तया दीनाः । शोकेन संदग्धः देहो येषां ते शोकसंदग्धदेहाः । चिन्तादिना स्वानि कार्याणि हित्वा विक्रोशन्तं पार्थिवं गर्हयन्ति निन्दन्ति अयोग्यं कर्म त्वया कृतमिति । शालिनी वृत्तम् । मात्तौ गौ चेच्छालिनी वेदलोकैः । इति लक्षणम् ॥ १३ ॥ युक्तमभिहितं मे राम इति ब्रुवता । सर्वलोकाभिरामं रामं वनं प्रहिण्वतो मम तस्य स्वपुत्रत्वेन निर्दोषोऽयुक्त इति भावः । **क्व ते** इति । हे प्रियसुत प्रियः सुतः रामः यस्य तत्सम्बुद्धिः । नाहं प्रियसुत इति ध्वनिः । गुरुजने श्वश्रूश्वशुरादौ निरतिशया भक्तिर्यस्याः सा निरतिशयभक्तिः विदेहानां दुहिता क्व । स सौमित्रिः वा क्व । आसन्नमरणं सकलजनशोकार्णवकरं हतपितृकं मां किमप्याहुः किम् । शिखरिणी वृत्तम् । रसैरुद्रैश्छिन्ना यमनस-

सुमन्त्रः—महाराज मा मैवममङ्गलवचनानि भाषिष्ठाः । अचिरादेव तान् द्रक्ष्यसि ।

राजा—सत्यमयुक्तमभिहितं मया । नायं तपस्विनामुचितः प्रश्नः । तत् कथ्यताम् । अपि तपस्विनां तपो वर्धते । अप्यरण्यानि स्वाधीनानि विचरन्ती वैदेही न परिखिद्यते ।

सुमन्त्रः—सुमन्त्र बहुवल्कलालङ्कृतशरीरा बालाप्यबालचारित्रा भर्तुः सहधर्मचारिणी अस्मान् महाराजं च किञ्चिन्नालपति । (सुमन्त बहु-वक्कलाळङ्किदसरीरा वाळा वि अवाळचारित्ता भत्तुणो सहधम्मआरिणी अह्मे महाराअं च किंचि णाळवदि)

सुमन्त्रः—सर्व एव महाराजम्—

राजा—न न । श्रोत्ररसायनैर्मम हृदयातुरौषधैस्तेषां नामधेयैरेव श्रावय ।

सुमन्त्रः—यदाज्ञापयति महाराजः । आयुष्मान् रामः ।

राजा—राम इति । अयं रामः । तन्नामश्रवणात् स्पृष्ट इव मे प्रतिभाति । ततस्ततः ।

सुमन्त्रः—आयुष्मान् लक्ष्मणः ।

राजा—अयं लक्ष्मणः । ततस्ततः ।

सुमन्त्रः—आयुष्मती सीता जनकराजपुत्री ।

भलागः शिखरिणी । इति लक्षणात् ॥ १४ ॥ मा भाषिष्ठाः मा भाषस्व । 'माङि लुङ्' इति माङ्योगे भाषतेर्लुङ् । तपस्विनां रामादीनामरण्यचारित्वात् । स्वस्मिन्नधि स्वाधीनम् । सप्तमी शौण्डैः इति समासः । अषडक्षा—इति खः । स्वाधीनानि स्वायत्तानि । ' स्वभुजवीर्यगुप्तिवशादात्मायत्तत्वं प्रापितानि अकुतोभयसञ्चाराणीत्यर्थः । इति ग. शा. । बहुवल्कलालंकृतशरीरा बहु अनेकविधं यथा तथा वल्कलाभ्यामलङ्कृतं शरीरं यस्याः सा । अबालाया इव चारित्रं यस्याः सा । चरित्रमेव चारित्रं शीलम् । प्रज्ञादिभ्यश्च इति अण् । महाराजमित्य पूर्णमिदं वाक्यम् । कर्णहृदयानन्दनानि तेषां नामानि पृथक् पृथक् निर्दिश्य कथयेत्याह श्रोत्रेति । श्रोत्रयोः रसायनानि । रसायनं नाम नानारसनिर्मितः भेषजविशेषः वैद्यके प्रसिद्धः । तस्य यथा रसमयत्वात्प्रीतिकरत्व-मौषधात्मकत्वाद्धितकरत्वं च तथा एतेषामपि प्रियत्वं हितत्वं चेति व्यञ्जयितुं रसायनत्व-

राजा—इयं वैदेही । रामो लक्ष्मणो वैदेहीत्ययमक्रमः ।

सुमन्त्रः—अथ कः क्रमः ।

राजा—रामो वैदेही लक्ष्मण इत्यभिधीयताम् ।

रामलक्ष्मणयोर्मध्ये तिष्ठत्वत्रापि मैथिली ।
बहुदोषाण्यरण्यानि सनाथैषा भविष्यति ॥ १५ ॥

सुमन्त्रः—यदाज्ञापयति महाराजः । आयुष्मान् रामः ।

राजा—अयं रामः ।

सुमन्त्रः—आयुष्मती जनकराजपुत्री ।

राजा—इयं वैदेही ।

सुमन्त्रः—आयुष्मान् लक्ष्मणः ।

राजा—अयं लक्ष्मणः । राम वैदेहि लक्ष्मण परिष्वजध्वं मां पुत्रकाः ।

सकृत् स्पृशामि वा रामं सकृत् पश्यामि वा पुनः ।
गतायुरमृतेनेव जीवामीति मतिर्मम ॥ १६ ॥

सुमन्त्रः—शृङ्गिबेरपुरे रथादवतीर्यायोध्याभिमुखाः स्थित्वा सर्व एव महाराजं शिरसा प्रणम्य विज्ञापयितुमारब्धाः ।

कमप्यर्थं चिरं ध्यात्वा वक्तुं प्रस्फुरिताधराः ।
बाष्पस्तम्भितकण्ठत्वादनुक्त्वैव वनं गताः ॥ १७ ॥

निर्देशः । हृदयातुरस्यौषधानीव सुखावहानि तैः । नामधेयैः नामभिः । **रामलक्ष्मणयोरिति** । अत्रापि वनस्थानामत्र नामग्रहणेपि । बहुदोषाणि बहवो दोषा अपाया येषु तानि । सनाथा उभयोर्मध्यगतत्वात्सुरक्षितेति यावत् । अतिस्नेहः पापशङ्कीति न्यायेनात्र राज्ञः सीताविषयकः स्नेहातिशयः सूचितः ॥१५॥ परिष्वजध्वमालिङ्गत । **सकृदिति** । सकृत् रामं स्पृशामि सकृद्वा रामं पश्यामि । गतायुर्गतप्रायायुरहममृतेनेव जीवामि इति मम मतिः ॥ १६ ॥ शृङ्गवेरं नाम गङ्गातीरस्थं किंचित्पुरं निषादानां वसतिस्थानं यत्र रामः गङ्गालङ्घनात्प्राक्कंचित्कालं स्थितः । अत्र रामायणं—आससाद महाबाहुः शृङ्गवेरपुरं प्रति । सुमन्त्रमब्रवीत्सूतमिहैवाद्य वसामहे ॥ इत्यादि । (अयो.५०–२६,२७) **कमप्यर्थमिति** । चिरं कमप्यर्थं ध्यात्वा इदं सन्देष्टव्यं किमयं संदेशार्होऽर्थः किमिति विचार्य वक्तुं प्रस्फुरिताधराः बाष्पेण स्तम्भितो निरुद्धः कण्ठो येषां तेषां भावः वाष्पस्तम्भितकण्ठत्वं तस्मात् । अनुक्त्वैव सन्देष्टव्यमर्थमकथयित्वैव वनं गताः । एतत्तु रामायणविरुद्धम् । अनेन पितुः पुत्रवात्सल्यं स्मृत्वा जातमनःपीडानां तेषां पितरि

राजा—कथमनुक्त्वैव वनं गताः । (इति द्विगुणं मोहमुपगतः ।)

सुमन्त्रः—(ससम्भ्रमम् ।) बालाके उच्यताममात्येभ्यः—अप्रतीकारायां दशायां वर्तते महाराज इति ।

काञ्चुकीयः—तथा । (निष्क्रान्तः ।)

देव्यौ—महाराज समाश्वसिहि समाश्वसिहि । (महाराअ समस्ससिहि समस्ससिहि ।)

राजा—(किञ्चित् समाश्वस्य ।)

अङ्गं मे स्पृश कौसल्ये न त्वां पश्यामि चक्षुषा ।
रामं प्रति गता बुद्धिरद्यापि न निवर्तते ॥ १८ ॥

पुत्र राम यत् खलु मया सन्ततं चिन्तितं

राज्ये त्वामभिषिच्य सन्नरपतेर्लाभात् कृतार्थाः प्रजाः
कृत्वा त्वत्सहजान् समानविभवान् कुर्वात्मनः सन्ततम् ।
इत्यादिश्य च ते तपोवनमितो गन्तव्यमित्येतया
कैकेय्या हि तदन्यथा कृतमहो निःशेषमेकक्षणे ॥ १९ ॥

सुमन्त्र उच्यतां कैकेय्याः—

गतो रामः प्रियं तेऽस्तु त्यक्तोऽहमपि जीवितैः ।
क्षिप्रमानीयतां पुत्रः पापं सफलमस्त्विति ॥ २० ॥

सुमन्त्रः—यदाज्ञापयति महाराजः ।

राजा—(ऊर्ध्वमवलोक्य ।) अये रामकथाश्रवणसन्दग्धहृदयं मामाश्वासयितुमागताः पितरः । कोऽत्र ।

प्रेमातिशयः सूचितः ॥ १७ ॥ अप्रतीकारायां प्रतीकाराक्षमायाम् । **अङ्गमिति ।** कौसल्ये मे अङ्गं स्पृश । त्वां चक्षुषा न पश्यामि । स्पर्शेन तव साभिध्यस्य ज्ञानं स्यादित्यर्थः । रामं प्रतीति । रामगतमना अहं नात्रस्थं किमपि वेद्मीति भावः ॥ एवं रामायणेपि–न त्वां पश्यामि कौसल्ये साधु मां पाणिना स्पृश । रामं मेनुगता दृष्टिरद्यापि न निवर्तते ॥ (अयो. ४२–३) ॥ १८ ॥ **राज्ये** इति । त्वां राज्ये अभिषिच्य सन्नरपतेः सुनृपतेः लाभात्प्रजाः कृतार्थाः कृत्वा त्वत्सहजान् लक्ष्मणादीन् सन्ततमात्मनः समानविभवान् कुरु इति ते । सम्बन्धे षष्ठी । त्वामादिश्य इतः तपोवनं गन्तव्यम् । इति यन्मया सन्ततं चिन्तितं तन्निःशेषम् अहो कष्टमनया 'बुध्युपस्थितया कैकय्या एकक्षणे अन्यथाकृतम् । शार्दूल० छन्दः ॥ १९ ॥ **गतो राम** इति । प्रियं रामवनगमनरूपम् । जीवितैः प्राणैः । पुत्रः भरतः । पापं रामनिर्वासनरूपं सफलं भरतस्य राज्याभिषेकादित्यर्थः ॥ २० ॥ पितरः पूर्वजाः । आसन्नमृत्योश्चित्त-

(प्रविश्य)

काञ्चुकीयः—जयतु महाराजः ।

राजा—आपस्तावत् ।

काञ्चुकीयः— यदाज्ञापयति महाराजः । (निष्क्रम्य प्रविश्य ।) जयतु महाराजः । इमा आपः ।

राजा—(आचम्यावलोक्य ।)

अयममरपतेः सखा दिलीपो रघुरयमत्रभवानजः पिता मे ।
किमभिगमनकारणं भवद्भिः सह वसने समयो ममापि तत्र ॥२१॥

राम वैदेहि लक्ष्मण अहमितः पितॄणां सकाशं गच्छामि । हे पितरः अयमयमागच्छामि । (मूर्छया परामृष्टः ।)

(काञ्चुकीयो यवनिकास्तरणं करोति ।)

सर्वे—हा हा महाराजः । (हा हा महाराओ ।)

(निष्क्रान्ताः सर्वे ।)

इति द्वितीयोऽङ्कः ।

अथ तृतीयोऽङ्कः ।

(ततः प्रविशति सुधाकारः ।)

सुधाकारः—(सम्मार्जनादीनि कृत्वा ।) भवतु इदानीं कृतमत्र कार्यमार्यसंभवकस्याज्ञप्तम् । यावन्मुहूर्तं स्वप्स्यामि । (स्वपिति ।) (भोदु दाणिं किदं एत्थ कय्यं अय्यसम्भवअस्स आणत्तं । जाव मुहुत्तं सुविस्सं ।)

विश्रमाद्दर्शनमिदमवगन्तव्यम् । **आचम्येति** । पूज्यानां देवपित्रादीनां दर्शनावसरे आचमनस्य विहितत्वात् । **अयमिति** । अमरपतेरिन्द्रस्य । तान्प्रति पृच्छति किमत्रागमनकारणम् यतो भवद्भिः सह तत्र स्वर्गे वसने ममापि समयः कालः उपस्थित इति शेषः । परामृष्ट आक्रान्तः । यवनिकास्तरणं वस्त्रेण नृपतेः शरीरावरणम् । इति द्वितीयाङ्क टीका ॥

अथ दशरथस्य स्वर्गगमनादूर्ध्वं क्षिप्रमानीयतां पुत्र इत्याज्ञानुसारेण रथेनायोध्यामानीयमानस्य भरतस्य मार्गे दशरथप्रतिमादर्शनं ततः पितृमरणज्ञानं ततो वनगमननिश्चयः इत्यादिकमर्थजातं तृतीयाङ्कोपनिबद्धं प्रस्तोतुकामः कविः प्रथमं तावत् दशरथप्रतिमागृहदर्शनार्थं कौसल्यादीनां गमनं सूचयितुं तत्र नियुक्तस्य सुधाकरस्य प्रवेशमाह

(प्रविश्य)

भटः—(चेटमुपगम्य ताडयित्वा ।) अङ्गो दास्याःपुत्र किमिदानीं कर्म न करोषि । (ताडयति ।) (अङ्गो दासीएपुत्त किं दाणिं कम्मं ण करेसि ।)

सुधाकारः—(बुद्ध्वा ।) ताडय मां ताडय माम् । (ताळेहि मं ताळेहि मं)

भटः—ताडिते त्वं किं करिष्यसि । (ताडिदे तुवं किं करिस्ससि ।)

सुधाकारः—अधन्यस्य मम कार्तवीर्यस्येव बाहुसहस्रं नास्ति । (अहण्णस्स मम कत्तवीअस्स विअ बाहुसहस्सं णत्थि ।)

भटः—बाहुसहस्रेण किं कार्यम् । (बाहुसहस्सेण किं कय्यं ।)

सुधाकारः—त्वां हनिष्यामि । (तुवं हणिस्सं ।)

भटः—एहि दास्याःपुत्र मृते मोक्ष्यामि । (पुनरपि ताडयति ।) (एहि दासीएपुत्त मुदे मुञ्चिस्सं ।)

सुधाकारः—(रुदित्वा ।) शक्यमिदानीं भर्तः मेऽपराधं ज्ञातुम् । (सक्कं दाणि भट्टा मे अवराहं जाणिदुम् ।)

भटः—नास्ति किलापराधो नास्ति । ननु मया सन्दिष्टो भर्तृदारकस्य रामस्य राज्यविभ्रष्टकृतसन्तापेन स्वर्गं गतस्य भर्तुर्दशरथस्य प्रतिमागेहं द्रष्टुमद्य कौसल्यापुरोगैः सर्वैरन्तःपुरैरिहागन्तव्यमिति । अत्रेदानीं त्वया किं कृतम् । (णत्थि किळ अवराहो णत्थि । णं मए सन्दिट्ठो भट्टिदारअस्स रामस्स रज्जविब्भट्टकिदसन्दावेण सग्गं गदस्स भट्टिणो दसरहस्स पडिमागेहं दट्ठुं अज्ज कोसळ्ळापुरोएहि सव्वेहि अन्तेउरेहि इह आअन्तव्वं त्ति । एत्थ दाणि तुए किं किदं ।)

सुधाकारः—पश्यतु भर्ता । अपनीतकपोतसन्दानकं तावद् गर्भ-

ततः प्रविशतीति । आर्यसंभवकस्य तन्नाम्नः कञ्चुकेः । अङ्गो इति सकोपामन्त्रणे । ताडय ताडयेति कृतकर्मणो मम ताडनं कथं युक्तमिति भावः । कार्तवीर्यो नाम कृतवीर्यस्य सूनुरर्जुनो नाम हैहयानां नृपः । स च श्रीदत्तप्रसादाद्बाहुसहस्रमाप्तवान् । मृते मोक्ष्यामि यावत्त्वं मृतो भवसि तावत्ताडयामि । अपराधं ज्ञातुं को ममापराध इति ज्ञातुम् । ममापराधं कथयेः किं यस्माद्मां ताडयसि । नास्ति किलापराधो नास्ति सत्यं तेऽपराधो नास्ति इति काकुः । राज्यात् विभ्रष्टं भ्रंशनम् । भावे क्तः । तेन कृतो जनितः सन्तापस्तेन । कौसल्या पुरोगा येषां तैः अन्तःपुरैरवरोधस्त्रीभिः अपनीतानि कपोतानां संदानानि बन्धाः कपोतागमनप्रतिबन्धार्थं निर्मिता यस्मात्तत् । गर्भगृहं प्रतिमागेहस्या-

गृहम् । सौधवर्णकदत्तचन्दनपञ्चाङ्गुला भित्तयः । अवसक्तमाल्यदामशोभीनि द्वाराणि । प्रकीर्णा वालुकाः । अत्रेदानीं मया किं न कृतम् । (पेक्खदु भट्टा । अवणीदकवोदसन्दाणअं दाव गब्भगिहं । सोहवण्णअदत्तचन्दणपञ्चाङ्गुला भित्तीओ । ओसत्तमल्लदामसोहीणि दुवाराणि । पइण्णा वालुआ । एत्थ दाणिं मए किं ण किदं ।)

भटः—यद्येवं विश्वस्तो गच्छ । यावदहमपि सर्वं कृतमित्यमात्याय निवेदयामि । (जइ एवं विस्सत्थो गच्छ । जाव अहं वि सव्वं किदं त्ति अमच्चस्स णिवेदेमि ।)

(निष्क्रान्तौ ।)

प्रवेशकः ।

(ततः प्रविशति भरतो रथेन सूतश्च ।)

भरतः—(सावेगम् ।) सूत चिरं मातुलपरिचयादविज्ञातवृत्तान्तोऽस्मि । श्रुतं मया दृढमकल्यशरीरो महाराज इति । तदुच्यतां

पितुर्मे को व्याधिः

सूतः— **हृदयपरितापः खलु महान्**

भरतः—**किमाहुस्तं वैद्याः**

सूतः— **न खलु भिषजस्तत्र निपुणाः**

भरतः—**किमाहारं भुङ्क्ते शयनमपि**

सूतः— **भूमौ निरशनः**

भरतः—**किमाशा स्याद्**

सूतः— **दैवं**

भरतः— **स्फुरति हृदयं वाहय रथम् ॥ १ ॥**

न्तर्गृहम् । सौधवर्णके सुधामये आलेपे दत्तानि चन्दनपञ्चांगुलानि शोभार्थं चन्दनपङ्कार्द्रैः पञ्चांगुलन्यासा यासु ताः । अवसक्तान्यालम्बितानि माल्यदामानि तैः शोभन्ते इति शोभीनि । प्रकीर्णा आस्तीर्णाः शोभार्थं चतुष्कादिरूपेणेत्यर्थः । विश्वस्तः ताडनभयरहितः । **प्रवेशकः** । तद्वदेवानुदात्तोक्त्या नीचपात्रप्रयोजितः । प्रवेशोऽङ्कद्वयस्यान्ते शेषार्थस्योपसूचकः ॥ इति दशरूपकम् । सावेगं सोत्पीडम् । मातुलपरिचयान्मातुलस्यान्तिके निवासात् । दृढमत्यन्तम् । अकल्यं कल्यं निरामयमकल्यं सामयं सरुक् शरीरं यस्य सोकल्यशरीरः । वार्तो निरामयः कल्य इत्यमरः । **पितुरिति** । पद्यमिदं प्रश्नोत्तरयुतम् । भिषजस्तत्र निपुणा भिषजामसाध्य इत्यर्थः । आशा जीविताशा । दैवं दैवाधीनमेव तस्य जीवितम् । स्फुरत्यन्तःपीडावशादिति भावः । शिखरिणी वृत्तम् । लक्षणं तूक्तम्

सूतः—यदाज्ञापयत्यायुष्मान् । (रथं वाहयति ।)

भरतः—(रथवेगं निरूप्य ।) अहोतुखलु रथवेगः । एते ते

द्रुमा धावन्तीव द्रुतरथगतिक्षीणविषया
नदीवोद्वृत्ताम्बुर्निपतति मही नेमिविवरे ।
अरव्यक्तिर्नष्टा स्थितमिव जवाच्चक्रवलयं
रजश्चाश्वोद्धूतं पतति पुरतो नानुपतति ॥ २ ॥

सूतः—आयुष्मन् सोपस्नेहतया वृक्षाणामभितः खल्वयोध्यया भवितव्यम् ।

भरतः—अहोतुखलु स्वजनदर्शनोत्सुकस्य त्वरता मे मनसः । सम्प्रति हि

पतितमिव शिरः पितुः पादयोः स्निह्यतेवास्मि राज्ञा समुत्थापितः
त्वरितमुपगता इव भ्रातरः क्लेदयन्तीव मामश्रुभिर्मातरः ॥ ३ ॥
सदृश इति महानिति व्यायतश्चेति भृत्यैरिवाहं स्तुतः सेवया
परिहसितमिवात्मनस्तत्र पश्यामि वेषं च भाषां च सौमित्रिणा ॥४॥

सूतः—(आत्मगतम्) भोः कष्टं यदयमविज्ञाय महाराजविनाश-

॥ १ ॥ **द्रुमा** इति । द्रुता शीघ्रा या रथगतिस्तया क्षीणः लघूकृतो विषयो येषां ते । द्रुमा वृक्षा धावन्तीव । भान्तीति शेषः । उद्वृत्तमुत्कूलगामि अम्बुजलं यस्याः सा नदी इव भूमिः नेमिविवरे निपतति इति भाति । अरव्यक्तिः नष्टा अरा व्यक्तं न भान्ति । जवात् रथवेगात् चक्रवलयं स्थितं निश्चलमिव भातीति शेषः । अश्वोद्धूतं अश्वखुरोत्क्षिप्तं पुरतः पतति न अनुपतति । शिखरिणी वृत्तम् ॥ २ ॥ सोपस्नेहतया पर्णशाखादीनां सुस्निग्धतया । स्वजनानां दर्शनं तत्र उत्सुकस्योत्कण्ठस्य । त्वरता संभ्रमवत्त्वम् । **सम्प्रतीति** । पितुः पादयोः शिरः मे इति शेषः । पतितमिव । त्वरातिशयात्तथा भातीत्यर्थः । एवमन्यत्र । स्निह्यता मयि प्रेम दर्शयता राज्ञा समुत्थापितः अस्मि । भ्रातरस्त्वरितमुपगता इव । मातरो मामश्रुभिः क्लेदयन्त्यार्द्रयन्ति । सदृश इति महान् वृद्ध इति व्यायतो दीर्घाङ्गश्चेति भृत्यैः सेवया मत्प्रीणनार्थमहंस्तुत इव । तत्र गृहे सौमित्रिणा लक्ष्मणेन आत्मनः वेषं केकयदेशोचितं परिहसितं भाषां च परिहसितामिव पश्यामि ॥ श्लोकद्वयस्य प्रभास्रग्विण्योर्मिश्रणादुपजातिश्छन्दः । एतयोर्लक्षणे–स्वरशरविरतिर्ननौ रौ प्रभा । कीर्तितैषा चतूरेफिका स्रग्विणी । इति । उक्तं च उपजातिलक्षणानन्तरम्–इत्थं किलान्यास्वपि मिश्रितासु वदन्ति जातिष्विदमेव नाम । इति । द्वितीयश्लोकस्य तृतीयचरणे यतिभङ्गः स्फुटएव

मुदर्के निष्फलामाशां परिवहन्नयोध्यां प्रवेक्ष्यति कुमारः । जानद्भिरप्यस्माभिर्न निवेद्यते । कुतः

पितुः प्राणपरित्यागं मातुरैश्वर्यलुब्धताम् ।
ज्येष्ठभ्रातुः प्रवासं च त्रीन् दोषान् कोऽभिधास्यति ॥ ५ ॥

(प्रविश्य)

भटः—जयतु कुमारः ।

भरतः—भद्र किं शत्रुघ्नो मामभिगतः ।

भटः—अभिगतः खलु वर्तते कुमारः । उपाध्यायास्तु भवन्तमाहुः ।

भरतः—किमिति किमिति ।

भटः—एकनाडिकावशेषः कृत्तिकाविषयः । तस्मात् प्रतिपन्नायामेव रोहिण्यामयोध्यां प्रवेक्ष्यति कुमारः ।

भरतः—बाढमेवम् । न मया गुरुवचनमतिक्रान्तपूर्वम् । गच्छ त्वम् ।

भटः—यदाज्ञापयति कुमारः । (निष्क्रान्तः ।)

भरतः—अथ कस्मिन् प्रदेशे विश्रमिष्ये । भवतु दृष्टम् । एतस्मिन् वृक्षान्तराविष्कृते देवकुले मुहूर्तं विश्रमिष्ये । तदुभयं भविष्यति दैवतपूजा विश्रमश्च । अथ च उपोपविश्य प्रवेष्टव्यानि नगराणीति सत्समुदाचारः । तस्मात् स्थाप्यतां रथः ।

सूतः—यदाज्ञापयत्यायुष्मान् । (रथं स्थापयति ।)

भरतः—(रथादवतीर्य ।) सूत एकान्ते विश्रामयाश्वान् ।

॥ ३।४ ॥ उदर्के अवसाने । गृहप्रवेशे इति यावत् । **पितुरिति** । कोभिधास्यतीति सामान्योक्त्या नाहमभिधातुं समर्थ इति ध्वनितम् ॥ ५ ॥ शत्रुघ्नो मामभिगतः ममागमनं श्रुत्वा मां सभाजयितुमुपस्थितः किम् इति प्रश्नः । अभित इति पाठान्तरम् । नाभिगतः किंतु आसन्नवर्ती तिष्ठतीत्यर्थः । एका नाडिका अवशेषो यस्य । कृत्तिकाविषयः कृत्तिकानक्षत्रकालावधिः । प्रतिपन्नायां रोहिण्यामिति कृत्तिकायां गृहप्रवेशनिषेधात् । बाढमित्यङ्गीकारे । पूर्वमतिक्रान्तमतिक्रान्तपूर्वम् । विश्रमिष्ये दीर्घप्रवासजन्यं खेदमपनेष्यामि । आत्मनेपदं चिन्त्यम् । वृक्षान्तरेण वृक्षमध्यावकाशेनाविष्कृते दर्शिते । देवकुले देवायतने । उपोपविश्योपकण्ठमुपविश्य । सत्समु-

---

१ अभितः ।

सूतः—यदाज्ञापयत्यायुष्मान् । (निष्क्रान्तः ।)

भरतः—(किञ्चिद् गत्वावलोक्य ।) साधुमुक्तपुष्पलाजाविष्कृता बलयः, दत्तचन्दनपञ्चाङ्गुला भित्तयः । अवसक्तमाल्यदामशोभीनि द्वाराणि । प्रकीर्णा वालुकाः । किन्नु खलु पार्वणोऽयं विशेषः अथवा आह्निकमास्तिक्यम् । कस्य नु खलु दैवतस्य स्थानं भविष्यति । नेह किञ्चित् प्रहरणं ध्वजो वा बहिश्चिह्नं दृश्यते । भवतु प्रविश्य ज्ञास्ये । (प्रविश्यावलोक्य।) अहो क्रियामाधुर्यं पाषाणानाम् । अहो भावगतिराकृतीनाम् । दैवतोद्दिष्टानामपि मानुषविश्वासतासां प्रतिमानाम् । किन्नु खलु चतुर्दैवतोऽयं स्तोमः । अथवा यानि तानि भवन्तु । अस्ति तावन्मे मनसि प्रहर्षः ।

कामं दैवतमित्येव युक्तं नमयितुं शिरः ।
वार्षलस्तु प्रणामः स्यादमन्त्रार्चितदैवतः ॥ ६ ॥

(प्रविश्य)

देवकुलिकः—भोः नैत्यकावसानप्राणिधर्ममनुतिष्ठति मयि कोनुखल्वयमासां प्रतिमानामल्पान्तराकृतिरिव प्रतिमागृहं प्रविष्टः । भवतु प्रविश्य ज्ञास्ये । (प्रविशति ।)

भरतः—नमोऽस्तु ।

दाचारः शिष्टाचारः । साधु सम्यग् यथा तथा मुक्तानि आवर्जितानि पुष्पाणि लाजाश्च तैराविष्कृताः प्रकटिताः बलयो देवतोपहाराः । दत्तेति व्याख्यातपूर्वम् । पार्वणः पर्वणि भवः विशेषो विशिष्टो विधिः । आह्निकं प्रतिदिनं क्रियमाणमास्तिक्यं कर्म । प्रहरणं यथा कार्त्तिकेयस्य शक्तिः । ध्वजः यथा चण्डिकायाः । अवलोक्य तत्रस्थाः प्रतिमा दृष्ट्वा । क्रियामाधुर्यं शिल्पसौष्ठवम् । भावगतिः हृद्गतविकाराविष्करणम् । अहो इत्याश्चर्ये । आसां प्रतिमानां देवतोद्दिष्टानां दैवतत्वेन कल्पितानाम् । मानुषविश्वासता मानुषताप्रतीतित्वम् । चतुर्दैवतः चत्वारि दैवतानि अवयत्वेनास्य । स्तोमः संघः । मनसि प्रहर्षः मम मनः प्रहृष्टम् । **काममिति** । दैवतमित्येव शिरः नमयितुं कामं युक्तम् । तु किंतु प्रणामः वृषलस्यायं वार्षलः शूद्रकृत इव स्यात् भवेत् । यतः मन्त्रैः मन्त्रपठनपूर्वमर्चितं दैवतं यस्मिन् तादृशः न भवतीत्यमन्त्रार्चितदैवतः । देववत्वानिश्चयात्समन्त्रको न कर्तव्य इत्याशयः ॥ ६ ॥ नैत्यस्य नित्यकर्मणः अवसाने अन्ते नित्यकर्माणि पूजादीनि कृत्वेत्यर्थः । प्राणिधर्मोऽन्नसेवनादिस्तमनुतिष्ठति कुर्वेति मयि । अल्पान्तराकृतिरिव अल्पं स्तोकमन्तरं यस्याः सा अल्पान्तरा सदृशप्राया आकृतिर्यस्य । प्रतिमासदृशाकृतिरित्यर्थः । नमोस्तु प्रतिमा उद्दिश्येयं नमस्कृतिः ।

देवकुलिकः—न खलु न खलु प्रणामः कार्यः।

भरतः—मा तावद् भोः।

वक्तव्यं किञ्चिदस्मासु विशिष्टः प्रतिपाल्यते।
किङ्कृतः प्रतिषेधोऽयं नियमप्रभविष्णुता॥ ७॥

देवकुलिकः—न खल्वेतैः कारणैः प्रतिषेधयामि भवन्तम्। किन्तु दैवतशङ्कया ब्राह्मणजनस्य प्रणामं परिहरामि। क्षत्रिया ह्यत्रभवन्तः।

भरतः—एवम्। क्षत्रिया ह्यत्रभवन्तः। अथ के नामात्रभवन्तः।

देवकुलिकः—इक्ष्वाकवः।

भरतः—(सहर्षम्।) इक्ष्वाकव इति। एते तेऽयोध्याभर्तारः।

एते ते दैवतानामसुरपुरवधे गच्छन्त्यभिसरी-
मेते ते शक्रलोके सपुरजनपदा यान्ति स्वसुकृतैः।
एते ते प्राप्नुवन्तः स्वभुजबलजितां कृत्स्नां वसुमती-
मेते ते मृत्युना ये चिरमनवसिताश्छन्दं मृगयता॥ ८॥

भोः यदृच्छया खलु मया महत् फलमासादितम्। अभिधीयतां कस्तावदत्रभवान्।

देवकुलिकः—अयं खलु तावत् सन्निहितसर्वरत्नस्य विश्वजितो यज्ञस्य प्रवर्तयिता प्रज्वलितधर्मप्रदीपो दिलीपः।

वक्तव्यमिति। अयं प्रतिषेधः किं कृतः कस्मात्कारणात् कृतः। मयि किंचिद्वक्तव्यं दोषार्हमस्ति किं येन नमस्कर्तुं मम नाधिकारः। विशिष्टः मत्तः श्रेष्ठः कश्चित्प्रतिपाल्यते प्रतीक्ष्यते किम्। नियमोऽनेन प्रणामः कार्योनेन नेत्येवंरूपं नियमनं तत्र प्रभविष्णुता सामर्थ्यं त्वन्निष्ठं किं येनाहं वारितः। आत्मगता तपोनुष्ठानप्रौढिः किम्। प्रतिषेधोयमात्मगततपोनुष्ठानप्रौढिकृतः किम्। इति ग० शा० ॥ ७॥ ब्राह्मणजनस्य भवन्तं ब्राह्मणं मन्यमानोहमित्यर्थः। **एते ते** इति। एते ते इक्ष्वाकवः ये असुरपुरवधे असुराणां तेषां पुराणां च वधे नाशे कर्तव्ये दैवतानामभिसरीं गच्छन्ति साहाय्यार्थमभिसरणं कुर्वन्ति। एते ते ये स्वसुकृतैः स्वपुण्यैः सपुरजनपदाः शक्रलोके यान्ति। ये स्वभुजबलजितां कृत्स्नां वसुमतीं पृथ्वीं प्राप्नुवन्तः। एते ते ये छन्दं इच्छां मृत्युविषयां मृगयताऽन्विष्यता। चिरमनवसिताः। स्वेच्छामरणाः दीर्घकालं नाशं न प्रापिताः। सुवदना वृत्तम्। एतल्लक्षणम्। ज्ञेया सप्ताश्वषड्भिर्मरभनययुता भ्लौ गः सुवदना। इति ॥ ८॥ यदृच्छया स्वैरगत्या प्रथमां प्रतिमां निर्दिश्य पृच्छति कस्तावदिति। सन्निहितानि उपस्थापितानि विश्वविजयात्सर्वाणि रत्नानि उत्कृष्टद्रव्याणि यस्मिन् तस्य

भरतः—नमोस्तु धर्मपरायणाय। अभिधीयतां कस्तावदत्रभवान्।

देवकुलिकः—अयं खलु तावत् संवेशनोत्थापनयोरनेकब्राह्मणजनसहस्रप्रयुक्तपुण्याहशब्दरवो रघुः।

भरतः—अहो बलवान् मृत्युरेतामपि रक्षामतिक्रान्तः। नमोस्तु ब्राह्मणजनविदितराज्यफलाय। अभिधीयतां कस्तावदत्रभवान्।

देवकुलिकः—अयं खलु तावत् प्रियावियोगनिर्वेदपरित्यक्तराज्यभारो नित्यावभृथस्नानप्रशांतरजा अजः।

भरतः—नमोऽस्तु श्लाघनीयपश्चात्तापाय। (दशरथस्य प्रतिमामवलोकयन् पर्याकुलो भूत्वा।) भोः बहुमानव्याक्षिप्तेन मनसा सुव्यक्तं नावधारितम्। अभिधीयतां कस्तावदत्रभवान्।

देवकुलिकः—अयं दिलीपः।

भरतः—पितृपितामहो महाराजस्य। ततस्ततः।

देवकुलिकः—अत्रभवान् रघुः।

भरतः—पितामहो महाराजस्य। ततस्ततः।

देवकुलिकः—अत्रभवानजः।

भरतः—पिता तातस्य। किमिति किमिति।

देवकुलिकः—अयं दिलीपः अयं रघुः अयमजः।

भरतः—भवन्त किञ्चित् पृच्छामि। धरमाणानामपि प्रतिमाः स्थाप्यन्ते।

देवकुलिकः—न खलु अतिक्रान्तानामेव।

विश्वजितः विश्वजिन्नामकस्य। प्रवर्तयिता कर्ता। नायं विश्वजितः कर्ता। दिलीपस्तु महातेजा यज्ञैर्बहुभिरिष्टवान्। इत्येवोक्तं रामायणे बालकाण्डे। प्रज्वलितः धर्मरूपः प्रदीपः धर्मप्रदीपो यस्य। धर्मपरायणाय धर्माचरणैकनिरताय। संवेशनं निद्रा उत्थापनं तस्मात्प्रबोधनं तयोः। तत्काले इत्यर्थः। अनेकैः ब्राह्मणजनसहस्रैः प्रयुक्तः पुण्याहशब्दः पुण्याहमन्त्रवाचनं तस्य रवः यस्य। एतां रक्षां पुण्याहवाचनपूर्वाशीर्वादकृताम्। अतिक्रान्तः अतिक्रम्य रघुं प्राप्तः। प्रियाया इन्दुमत्या वियोगस्तेन निर्वेदस्तेन परित्यक्तो राज्यभारो येन। नित्यं यदवभृथस्नानम्। अवभृथो दीक्षान्ते यज्ञविशेषस्तत्र स्नानं तेन प्रशान्तं रजः रजोगुणविकारो यस्य सः। श्लाघनीयः पश्चात्तापो राज्योपभोगतृष्णाराहित्यं यस्य तस्मै। पर्याकुल उद्विग्नः। बहुमानः पुरुषविशेषेष्वादरस्तेन व्याक्षिप्तमन्यतो नीतं

भरतः—तेन ह्यापृच्छे भवन्तम् ।

देवकुलिकः—तिष्ठ ।

येन प्राणाश्च राज्यं च स्त्रीशुल्कार्थे विसर्जिताः ।
इमां दशरथस्य त्वं प्रतिमां किं न पृच्छसे ॥ ९ ॥

भरतः—हा तात । (मूर्छितः पतति । पुनः प्रत्यागत्य ।)

हृदय भव सकामं यत्कृते शङ्कसे त्वं
शृणु पितृनिधनं तद् गच्छ धैर्यं च तावत् ।
स्पृशति तु यदि नीचो मामयं शुल्कशब्द-
स्त्वथ च भवति सत्यं तत्र देहो विशोध्यः ॥ १० ॥

आर्य ।

देवकुलिकः—आर्येति इक्ष्वाकुकुलालापः खल्वयम् । कच्चित् कैकेयीपुत्रो भरतो भवान् ननु ।

भरतः—अथ किमथ किम् । दशरथपुत्रो भरतोऽस्मि न कैकेय्याः ।

देवकुलिकः—तेन ह्यापृच्छे भवन्तम् ।

भरतः—तिष्ठ । शेषमभिधीयताम् ।

देवकुलिकः—का गतिः । श्रूयताम् । उपरतस्तत्रभवान् दशरथः । सीतालक्ष्मणसहायस्य रामस्य वनगमनप्रयोजनं न जाने ।

भरतः—कथं कथमार्योऽपि वनं गतः । (द्विगुणं मोहमुपगतः ।)

देवकुलिकः—कुमार समाश्वसिहि समाश्वसिहि ।

तेन । धरमाणानां जीवताम् । अतिक्रान्तानां मृतानाम् । **येनेति** । स्त्रीशुल्कार्थे विवाहकाले भार्याप्रतिश्रुतार्थे । विसर्जिता दत्ताः । स्पष्टमन्यत् । पृच्छसे पृच्छसीति पाठो युक्तः ॥ ९ ॥ **हृदयेति** । सकामं लब्धेच्छं भव । तव शङ्कायाः सफलत्वात् । यत्कृते त्वं शङ्कसे तत् पितृनिधनं पितुर्मरणं शृणु धैर्यं च तावद् गच्छावलम्बस्वेत्यर्थः । यदि अयं नीचः तुच्छः शुल्कशब्दो मां स्पृशति स्पृशेत् मद्विषयकः स्यात् । मत्प्रेरिता माता मम राज्याभिषेकं प्रार्थितवतीति स्यात् । अथ च सत्यं भवेत्सत्यत्वेन गृह्येत तत्र मम देहो विशोध्यः अग्निधारणादिदिव्येन निर्दोषतां प्रापयितव्यः । मालिनी वृत्तम् । लक्षणमुक्तम् ॥ १० ॥ इक्ष्वाकुकुलालापः इक्ष्वाकुकुलस्य आलापः सगौरवमामन्त्रणम् । कैकेय्याः कैकेयीपुत्र इति तु साधीयः । आपृच्छे यामीति भवन्तमामन्त्र्य यास्यामीत्यर्थः । 'आङि नुप्रच्छयोरुपसंख्यानम्' इत्यात्मनेपदम् ।

भरतः—(समाश्वस्य ।)

अयोध्यामटवीभूतां पित्रा भ्रात्रा च वर्जिताम् ।
पिपासार्तोऽनुधावामि क्षीणतोयां नदीमिव ॥ ११ ॥

आर्य विस्तरश्रवणं मे मनसः स्थैर्यमुत्पादयति । तत् सर्वमनवशेषमभिधीयताम् ।

देवकुलिकः—श्रूयताम् । तत्रभवता राज्ञाभिषिच्यमाने तत्रभवति रामे भवतो जनन्याभिहितं किल ।

भरतः—तिष्ठ ।

तं स्मृत्वा शुल्कदोषं भवतु मम सुतो राजेत्यभिहितं
तद्धैर्येणाश्वसत्या व्रज सुत वनमित्यार्योऽप्याभिहितः ।
तं दृष्ट्वा बद्धचीरं निधनमसदृशं राजा ननु गतः
पात्यन्ते धिक्प्रलापा ननु मयि सदृशाः शेषाः प्रकृतिभिः॥१२॥

(मोहमुपगतः ।)

(नेपथ्ये)

उत्सरतार्याः उत्सरत । (उस्सरह अय्या उस्सरह ।)

देवकुलिकः—(विलोक्य ।) अये

काले खल्वागता देव्यः पुत्रे मोहमुपागते ।
हस्तस्पर्शो हि मातॄणामजलस्य जलाञ्जलिः ॥ १३ ॥

अयोध्यामिति । पित्रा भ्रात्रा च वर्जितां हीनामत एवाटवीभूतामटव्या समामरण्यतुल्याम् ' भूतं प्राण्यतीते समे त्रिषु । इत्यमरः । अयोध्यां पिपासया तृष्णया आर्तः पीडितः कश्चित् क्षीणतोयां शुष्कजलां नदीमिवानुधावामि । उपमालङ्कारः । ' तदनुरोधात् पितृमातृदर्शनोत्कण्ठितत्वरूपमुपमेये गम्यम् ' इति ग० शा० ॥ ११ ॥ अनवशेषं साकल्येन । तिष्ठ कथनाद्विरम । अवगतं मया यज्जनन्योक्तमित्याह—**तं स्मृत्वा** इति । तं शुल्कदोषं दुष्टशुल्कं स्मृत्वा मम सुतो राजा भवतु इति तया अभिहितम् । तस्मिन्राज्ञानुमते तद्धैर्येण आश्वसत्या विश्वासं गतया सुत वनं गच्छेति आर्यो रामोपि अभिहितः । तं बद्धचीरं धृतवल्कलं दृष्ट्वा राजापि असदृशं अननुरूपं निधनं गतो ननु । प्रकृतिभिः प्रजाभिः शेषाः कैकेय्या उपरिनिपात्यावशिष्टाः धिक्प्रलापा मयि ननु पात्यन्ते । सुवदनावृत्तम् । लक्षणमुक्तम् ॥१२॥ **काले** इति । पुत्रे मोहमुपागते मातरः काले योग्यसमये आगताः खलु । हि यतः मातॄणां हस्तस्पर्शः अजलस्य जलार्थिनः

(ततः प्रविशन्ति देव्यः सुमन्त्रश्च ।)

सुमन्त्रः—इत इतो भवत्यः ।

इदं गृहं तत् प्रतिमानृपस्य नः समुच्छ्रयो यस्य स हर्म्यदुर्लभः ।
अयन्त्रितैरप्रतिहारिकागतैर्विना प्रणामं पथिकैरुपास्यते ॥ १४ ॥

(प्रविश्यावलोक्य) भवत्यः न खलु न खलु प्रवेष्टव्यम् ।

अयं हि पतितः कोऽपि वयस्स्थ इव पार्थिवः ।

देवकुलिकः—

परशङ्कामलं कर्तुं गृह्यतां भरतो ह्ययम् ॥ १५ ॥

(निष्क्रान्तः ।)

देव्यः—(सहसोपगम्य ।) हा जात भरत । (हा जाद भरद ।)

भरतः—(किञ्चित् समाश्वस्य ।) आर्य ।

सुमन्त्रः—जयतु महा—(इत्यर्धोक्ते सविषादम् ।) अहो स्वरसादृश्यम् ! मन्ये प्रतिमास्थो महाराजो व्याहरतीति ।

भरतः—अथ मातॄणामिदानीं कावस्था ।

देव्यः—जात एषा नोऽवस्था । (जाद एसा णो अवत्था ।) (अवगुण्ठनमपनयन्ति ।)

सुमन्त्रः—भवत्यः निगृह्यतामुत्कण्ठा ।

भरतः—(सुमन्त्रं विलोक्य ।) सर्वसमुदाचारसन्निकर्षस्तु मां सूचयति । कच्चित् तात सुमन्त्रो भवान् ननु ।

जलाञ्जलिः जीवप्रद इत्यर्थः ॥ १३ ॥ **इदं गृहमिति** । तत् प्रतिमानृपस्य प्रतिमारूपो नृपः प्रतिमानृपस्तस्य । इदं तद् गृहं यस्य हर्म्यदुर्लभः हर्म्ये दुष्प्रापः उच्छ्रय उत्सेधः । यद् अयन्त्रितैरनिषिद्धैः अप्रतिहारिकागतैः प्रतिहारिकानिर्देशं विनैव प्रविष्टैः पथिकैः पान्थैः प्रणामं विना उपास्यते सेव्यते । साक्षान्नृपस्य गृहं तु यन्त्रितैः प्रतिहारीकृतप्रवेशैः सप्रणामं सेव्यते इत्यस्य तस्माद्व्यतिरेकः । वंशस्थं वृत्तम् । जतौ तु वंशस्थमुदीरितं जरौ । इति तस्य लक्षणम् ॥ १४ ॥ **अयं हि** इति । वयसि तिष्ठतीति वयस्थः तरुणः । वयस्थस्तरुणो युवा इत्यमरः । पार्थिव इव । उत्प्रेक्षा । परशङ्कां परोयमिति शङ्कां कर्तुमलं शङ्का न कर्तव्या । गृह्यताम् हि । अयं भरतः ॥ १५ ॥ अवगुण्ठनमपनयन्ति शोकम्लानमुखदर्शनेनैवावस्थाज्ञानार्थम् । उत्कण्ठा मनसः पर्याकुलत्वम् । सर्वो यः समुदाचार आप्तजनोचिताचारस्तस्य सन्निकर्ष उपस्थितिः ।

सुमन्त्रः—कुमार अथ किम् । सुमन्त्रोऽस्मि ।

अन्वास्यमानश्चिरजीवदोषैः
कृतघ्नभावेन विडम्ब्यमानः ।
अहं हि तस्मिन् नृपतौ विपन्ने
जीवामि शून्यस्य रथस्य सूतः ॥ १६ ॥

भरतः—हा तात । (उत्थाय ।) तात अभिवादनक्रममुपदेष्टुमिच्छामि मातॄणाम् ।

सुमन्त्रः—बाढम् । इयं तत्रभवतो रामस्य जननी देवी कौसल्या ।

भरतः—अम्ब अनपराद्धोऽहमभिवादये ।

कौसल्या—जात निःसन्तापो भव । (जाद णिस्सन्दावो होहि ।)

भरतः—(आत्मगतम् ।) आक्रुष्ट इवास्म्यनेन । (प्रकाशम् ।) अनुगृहीतोऽस्मि । ततस्ततः ।

सुमन्त्रः—इयं तत्रभवतो लक्ष्मणस्य जननी देवी सुमित्रा ।

भरतः—अम्ब लक्ष्मणेन अतिसन्धितोऽहमभिवादये ।

सुमित्रा—जात यशोभागी भव । (जाद जसोभाई होहि ।)

भरतः—अम्ब । इदं प्रयतिष्ये । अनुगृहीतोऽस्मि । ततस्ततः ।

सुमन्त्रः—इयं ते जननी ।

भरतः—(सरोषमुत्थाय ।) आः पापे

मम मातुश्च मातुश्च मध्यस्था त्वं न शोभसे ।
गङ्गायमुनयोर्मध्ये कुनदीव प्रवेशिता ॥ १७ ॥

कैकेयी—जात किं मया कृतम् । (जाद किं मए किदं ।)

अन्वास्यमान इति । चिरजीवश्चिरजीवनं तस्य दोषैरन्वास्यमानोऽनुबध्यमानः । भावेन कृतघ्नतयापि विडम्ब्यमान उपहस्यमानः । कृतघ्नतां दर्शयति । तस्मिन्नृपतौ उपरतेऽपि शून्यस्य रथस्य सूतः सन् जीवामि । उपजातिश्छन्दः ॥ १६ ॥ निःसन्तापो शरहितः । आक्रुष्टः निन्दितः । सन्तापस्यापराधजन्यत्वात् । अनेन निःसंन्तापो भव वचनेन । अतिसंहितः वञ्चितः । स्वयं गत्वा रामेण सह वनं गमनाय मामवसरमदत्वेति भावः । प्रयतिष्ये राज्यं त्यक्त्वा भरतोपि राममनुगत इति यशो लब्धुमिति भावः । **मम मातुः** इति । मातुश्च सुमित्रायाश्च । कुत्सिता कलुषजला नदी कुनदी ।

भरतः—किं कृतमिति वदसि ।

वयमयशसा चीरेणार्यो नृपो गृहमृत्युना
प्रततरुदितैः कृत्स्नायोध्या मृगैः सह लक्ष्मणः ।
दयिततनयाः शोकेनाम्बाः स्नुषाध्वपरिश्रमै-
र्धिगिति वचसा चोग्रेणात्मा त्वया ननु योजिताः ॥ १८ ॥

कौसल्या—जात सर्वसमुदाचारमध्यस्थः किं न वन्दसे मातरम् ।
(जाद सव्वसमुदाआरमज्झत्थो किं ण वन्दसि मादरं ।)

भरतः—मातरमिति । अम्ब त्वमेव मे माता । अम्ब अभिवादये ।

कौसल्या—नहि नहि । इयं ते जननी । (णहि णहि इअं दे जणणी ।)

भरतः—आसीत् पुरा । न त्विदानीम् । पश्यतु भवती

त्यक्त्वा स्नेहं शीलसङ्क्रान्तदोषैः
पुत्रास्तावत्सन्त्वपुत्राः क्रियन्ते ।
लोकेऽपूर्वं स्थापयाम्येष धर्मं
भर्तृद्रोहादस्तु माताप्यमाता ॥ १९ ॥

कैकेयी—जात महाराजस्य सत्यवचनं रक्षन्त्या मया तथोक्तम् ।
(जाद महाराअस्स सच्चवअणं रक्खन्तीए मए तह उत्तं ।)

भरतः—किमिति किमिति ।

कैकेयी—पुत्रको मे राजा भवत्विति । (पुत्तओ मे राजा होदु त्ति ।)

भरतः—अथ स इदानीमार्योऽपि भवत्याः कः ।

वयमिति । वयमयशसाऽकीर्त्या योजिताः । आर्यः रामश्चीरेण योजितः । एवमन्यत्र । प्रततैरनवरतैः रुदितैः । कृत्स्ना संपूर्णा । दयितः प्रियस्तनयो यस्याः सा दयिततनया । अम्बा कौसल्या । स्नुषा सीता । अध्वपरिश्रमैर्वनमार्गसंचरणखेदैः योजिता । उग्रेण दुःसहेन । धिक् कैकेयीमिति । त्वया आत्मा योजितः ननु । हरिणी वृत्तम् । लक्षणमुक्तम् ॥ १८ ॥ सर्वः यः समुदाचार उचिताचारोऽभिवादनारूपस्तस्य मध्यस्थः तमनुवर्तमानः । **त्यक्त्वेति** । ननु शीलसंक्रान्तदोषैः शीलं स्वभावस्तेन संक्रान्तैः दोषैः । स्नेहं त्यक्त्वा पुत्रा अपुत्राः क्रियन्त । पुत्रत्वसम्बन्धं त्याज्यन्ते अतो नेयं मम मातेति भावः । न केवलमेतत् किंतु एषोहं भर्तृद्रोहात् भर्तुमरणमावहन्त्याऽतो भर्तृद्रोहं कुर्वाणा मातापि अमातास्तु भवतु । मातरि मातृवन्नाचरितव्यमिति लोके अपूर्वं धर्मं स्थापयामि । शालिनी वृत्तम् । लक्षणमुक्तम् ॥ १९ ॥ सत्यवचनं रक्षन्त्या राजा सत्यप्रतिज्ञ इति लोके प्रथितं यथा स्यात्तथा कुर्वत्येत्यर्थः ॥

पितुर्मे नौरसः पुत्रो न क्रमेणाभिषिच्यते ।
दयिता भ्रातरो न स्युः प्रकृतीनां न रोचते ॥ २० ॥

कैकेयी—जात शुल्कलुब्धा ननु प्रष्टव्या । (जाद सुक्कलुद्धा णणु पुच्छिदव्वा ।)

भरतः—

वल्कलैर्हृतराजश्रीः पदातिः सह भार्यया ।
वनवासं त्वयाज्ञप्तः शुल्केऽप्येतदुदाहृतम् ॥ २१ ॥

कैकेयी—जात देशकाले निवेदयामि । (जाद देसकाले णिवेदेमि ।)

भरतः ।

अयशसि यदि लोभः कीर्तयित्वा किमस्मान्
किमु नृपफलतर्षः किं नरेन्द्रो न दद्यात् ।
अथ तु नृपतिमातेत्येष शब्दस्तवेष्टो
वदतु भवति सत्यं किं तवार्यो न पुत्रः ॥ २२ ॥

कष्टं कृतं भवत्या ।

त्वया राज्यैषिण्या नृपतिरसुभिर्नैव गणितः
सुतं ज्येष्ठं च त्वं व्रज वनमिति प्रेषितवती ।

पितुरिति। स आर्यः रामः मे पितुः औरसः पुत्रो न किम् । येन भवत्या अपि पुत्रो न स्यात् । सक्रमेण ज्येष्ठक्रमेण राज्ये नाभिषिच्यते किम् । तस्मिन्नभिषिक्ते भ्रातरः । वयमित्यर्थः । दयिता स्नेहपूर्णा न स्युः किम् । अपि तु स्युरेव । आर्याभिषेचनं प्रकृतीनां न रोचते प्रीत्यै न किम् । सर्वथातिगर्हणीयं तव चेष्टितमिति भावः ॥ २० ॥ शुल्कलुब्धा शुल्कलोभः । शुल्कलुब्धया मयैतत्कृतमित्यभिप्रायः । यद्येवमस्तु राज्यप्रार्थना । रामविवासनं प्रति को-हेतुस्तदपि शुल्कान्तर्गतमासीत् किमित्याह **वल्कलैः** इति । हता राज्यश्रीर्यस्य स तथा-भूतः वल्कलैर्युक्तः भार्यया सह पदातिः पदचारी त्वया वनवासमाज्ञप्तः । एतदपि शुल्के शुल्कपणे उदाहृतं प्रतिश्रुतमासीत् किम् । देशकाले देशयुक्तः कालो देशकालः तस्मिन् समु-चिते देशे काले चेत्यर्थः । **अयशसि** इति । यदि अयश इष्टं तर्हि अस्मान् कीर्तयित्वा मम नामोद्घोष्य किं किं लब्धम् । अयं नृपफलतर्षः नृपस्य । राज्यप्राप्तेरित्यर्थः । यत्फ-लमभिमतवस्तुप्राप्तिरूपं तस्य तर्षः तृष्णा किमु । एवं चेत् नरेन्द्रः किं न दद्यात् । राम-विवासनमन्तरेणापि किं तेऽभिलषितं न पूरयेत् । अथेति । भवति भवती सत्यं वदतु आर्यस्तव पुत्रो न किमिति । भवति इति क्रियापदं वा पुत्रो न भवति किम् । मालिनी वृत्तम् ॥ २२ ॥ **त्वयेति** । भवति राज्यैषिण्या राज्यं काङ्क्षन्त्या त्वया असुभिः वियु-ज्यमान इति शेषः । न गणितः । त्वं ज्येष्ठं सुतं वनं व्रजेति प्रेषितवती । जनकतनया

न शीर्णं यद् दृष्ट्वा जनकतनयां वल्कलवती-
महो धात्रा सृष्टं भवति हृदयं वज्रकठिनम् ॥ २३ ॥

सुमन्त्रः—कुमार एतौ वसिष्ठवामदेवौ सह प्रकृतिभिरभिषेकं पुरस्कृत्य भवन्तं प्रत्युद्गतौ विज्ञापयतः ।

गोपहीना यथा गावो विलयं यान्त्यपालिताः ।
एवं नृपतिहीना हि विलयं यान्ति वै प्रजाः ॥ २४ ॥

भरतः—अनुगच्छन्तु मां प्रकृतयः ।

सुमन्त्रः—अभिषेकं विसृज्य क्व भवान् यास्यति ।

भरतः—अभिषेकमिति । इहात्रभवत्यै प्रदीयताम् ।

सुमन्त्रः—क्व भवान् यास्यति ।

भरतः—

तत्र यास्यामि यत्रासौ वर्तते लक्ष्मणप्रियः ।
नायोध्या तं विनायोध्या सायोध्या यत्र राघवः ॥ २५ ॥

(निष्क्रान्ताः सर्वे ।)

तृतीयोऽङ्कः ॥

वल्कलवतीं दृष्ट्वा यत् तव हृदयं न शीर्णम् । अहो धात्रा विधात्रा तद् वज्रकठिनं सृष्टम् । शिखरिणी वृत्तम् ॥ २३ ॥ **गोपहीना** इति । यथा गोपेन रक्षकेण हीना गावोऽपालिता विलयं नाशं यान्ति एवमित्यादि ॥ २४ ॥ **तत्रेति** । असौ राघवः वर्तते । लक्ष्मणः प्रियः यस्य स लक्ष्मणप्रियः । तं विना अयोध्या अयोध्या न । अटवी एवेत्यभिप्रायः ॥ २५ ॥ इति प्रतिमाटीकायां तृतीयोऽङ्कः ॥

अथ चतुर्थोऽङ्कः ।

(ततः प्रविशतश्चेट्यौ ।)

विजया—हला नन्दिनिके भण भण । अद्य कौसल्यापुरोगैः सर्वैरन्तःपुरैः प्रतिमागेहं द्रष्टुं गतैस्तत्र किल भर्तृदारको भरतो दृष्टः । अहं च मन्दभागा द्वारे स्थिता । (हळा णन्दिणिए भणेहि भणेहि । अज्ज कोसल्लापुरोगेहि सव्वेहि अन्तेवुरेहि पडिमागेहं दट्ठुं गदेहि तहिं किळ भट्टिदारओ भरदो दिट्ठो । अहं च मन्दभाआ दुवारे ट्ठिदा ।

नन्दिनिका—हला दृष्टोऽस्माभिः कौतूहलेन भर्तृदारको भरतः । (हळा दिट्ठो अह्मेहि कोदूहळेण भट्टिदारओ भरदो ।)

विजया—भट्टिनी कुमारेण किं भणिता । (भट्टिणी कुमारेण किं भणिदा ।

नन्दिनिका—किं भणितम् । अवलोकितुमपि नेच्छति कुमारः । (किं भणिदं । ओळोइदुं वि णेच्छदि कुमारो ।)

विजया—अहो अत्याहितम् । राज्यलुब्धया भर्तृदारकस्य रामस्य राज्यविभ्रष्टं कुर्वत्यात्मनो वैधव्यमादिष्टम् । लोकोऽपि विनाशं गमितः । निर्घृणा खलु भट्टिणी । पापकं कृतम् । (अहो अच्चाहिदम् । रज्जलुद्धाए भट्टिदारअस्स रामस्स रज्जविब्भट्टं करन्तीए अत्तणो वेहव्वं आदिट्टं । लोवो वि विणासं गमिओ । णिग्घिणा हु भट्टिणी । पापअं किदं ।)

नन्दिनिका—हला श्रृणु । प्रकृतिभिरानीतमभिषेकं विसृज्य रामतपोवनं गतः कुमारः । (हळा सुणाहि । पइदीहि आणीदं अभिसेअं विसज्जिअ रामतवोवणं गदो कुमारो ।)

विजया—(सविषादम् ।) हम् । एवं गतः कुमारः । नन्दिनिके एह्यावां भट्टिनीं पश्यावः । (हम् । एवं गदो कुमारो । णन्दिणिए एहि अह्मे भट्टिणिं पेक्खामो ।)

(निष्क्रान्ते ।)

अथ पूर्वाङ्के निर्दिष्टं भरतस्य वनप्रयाणं तत्र रामं दृष्ट्वा तत्पादुके गृहीत्वा निक्षेपभूतं राज्यं परिपालयितुं पुनरयोध्यामागमनमित्याद्यर्थजातं प्रतिपादयितुं चतुर्थाङ्कमारभते । तत्रादौ प्रवेशके चेट्योः प्रवेशः । कौसल्या पुरोगाऽग्रगा येषां तैः । किलेति वार्तायाम् । मन्दः भागो यस्याः सा । द्वारे स्थिता तं द्रष्टुं नाशक्नवम् । भट्टिणी कैकेयी । अत्याहितं महती आपत् । राज्यविभ्रष्टं राज्याद्विभ्रंशनम् । निर्घृणा निर्दया । प्रकृतिभिरानीतमभिषेकमभिषेकसंभारम् । हमित्याश्चर्ये । एवं कुमारः वनं गतः । यद्वा एवमवस्थामापन्नः ।

प्रवेशकः ।

(ततः प्रविशति भरतो रथेन सुमन्त्रः सूतश्च ।)

भरतः—

स्वर्गं गते नरपतौ सुकृतानुयात्रे
पौराश्रुपातसलिलैरनुगम्यमानः ।
द्रष्टुं प्रयाम्यकृपणेषु तपोवनेषु
रामाभिधानमपरं जगतः शशाङ्कम् ॥ १ ॥

सुमन्त्रः—एष एष आयुष्मान् भरतः ।

दैत्येन्द्रमानमथनस्य नृपस्य पुत्रो
यज्ञोपयुक्तविभवस्य नृपस्य पौत्रः ।
भ्राता पितुः प्रियकरस्य जगत्प्रियस्य
रामस्य रामसदृशेन पथा प्रयाति ॥ २ ॥

भरतः—भोस्तात ।

सुमन्त्रः—कुमार अयमस्मि ।

भरतः—क्व तत्रभवान् ममार्यो रामः । क्वासौ महाराजस्य प्रतिनिधिः क्व सन्निदर्शनं सारवताम् । क्वासौ प्रत्यादेशो राज्यलुब्धायाः कैकेय्याः । क्व तत् पात्रं यशसः । क्वासौ नरपतेः पुत्रः । क्वासौ सत्यमनुव्रतः ।

स्वर्गमिति । सुकृतानुयात्रे सुकृतं पुण्यमनुयात्रमनुगामि यस्य तस्मिन् नरपतौ दशरथे स्वर्गं याते । पौराणामश्रुपातसलिलैः गलिताश्रुजलैः अनुगम्यमानोहम् । अकृपणेषु उदारेषु तपोवनेषु वर्तमानं राम इति अभिधानं यस्य तं रामाभिधानमपरं प्रसिद्धाच्छशाङ्कादन्यं जगतः शशाङ्कं चन्द्रं सकललोकाह्लादकरत्वात् । द्रष्टुं प्रयामि । रूपकमलंकारः ॥१॥ एष एष इति द्विरुक्तिरादरातिशयार्था । एषः । **दैत्येन्द्रेति** । दैत्येन्द्राणां मानस्य मथ्नातीति मथनः ध्वंसकः दैत्येन्द्रमानमथनस्तस्य नृपस्य दशरथस्य पुत्रः । यज्ञेषूपयुक्तो विभवो येन तस्य नृपस्याजस्य पौत्रः । पितुः प्रियकरस्य जगत्प्रियस्य रामस्य भ्राता रामसदृशेन रामस्यानुरूपेण पथा न्यायमार्गेण प्रयाति । रामेण यथा पित्राज्ञया राज्यं त्यक्तं तथानेनाप्यन्यायप्राप्तं राज्यं त्यक्तमिति भावः । श्लोकद्वयस्य वसन्ततिलकं वृत्तम् । ॥ २ ॥ औत्सुक्यातिशयात्पृच्छति क्वेति । प्रतिनिधिः पुत्रः । सारः मनःस्थैर्यम् । अक्षोभ्यं धैर्यमिति यावत् । तद्वतां सन्निदर्शनमुत्कृष्टमुदाहरणम् । प्रत्यादेशो निराकृतिः । अनुव्रतः अनुकूलं व्रतं कर्म यस्यासौ अनुव्रतः सत्यस्य पालयिता ।

मम मातुः प्रियं कर्तुं येन लक्ष्मीर्विसर्जिता ।
तमहं द्रष्टुमिच्छामि दैवतं परमं मम ॥ ३ ॥

सुमन्त्रः—कुमार एतस्मिन्नाश्रमपदे ।

अत्र रामश्च सीता च लक्ष्मणश्च महायशाः ।
सत्यं शीलं च भक्तिश्च येषु विग्रहवत् स्थिता ॥ ४ ॥

भरतः—तेन हि स्थाप्यतां रथः ।

सूतः—यदाज्ञापयत्यायुष्मान् । (तथा करोति ।)

भरतः—(रथादवतीर्य ।) सूत एकान्ते विश्रामयाश्वान् ।

सूतः—यदाज्ञापयत्यायुष्मान् । (निष्क्रान्तः ।)

भरतः—भोस्तात निवेद्यतां निवेद्यताम् ।

सुमन्त्रः—कुमार किमिति निवेद्यते ।

भरतः—राज्यलुब्धायाः कैकेय्याः पुत्रो भरतः प्राप्त इति ।

सुमन्त्रः—कुमार अलं गुरुजनापवादमभिधातुम् ।

भरतः—सुष्ठु न न्याय्यं परदोषमभिधातुम् । तेन हि उच्यतामिक्ष्वाकुकुलन्यङ्गभूतो भरतो दर्शनमभिलषतीति ।

सुमन्त्रः—कुमार नाहमेवं वक्तुं समर्थः । अथ पुनर्भरतः प्राप्त इति ब्रूयाम् ।

भरतः—न न । नाम केवलमभिधीयमानमकृतप्रायश्चित्तमिव मे प्रतिभाति । किं ब्रह्मघ्नानामपि परेण निवेदनं क्रियते । तस्मात् तिष्ठतु तातः। अहमेव निवेदयिष्ये । भो भोः निवेद्यतां निवेद्यतां तत्रभवते पितृवचनकराय राघवाय—

निर्घृणश्च कृतघ्नश्च प्राकृतः प्रियसाहसः ।
भक्तिमानागतः कश्चित् कथं तिष्ठतु यात्विति ॥ ५ ॥

ममेति । लक्ष्मी राज्यलक्ष्मीः । विसर्जिता त्यक्ता ॥ ३ ॥ **अत्रेति** । महद्यशो यस्य स महायशा रामः सीता लक्ष्मणश्च वसन्ति इति शेषः । येषु सत्यं शीलं भक्तिश्चेति त्रयं विग्रहवन्मूर्तिमत् स्थितम् । येषु यथाक्रमं स्थितमिति वा ॥ ४ ॥ गुरुजनापवादं मातुर्निन्दाम् । न्याय्यं युक्तम् । न्यङ्गभूतः कलङ्कभूतः । केवलं दोषदर्शकविशेषणरहितम् । अकृतं प्रायश्चित्तं यस्य । परेण अन्येन । आत्मनैव कर्तव्यमित्यर्थः । **निर्घृणश्च** इति । प्रियं साहसं यस्य । एतादृशो भक्तिमान् भवद्दर्शनापेक्षी कश्चिदागतः । स कथं तिष्ठतु उत दर्शनेऽदीयमाने यातु इति निवेद्यतामिति पूर्वेण सम्बन्धः ॥ ५ ॥

(ततः प्रविशति रामः सीतालक्ष्मणाभ्याम् ।)

रामः—(आकर्ण्य सहर्षम् ।) सौमित्रे किं श्रृणोषि । अयि विदेहराजपुत्रि त्वमपि श्रृणोषि ।

कस्यासौ सदृशतरः स्वरः पितुर्मे
गाम्भीर्यात् परिभवतीव मेघनादम् ।
यः कुर्वन् मम हृदयस्य बन्धुशङ्कां
सस्नेहः श्रुतिपथमिष्टतः प्रविष्टः ॥ ६ ॥

लक्ष्मणः—आर्य ममापि खल्वेष स्वरसंयोगो बन्धुजनबहुमानमावहति । एष हि

घनः स्पष्टो धीरः समदवृषभास्निग्धमधुरः
कलः कण्ठे वक्षस्यनुपहतसञ्चाररभसः ।
यथास्थानं प्राप्य स्फुटकरणनानाक्षरतया
चतुर्णां वर्णानामभयमिव दातुं व्यवसितः ॥ ७ ॥

रामः—सर्वथा नायमबान्धवस्य स्वरसंयोगः क्लेदयतीव मे हृदयम् । वत्स लक्ष्मण दृश्यतां तावत् ।

लक्ष्मणः—यदाज्ञापयत्यार्यः । (परिक्रामति ।)

भरतः—अये कथं न कश्चित् प्रतिवचनं प्रयच्छति । किन्नु खलु विज्ञातोऽस्मि कैकेय्याः पुत्रो भरतः प्राप्त इति ।

कस्येति । अयं मे पितुः सदृशतरोऽत्यन्तसदृशः स्वरः गाम्भीर्यान्मेघनादं घनगर्जितं परिभवति तिरस्करोति । यः सस्नेहः मम हृदयस्य बन्धुशङ्कां बन्धुरयं भवेदिति शङ्कां कुर्वन् मम श्रुतिपथमिष्टतः इष्टत्वेन प्रविष्टः । प्रहर्षणी वृत्तम् । लक्षणमुक्तम् ॥ ६ ॥ बन्धुजनबहुमानं बन्धुजनोचितं बहुमानम् । **घनः** इति । एष स्वरसंयोगः **घनः** सान्द्रः स्पष्टः स्फुटः धीरो गम्भीरः मदेन सहितः समदो यः वृषभस्तस्य इव स्निग्धो मसृणो मधुरो हृद्यश्च । कलो मृदुः । यथा स्थानं प्राप्य वर्णानामष्टौ स्थानानि । तदुक्तं—अष्टौ स्थानानि वर्णानामुरः कण्ठः शिरस्तथा । जिह्वामूलं च दन्ताश्च नासिकौष्ठौ च तालु च ॥ इति । तेषां मध्ये स्वस्य स्वस्योचितं स्थानं प्राप्यासाद्य । स्फुटं करणमिन्द्रियकर्मात्रोच्चारणप्रयत्नो येषां तानि स्फुटकरणानि नानाक्षराणि यस्मिन्स स्फुटकरणनानाक्षरस्तस्य भावस्तत्ता तया । करणं कारणे काये साधनेन्द्रियकर्मसु । इत्यजयः । कण्ठे वक्षसि हृदयेऽनुपहतोऽस्खलितः सञ्चारस्य वेगो यस्य तादृशः चतुर्णां वर्णानां ब्राह्मणादीनामभयं दातुं व्यवसितः कृतप्रयत्न इव । शिखरिणी वृत्तम् । लक्षणमुक्तम् ॥ ७ ॥ क्लेदयति स्नेहार्द्रं

लक्ष्मणः—(विलोक्य ।) अये अयमार्यो रामः । न न । रूपसादृश्यम् ।

मुखमनुपमं त्वार्यस्याभं शशाङ्कमनोहरं
मम पितृसमं पीनं वक्षः सुरारिशरक्षतम् ।
द्युतिपरिवृतस्तेजोराशिर्जगत्प्रियदर्शनो
नरपतिरयं देवेन्द्रो वा स्वयं मधुसूदनः ॥ ८ ॥

(सुमन्त्रं दृष्ट्वा ।) अये तातः ।

सुमन्त्रः— अये कुमारो लक्ष्मणः ।

भरतः—एवं गुरुरयम् । आर्य अभिवादये ।

लक्ष्मणः—एह्येहि । आयुष्मान् भव । (सुमन्त्रं वीक्ष्य ।) तात कोऽत्रभवान् ।

सुमन्त्रः—कुमार

रघोश्चतुर्थोऽयमजात् तृतीयः
पितुः प्रकाशस्य तव द्वितीयः ।
यस्यानुजस्त्वं स्वकुलस्य केतो-
स्तस्यानुजोऽयं भरतः कुमारः ॥ ९ ॥

लक्ष्मणः—एह्येहीक्ष्वाकुकुमार । वत्स स्वस्ति । आयुष्मान् भव ।

असुरसमरदक्षैर्वज्रसंघृष्टचापै-
रनुपमबलवीर्यैः स्वैः कुलैस्तुल्यवीर्यः ।
रघुरिव स नरेन्द्रो यज्ञविश्रान्तकोशो
भव जगति गुणानां भाजनं भ्राजितानाम् ॥ १० ॥

करोति । रूपसादृश्यं रूपेण रामसदृश इत्यर्थः । **मुखमिति** । अस्य मुखमनुपममतुलम् । आर्यास्याभमार्यस्यास्यं तस्येव आभा कान्तिर्यस्य । पीनं वक्षः सुरारीणां दानवानां शरैः देवदानवानां युद्धे देवसाहाय्यकरणात् । क्षतम् । पितृसमं पितृवक्षःसममित्यर्थः । द्युत्या दीप्त्या परिवृतः तेजोराशिः जगतः प्रियदर्शनः अयं नरपतिः किं देवेन्द्रः वा स्वयं मधुसूदनो विष्णुः किम् ॥ हरिणी वृत्तम् । लक्ष्मणमुक्तम् ॥ ८ ॥ **रघोरिति** । प्रकाशस्य विख्यातस्य स्वकुलस्य केतोः ध्वजभूतस्य यस्य रामस्य त्वमनुजस्तस्य । उपेन्द्रवज्रा वृत्तम् ॥ ९ ॥ आयुष्मान्दीर्घायुः । **असुरैरिति** । असुरैः सह समरे दक्षैः पटुभिः । वज्रेण पविना संघृष्टं जातघर्षणमेकत्र युद्धकरणात् । जातस्पर्धं वा चापं येषां तैः । अनुपमबलवीर्यैः स्वैः कुलैः वंश्यैः तुल्यवीर्यः । स प्रसिद्धः यज्ञे विश्वजिति विश्रान्तः निःशेषः कोशो यस्य स नरेन्द्रो रघुरिव । जगति भ्राजितानां दीप्तिमतां श्लाघनीयाना-मित्यर्थः । गुणानां भाजनमाश्रयो भव । मालिनी छन्दः । लक्ष्मणमुक्तम् ॥ १० ॥

भरतः—अनुगृहीतोऽस्मि ।

लक्ष्मणः—कुमार इह तिष्ठ । त्वदागमनमार्याय निवेदयामि ।

भरतः—आर्य अचिरमिदानीमभिवादयितुमिच्छामि । शीघ्रं निवेद्यताम् ।

लक्ष्मणः—बाढम् । (उपेत्य ।) जयत्वार्यः । आर्य

अयं ते दयितो भ्राता भरतो भ्रातृवत्सलः ।
संक्रान्तं यत्र ते रूपमादर्श इव तिष्ठति ॥ ११ ॥

रामः—वत्स लक्ष्मण । किमेवं भरतः प्राप्तः ।

लक्ष्मणः—आर्य । अथ किम् ।

रामः—मैथिलि भरतावलोकनार्थं विशालीक्रियतां ते चक्षुः ।

सीता—आर्यपुत्र किं भरत आगतः। (अय्यउत्त किं भरदो आअदो ।)

रामः—मैथिलि अथ किम् ।

अद्य खल्ववगच्छामि पित्रा मे दुष्करं कृतम् ।
कीदृशस्तनयस्नेहो भ्रातृस्नेहोऽयमीदृशः ॥ १२ ॥

लक्ष्मणः—आर्य । किं प्रविशतु कुमारः ।

रामः—वत्स लक्ष्मण इदमपि तावदात्माभिप्रायमनुवर्तयितुमिच्छसि। गच्छ सत्कृत्य शीघ्रं प्रवेश्यतां कुमारः ।

लक्ष्मणः—यदाज्ञापयत्यार्यः ।

रामः—अथवा तिष्ठ त्वम् ।

इयं स्वयं गच्छतु मानहेतोर्मातेव भावं तनये निवेश्य ।
तुषारपूर्णोत्पलपत्रनेत्रा हर्षास्रमासारमिवोत्सृजन्ती ॥ १३ ॥

अचिरमकालहीनम् । **अयं ते** इति । दयितः प्रियः । भ्रातरि वत्सलः भ्रातृवत्सलः । आदर्शे मुकुले इव यत्र यस्मिन् संक्रान्तं तिष्ठति ॥ ११ ॥ विशालीक्रियतां विस्फार्यताम् । **अद्येति** । मे मम पित्राद्य दुष्करं मदर्थं प्राणत्यागादिकं कृतमित्यवगच्छामि । यतः अयं भ्रातृस्नेह ईदृशः । यत्प्राप्तमपि राज्यं त्यक्त्वा मदनुगमनार्थं भरतोऽत्रागतः । ततः तनयस्नेहः कीदृशो भवेत् । कामापदमावहेत् ॥१२॥ आत्माभिप्रायं मयानुवर्तयितुं तवाभिप्रायानुसारेण मम वर्तनार्थमित्यर्थः । **इयामिति** । मानहेतोः भरतसम्माननार्थं माता तनये इव भावं चित्तवृत्तिं निवेश्य । पुत्रवात्सल्येनेत्यर्थः । तुषारेण हिमेन पूर्णे उत्पलपत्रे इव नेत्रे यस्याः सा । हर्षास्रमानन्दाश्रु आसारं धारासम्पातमिव उत्सृजन्ती इयं सीता स्वयं गच्छतु ।

सीता—यदार्यपुत्र आज्ञापयति। (जं अय्यउत्तो आणवेदि।) (उत्थाय परिक्रम्य भरतमवलोक्य।) हं ततस्तां वेलामिदानीं निष्क्रान्त आर्यपुत्रः। नहि। नहि। रूपसादृश्यम्। (हं तदो तं वेळं दाणि णिक्कन्तो अय्यउत्तो। णहि णहि। रूवसदिस्सं।)

सुमन्त्रः—अये वधूः।

भरतः—अये इयमत्रभवती जनकराजपुत्री।

इदं तत् स्त्रीमयं तेजो जातं क्षेत्रोदराद्धलात्।
जनकस्य नृपेन्द्रस्य तपसः सन्निदर्शनम्॥ १४॥

आर्ये अभिवादये। भरतोऽहमस्मि।

सीता—(आत्मगतम्।) नहि रूपमेव। स्वरयोगोऽपि स एव। (प्रकाशम्।) वत्स। चिरं जीव। (णहि रूवं एव्व। सरजोओ वि सो एव्व) वच्छ चिरं जीव।)

भरतः—अनुगृहीतोऽस्मि।

सीता—एहि वत्स। भ्रातृमनोरथं पूरय। (एहि वच्छ। भादुमणोरहं पूरेहि।)

सुमन्त्रः—प्रविशतु कुमारः।

भरतः—तात इदानीं किं करिष्यसि।

सुमन्त्रः—

अहं पश्चात् प्रवेक्ष्यामि स्वर्गं याते नराधिपे।
विदितार्थस्य रामस्य ममैतत् पूर्वदर्शनम्॥ १५॥

भरतः—एवमस्तु। (राममुपगम्य।) आर्य अभिवादये भरतोऽहमस्मि।

रामः—(सहर्षम्।) एह्येहि इक्ष्वाकुकुमार। स्वस्ति। आयुष्मान् भव।

उपेन्द्रवज्रा छन्दः॥१३॥ हमिति विस्मये। भरते रामभ्रमाद्विस्मयः। विस्मिताहं ततः उटजात्। तां वेलां यस्यामहं निष्क्रान्ता तस्यां वेलायां तत्र स्थितः आर्यपुत्रः कथमिदानीं निष्क्रान्तः निष्क्रम्येह स्थितः। निरीक्ष्याह नहि नहि इति। **इदं तदिति**। हलात् लाङ्गलात् हलकृष्टादिति यावत्। क्षेत्रोदराज्जातमिदं तत्स्त्रीमयं तेजः। यद् नृपेन्द्रस्य जनकस्य तपसः सन्निदर्शनमुत्कृष्टोदाहरणम्॥१४॥ **अहमिति**। नराधिपे दशरथे स्वर्गं याते मृते ममैतत्पूर्वदर्शनं प्रथमदर्शनं विदितार्थस्य त्वद्दर्शनाज्ज्ञातपितृमरणरूपार्थस्य रामस्य स्यादिति अहं पश्चात्प्रवेक्ष्यामि। नाहं नराधिपमरणस्य प्रथमनिवेदको भवेयमित्यर्थः

वक्षः प्रसारय कपाटपुटप्रमाण-
मालिङ्ग मां सुविपुलेन भुजद्वयेन ।
उन्नामयाननमिदं शरदिन्दुकल्पं
प्रह्लादय व्यसनदग्धमिदं शरीरम् ॥ १६ ॥

भरतः—अनुगृहीतोऽस्मि ।

सुमन्त्रः—(उपेत्य ।) जयत्वायुष्मान् ।

रामः—हा तात ।

गत्वा पूर्वं स्वसैन्यैरभिसरिसमये खं समानैर्विमानै—
र्विख्यातो यो विमर्दे स स इति बहुशः सासुराणां सुराणाम् ।
स श्रीमांस्त्यक्तदेहो दयितमपि विना स्नेहवन्तं भवन्तं
स्वर्गस्थः साम्प्रतं किं रमयति पितृभिः स्वैर्नरेन्द्रैर्नरेन्द्रः ॥ १७ ॥

सुमन्त्रः—(सशोकम् ।)

नरपतिनिधनं भवत्प्रवासं भरतविषादमनाथतां कुलस्य ।
बहुविधमनुभूय दुष्प्रसह्यं गुण इव बद्धपराद्धमायुषा मे ॥ १८ ॥

सीता—रुदन्तमार्यपुत्रं पुनरपि रोदयति तातः । (रोदन्तं अय्यउत्तं पुणो वि रोदावीअदि तादो ।)

रामः—मैथिलि एष पर्यवस्थापयाम्यात्मानम् । वत्स लक्ष्मण आपस्तावत् ।

॥ १५ ॥ **वक्ष** इति । कपाटपुटं प्रमाणं यस्य तत्कपाटपुटप्रमाणं वक्षः प्रसारय । सुविपुलेन वृहता भुजद्वयेन मामालिङ्ग । शरदिन्दुकल्पं ईषदसमाप्तः शरदिन्दुः तत्तुल्यम् । इदं तवाननमुन्नमय । व्यसनदग्धं इदं मम शरीरं प्रह्लादय । वसन्ततिलकं वृत्तम् ॥ १६ ॥ **गत्वेति** । यः पूर्वं सासुराणां सुराणां विमर्दे युद्धे अभिसरिसमये सुरसाह्यार्थं गमनकाले समानैः देवविमानसमानैः विमानैः स्वसैन्यैः स्वं स्वर्गं गत्वा सः सः स दशरथः यस्तत्र दृश्यते स दशरथ यस्तत्र दृश्यते इति बहुशः विख्यातः निर्दिष्टः । यद्वा स स इति अनेकैः निर्दिश्यमानत्वाद्वीप्सा । स श्रीमान् त्यक्तदेहः नरेन्द्रः दयितं स्नेहवन्तमपि भवन्तं विना स्वर्गस्थः सन् साम्प्रतं पितृभिः पितृभूतैः स्वैः **पूर्वजैर्नरेन्द्रैः** रमयति । आत्मानमिति शेषः । किम् । स्रग्धरा वृत्तम् । म्रभ्नैर्यानां त्रयेण त्रिमुनियतियुता स्रग्धरा कीर्तितेयम् । इति लक्षणम् ॥१७॥ **नरपतीति** । मे आयुषा नरपतिनिधनं भवतां प्रवासं भरतविषादं कुलस्य अनाथतां च एवं बहुविधमनेकप्रकारं दुष्प्रसह्यं अनर्थजातमनुभूय गुणेऽपराद्धमिव । दीर्घत्वं गुण एव तस्य महानपराधो जात इत्यर्थः । पुष्पिताग्रा वृत्तम् । लक्षणमुक्तम् ॥ १८ ॥ पर्यवस्थापयामि शोकं निगृह्णामीत्यर्थः । आपस्तावदानीयन्तामिति

लक्ष्मणः—यदाज्ञापयत्यार्यः ।

भरतः—आर्य न खलु न्याय्यम् । क्रमेण शुश्रूषयिष्ये । अहमेव यास्यामि । (कलशं गृहीत्वा निष्क्रम्य प्रविश्य ।) इमा आपः ।

रामः—(आचम्य ।) मैथिलि विशीर्यते खलु लक्ष्मणस्य व्यापारः ।

सीता—आर्यपुत्र नन्वेतेनापि शुश्रूषयितव्यः । (अय्यउत्त णं एदिणा पि सुस्सूसइदव्वो ।)

रामः—सुष्ठु खल्विह लक्ष्मणः शुश्रूषयतु । तत्रस्थो मां भरतः शुश्रूषयतु ।

भरतः—प्रसीदत्वार्यः ।

इह स्थास्यामि देहेन तत्र स्थास्यामि कर्मणा ।
नाम्नैव भवतो राज्यं कृतरक्षं भविष्यति ॥ १९ ॥

रामः—वत्स कैकेयीमातः । मा मैवम् ।

पितुर्नियोगादहमागतो वनं
न वत्स दर्पान्न भयान्न विभ्रमात् ।
कुलं च नः सत्यधनं ब्रवीमि ते
कथं भवान् नीचपथे प्रवर्तते ॥ २० ॥

सुमन्त्रः—अथेदानीमभिषेकोदकं क्व तिष्ठतु ।

रामः—यत्र मे मात्राभिहितं तत्रैव तावत् तिष्ठतु ।

भरतः—प्रसीदत्वार्यः । आर्य अलमिदानीं व्रणे प्रहर्तुम् ।

शेषः । न्याय्यं योग्यम् । कनीयसि मयि स्थिते लक्ष्मणेन जलानयनम् । क्रमेण पूर्वापरक्रमेण । विशीर्यते विच्छिद्यते । सुष्ठु खलु शोभनं खलु इदं यत् । तत्रस्थो नगरस्थः । **इहेति** । इह अस्मिन्वने देहेन स्थास्यामि । तत्र शुश्रूषणार्थमिति भावः । तत्रायोध्यायां कर्मणा राज्यपरिपालनकर्म कुर्वन् सचिवादिद्वारेणेत्यर्थः । तत्कस्य नाम्नेति चेत् भवतो नाम्ना रामस्यैवेदं राज्यमिति कृतरक्षं भविष्यति ॥ १९ ॥ भरतोक्तमयुक्तं मन्यमान आह मामैवमिति । **पितुरिति** । वत्स अहं पितुर्नियोगादाज्ञया वनमागतः । न दर्पात् ज्येष्ठो गुणसम्पन्नोऽहं कथं पित्रावमानितोऽतो न तत्संमुखे स्थास्यामीत्यवलेपान्न । न भयाद्बलवतः पितुर्भयात् । नापि विभ्रमाद्बुद्धिभ्रंशात् । ज्येष्ठः सन्नप्यहं पित्रा राज्यात्प्रच्यावितो च किं करिष्ये इति किंकर्तव्यतामूढतया न । किंतु पितृनियोगः सर्वथानुष्ठातव्य इति । अस्माकं कुलं सत्यधनमतस्ते ब्रवीमि । भवान् कथं नीचानां पन्था नीचपथः पितृनियोगापरिपालनरूपः तत्र प्रवर्तसे ॥ वंशस्थं वृत्तम् ॥ २० ॥ क्व तिष्ठतु । भवतः शिरसि भरतस्य शिरसि वा इत्यर्थः ।

अपि सुगुण ममापि त्वत्प्रसूतिः प्रसूतिः
स खलु निभृतधीमांस्ते पिता मे पिता च ।
सुपुरुष पुरुषाणां मातृदोषो न दोषो
वरद भरतमार्तं पश्य तावद् यथावत् ॥ २१ ॥

सीता—आर्यपुत्र । अतिकरुणं मन्त्रयते भरतः । किमिदानीमार्यपुत्रेण चिन्त्यते । (अय्यउत्त । अदिकरुणं मन्तेअइ भरदो । किं दाणिं अय्यउत्तेण चिन्तीअदि ।)

रामः—मैथिलि

तं चिन्तयामि नृपतिं सुरलोकयातं
येनायमात्मजविशिष्टगुणो न दृष्टः ।
ईदृग्विधं गुणनिधिं समवाप्य लोके
धिग् भो विधेर्यदि बलं पुरुषोत्तमेषु ॥ २२ ॥

वत्स कैकेयीमातः ।

यत्सत्यं परितोषितोऽस्मि भवता निष्कलमषात्मा भवां-
स्त्वद्वाक्यस्य वशानुगोऽस्मि भवतः ख्यातैर्गुणैर्निर्जितः ।

अपि सुगुणेति हे सुगुण प्रसूयते अनया इति प्रसूतिः प्रभवः । मूलपुरुष इत्यर्थः । तव प्रसूतिः वंश इत्यर्थः । ममापि प्रसूतिः अपि । न किमित्यर्थः । अपि शब्दो यद्यर्थे इति ग० शा० । निभृतधीमान् नितरां भृता निभृता श्रेष्ठा निश्चला वा धीः बुद्धिस्तद्वान् । स खलु ते पिता मम च पिता । हे सुपुरुष मातृदोषः मातृकृतापराधः पुरुषाणां नराणां न दोषः । न तेषु प्रसज्यते । हे वरद । अनेन ममाभीष्टं कर्तुं त्वं समर्थ इति ध्वनितम् । आर्तमापन्नं भरतं यथावत यथार्थरूपेण पश्य तावत् । तस्यान्तर्भावं विदित्वा तत्समीहितं सम्पादयेति यावत् । मालिनी वृत्तम् ॥ २१ ॥ अतिकरुणमतिदीनम् । चिन्त्यते विचार्यते । अस्याभिमतानुष्ठाने कोऽपि विचार इत्यर्थः । **तमिति** । हे मैथिलि सुरलोकयातं तं नृपतिं चिन्तयामि येन अयमात्मजस्य विशिष्टः उदात्तः गुणः । अतुलभ्रातृप्रेमान्यायाचरणपराङ्मुखतादिरूपः । न दृष्टो लक्षितः । वस्तुतस्तु आत्मजश्चासौ विशिष्टगुणश्चेति कवेर्मनस्यासीदिति भाति । 'आत्मजेषु विशिष्टगुणः' इति ग० शा० । एतत्तु विधिबलादित्याह—लोके ईदृग्विधं भरतसदृशं गुणनिधिं पुत्रं समवाप्य । स्थितेषु पुरुषोत्तमेषु यदि विधेर्बलं । स्यात् । एतानपि विधिर्न्याय्यात्पथः प्रविचालयितुं प्रभवेद्यदि । भो धिक् । सर्वथा निन्द्यमिदम् ॥ वसन्ततिलका वृत्तम् ॥ २२ ॥ **यत्सत्यमिति** । यत्सत्यं भवता परितोषितः साकल्येन तुष्टिं नीतोस्मि । भवान् निष्कल्मषात्मा न ते मनसि पापलेशोपि । भवतः ख्यातैः गुणैर्निर्जितोहं त्वद्वाक्यस्य वशानु-

किन्त्वेतन्नृपतेर्वचस्तदनृतं कर्तुं न युक्तं त्वया
किञ्चोत्पाद्य भवाद्विधं भवतु ते मिथ्याभिधायी पिता ॥ २३ ॥

भरतः—

यावद् भविष्यति भवन्नियमावसानं
तावद् भवेयमिह ते नृप पादमूले ।

रामः—

मैवं नृपः स्वसुकृतैरनुयातु सिद्धिं
मे शापितो न परिरक्षसि चेत् स्वराज्यम् ॥ २४ ॥

भरतः—हन्त अनुत्तरमभिहितम् । भवतु समयतस्ते राज्यं परिपालयामि ।

रामः—वत्स कः समयः ।

भरतः—मम हस्ते निक्षिप्तं तव राज्यं चतुर्दशवर्षान्ते प्रतिग्रहीतुमिच्छामि ।

रामः—एवमस्तु ।

भरतः—आर्य श्रुतम् । आर्ये श्रुतम् । तात श्रुतम् ।

सर्वे—वयमपि श्रोतारः ।

भरतः—आर्य अन्यमपि वरं हर्तुमिच्छामि ।

रामः—वत्स किमिच्छसि । किमहं ददामि । किमहमनुष्ठास्यामि ।

गोस्मि । किंतु भरत एव राजा भवतु इत्येतन्नृपतेर्वचः । तत्त्वयाऽनृतं कर्तुं न युक्तम् । किंच एतत्कथय—भवाद्विधं गुणसम्पन्नमुत्पाद्य पुत्रं लब्ध्वा ते पिता मिथ्याभिधायी भवतु भवतु किम् । शार्दूलविक्रीडितम् ॥ २३ ॥ **यावदिति** । यावत् भवतश्चतुर्दशवर्षवनवासरूपस्य नियमस्य अवसानं समाप्तिः भविष्यति तावत् । हे नृप । अनेन त्वमेव राजेति सूचितम् । इह ते पादमूले भवेयं स्थास्यामि । **मैवमिति** । एवं मा ब्रूहि नृपः स्वसुकृतैः सिद्धिमनुयातु । राज्यं न परिरक्षसि चेन्मे मत्सम्बन्धेन । मम जीवितेनेति यावत् । शापितोसि ॥ वसन्ततिलकेयम् ॥ २४ ॥ अनुत्तरं शापितोस्मीत्यतोत्र उत्तरं नास्ति । निक्षिप्तं न्यासीकृतं निक्षेपत्वेन स्वीकृतमित्यर्थः । प्रतिग्रहीतुं प्रतिग्राहयितुमित्यर्थः । श्रुतम् युष्माकं साक्ष्येभिहितमित्यर्थः । किमिच्छसीत्यादि प्रेमातिशयं सूचयति ।

भरतः—

पादोपभुक्ते तव पादुके मे
एते प्रयच्छ प्रणताय मूर्ध्ना।
यावद् भवानेष्यति कार्यसिद्धिं
तावद् भविष्याम्यनयोर्विधेयः॥ २६॥

रामः—(स्वगतम्।) हन्त भोः।

सुचिरेणापि कालेन यशः किञ्चिन्मयार्जितम्।
अचिरेणैव कालेन भरतेनाद्य सञ्चितम्॥ २६॥

सीता—आर्यपुत्र ननु दीयते खलु प्रथमयाचनं भरताय।
(अय्यउत्त णं दीयदि खु पुढमजाअणं भरदस्स।)

रामः—तथास्तु। वत्स गृह्यताम्। (पादुके अर्पयति।)

भरतः—अनुगृहीतोऽस्मि (गृहीत्वा।) आर्य अत्राभिषेकोदकमावर्जयितुमिच्छामि।

रामः—तात यदिष्टं भरतस्य तत् सर्वं क्रियताम्।

सुमन्त्रः—यदाज्ञापयत्यायुष्मान्।

भरतः—(आत्मगतम्।) हन्त भोः

श्रद्धेयः स्वजनस्य पौररुचितो लोकस्य दृष्टिक्षमः
स्वर्गस्थस्य नराधिपस्य दयितः शीलान्वितोऽहं सुतः।

पादोपभुक्ते इति। मूर्ध्ना प्रणताय मे मह्यमेते पादोपभुक्ते तव पादुके प्रयच्छ। यावद्भवान्कार्यसिद्धिमेष्यति स्वकार्यं सम्पाद्यागमिष्यतीति यावत्। तावदनयोः विधेय आज्ञाकरः भविष्यामि। अत्र रामायणम्—अधिरोहार्य पादाभ्यां पादुके हेमभूषिते। एते हि सर्वलोकस्य योगक्षेमं विधास्यतः॥ ** चतुर्दश हि वर्षाणि जटाचीरधरो ह्यहम्। फलमूलाशनो वीर भवेयं रघुनन्दन। तव पादुकयोर्न्यस्य राज्यतन्त्रं परंतप॥ इति। **सुचिरेणेति**। मया सुचिरेणापि कालेन किंचित्स्वल्पं यशः पित्राज्ञानुरोधाद्वनमागच्छता अर्जितम्। भरतेन तु अचिरेणैव कालेनाद्य सुमहदिति शेषः यशः सञ्चितं सम्पादितम्। निःसीमभ्रातृभक्तिमाविष्कुर्वता स्वयमेव प्राप्तमपि राज्यं परित्यजतेति भावः॥ २६॥ अत्र अनयोः पादुकयोः। आवर्जयितुं पातयितुम्। अत्र रामायणम्-ततस्तु भरतः श्रीमानभिषिच्यार्यपादुके। तदधीनस्तदा राज्यं कारयामास सर्वदा॥ (अयो० ११५-२३) रामेणानुगृहीतः आत्मानं धन्यं मन्यमान आह **श्रद्धेय इति**। शीलान्वितः अहं स्वजनस्य बन्धुजनस्य श्रद्धेयो विश्वासपात्रम्। पौराणां रुचितः प्रियः। लोकस्य दृष्टिक्षमो दर्शनयोग्यः। स्वर्गस्थस्य नराधिपस्य दयितः सुतः रामाय राज्य-

भ्रातॄणां गुणशालिनां बहुमतः कीर्तेर्महद् भाजनं
संवादेषु कथाश्रयो गुणवतां लब्धप्रियाणां प्रियः ॥ २७ ॥

रामः—वत्स कैकेयीमातः राज्यं नाम मुहूर्तमपि नोपेक्षणीयम् । तस्मादद्यैव विजयाय प्रतिनिवर्ततां कुमारः ।

सीता—हम् अद्यैव गमिष्यति कुमारो भरतः । (हं अज्ज एव्व गमिस्सदि कुमारो भरदो ।)

रामः—अलमतिस्नेहेन । अद्यैव विजयाय प्रतिनिवर्ततां कुमारः ।

भरतः—आर्य अद्यैवाहं गमिष्यामि ।

आशावन्तः पुरे पौराः स्थास्यन्ति त्वद्दिदृक्षया ।
तेषां प्रीतिं करिष्यामि त्वत्प्रसादस्य दर्शनात् ॥ २८ ॥

सुमन्त्रः—आयुष्मन् मयेदानीं किं कर्तव्यम् ।

रामः—तात महाराजवत् परिपाल्यतां कुमारः ।

सुमन्त्रः—यदि जीवामि तावत् प्रयतिष्ये ।

रामः—वत्स कैकेयीमातः आरुह्यतां ममाग्रतो रथः ।

भरतः—यदाज्ञापयत्यार्यः । (रथमारोहतः ।)

रामः—मैथिलि इतस्तावत् । वत्स लक्ष्मण इतस्तावत् । आश्रमपदद्वारमात्रमपि भरतस्यानुयात्रं भविष्यामः ।

(इति निष्क्रान्ताः सर्वे ।)

चतुर्थोऽङ्कः ।

प्रत्यर्पणात् । गुणशालिनां गुणशोभिनां भ्रातॄणां बहुमतः परं मान्यः । कीर्तेः महद्भाजनं पात्रम् । गुणवतां संवादेषु संभाषणेषु कथाश्रयः वाग्विषयीभूतः सौभ्रात्रात् । लब्धप्रियाणां लब्धं प्रियं रामस्य राज्याप्तिरूपं यैस्तेषां सुमन्त्रादीनां प्रियः प्रियकरणात् ॥ शार्दूलविक्रीडितम् ॥ २७ ॥ विजयायोत्कृष्टयशलाभायेत्यर्थः । **आशावन्तः** इति । पुरे आशावन्तः भरतो गतोऽतो राममनुनीयानयेदित्याशां कुर्वन्तः त्वद्दिदृक्षया तव दर्शनेच्छया स्थास्यन्ति तिष्ठेयुः । तेषां त्वत्प्रसादस्य त्वत्प्रसादलब्धपादुकयोः दर्शनात् प्रीतिं तोषं करिष्यामि ॥ २८ ॥ तावत् साकल्येन । यद्वा यावदायुस्तावत् । आश्रमद्वारमात्रमाश्रमद्वारावधि । अनुयात्रं यात्रायाः पश्चादनुयात्रं यात्रामनुगमनेन संभावयिष्यामः । इति ग० शा० । इति प्रतिमाटीकायां चतुर्थोऽङ्कः ॥

अथ पञ्चमोऽङ्कः ।

(ततः प्रविशति सीता तापसी च ।)

सीता—आर्ये उपहारसुमनआकीर्णः संमार्जित आश्रमः । आश्रमपदविभवेनानुष्ठितो देवसमुदाचारः । तद् यावदार्यपुत्रो नागच्छति तावदिमान् बालवृक्षानुदकप्रदानेनानुक्रोशयिष्यामि । (अय्ये उवहारसुमणाइण्णो सम्मज्जिदो अस्समो । अस्समपदविभवेण अणुट्ठिओ देवसमुदाआरो । ता जाव अय्यउत्तो ण आअच्छदि दाव इमाणं बालरुक्खाणं उदअप्पदाणेण अणुक्कोसइस्सं ।)

तापसी—अविघ्नमस्य भवतु । (अविग्घं से होदु ।)

(ततः प्रविशति रामः ।)

रामः—(सशोकम् ।)

त्यक्त्वा तां गुरुणा मया च रहितां रम्यामयोध्यां पुरी-
मुद्यम्यापि ममाभिषेकमखिलं मत्सन्निधावागतः ।
रक्षार्थं भरतः पुनर्गुणनिधिस्तत्रैव सम्प्रेषितः
कष्टं भो नृपतेर्धुरं सुमहतीमेकः समुत्कर्षति ॥ १ ॥

(विमृश्य ।) ईदृशमेवैतत् । यावदिदानीमीदृशशोकविनोदनार्थमवस्थाकुटुम्बिनीं मैथिलीं पश्यामि । तत् क्व नु खलु गता वैदेही । (परिक्रम्यावलोक्य ।) अये इमानि खलु प्रत्यग्राभिषिक्तानि वृक्षमूलानि अदूरगतां मैथिलीं सूचयन्ति । तथाहि ।

भ्रमति सलिलं वृक्षावर्ते सफेनमवस्थितं
तृषितपतिता नैते क्लिष्टं पिबन्ति जलं खगाः ।

अथ पञ्चमोऽङ्कः । अस्मिन्नतिथिरूपेण रावणेन सीताहरणं वर्ण्यते । आर्ये इति । उपहारार्थं पूजार्थं सुमनस उपहारसुमनसस्ताभिराकीर्णः व्याप्तः । यद्वा उपहारभूताः सुमनसः निर्माल्यकुसुमानि इत्यर्थः । आश्रमपदविभवेन पुष्पफलाद्युपकरणजातेन । देवसमुदाचारो देवपूजा । अनुक्रोशयिष्यामि सदयमनुग्रहीष्यामि । विघ्नस्याभावः अविघ्नम् । अव्ययंविभक्ति–इत्यादिनार्थाभावेऽव्ययीभावः । **त्यक्त्वेति** । गुरुणा पित्रा मयापि रहितां तां रम्यामयोध्यां पुरीं त्यक्त्वा मम अखिलमभिषेकमुद्यम्य उपसंगृह्य मम सन्निधौ आगतः गुणनिधिः भरतः पुनः रक्षार्थं तत्रैव अयोध्यामेव संप्रेषितः सन् एकः सुमहतीं गुर्वीं नृपतेर्धुरं उद्वहति धारयतीति **कष्टम्** । शार्दूलविक्रीडितम् ॥ १ ॥ ईदृशमेवैतद्राज्यतन्त्रं कष्टप्रदमेवेत्यर्थः । अवस्थाकुटुम्बिनीं सर्वावस्थासखीम् । प्रत्यग्राभिषिक्तानि नूतनाभिषिक्तानि । **भ्रमतीति** । वृक्षावर्ते वृक्षालवाले सफेनमवस्थितं सलिलं भ्रमति । तृषिताश्च ते पतिता अवतीर्णाश्च तृषितपतिता एते खगाः क्लिष्टं कलुषं जलं न पिबन्ति ।

स्थलमभिपतन्त्यार्द्राः कीटा बिले जलपूरिते
नववलयिनो वृक्षा मूले जलक्षयरेखया ॥ २ ॥

(विलोक्य ।) अये इयं वैदेही । भोः कष्टम् ।

योऽस्याः करः श्राम्यति दर्पणेऽपि
स नैति खेदं कलशं वहन्त्याः ।
कष्टं वनं स्त्रीजनसौकुमार्यं
समं लताभिः कठिनीकरोति ॥ ३ ॥

(उपेत्य ।) मैथिलि अपि तपो वर्धते ।

सीता—हम् आर्यपुत्रः । जयत्वार्यपुत्रः । (हं अय्यउत्तो । जेदु अय्यउत्तो ।)

रामः—मैथिलि यदि ते नास्ति धर्मविघ्नः आस्यताम् ।

सीता—यदार्यपुत्र आज्ञापयति । (जं अय्यउत्तो आणवेदि।) (उपविशति ।)

रामः—मैथिलि प्रतिवचनार्थिनीमिव त्वां पश्यामि । किमिदम् ।

सीता—शोकशून्यहृदयस्येवार्यपुत्रस्य मुखरागः । किमेतत् । (सोअसुण्णहिअअस्स विअ अय्यउत्तस्स मुहराओ । किं एदं ।)

रामः—मैथिलि स्थाने खलु कृता चिन्ता ।

कृतान्तशल्याभिहते शरीरे तथैव तावद्धृदयव्रणो मे ।
नानाफलाः शोकशराभिघातास्तत्रैव तत्रैव पुनः पतन्ति ॥ ४ ॥

यद्वा जलं क्लिष्टं क्लेशेन यथा तथा न पिबन्ति । सुलभत्वात्सौकर्येण पिबन्ति इत्यर्थः । बिले जलपूरिते आर्द्राः कीटाः स्थलमभिपतन्ति । वृक्षा मूले जलरेखया नववलयिनः नववलयधारिणः सन्ति । हरिणी वृत्तम् ॥ २ ॥ **योस्याः** इति । यः अस्याः करो दर्पणेपि दर्पणधारणेपि श्राम्यति स जलपूर्णं कलशं वहन्त्याः खेदं न एति न श्राम्यति । कष्टं कष्टपूर्णं वनं स्त्रीजनसौकुमार्यं लताभिः समं कठिणीकरोति । यद्वा वनं कठिणीकरोति इति कष्टम् । उपजातिर्वृत्तम् ॥ ३ ॥ तपो वृक्षसेचनादि-शरीरायासकरं कर्म । धर्मविघ्नः वृक्षसेचनादिपुण्यकर्मप्रत्यूहः । धर्मो न उपरुध्येते-त्यर्थः । प्रतिवचनार्थिनीं मत्तः प्रतिवचनकांक्षिणीं प्रष्टुकामामित्यर्थः । शोकेन शून्यं हृदयं यस्य । मुखराग आननवर्णः । स्थाने युक्तविषये खलु चिन्ता हृदयखेदः कृता क्रियते । **कृतान्तेति** । कृतान्तस्य शल्यैः शल्यवत्पीडाकरैरुपतापैः अभिहते शरीरे मे हृदयव्रणः हृदयशोकरूपो व्रणः तथैव अद्यापि नव एव । तथाहि नानाफला अने-कविधदुःखकारिणः । यद्वा फलं बाणाग्रं नानाफला विविधाग्रोत्पन्नाः । अर्थः स एव । फलं हेतुसमुत्थे स्यात्......सस्यबाणाग्रयोरपि । इति विश्वः । शोकशराभिघाताः ।

सीता—आर्यपुत्रस्य क इव सन्तापः। (अय्यउत्तस्स को विअ सन्दावो ।)

रामः—श्वस्तत्रभवतस्तातस्यानुसंवत्सरश्राद्धविधिः । कल्पविशेषेण निवपनक्रियामिच्छन्ति पितरः । तत् कथं निर्वर्तयिष्यामीत्येतच्चिन्त्यते । अथवा

गच्छन्ति तुष्टिं खलु येन केन
त एवजानन्ति हि तां दशां मे ।
इच्छामि पूजां च तथापि कर्तुं
तातस्य रामस्य च सानुरूपाम् ॥ ५ ॥

सीता—आर्यपुत्र निर्वर्तयिष्यति श्राद्धं भरत ऋद्ध्या अवस्थानुरूपं फलोदकेनाप्यार्यपुत्रः । एतत् तातस्य बहुमततरं भविष्यति । (अय्यउत्त णिव्वत्तइस्सिदि सद्धं भरदो रिद्धीए अवत्थाणुरूवं फलोदएण वि अय्यउत्तो । एदं तादस्स बहुमदअरं भविस्सदि ।

रामः—मैथिलि ।

फलानि दृष्ट्वा दर्भेषु स्वहस्तरचितानि नः ।
स्मारितो वनवासं च तातस्तत्रापि रोदिति ॥ ६ ॥

(ततः प्रविशति परिव्राजकवेषो रावणः ।)

रावणः—एष भोः ।

नियतमनियतात्मा रूपमेतद् गृहीत्वा
खरवधकृतवैरं राघवं वञ्चयित्वा ।
स्वरपदपरिहीणां हव्यधारामिवाहं
जनकनृपसुतां तां हर्तुकामः प्रयामि ॥ ७ ॥

तत्रैव तत्रैव पुनः पतन्ति ॥ ४ ॥ क इव कीदृशः इव । संवत्सरे संवत्सरे भवमनुसंवत्सरं प्रातिसांवत्सरिकं श्राद्धं तस्य विधिः । कल्पविशेषेण क्रियाप्रकारविशेषेण । निवपनक्रिया पिण्डादिपितृदानक्रिया । **गच्छन्तीति** । ते मम पितरः येन केन प्रकारेण तुष्टिं गच्छन्ति गच्छेयुः । ते एव हि तां मे दशां जानन्ति । तथापि तातस्य रामस्य च सानुरूपां पूजां कर्तुमिच्छामि हि । उपजातिश्छन्दः ॥ ५ ॥ ऋद्धया महार्घवस्तुभिः । **फलानि** इति । नः दर्भेषु न तु सौवर्णादिपात्रेषु स्वहस्तरचितानि फलानि दृष्ट्वा तातः अस्माकं वनवासं स्मारितः तत्र स्वर्गे अपि रोदिति रोदिष्यति ॥ ६ ॥ **नियतमिति** । अनियतात्मा अवशीकृतान्तःकरणः एतदतिथे रूपं गृहीत्वा नियतं वशिनं खरवधेन कृतं वैरं येन तं रामं वञ्चयित्वा प्रतार्य तां जनकसुतां स्वरपदपरिहीणां मन्त्राक्षरोच्चारणपूर्वमदीयमानाम् । वक्ष्यति च परस्तात्—अमन्त्राक्तामिवाहुतिमिति । हव्यधारामिव हर्तुकामः प्रयामि । मालिनी वृत्तम् । लक्षणमुक्तम् ॥ ७ ॥

(परिक्रम्याधो विलोक्य ।) इदं रामस्याश्रमपदद्वारम् । यावदवतरामि । (अवतरति ।) यावदहमप्यतिथिसमुदाचारमनुष्ठास्यामि । अहमतिथिः । कोऽत्र भोः ।

रामः—(श्रुत्वा ।) स्वागतमतिथये ।

रावणः—साधु विशेषितं खलु रूपं स्वरेण ।

रामः—(विलोक्य ।) अये भगवान् । भगवन् अभिवादये ।

रावणः—स्वस्ति ।

रामः—भगवन् एतदासनमास्यताम् ।

रावणः—(आत्मगतम् ।) कथमाज्ञप्त इवास्म्यनेन । (प्रकाशम् ।) बाढम् । (उपविशति ।)

रामः—मैथिलि पाद्यमानय भगवते ।

सीता—यदार्यपुत्र आज्ञापयति । (जं अय्यउत्तो आणवेदि ।) (निष्क्रम्य प्रविश्य ।) इमा आपः । (इमा आवो ।)

रामः—शुश्रूषय भगवन्तम् ।

सीता—यदार्यपुत्र आज्ञापयति । (जं अय्यउत्तो आणवेदि ।)

रावणः—(मायाप्रकाशनपर्याकुलो भूत्वा ।) भवतु भवतु ।

इयमेका पृथिव्यां हि मानुषीणामरुन्धती ।
यस्या भर्तेति नारीभिः सत्कृतः कथ्यते भवान् ॥ ८ ॥

रामः—तेन हि आनय अहमेव शुश्रूषयिष्ये ।

रावणः—अयि छायां परिहृत्य शरीरं न लङ्घयामि । वाचानुवृत्तिः खल्वतिथिसत्कारः । पूजितोऽस्मि । आस्यताम् ।

अतिथिसमुदाचारमतिथ्युचितमाचारम् । विशेषितं सुन्दरतरं कृतम् । यद्वा ममातिथिरूपं मम स्वरेण विशेषितं विशेषेण समर्थितम् । पाद्यं पादप्रक्षालनार्थमुदकम् मायाप्रकाशनेति—सीतया कृते पादस्पर्शे रोमाञ्चादिविकाराविर्भावेनात्मनो माया प्रकाशिता भवेदिति शङ्कया । **इयमेकेति** । मानुषीणां मध्ये इयमेका अरुन्धती पतिव्रताश्रेष्ठा । यस्या भर्तेति भवान् नारीभिः सत्कृतः पूजितः सन् कथ्यते वर्ण्यते । यस्याः पातिव्रत्येन भवानपि लोके माहात्म्यं गतः ॥ ८ ॥ छायां सर्वदानुवृत्त्या छायावस्थितां ते भार्यां सीताम् । शरीरं त्वां रामम् । छायापेक्षया शरीरस्य प्राधान्यात्कथं तव सकाशादहं सेवाग्रहणं करिष्यामीत्याशयः । वाचानुवृत्तिः अतिसत्कारोचितं भाषणम् ।

रामः—बाढम् । (उपविशति ।)

रावणः— (आत्मगतम् ।) यावदहमपि ब्राह्मणसमुदाचारमनुष्ठास्यामि । (प्रकाशम् ।) भोः । काश्यपगोत्रोऽस्मि । साङ्गोपाङ्गं वेदमधीये मानवीयं धर्मशास्त्रं माहेश्वरं योगशास्त्रं बार्हस्पत्यमर्थशास्त्रं मेधातिथेर्न्यायशास्त्रं प्राचेतसं श्राद्धकल्पं च ।

रामः—कथं कथं श्राद्धकल्पमिति ।

रावणः—सर्वाः श्रुतीरतिक्रम्य श्राद्धकल्पे स्पृहा दर्शिता । किमेतत् ।

रामः—भगवन् भ्रष्टायां पितृमत्तायामागम इदानीमेषः ।

रावणः—अलं परिहृत्य । पृच्छतु भवान् ।

रामः—भगवन् निवपनक्रियाकाले केन पितृंस्तर्पयामि ।

रावणः—सर्वं श्रद्धया दत्तं श्राद्धम् ।

रामः—भगवन् अनादरतः परित्यक्तं भवति । विशेषार्थं पृच्छामि ।

रावणः—श्रूयताम् । विरूढेषु दर्भाः ओषधीषु तिलाः कलायं शाकेषु मत्स्येषु महाशफरः पक्षिषु वार्ध्राणसः पशुषु गौः खड्गो वा इत्येते मानुषाणां विहिताः ।

बाढमित्यङ्गीकारे । साङ्गोपाङ्गं–अङ्गैः षड्भिः शिक्षाकल्पव्याकरणनिरुक्तछन्दोज्योतिर्भिः उपाङ्गैः पुराणन्यायमीमांसाधर्मशास्त्रसंज्ञैः सहितस्तम् । मानवीयं मनुना प्रणीतम् । माहेश्वरं महेश्वरेण शिवेन प्रोक्तम् । बार्हस्पत्यं बृहस्पतिना प्रणीतम् । मेधातिथिर्नाम ऋषिविशेषः । प्रचेतसा वरुणेन प्रोक्तं प्राचेतसम् । श्रुती वेदान् । यद्यपि श्रुतिशब्दो वेदपरस्तथाऽप्यनन्तरप्रोक्तानि शास्त्राण्यपि वक्तुरिष्टानि । भ्रष्टायां पितृमत्तायां पितास्य विद्यते इति पितृमान् तस्य भावः पितृमत्ता । पितरि विनष्टे इत्यर्थः । एष आगमः श्राद्धकल्प एव इष्यते इति शेषः । अलं परिहृत्य प्रष्टव्यं पृच्छेत्यर्थः । सर्वं श्रद्धया दत्तं पितृंस्तर्पयतीत्यर्थः । अत्र मनुः–यद्ददाति विधिवत्सम्यक् श्रद्धासमन्वितः । तत्तत्पितृणां भवति परत्रानन्तमक्षयम् ॥ अनादरतः अश्रद्धया दत्तं परित्यक्तं भवतीत्यर्थः । विशेषार्थं श्रद्धया दत्तेष्वर्थेषु को विशेषेणाद्रियते इति पृच्छामीत्याशयः । विरूढेषु यानि रोहन्ति तेषु तृणेषु । कलायः धान्यविशेषः । स तु अत्र नाभिप्रेतः । अतोऽत्र कलायशब्दे कालशाकपरः । तथा च मनुः–कालशाकं महाशल्काः खड्गलोहामिषं मधु । आनन्त्यायैव कल्प्यन्ते मुन्यन्नानि च सर्वशः ॥ इति । वार्ध्राणसः पक्षिविशेषः । नीलग्रीवो रक्तशीर्षः कृष्णपादः सितच्छदः । वार्ध्राणसः स्यात्पक्षीशः (मम विष्णोरतिप्रियः ॥) इति कालिकापुराणम् ॥ रक्तपादो रक्तशिरा रक्तचञ्चुर्विहंगमः । कृष्णवर्णेन च तथा पक्षी

रामः—भगवन् वाशब्देनावगतमप्यदन्यस्तीति ।

रावणः—अस्ति प्रभावसम्पाद्यम् ।

रामः—भगवन् एष एव मे निश्चयः ।

उभयस्यास्ति सान्निध्यं यद्येतत् साधयिष्यति ।
धनुर्वा तपसि श्रान्ते श्रान्ते धनुषि वा तपः ॥ ९ ॥

रावणः—सन्ति । हिमवति प्रतिवसन्ति ।

रामः—हिमवतीति । ततस्ततः ।

रावणः—हिमवतः सप्तमे शृङ्गे प्रत्यक्षस्थाणुशिरःपतितगङ्गाम्बुपायिनो वैदूर्यश्यामपृष्ठाः पवनसमजवाः काञ्चनपार्श्वा नाम मृगाः यैर्वैखानसवालखिल्यनैमिशीयादयो महर्षयश्चिन्तितमात्रोपस्थितविपन्नैः श्राद्धान्यभिवर्धयन्ति ।

तैस्तर्पिताः सुतफलं पितरो लभन्ते
हित्वा जरां खमुपयान्ति हि दीप्यमानाः ।
तुल्यं सुरैः समुपयान्ति विमानवास-
मावर्तिभिश्च विषयैर्न बलाद् ध्रियन्ते ॥ १० ॥

रामः—मैथिलि ।

वार्ध्रीणसो मतः ॥ इति मार्कण्डेये । वार्ध्रीणसस्य मांसेन तृप्तिर्द्वादशवार्षिकी । इति मनुः । खड्गः गण्डकः । प्रभावसम्पाद्यं प्रभावेण तेजोविशेषेण सम्पाद्यम् । एष एव यत्पितॄन्प्रभावप्राप्तेन द्रव्येण तर्पयामि । **उभयस्येति** । उभयस्य द्विप्रकारस्य । तपोबलस्य क्षात्रतेजसश्च । तपसि श्रान्ते तपसः कुण्ठत्वे धनुः । धनुषि श्रान्ते तपः तपःसामर्थ्यम् ॥ ९ ॥ सन्ति प्रभावसम्पाद्यानि इत्यर्थात् । प्रत्यक्षेति । प्रत्यक्षः साक्षाद्वर्तमानः यः स्थाणुः शिवस्तस्य शिरःपतितं गङ्गाम्बु पातुं शीलं येषां ते पायिनः । वैदूर्यं रत्नविशेषो बालवायजाख्यः । तद्वत् श्यामं पृष्ठं येषां ते । पवनेन समः जवो वेगो येषां ते । वैखानसाः तापसविशेषाः । वालखिल्या अङ्गुष्ठोदरप्रमाणा ऋषिविशेषाः । नैमिशीया निमिशारण्यवासिनो मुनयः । चिन्तितमात्रा उपस्थिताश्च ते विपन्ना मृताश्च तैः । अभिवर्धयन्ति ऋद्ध्या सम्पादयन्ति । **तैस्तर्पिता** इति । तैस्तन्मांसैः तर्पिताः पितरः सुतफलं सुतप्राप्तिफलं लभन्ते । जरां हित्वा निर्जरा इत्यर्थः । दीप्यमाना भ्राजमानाः खं स्वर्गमुपयान्ति । सुरैस्तुल्यं विमानवासं समुपयान्ति । आवर्तिभिः भ्रमकारिभिः विषयैर्बलान्न ध्रियन्ते च । वसन्ततिलका वृत्तम् ॥ १० ॥ काञ्चनपार्श्वमृगलोभाज्जातहिमाल-

आपृच्छ पुत्रकृतकान् हरिणान् द्रुमांश्च
विन्ध्यं वनं तव सखीर्दयिता लताश्च ।
वत्स्यामि तेषु हिमवद्गिरिकाननेषु
दीप्तैरिवौषधिवनैरुपरञ्जितेषु ॥ ११ ॥

सीता—यदार्यपुत्र आज्ञापयति । (जं अय्यउत्तो आणवेदि ।)

रावणः—कौसल्यामात अलमतिमनोरथेन । न ते मानुषैर्दृश्यन्ते ।

रामः—भगवन् किं हिमवति प्रतिवसन्ति ।

रावणः—अथ किम् ।

रामः—तेन हि पश्यतु भवान् ।

सौवर्णान् वा मृगांस्तान् मे हिमवान् दर्शयिष्यति ।
भिन्नो मद्बाणवेगेन क्रौञ्चत्वं वा गमिष्यति ॥ १२ ॥

रावणः—(स्वगतम् ।) अहो अमह्यः खल्वस्यावलेपः ।

रामः—(दिशो विलोक्य ।) अये विद्युत्सम्पात इव दृश्यते ।

रावणः—(प्रकाशम् ।) कौसल्यामात इहस्थमेव भवन्तं पूजयति हिमवान् । एष काञ्चनपार्श्वः ।

रामः—भगवतो वृद्धिरेषा ।

सीता—दिष्ट्यार्यपुत्रो वर्धते । (दिट्ठिआ अय्यउत्तो वड्ढइ ।)

रामः—न न ।

तातस्यैतानि भाग्यानि यदि स्वयमिहागतः ।
अर्हत्येष हि पूजायां लक्ष्मणं ब्रूहि मैथिलि ॥ १३ ॥

सीता—आर्यपुत्र ननु तीर्थयात्रात उपावर्तमानं कुलपतिं प्रत्युद्ग-

---

यकाननवासस्पृहः आह **आपृच्छेति** । पुत्रकृतकान् हरिणानित्यादि । आपृच्छ आमन्त्रयस्व । अत्र परस्मैपदप्रयोग आर्षः । आङिनुप्रच्छ्योः इति आपृच्छस्वेत्येव स्यात् । दीप्तैः ज्वलद्भिः इव ओषधिवनैः उपरञ्जितेषु तेषु हिमवद्गिरिकाननेषु वत्स्यामि । वसन्ततिलका वृत्तम् ॥ ११ ॥ अतिमनोरथेनासाध्यमनोरथेन । **सौवर्णानिति** । हिमालयः सौवर्णान्मृगान् मे दर्शयिष्यति । वा अथवा मद्बाणवेगेन मम शरवेगेन भिन्नो दारितः क्रौञ्चत्वं क्रौञ्चपर्वततुल्यावस्थामेष्यति । पुरा किल कार्तिकेयेन परशुरामेण च क्रौञ्चपर्वतः विशिखेन विदारितस्तदनुरोधादिदमुक्तम् ॥ १२ ॥ वृद्धिः प्रभावः । **तातस्येति** । यदि काञ्चनपार्श्वः स्वयमागतः तर्हि एतानि तातस्य भाग्यानि । एष अर्हति पूजामिति शेषः । पूजायां पूजाविषये लक्ष्मणं ब्रूहि अर्घ्यदानादिना सत्कृत्यानीयतामयामिति यावत् ॥ १३ ॥ उपावर्तमानं निवर्तमानम् । कुलपतिं तपोवनवासिमुनि-

च्छेति सन्दिष्टः सौमित्रिः । (अय्यउत्त णं तित्थअत्तादो उत्रावत्तमाणं कुळवंदिं पच्चुग्गच्छेहित्ति सन्दिट्ठो सोमित्ती ।)

रामः--तेन हि अहमेव यास्यामि ।

सीता—आर्यपुत्र अहं किं करिष्यामि । (अय्यउत्त अहं किं करिस्सं)

रामः—शुश्रूषयस्व भगवन्तम् ।

सीता—यदार्यपुत्र आज्ञापयति । (जं अय्यउत्तो आणवेदि ।)

(निष्क्रान्तो रामः ।)

रावणः—अये अयमर्घ्यमादायोपसर्पति राघवः । एष इदानीं पूजामनवेक्ष्य धावन्तं मृगं दृष्ट्वा धनुरारोपयति राघवः ।

अहो बलमहो वीर्यमहो सत्त्वमहो जवः ।
राम इत्यक्षरैरल्पैः स्थाने व्याप्तमिदं जगत् ॥ १४ ॥

एष मृगः एकप्लुतातिक्रान्तशरविषयो वनगहनं प्रविष्टः ।

सीता—(आत्मगतम् ।) आर्यपुत्रविरहिताया भयं मेऽत्रोत्पद्यते । (अय्यउत्तविरहिदाए भअं मे एत्थ उप्पज्जइ ।)

रावणः—(आत्मगतम् ।)

मायया पहृते रामे सीतामेकां तपोवनात् ।
हरामि रुदतीं बालाममन्त्रोक्तामिवाहुतिम् ॥ १५ ॥

सीता—यावदुटजं प्रविशामि । (गन्तुमीहते ।) (जाव उडजं पविसामि ।)

रावणः—(स्वरूपं गृहीत्वा ।) सीते तिष्ठ तिष्ठ ।

सीता—(सभयम् ।) हं क इदानीमयम् । (हं को दाणि अअं ।)

रावणः—किं न जानीषे ।

युद्धे येन सुराः सदानवगणाः शक्रादयो निर्जिता
दृष्ट्वा शूर्पणखाविरूपकरणं श्रुत्वा हतौ भ्रातरौ ।

मुख्यम् । **अहो बलमिति** । अहो इत्याश्चर्ये सत्त्वं धैर्यम् । रामः इत्यल्पैः इत्यादि । स्थाने युक्तम् ॥ १४ ॥ एकेन प्लुतेनोड्डयनेन अतिक्रान्तः शरस्य विषयः येन । **माययेति** । मायया मायां प्रयुज्य । काञ्चनमृगच्छलेनेत्यर्थः । अमन्त्रोक्तां मन्त्रोच्चारणपूर्वमदत्ताम् । उपमाबलादरक्षितां सीतामित्यर्थो लभ्यते ॥ १५ ॥ **युद्धे येनेति** । हे विशालनयने येन शक्रादयः सुराः सदानवगणाः दानवगणाश्च युद्धे निर्जिताः सोऽहं रावणः शूर्पणखाया विरूपकरणं कर्णनासिकाकर्तनेन दृष्ट्वा भ्रातरौ हतौ श्रुत्वा

दर्पाद् दुर्मतिमप्रमेयबलिनं रामं विलोभ्य च्छलैः
स त्वां हर्तुमना विशालनयने प्राप्तोऽस्म्यहं रावणः ॥ १६ ॥

सीता—हं रावणो नाम । (हं ळावणो णाम ।) (प्रतिष्ठते ।)

रावणः—आः रावणस्य चक्षुर्विषयमागता क्व यास्यसि ।

सीता—आर्यपुत्र परित्रायस्व परित्रायस्व । सौमित्रे परित्रायस्व परित्रायस्व । (अय्यउत्त परित्ताअहि परित्ताअहि । सोमित्ती परित्ताअहि परित्ताअहि ।)

रावणः— सीते श्रूयतां मत्पराक्रमः ।

भग्नः शक्रः कम्पितो वित्तनाथः
क्रुष्टः सोमो मर्दितः सूर्यपुत्रः ।
धिग् भोः स्वर्गं भीतदेवैर्निविष्टं
धन्या भूमिर्वर्तते यत्र सीता ॥ १७ ॥

सीता—आर्यपुत्र परित्रायस्व परित्रायस्व । सौमित्रे परित्रायस्व परित्रायस्व माम् । (अय्यउत्त परित्ताअहि परित्ताअहि । सोमित्ती परित्ताअहि परित्ताअहि मं ।)

रावणः—

रामं वा शरणमुपेहि लक्ष्मणं वा
स्वर्गस्थं दशरथमेव वा नरेन्द्रम् ।
किं वा स्यात् कुपुरुषसंश्रितैर्वचोभि-
र्न व्याघ्रं मृगशिशवः प्रधर्षयन्ति ॥ १८ ॥

सीता—आर्यपुत्र परित्रायस्व परित्रायस्व । सौमित्रे परित्रायस्व परित्रायस्व माम् । (अय्यउत्त । परित्ताअहि परित्ताअहि । सोमित्ती परित्ताअहि परित्ताअहि मं ।)

रावणः—

विलपसि किमिदं विशालनेत्रे
विगणय मां च यथा तवार्यपुत्रम् ।

दर्पाद् दुर्मतिमप्रमेयबलिनं रामं छलैः विलोभ्य त्वां हर्तुमनाः हर्तुं मनो यस्य सः । तुं काममनसोरपि इति मकारलोपः । प्राप्तोस्मि । शार्दूल० ॥ १६ ॥ **भग्न इति** । भग्नः युद्धे पराजितः । वित्तनाथः कुबेरः । सोमः चन्द्रः । ब्रह्मा इति ग० शा० । चिन्त्यमिदं ब्रह्मणो रावणस्य लब्धश्रीकत्वात् । सूर्यपुत्रो यमः । निविष्टमधिष्ठितम् । शालिनीवृत्तम् । लक्षणमुक्तम् ॥१७॥ **रामं वेति** । शरणं रक्षितारम् । कुपुरुषसंश्रितैः वचोभिः तवक्रन्दितैः मे किं स्यात् । मृगशिशवो व्याघ्रं न प्रधर्षयन्ति । एवं रामादयो मां धर्षयितुं न प्रभवेयुरित्युक्तम् । प्रहर्षिणी छन्दः ॥ १८ ॥ **विलपसीति** । मामार्यपुत्रं यथा

विपुलबलयुतो ममैष योद्धुं
ससुरगणोऽप्यसमर्थ एव रामः ॥ १९ ॥

सीता—(सरोषम् ।) शप्तोऽसि । (सत्तो सि ।)

रावणः—हहह । अहो पतिव्रतायास्तेजः ।

योऽहमुत्पतितो वेगान्न दग्धः सूर्यरश्मिभिः ।
अस्याः परिमितैर्दग्धः शप्तोऽसीत्येभिरक्षरैः ॥ २० ॥

सीता—आर्यपुत्र परित्रायस्व परित्रायस्व । (अय्यउत्त परित्ताआहि परित्ताआहि ।)

रावणः—(सीतां गृहीत्वा ।) भो भो जनस्थानवासिनस्तपस्विनः । शृण्वन्तु शृण्वन्तु भवन्तः ।

बलादेष दशग्रीवः सीतामादाय गच्छति ।
क्षात्रधर्मे यदि स्निग्धः कुर्याद् रामः पराक्रमम् ॥ २१ ॥

सीता—आर्यपुत्र परित्रायस्व परित्रायस्व । (अय्यउत्त परित्ताआहि परित्ताआहि ।)

रावणः—(परिक्रामन् विलोक्य ।) अये स्वपक्षपवनोत्क्षेपक्षुभितवनषण्डश्चण्डचञ्चुरभिधावत्येष जटायुः । आः तिष्ठेदानीम् ।

मद्भुजाकृष्टनिस्त्रिंशकृत्तपक्षक्षतच्युतैः ।
रुधिरैरार्द्रगात्रं त्वां नयामि यमसादनम् ॥ २२ ॥

(निष्क्रान्तौ ।)

पञ्चमोऽङ्कः ।

इव विगणय मन्यस्व । विपुलबलयुतः ससुरगणः अपि एष रामो योद्धुं ममासमर्थः । पुष्पिताग्रा वृत्तम् । लक्षणमुक्तम् ॥ १९ ॥ **योहमिति** । वेगादुत्पतितः योहं सूर्यरश्मिभिः न दग्धः सोहमस्याः शप्तोसीति एभिः परिमितैरक्षरैः दग्धः स्यां किम् । अथवा दग्ध इत्युपहासः ॥ २० ॥ **बलादिति** । क्षात्रधर्मे अपकृते युद्धं कृत्वा निराकृतिः क्षात्रधर्मस्तस्मिन् । स्निग्धः रतः ॥ २१ ॥ स्वपक्षयाः पवनस्तेनोत्क्षेपस्तेन क्षुभिता वनषण्डा वृक्षसमूहाः येन । चण्डा भीषणा चञ्चुर्यस्य । **मद्भुजेति** । मम भुजेनाकृष्टः यो निस्त्रिंशः खड्गस्तेन कृत्तपक्षक्षतात् च्युतैः रुधिरैः आर्द्रगात्रं त्वां यमसादनं यमगृहं नेष्यामि ॥ २२ ॥ इति प्रतिमाटीकायां पञ्चमोङ्कः ।

अथ षष्ठोऽङ्कः ।

(ततः प्रविशतो वृद्धतापसौ)

उभौ—परित्रायतां परित्रायतां भवन्तः ।

प्रथमः—

इयं हि नीलोत्पलदामवर्चसा
मृणालशुक्लोज्ज्वलदंष्ट्रहासिना ।
निशाचरेन्द्रेण निशार्धचारिणा
मृगीव सीता परिभूय नीयते ॥ १ ॥

द्वितीयः—एषा खलु तत्रभवती वैदेही

विचेष्टमानेव भुजङ्गमाङ्गना
विधूयमानेव च पुष्पिता लता ।
प्रसह्य पापेन दशाननेन सा
तपोवनात् सिद्धिरिवापनीयते ॥ २ ॥

उभौ—परित्रायतां परित्रायतां भवन्तः ।

प्रथमः—(ऊर्ध्वमवलोक्य ।) अये वचनसमकाल एव दशरथस्यानृण्यं कर्तुं मयि स्थिते क्व यास्यसीति रावणमाहूयान्तरिक्षमुत्पतितो जटायुः ।

द्वितीयः—एष रोषादुद्वृत्तनयनः प्रतिनिवृत्तो रावणः ।

प्रथमः—एष रावणः ।

द्वितीयः—एष जटायुः ।

अथ पञ्चमाङ्कान्ते उपक्षिप्तं रावणस्य जटायुना युद्धं विष्कम्भके वर्णयितुं द्वयोः वृद्धतापसयोः प्रवेशं निर्दिशति ततः प्रविशत इति । **इयं हि** इति । नीलोत्पलदामवत् वर्चः अङ्गकान्तिर्यस्य तेन । मृणालवत् शुक्ला शुभ्रा उज्ज्वला च दंष्ट्रा यस्मिन्कर्मणि तथा हसितुं शीलं यस्य तेन । निशार्धचारिणा निशाचरेन्द्रेण रावणेन सिंहेन च मृगीव सीता परिभूय तां युष्मान् वा । नीयते । वंशस्थं वृत्तम् । लक्षणमुक्तम् ॥ २१ ॥ **विचेष्टमानेव इति** । विचेष्टमाना प्रयासं कुर्वती भुजङ्गमाङ्गना सर्पिणी इव विधूयमाना कम्प्यमाना पुष्पिता सञ्जातपुष्पा लता इव प्रसह्य बलात् पापेन दशाननेन सा तपोवनात् सिद्धिः तपःफलमिव अपनीयते । वृत्तं पूर्वोक्तम् ॥ २ ॥ अनृणस्य भाव आनृण्यं कर्तुं प्रत्युपकारकरणार्थम् । उद्वृत्तनयन उद्भ्रान्तचक्षुः ।

उभौ—हन्तैतदन्तरिक्षे प्रवृत्तं युद्धम् ।

प्रथमः—काश्यप काश्यप पश्य क्रव्यादीश्वरस्य सामर्थ्यम् ।

पक्षाभ्यां परिभूय वीर्यविषयं द्वन्द्वं प्रतिव्यूहते
तुण्डाभ्यां सुनिघृष्टतीक्ष्णमचलः संवेष्टनं चेष्टते ।
तीक्ष्णैरायसकण्टकैरिव नखैर्भीमान्तरं वक्षसो
वज्राग्रैरिव दार्यमाणविषमाच्छैलाच्छिला पाट्यते ॥ ३ ॥

द्वितीयः—हन्त संक्रुद्धेन रावणेनासिना क्रव्यादीश्वरः स दक्षिणांसदेशे हतः ।

उभौ—हा धिक् । पतितोऽत्रभवान् जटायुः ।

प्रथमः—भोः कष्टम् । एष खलु तत्रभवान् जटायुः

कृत्वा स्ववीर्यसदृशं परमं प्रयत्नं
क्रीडामयूरमिव शत्रुमचिन्तयित्वा ।
दीप्तं निशाचरपतेरवधूय तेजो
नागेन्द्रभग्नवनवृक्ष इवावसन्नः ॥ ४ ॥

उभौ—स्वर्ग्योऽयमस्तु ।

प्रथमः—काश्यप आगम्यताम् । इमं वृत्तान्तं तत्रभवते राघवाय निवेदयिष्यावः ।

द्वितीयः—बाढम् । प्रथमः कल्पः ।

(निष्क्रान्तौ ।)

क्रव्यं मांसमत्तुं शीलं येषां ते क्रव्यादिनस्तेषां ईश्वरस्य गृध्रराजस्य । **पक्षाभ्यामिति ।** अचलः अकम्पमानः पक्षाभ्यां परिभूय प्रहृत्य रावणमिति शेषः । पराभवोऽत्र धर्षणम् । वीर्यविषयं वीर्यविषयभूतं द्वंद्वं प्रतिव्यूहते प्रतियुध्यते । द्वंद्वे महता वीर्येण प्रहारं ददातीत्यर्थः । तदनन्तरं तुण्डाभ्यां चञ्चुदलाभ्यां सुविघृष्टं च तत्तीक्ष्णं च संवेष्टनं संवरणं तच्चेष्टते ग्रसितुं प्रयतते । आयसकण्टकैः अयोनिर्मितैः कण्टकैः इव तीक्ष्णैः नखैः रावणस्य वक्षसः भीमांतरं भीमो विस्तारः पाट्यते विदीर्यते । तत्रोपमामाह वज्राग्रैः वज्रकोटिभिः दार्यमाणश्चासौ विषमश्च तस्मात् शैलात् शिला इव ॥ शार्दूलविक्रीडितं वृत्तम् ॥ ३ ॥ हन्त विषादे । **कृत्वेति** । क्रीडार्थः मयूरः क्रीडामयूरः । सुकुमार इत्यर्थः । तमिव शत्रुमचिन्तयित्वा अगणयित्वा स्ववीर्यसदृशं परमं पराक्रमं कृत्वा निशाचरपतेः दीप्तं तेजः वीर्यमवधूय । कृततद्वीर्यतिरस्कारः इत्यर्थः । नागेन्द्रेण मत्तगजेन भग्नः वनवृक्ष इव अवसन्नः नाशं गतः । वसन्ततिलकं वृत्तम् ॥४॥ स्वर्ग्यः स्वर्गवासोचितः ।

विष्कम्भकः ।

(ततः प्रविशति काञ्चुकीयः ।)

काञ्चुकीयः—क इह भोः काञ्चनतोरणद्वारमशून्यं कुरुते ।

(प्रविश्य)

प्रतिहारी—आर्य अहं विजया । किं क्रियताम् । (अय्य अहं विजया । किं करीअदु ।)

काञ्चुकीयः—विजये निवेद्यतां निवेद्यतां भरतकुमाराय—एष खलु रामदर्शनार्थं जनस्थानं प्रस्थितः प्रतिनिवृत्तस्तत्रभवान् सुमन्त्र इति ।

प्रतिहारी—आर्य अपि कृतार्थस्तातसुमन्त्र आगतः । (अय्य अवि किदत्थो तादसुमन्तो आअदो ।)

काञ्चुकीयः—भवति न जाने ।

हृदयस्थितशोकाग्निशोषिताननमागतम् ।
दृष्ट्वैवाकुलमासीन्मे सुमन्त्रमधुना मनः ॥ ५ ॥

प्रतिहारी—आर्य एतच्छ्रुत्वा पर्याकुलमिव मे हृदयम् । (अय्य एदं सुणिअ पय्याउळं विअ मे हिअअं ।)

काञ्चुकीयः—भवति किमिदानीं स्थिता । शीघ्रं निवेद्यताम् ।

प्रतिहारी—आर्य इयं निवेदयामि । (निष्क्रान्ता ।) (अय्य इअं णिवेदेमि ।)

काञ्चुकीयः—(विलोक्य ।) अये अयमत्रभवान् भरतकुमारः सुमन्त्रागमनजनितकुतूहलहृदयश्चीरवल्कलवसनश्चित्रजटापुञ्जपिञ्जरितोत्तमाङ्ग इत एवाभिवर्तते । य एषः

प्रख्यातसद्गुणगणः प्रतिपक्षकाल-
स्तिग्मांशुवंशतिलकस्त्रिदशेन्द्रकल्पः ।

काञ्चनतोरणद्वारं सुवर्णनिर्मितं वहिर्द्वारम् । कृतार्थः कृतकार्यः । लब्धरामदर्शन इत्यर्थः । **हृदयस्थितेति** । हृदयस्थितः यः शोकाग्निः तेन शोषितमाननं मुखं यस्य तम् । आगतं सुमन्त्रं दृष्ट्वैव अधुना मम मन आकुलमासीदुद्विग्नमभवत् ॥ ५ ॥ सुमन्त्रागमनेन जनितं कुतूहलं यस्मिन् तथा हृदयं यस्य । चीरवल्कले वसने यस्य । चित्रः यः जटापुञ्जस्तेन पिञ्जरितं पीतरक्तीकृतमुत्तमाङ्गं शीर्षं यस्य स तथोक्तः । **प्रख्यातेति** । प्रख्यातः सद्गुणगणः यस्य । प्रतिपक्षाणां शत्रूणां कालः संहर्ता । तिग्माः चण्डा अंशवो यस्य स तिग्मांशुः सूर्यः तस्य वंशस्य तिलकः भूषणम् । ईषदसमाप्तः त्रिदशेन्द्रः त्रिदशेन्द्रकल्पः इन्द्रतुल्यः ।

आज्ञावशादखिलभूपरिरक्षणस्थः
श्रीमानुदारकलभेभसमानयानः ॥ ६ ॥

(ततः प्रविशति भरतः प्रतिहारी च ।)

भरतः—विजये एवमुपगतस्तत्रभवान् सुमन्त्रः ।

गत्वा तु पूर्वमयमार्यनिरीक्षणार्थं
लब्धप्रसादशपथे मयि सन्निवृत्ते ।
दृष्ट्वा किमागत इहात्रभवान् सुमन्त्रो
रामं प्रजानयनबुद्धिमनोभिरामम् ॥ ७ ॥

काञ्चुकीयः—(उपगम्य ।) जयतु कुमारः ।

भरतः—अथ कस्मिन् प्रदेशे वर्तते तत्रभवान् सुमन्त्रः ।

काञ्चुकीयः—असौ काञ्चनतोरणद्वारे ।

भरतः—तेन हि शीघ्रं प्रवेश्यताम् ।

काञ्चुकीयः—यदाज्ञापयति कुमारः । (निष्क्रान्तौ ।)

(ततः प्रविशति सुमन्त्रः प्रतिहारी च ।)

सुमन्त्रः—(सशोकम् ।) कष्टं भोः कष्टम् ।

नरपतिनिधनं मयानुभूतं
नृपतिसुतव्यसनं मयैव दृष्टम् ।
श्रुत इह स च मैथिलीप्रणाशो
गुण इव बह्वपराद्धमायुषा मे ॥ ८ ॥

प्रतिहारी—(सुमन्त्रमुद्दिश्य ।) एत्वेत्वार्यः । एष भर्ता । उपसर्पत्वार्यः । (एदु एदु अय्यो । एसो भट्टा । उपसप्पदु अय्यो ।)

सुमन्त्रः—(उपसृत्य ।) जयतु कुमारः ।

आज्ञावशाद्रामस्याज्ञानुरोधादखिला या भूः तस्याः परिरक्षणे तिष्ठति स्मेति अखिलभूपरिरक्षणस्थः । श्रीमान् उदारः यः कलभेभः त्रिंशद्वर्षः हस्ती तेन समानं यानं गतिर्यस्य । वसन्ततिलकम् ॥ ६ ॥ गत्वेति । लब्धः प्रसादः पादुकाप्राप्तिरूपः शपथः चतुर्दशवर्षान्ते राज्यं प्रतिग्रहीष्यामीति प्रतिज्ञानं च येन तस्मिन्मयि सन्निवृत्ते । आर्यदर्शनार्थं अयं पूर्वं गत्वा अत्रभवान् सुमन्त्रः प्रजानां नयनयोः बुद्धेः मनसश्चाभिरामं रमणीयं रामं दृष्ट्वा आगतः किम् । वृत्तमनन्तरोक्तम् ॥ ७ ॥ नरपतिनिधनमिति । मया नरपतिनिधनमनुभूतम् । नृपतिसुतस्य रामस्य व्यसनं मयैव दृष्टम् । इह स च मैथिलीप्रणाशः सीतापहरणं श्रुतः ; मे ममायुषा गुणे बहु अपराद्धमिव । पुष्पिताग्रा वृत्तम् ॥८॥

भरतः—तात अपि दृष्टस्त्वया लोकाविष्कृतपितृस्नेहः । अपि दृष्टं द्विधाभूतमरुन्धतीचारित्रम् । अपि दृष्टं त्वया निष्कारणावहितवनवासं सौभ्रात्रम् ।

(सुमन्त्रः सचिन्तस्तिष्ठति ।)

प्रतिहारी—भर्तृदारकः खल्वार्यं पृच्छति । (भट्टिदारओ क्खु अय्यं पुच्छति ।)

सुमन्त्रः—भवति किं माम् ।

भरतः—(स्वगतम् ।) अतिमहान् खल्वायासः । सन्तापाद् भ्रष्टहृदयः । (प्रकाशम् ।) अपि मार्गात् प्रतिनिवृत्तस्तत्रभवान् ।

सुमन्त्रः—कुमार त्वन्नियोगाद् रामदर्शनार्थं जनस्थानं प्रस्थितः कथमहन्मतरा प्रतिनिवर्तिष्ये ।

भरतः—किन्नु खलु क्रोधेन वा लज्जया वात्मानं न दर्शयन्ति ।

सुमन्त्रः—कुमार

कुतः क्रोधो विनीतानां लज्जा वा कृतचेतसाम् ।
मया दृष्टं तु तच्छून्यं तैर्विहीनं तपोवनम् ॥ ९ ॥

भरतः—अथ क्व गता इति श्रुताः ।

सुमन्त्रः—अस्ति किल किष्किन्धा नाम वनौकसां निवासः । तत्र गता इति श्रुताः ।

भरतः—हन्त अविज्ञातपुरुषविशेषाः खलु वानराः । दुःखिताः प्रतिवसन्ति ।

सुमन्त्रः—कुमार तिर्यग्योनयोऽप्युपकृतमवगच्छन्ति ।

भरतः—तात कथमिव ।

सुमन्त्रः—

सुग्रीवो भ्रंशितो राज्याद् भ्राता ज्येष्ठेन वालिना ।
हृतदारो वसञ्छैले तुल्यदुःखेन मोक्षितः ॥ १० ॥

लोके आविष्कृतः पितरि स्नेहः येन सः । द्विप्रकारेण स्थितम् । सीतया संविभक्तम् । निष्कारणमवहितः वनवासो यस्मिन् । सौभ्रात्रं भ्रातृस्नेहः । लक्ष्मण इत्यर्थः । आयासः मनःक्लेशः । अन्तरा मार्गमध्यात् । **कुत इति** । विनीतानां संयमिनां कुतः क्रोधः । कृतचेतसां कृतमतीनाम् । तपोवनं रामनिवासस्थानम् ॥ ९ ॥ वनौकसां वानराणाम् । अविज्ञातः पुरुषाणां विशेषः यैस्ते । **सुग्रीव इति** । ज्येष्ठेन भ्रात्रा वालिना राज्याद् भ्रंशितः हृतदारः हृता दारा यस्य स तादृशः सुग्रीवः तुल्यदुःखेन हृतदारत्वादित्यार्थम् । रामेण मोक्षितः ॥ १० ॥

भरतः—तात कथं तुल्यदुःखेन नाम ।

सुमन्त्रः—(आत्मगतम् ।) हन्त सर्वमुक्तमेव मया । (प्रकाशम् ।) कुमार न खलु किञ्चित् । ऐश्वर्यभ्रंशतुल्यता ममाभिप्रेता ।

भरतः—तात किं गूहसे । स्वर्गं गतेन महाराजपादमूलेन शापितः स्याः यदि सत्यं न ब्रूयाः ।

सुमन्त्रः—का गतिः । श्रूयताम्

वैरं मुनिजनस्यार्थे रक्षसा महता कृतम् ।
सीता मायामुपाश्रित्य रावणेन ततो हृता ॥ ११ ॥

भरतः—कथं हृतेति । (मोहमुपगतः ।)

सुमन्त्रः—समाश्वासिहि समाश्वासिहि ।

भरतः—(पुनः समाश्वस्य ।) भोः कष्टम् ।

पित्रा च बान्धवजनेन च विप्रयुक्तो
दुःखं महत् समनुभूय वनप्रदेशे ।
भार्यावियोगमुपलभ्य पुनर्ममार्यो
जीमूतचन्द्र इव खे प्रभया वियुक्तः ॥ १२ ॥

भोः किमिदानीं करिष्ये । भवतु दृष्टम् । अनुगच्छतु मां तातः ।

सुमन्त्रः—यदाज्ञापयति कुमारः ।

(उभौ परिक्रामतः ।)

सुमन्त्रः—कुमार न खलु न खलु गन्तव्यम् । देवीनां चतुश्शालमिदम् ।

भरतः—अत्रैव मे कार्यम् । भोः क इह प्रतिहारे ।

(प्रविश्य)

प्रतिहारी—जयतु भर्तृदारकः । विजया खल्वहम् । (जेदु भट्टिदारओ । विजआ खु अहं ।)

उक्तमेव अनवधानत्वात् । तुल्यदुःखेन इति वदता । ऐश्वर्यभ्रंशेन तुल्यता । **वैरमिति** । मुनिजनस्यार्थे मुनिजनरक्षणहेतोः । रामेण महता बलवता रक्षसा रावणेन सह वैरं कृतम् । ततो रावणेन मायामुत्पाद्य सीता हृता ॥ ११ ॥ **पित्रा चेति** । मम आर्यः रामः पित्रा च बान्धवजनेन च विप्रयुक्तः वनप्रदेशे महद् दुःखं समनुभूय भार्यावियोगम् उपलभ्य खे आकाशे जीमूतो मेघः जीमूतच्छन्नः चन्द्रः जीमूतचन्द्रः । इव प्रभया वियुक्तोऽस्ति । वसन्ततिलका वृत्तम् ॥ १२ ॥ चतुःशालं चतस्रः शालाः समाहृताश्चतुःशालं अन्योन्याभिमुखशालाचतुष्टयगृहम् ।

भरतः—विजये ममागमनं निवेदयात्रभवत्यै ।

प्रतिहारी—कतमस्यै भट्टिन्यै निवेदयामि । (कदमाए भट्टिणीए णिवेदेमि।)

भरतः—या मां राजानमिच्छति ।

प्रतिहारी—(आत्मगतम् ।) हं किं नु खलु भवेत् । (हं किं णुखु भवे ।) (प्रकाशम् ।) भर्तः तथा । (भट्टा तह ।) (निष्क्रान्ता ।)

(ततः प्रविशति कैकेयी प्रतिहारी च ।)

कैकेयी—विजये मां प्रेक्षितुं भरत आगतः । (विजए मं पेक्खिदुं भरदो आअदो ।)

प्रतिहारी—भट्टिनि तथा । भर्तृदारकस्य रामस्य सकाशात् तात-सुमन्त्र आगतः । तेन सह भर्तृदारको भरतो भट्टिनीं प्रेक्षितुमिच्छति किल । (भट्टिणि तह । भट्टिदारअस्स रामस्स सआसादो तादसुमन्तो आअदो । तेण सह भट्टिदारओ भरदो भट्टिणिं पेक्खिदुं इच्छदि किळ ।)

कैकेयी—(स्वगतम् ।) केन खलूद्घातेन मामुपालप्स्यते भरतः । (केण खु उग्घादेण मं उवालम्भिस्सिदि भरदो ।)

प्रतिहारी—भट्टिनि किं प्रविशतु भर्तृदारकः । (भट्टिणि किं पविसदु भट्टिदारओ ।)

कैकेयी—गच्छ । प्रवेशयैनम् । (गच्छ । पवेसेहि णं ।)

प्रतिहारी—भट्टिनि तथा । (भट्टिणि तह ।) (परिक्रम्योपसृत्य) जयतु भर्तृदारकः । प्रविशतु किल । (जेदु भट्टिदारओ । पविसदु किळ ।)

भरतः—विजये किं निवेदितम् ।

प्रतिहारी—आम् । (आम ।)

भरतः—तेन हि प्रविशावः ।

(प्रविशतः ।)

कैकेयी—जात विजया मन्त्रयते—रामस्य सकाशात् सुमन्त्र आगत इति । (जाद विअआ मन्तेदि-रामस्स सआसादो सुमन्तो आअदोत्ति ।)

भरतः—अतः परं प्रियं निवेदयाम्यत्रभवत्यै ।

कैकेयी—जात अपि कौसल्या सुमित्रा च शब्दयितव्या । (जाद अवि कोसळ्ळा सुमित्ता अ सद्दावइदव्वा ।)

भरतः—न खलु ताभ्यां श्रोतव्यम् ।

कैकेयी—(आत्मगतम् ।) हुं किं नु खलु भवेत् । (हं किं णुहु भवे ।) (प्रकाशम् ।) भण जात । (भणाहि जाद ।)

भरतः—श्रूयताम्

यः स्वराज्यं परित्यज्य त्वन्नियोगाद् वनं गतः ।
तस्य भार्या हृता सीता पर्याप्तस्ते मनोरथः ॥ १३ ॥

कैकेयी—हं ।

भरतः—

हन्त भोः सत्वयुक्तानामिक्ष्वाकूणां मनस्विनाम् ।
वधूप्रधर्षणं प्राप्तं प्राप्याग्रभवतीं वधूम् ॥ १४ ॥

कैकेयी—(आत्मगतम् ।) भवतु इदानीं कालः कथयितुम् (प्रकाशम् ।) जात त्वं न जानासि महाराजस्य शापम् । (भोदु दाणि काळो कहेउं ।) (जाद तुवं ण आणासि महाराअस्स सावं ।)

भरतः—किं शप्तो महाराजः ।

कैकेयी—सुमन्त्र आचक्ष्व विस्तरेण । (सुमन्त आअक्ख वित्थरेण)

सुमन्त्रः—यदाज्ञापयति भवती । कुमार श्रूयताम्—पुरा मृगयागतेन महाराजेन कस्मिंश्चित् सरसि कलशं पूरयमाणो वनगजबृंहितानुकारिशब्दसमुत्पन्नवनगजशङ्कया शब्दवेधिना शरेण विपन्नचक्षुषो महर्षेश्चक्षुर्भूतो मुनितनयो हिंसितः ।

यः स्वराज्यमिति । यः त्वन्नियोगात्स्वराज्यं परित्यज्य वनं गतस्तस्य भार्या सीता हृता । रावणेन इति शेषः । तस्य भार्यावियोगदुःखमपि संजातमित्यर्थः । अतः ते मनोरथः पर्याप्तः साकल्येन पूर्णः ॥ १३ ॥ **हन्त भोः** इति । हन्तेति खेदे । अत्रभवतीं त्वां वधूं प्राप्य । त्वमस्मत्कुले आगता त्वत्कारणाद्रामो वनं प्रेषितः तत्र च एकाकिना अरक्षिता सीतापहृता । राज्यस्था चेन्नाहारिष्यतेति भरतस्याभिप्रायः । सत्त्वयुक्तानां मनस्विनां इक्ष्वाकूणां वधूप्रधर्षणं वध्वाः प्रधर्षणं बलादपहरणं प्राप्तम् । तद्रूपावमानना प्राप्तेति साधिक्षेपोक्तिः ॥ १४ ॥ देशकाले निवेदयामि इति यत्तृतीयाङ्क उक्तं तदनुरोधादाह कालः कथयितुमिति । सीतापहरणप्रवृद्धं । रामवनगमनोत्पन्नं भरतस्य शोकं रामस्य वनप्रयाणं यथाऽवश्यं भाव्यासीत्तथा कथनेन लघूकर्तुमुचितः काल इत्यर्थः । वनगजस्य बृंहितं गर्जितं तदनुकरोतीति अनुकारी शब्दः कलशपूरणोत्पन्नः तेन समुत्पन्ना वनगजस्य शङ्का तया । शब्दवेधिना शब्दानुसारेण लक्ष्यवेधिना । विपन्ने

भरतः—हिंसित इति । शान्तं पापं शान्तं पापम् । ततस्ततः ।

सुमन्त्रः—ततस्तमेवं गतं दृष्ट्वा

> तेनोक्तं रुदितस्यान्ते मुनिना सत्यभाषिणा ।
> यथाहं भोस्त्वमप्येवं पुत्रशोकाद् विपत्स्यसे ॥ १५ ॥

इति ।

भरतः—नन्विदं कष्टं नाम ।

कैकेयी—जात एतन्निमित्तमपराधे मां निक्षिप्य पुत्रको रामो वनं प्रेषितः । न खलु राज्यलोभेन । अपरिहरणीयो महर्षिशापः पुत्रविप्रवासं विना न भवति । (जाद एदण्णिमित्तं अवराहे मं णिक्खिविअ पुत्तओ रामो वणं पेसिदो । णहु रज्जळोहेण । अपरिहरणीओ महरिसिसावो पुत्तविप्पवासं विणा ण होइ ।

भरतः—अथ तुल्ये पुत्रविप्रवासे कथमहमरण्यं न प्रेषितः ।

कैकेयी—जात मातुलकुले वर्तमानस्य प्रकृतीभूतस्ते विप्रवासः । (जाद मादुळकुळे वत्तमाणस्स पइदीहूदो दे विप्पवासो)

भरतः—अथ चतुर्दश वर्षाणि किं कारणमवेक्षितानि ।

कैकेयी--जात चतुर्दश दिवसा इति वक्तुकामया पर्याकुलहृदयया चतुर्दश वर्षाणीत्युक्तम् । (जाद चउद्दस दिअस त्ति वत्तुकामाए पय्याउळहिअआए चउद्दस वरिसाणि त्ति उत्तं ।)

भरतः—अस्ति पाण्डित्यं सम्यग् विचारयितुम् । अथ विदितमेतद् गुरुजनस्य ।

सुमन्त्रः—कुमार वसिष्ठवामदेवप्रभृतीनामनुमतं विदितं च ।

गते चक्षुषी यस्य तस्य । अन्धस्येत्यर्थः । एवं गतं शरेण हतम् । **तेनोति** । सत्यभाषिणा अन्यथाभवनानर्हवचसा तेन मुनिना रुदितस्यान्ते उक्तम् । भोः यथाहं पुत्रशोकादद्य विपद्ये तथा त्वमपि पुत्रशोकाद् विपत्स्यसे इति । अत्र रामायणम् । पुत्रव्यसनजं दुःखं यदेतन्मम साम्प्रतम् । एवं त्वं पुत्रशोकेन राजन्कालं करिष्यसि ॥ इति ॥ १५ ॥ एतन्निमित्तं मुनिशापो यथार्थः स्यादिति । मामात्मानमपराधे निक्षिप्य मया पुत्रकः इत्यादि । अपरिहरणीयोऽवश्यं-भावी । प्रकृतीभूतः स्वाभाविकः सम्पन्नः परिचितत्वात् । आकस्मिकः पुत्रवियोग एव मृत्युमावहेदिति हेतोः । अस्ति पाण्डित्यं भवत्या इति शेषः । सम्यग् विचारयितुमेवं कृते एवं भवेदिति बुद्ध्या विमर्शयितुम् । विदितमेतद् यदनेन

रतः---हन्त त्रैलोक्यसाक्षिणः खल्वेते। दिष्टयाऽनपराद्धात्रभवती। अम्ब यद् भ्रातृस्नेहात् समुत्पन्नमन्युना मया दूषितात्रभवती तत् सर्वं मर्षयितव्यम्। अम्ब अभिवादये।

कैकेयी—जात का नाम माता पुत्रकस्यापराधं न मर्षयति। उत्तिष्ठोत्तिष्ठ। कोऽत्र दोषः। (जाद का णाम मादा पुत्तअस्स अवराहं ण मरिसेदि। उट्ठेहि उट्ठेहि। को एत्थ दोसो।)

भरतः—अनुगृहीतोऽस्मि। आपृच्छाम्यत्रभवतीम्। अद्यैवाहमार्यस्य साहाय्यार्थं कृत्स्नं राजमण्डलमुद्योजयामि। अयमिदानीं

वेलामिमां मत्तगजान्धकारां
करोमि सैन्यौघनिवेशनद्धाम्।
बलैस्तरङ्गिश्च नयामि तुल्यं
ग्लानिं समुद्रं सह रावणेन॥ १६॥

अये शब्द इव। तूर्णं ज्ञायतां शब्दः।

(प्रविश्य)

प्रतिहारी— जयतु कुमारः। इमं वृत्तान्तं श्रुत्वा ज्येष्ठभट्टिनी मोहं गता। (जेदु कुमारो। इयं वुत्तन्तं सुणिअ जेट्ठभट्टिणी मोहं गआ।)

कैकेयी—हं।

भरतः—कथं मोहमुपगताम्बा।

कैकेयी—एहि जात। आर्यामाश्वासयिष्यावः। (एहि जाद। अय्यं अस्सासइस्सामो)

भरतः—यदाज्ञापयत्यम्बा।

(निष्क्रान्ताः सर्वे।)

षष्ठोऽङ्कः।

हेतुना भवत्यैतत्कृतमिति। त्रैलोक्यदर्शिनः अतो भवत्या अभिप्रायं ज्ञातुं समर्थाः। समुत्पन्नो मन्युः क्रोधो यस्य तेन। आपृच्छामि आमन्त्रये। आपृच्छे इति युक्ततरं पठितुम्। कृत्स्नं सप्तप्रकृतिकम्। उद्योजयामि प्रोत्साहयिष्ये। अमात्यानुमत्या ससामन्तबलवाहनो गमिष्यामीत्यर्थः। **वेलामिति**। इमां बुद्धिस्थां वेलां समुद्रकूलं मत्तगजा एव कृष्णवर्णत्वादन्धकारो यस्यां तथाभूताम्। सैन्यौघस्य बलसमुदायस्य निवेशेन नद्धां व्याप्तां च करोमि। तरङ्गिः बलैः रावणेन सह समुद्रं तुल्यं यथास्यात्तथा ग्लानिं व्याकुलतां नयामि। रावणपक्षे ग्लानिः हर्षक्षयः। हर्षक्षयो धातुक्षय इति सि. कौ०। तूर्णं शीघ्रम्। ज्येष्ठभट्टिनी कौसल्या। इति प्रतिमाटीकायां षष्ठोऽङ्कः।

अथ सप्तमोऽङ्कः ।

(ततः प्रविशति तापसः ।)

तापसः—नन्दिलक नन्दिलक ।

(प्रविश्य)

नन्दिलकः—आर्य अयमस्मि । (अय्य अअं म्हि ।)

तापसः—नन्दिलक कुलपतिर्विज्ञापयति—एष खलु स्वदारापहारिणं त्रैलोक्यविद्रावणं रावणं नाशयित्वा राक्षसगणविरुद्धवृत्तं गुणगणविभूषणं विभीषणमभिषिच्य देवदेवर्षिसिद्धविमलचारित्रां तत्रभवतीं सीतामादाय ऋक्षराक्षसवानरमुख्यैः परिवृतः सम्प्राप्तस्तत्रभवान् शरद्विमलगगनचन्द्राभिरामो रामः । तदद्यास्मिन्नाश्रमपदेऽस्मद्विभवेन यत् सङ्कल्पयितव्यं तत् सर्वं सज्जीक्रियताम् इति ।

नन्दिलकः—आर्य सर्वं सज्जीकृतम् । किन्तु (अय्य सव्वं सज्जीकिदं । किन्तु—)

तापसः—किमेतत् ।

नन्दिलकः—अत्र बिभीषणसम्बन्धिनो राक्षसाः । तेषां भक्षणनिमित्तं कुलपतिः प्रमाणम् । (एत्थ बिभीसणकेरआ रक्खसा । तेसं भक्खणणिमित्तं कुळवदि पमाणं ।)

तापसः—किमर्थम् ।

नन्दिलकः—ते खलु खादन्ति । (ते खु खज्जन्ति)

अथ विहतरावणस्य निरस्तसकलविघ्नस्य रामस्य सीतया सह तपोवनं प्रति पुनरागमनं तत्र मातृसहितस्य भरतस्य समागमो रामस्याभिषेचनं सर्वैः सह पुनरयोध्यां प्रति निवर्तनं चेत्याद्यर्थजातं प्रदर्शयितुं सप्तमाङ्कमारभते । तत्रादौ रामस्य तपोवनागमनं वर्णयति मिश्रविष्कम्भकेन । त्रयो लोकास्त्रैलोक्यम् । चातुर्वर्ण्यादित्वात्स्वार्थे ष्यञ् । तद् विद्रावयति भयात्पलायनपरं करोतीति त्रैलोक्यविद्रावणस्तम् । राक्षसगणेन विरुद्धं सात्त्विकं सज्जनानुरूपं वृत्तं यस्य तम् । गुणगणो विभूषणं यस्य तम् । देवदेवर्षिषु सिद्धं देवदेवर्षिसिद्धेषु वा विमलं चारित्रं यस्यास्ताम् । ऋक्षाः जाम्बवदादयः । शरदः विमलं यद्गगनं तत्र चन्द्रस्तद्वदभिरामः । अस्मद्विभवेन अस्मद्विभवानुरूपमित्यर्थः । भक्षणनिमित्तं भक्ष्यवस्तूनां संविधानार्थम् । अन्यथा मानुषान् भक्षयेयुरिति भावः ।

तापसः—अलमलं सम्भ्रमेण । बिभीषणविधेयाः खलु राक्षसाः ।

नन्दिलकः—नमो राक्षससज्जनाय । (णमो रक्खससज्जणाअ ।
(निष्क्रान्तः ।)

तापसः—(विलोक्य ।) अये अयमत्रभवान् राघवः । य एष

जय नरवर जेयः स्याद् द्वितीयस्तवारि-
स्तव भवतु विधेया भूमिरेकातपत्रा ।
इति मुनिभिरनेकैः स्तूयमानः प्रसन्नैः
क्षितितलमवतीर्णो मानवेन्द्रो विमानात् ॥ १ ॥

जयतु भवान् जयतु । (निष्क्रान्तः ।)

मिश्रविष्कम्भकः ।

(ततः प्रविशति रामः)

रामः— भोः ।

समुदितबलवीर्यं रावणं नाशयित्वा
जगति गुणसमग्रां प्राप्य सीतां विशुद्धाम् ।
वचनमपि गुरूणामन्तशः पूरयित्वा
मुनिजनवनवासं प्राप्तवानस्मि भूयः ॥ २ ॥

तापसीनामभिवन्दनार्थमभ्यन्तरं प्रविष्टा चिरायते खलु मैथिली । (विलोक्य ।) अये इयं वैदेही ।

सखीति सीतेति च जानकीति
यथावयः स्निग्धतरं स्नुषेति ।
तपस्विदारैर्जनकेन्द्रपुत्री
सम्भाष्यमाणा समुपैति मन्दम् ॥ ३ ॥

बिभीषणविधेया बिभीषणाज्ञानुविधायिनः । अतस्तदाज्ञप्ता मानुषान्न खादेयुः । **जयेति** । नरवर जय तवोत्कर्षोऽस्तु । तव द्वितीयः अरिः उत्पद्येत चेत् जेयः स्यात् जेतुं योग्यो भवेत् । तमपि त्वं जीया इत्याशीर्वचनम् । भूमिः एकमातपत्रं छत्रं यस्यां सा एकातपत्राऽनन्यशासनेत्यर्थः । तव विधेया वश्या भवतु । इति अनेन प्रकारेण अनेकैः प्रसन्नैः मुनिभिः स्तूयमानः मानवेन्द्रो रामः विमानात्पुष्पकात्क्षितितलमवतीर्णः । मालिनी वृत्तम् ॥ १ ॥ **समुदितेति** । समुदितं प्रकटं बलं वीर्यं च यस्य तं रावणं नाशयित्वा जगति गुणसमग्रां गुणाढ्यां विशुद्धां सीतां प्राप्य अन्तशः साकल्येन गुरूणा वचनमपि पूरयित्वा मुनिजनवनवासं भूयः पुनः प्राप्तवानस्मि । वृत्तमनन्तरोक्तम् ॥ २ ॥ **सखीतीति** यथावयः वयसोनतिक्रमेण स्वस्ववयोनुरूपं तपस्विदारैः सखीति सीतेति जानकीति स्नुषेति स्निग्धतरमतिस्नेहेन सम्भाष्यमाणा जनकेन्द्रपुत्री मन्दं समुपैति । उपजातिश्छन्दः ॥ ३ ॥

(ततः प्रविशति सीता तापसी च ।)

तापसी—हला एष ते कुटुम्बिकः । उपसर्पैनम् । न शक्यं त्वामेकाकिनीं प्रेक्षितुम् । (हळा एसो दे कुडुम्बिओ । उवसप्प णं । ण सक्कं तुमं एआइणिं पेक्खिदुं ।)

सीता—हम् । अद्याप्यविश्वसनीयमिव मे प्रतिभाति । (उपसृत्य ।) जयत्वार्यपुत्रः । (हं । अज्ज वि अविस्सप्तणीअं विअ मे पडिभादि । (जेदु अय्यउत्तो ।)

रामः—मैथिलि अपि जानासि पूर्वाधिष्ठानमस्माकं जनस्थानमासीत् । अप्यत्र ज्ञायन्ते पुत्रकृतका वृक्षाः ।

सीता—जानामि जानामि अवलोकितपत्रका उल्लोकयितव्या इदानीं संवृत्ताः । (जाणामि जाणामि आलोइअपत्तआ उल्लोअइदव्वा दाणिं संवुत्ता ।)

रामः—एवमेतत् । निम्नस्थलोत्पादको हि कालः । मैथिलि । अप्युपलभ्यतेऽस्य सप्तपर्णस्याधस्ताच्छुक्लवाससं भरतं दृष्ट्वा परित्रस्तं मृगयूथमासीत् ।

सीता—आर्यपुत्र दृढं खलु स्मरामि । (अय्यउत्त । दिढं खु सुमरामि)

रामः—अयं तु नस्तपसः साक्षिभूतो महाकच्छः । अत्रास्माभिरासीनैस्तातस्य निवपनक्रियां चिन्तयद्भिः काञ्चनपार्श्वो नाम मृगो दृष्टः ।

सीता—हम् आर्यपुत्र मा खलु मा खल्वेवं भणितुम् । (हं अय्यउत्त । मा खु मा खु एवं भणिदुं । (भीता वेपते ।)

रामः—अलमलं सम्भ्रमेण । अतिक्रान्तः खल्वेष कालः (दिशो विलोक्य ।) अये कुतो नु

कुटुम्बमस्यास्तीति कुटुम्बिकः भर्ता । न शक्यं त्वामिति । एकाकिनीं भर्तृरहिताम् । भर्तृसहिताया एव तव चिरवियुक्ताया दर्शनमस्माकं प्रीतिकरमिति भावः । हमित्यङ्गीकारे । एवं कुर्यामित्यर्थः । अद्यापि हते रावणेपि । अविश्वसनीयं भर्तृविनाकृताया अवस्थानं न विश्वासार्हं सुरक्षितमिव । पुत्रकृतकाः पुत्रवत्परिपालितत्वात् कृत्रिमपुत्रा इव स्थिताः । आहिताग्निपाठात्परनिपातः । अवलोकितपत्रका अवलोकितानि पत्रकाणि बालत्वादल्पपत्राणि येषां ते । उल्लोकयितव्या उदुच्चक्षुषावलोकयितव्याः । संवृत्ता इत्यर्थः । निम्नस्थलोत्पादकः निम्नं च स्थलं स्थलभूतं च तस्योत्पादकः । स्थलमत्रोच्चभूभागः । निम्नमुच्चतां नयतीत्यर्थः । कालान्तरेण ह्रस्वं दीर्घतामापद्यते इति यावत् । अत्र रामः सीताया वचनमर्थान्तरेण समर्थयतीत्ययमेवार्थः साधीयान् । 'निम्नोत्पादकः स्थलोत्पादकश्च । कश्चिद्धि देशः स्थलरूपः कालतो निम्नो भवति कश्चिच्च निम्नरूपः स्थलतामापद्यते इत्यर्थः । इति ग० शा० । वस्तूनामुच्चनीचसंनिवेशः कालकृत एवेति शास्त्रिणामाशयः । उपलभ्यते स्मृतिविषयीभवति । स्मर्यते इत्यर्थः । परित्रस्तं भीतं शुक्लवस्त्रस्यादृष्टपूर्वत्वात् । महाकच्छः महांस्तटप्रदेशः । कुतो नु इति श्लोकान्वायं ।

रेणुः समुत्पतति लोध्रसमानगौरः
सम्प्रावृणोति च दिशः पवनावधूतः ।
शङ्खध्वनिश्च पटहस्वनधीरनादैः
सम्मूर्च्छितो वनमिदं नगरीकरोति ॥ ४ ॥

(प्रविश्य)

लक्ष्मणः—जयत्वार्यः । आर्य

अयं सैन्येन महता त्वद्दर्शनसमुत्सुकः ।
मातृभिः सह सम्प्राप्तो भरतो भ्रातृवत्सलः ॥ ५ ॥

रामः—वत्स लक्ष्मण किमेवं भरतः प्राप्तः ।

लक्ष्मणः—आर्य अथ किम् ।

रामः—मैथिलि श्वश्रूजनपुरोगं भरतमवलोकयितुं विशालीक्रियतां ते चक्षुः।

सीता—आर्यपुत्र एष्टव्ये काले भरत आगतः । (अय्यउत्त इच्छिदव्वे काले भरदो आददो ।)

(ततः प्रविशति भरतः समातृकः ।)

भरतः—

तैस्तैः प्रवृद्धविषयैर्विषमैर्विमुक्तं
मेघैर्विमुक्तममलं शरदीव सोमम् ।
आर्यासहायमहमद्य गुरुं दिदृक्षुः
प्राप्तोऽस्मि तुष्टहृदयः स्वजनानुबद्धः ॥ ६ ॥

रामः—अम्बाः अभिवादये ।

सर्वाः—जात चिरं जीव । दिष्ट्या वर्धामहे अवसितप्रतिज्ञं त्वां कुशलिनं सह वध्वा प्रेक्ष्य । (जाद चिरंजीव । दिट्ठिआ वड्ढामो अवसिदपडिण्णं तुमं कुसलिणं सह वहूए पेक्खिअ ।)

रेणुरिति । कुतो नु लोध्रसमानगौरः लोध्रतुल्यगौरः रेणुः समुत्पतति । पवनावधूतः वायुना विधुतः दिशः संप्रावृणोति च । पटहस्वनस्य धीरैः गभीरैः नादैः सम्मूर्च्छितः वर्धितः । शङ्खध्वनिश्च इदं वनं नगरीकरोति । नगरे एवैतादृशानां शब्दानामुपलम्भादिति भावः । वसन्ततिलका वृत्तम् ॥ ४ ॥ **अयमिति** । अयं भ्रातृवत्सलः त्वद्दर्शनसमुत्सुकः महता सैन्येन युक्तः भरतः मातृभिः सह सम्प्राप्तः ॥ ५ ॥ श्वश्रूजनपुरोगं श्वश्रूजनपुरःसरम् । एष्टव्ये अभिलषितव्ये । **तैस्तैरिति** । अद्य तुष्टहृदयः स्वजनेनानुबद्धः अनुगतः तैस्तैः प्रवृद्धः विषयो येषां तैः प्रवृद्धविषयैः वृद्धिं गतैः विषमैः संकटैः विमुक्तम् । शरदि मेघैः विमुक्तममलं सोममिव आर्यासहायं सीतासखं गुरुं रामं दिदृक्षुर्द्रष्टुमिच्छुः प्राप्तोऽस्मि ॥ वसन्ततिलकं वृत्तम् ॥ ६ ॥ अवसिता

रामः—अनुगृहीतोऽस्मि ।

लक्ष्मणः—अम्बाः अभिवादये ।

सर्वाः—जात चिरं जीव । (जाद चिरं जीव ।)

लक्ष्मणः—अनुगृहीतोऽस्मि ।

सीता—आर्याः वन्दे । (अय्या वन्दामि ।)

सर्वाः—वत्से चिरमङ्गला भव । (वच्छे चिरमङ्गला होहि)

सीता—अनुगृहीतास्मि । (अणुग्गहिदह्मि ।)

भरतः—आर्ये अभिवादये भरतोऽहमस्मि ।

रामः—एह्येहि वत्स इक्ष्वाककुमार । स्वस्ति । आयुष्मान् भव ।

वक्षः प्रसारय कवाटपुटप्रमाण—
मालिङ्ग मां सुविपुलेन भुजद्वयेन ।
उन्नामयाननमिदं शरदिन्दुकल्पं
प्रह्लादय व्यसनदग्धमिदं शरीरम् ॥ ७ ॥

भरतः—अनुगृहीतोऽस्मि । आर्ये अभिवादये भरतोऽहमस्मि ।

सीता—आर्यपुत्रेण चिरसञ्चारी भव । (अय्यउत्तेण चिरसञ्चारी होहि ।)

भरतः—अनुगृहीतोऽस्मि । आर्य अभिवादये ।

लक्ष्मणः—एह्येहि वत्स दीर्घायुर्भव । परिष्वजस्व गाढम् । (आलिङ्गति ।)

भरतः—अनुगृहीतोऽस्मि । आर्य प्रतिगृह्यतां राज्यभारः ।

रामः—वत्स कथमिव ।

कैकेयी—जात चिराभिलषितः खल्वेष मनोरथः । (जाद चिराहिलसिदो खु एसो मणोरहो ।)

(ततः प्रविशति शत्रुघ्नः ।)

शत्रुघ्नः—

विविधैर्व्यसनैः क्लिष्टमक्लिष्टगुणतेजसम् ।
द्रष्टुं मे त्वरते बुद्धी रावणान्तकरं गुरुम् ॥ ८ ॥

पूर्णा प्रतिज्ञा यस्य तम् । **वक्षः प्रसारय** इति । व्याख्यातपूर्वमिदम् (अं. ४-१६) ॥७॥ **विविधैः इति** । विविधैरनेकप्रकारैः व्यसनैः संकटैः क्लिष्टं पीडितम् । अक्लिष्टा अबाधा गुणाः तेजश्च यस्य तमक्लिष्टगुणतेजसं रावणान्तकरं गुरुं द्रष्टुं मे बुद्धिः त्वरति ॥८॥

(उपगम्य ।) आर्य शत्रुघ्नोऽहमभिवादये ।

रामः—एह्येहि वत्स । स्वस्ति । आयुष्मान् भव ।

शत्रुघ्नः—अनुगृहीतोऽस्मि । आर्ये अभिवादये ।

सीता—वत्स चिरं जीव । (वच्छ चिरं जीव ।)

शत्रुघ्नः—अनुगृहीतोऽस्मि । आर्य अभिवादये ।

लक्ष्मणः—स्वस्ति । आयुष्मान् भव ।

शत्रुघ्नः—अनुगृहीतोऽस्मि । आर्य एतौ वसिष्ठवामदेवौ सह प्रकृतिभिरभिषेकं पुरस्कृत्य त्वद्दर्शनमभिलषतः ।

तीर्थोदकेन मुनिभिः स्वयमाहृतेन
नानानदीनदगतेन तव प्रसादात् ।
इच्छन्ति ते मुनिगणाः प्रथमाभिषिक्तं
द्रष्टुं मुखं सलिलसिक्तमिवारविन्दम् ॥ ९ ॥

कैकेयी—गच्छ जात । अभिलषाभिषेकम् । (गच्छ जाद । अभिलसेहि अभिसेअं ।)

रामः—यदाज्ञापयत्यम्बा । (निष्क्रान्तः ।)

(नेपथ्ये ।)

जयतु भवान् । जयतु स्वामी । जयतु महाराजः । जयतु देवः । जयतु भद्रमुखः । जयत्वार्यः । जयतु रावणान्तकः ।

कैकेयी—एते पुरोहिताः कञ्चुकिनः पुत्रकस्य मे विजयघोषं वर्धयन्त आशीर्भिः पूजयन्ति । (एदे पुरोहिदा कञ्चुइणो पुत्तअस्स मे विजअघोसं वड्ढअन्तो आसीहि पूजअन्ति ।)

सुमित्रा—प्रकृतयः परिचारकाः सज्जनाश्च पुत्रकस्य मे विजयं वर्धयन्ति । (पइदीओ परिचारआ सज्जणा अ पुत्तअस्स मे विजअं वड्ढअन्ति ।)

(नेपथ्ये ।)

भो भो जनस्थानवासिनस्तपस्विनः । शृण्वन्तु शृण्वन्तु भवन्तः ।

हत्वा रिपुप्रभवमप्रतिमं तमौघं
सूर्योऽन्धकारमिव शौर्यमयैर्मयूखैः ।

तीर्थोदकेनेति । मुनिगणाः तव प्रसादान्मुनिभिः स्वयमाहृतेन नानानदीनदगतेन तीर्थोदकेन प्रथमाभिषिक्तं ते मुखं सलिलसिक्तमरविन्दमिव द्रष्टुमिच्छन्ति । वसन्ततिलकम् ॥९॥ **हत्वेति** । अप्रतिममतुलं रिपुप्रभवं तमौघं सूर्य अधकारमिव शौर्यमयैः मयूखैः

सीतामवाप्य सकलाशुभवर्जनीयां
रामो महीं जयति सर्वजनाभिरामः ॥ १० ॥

कैकेयी—अम्महे पुत्रस्य मे विजयघोषणा वर्धते । (अम्महे पुत्तस्स मे विजअघोषणा वड्ढइ ।)

(ततः प्रविशति कृताभिषेको रामः सपरिवारः ।)

रामः—(विलोक्याकाशे ।) भोस्तात ।

स्वर्गेऽपि तुष्टिमुपगच्छ विमुञ्च दैन्यं
कर्म त्वयाभिलषितं मयि यत् तदेतत् ।
राजा किलास्मि भुवि सत्कृतभारवाही
धर्मेण लोकपरिरक्षणमभ्युपेतम् ॥ ११ ॥

भरतः—

अधिगतनृपशब्दं धार्यमाणातपत्रं
विकसितकृतमौलिं तीर्थतोयाभिषिक्तम् ।
गुरुमधिगतलीलं वन्द्यमानं जनौघै-
र्नवशशिनमिवार्यं पश्यतो मे न तृप्तिः ॥ १२ ॥

शत्रुघ्नः—

एतदार्याभिषेकेण कुलं मे नष्टकल्मषम् ।
पुनः प्रकाशतां याति सोमस्येवोदये जगत् ॥ १३ ॥

रामः—वत्स लक्ष्मण । अधिगतराज्योऽहमस्मि ।

लक्ष्मणः—दिष्ट्या भवान् वर्धते ।

(प्रविश्य)

काञ्चुकीयः—जयतु महाराजः । एष खलु तत्रभवान् बिभीषणो

किरणैः हत्वा सकलैरशुभैर्वर्जनीयां कल्याणमयीमित्यर्थः । सीतामवाप्य सर्वजनाभिरामो रामो महीं जयति । वसन्ततिलकं वृत्तम् ॥१०॥ **स्वर्गेपीति** । स्वर्गेपि तुष्टिमुपगच्छ । दैन्यं विमुञ्च । यत्कर्म राज्याभिषेचनरूपं त्वया मयि अभिलषितं तदेतन्निर्वृत्तम् । भुवि सत्कृतो भारो राज्यतन्त्ररूपस्तं वहतीति सत्कृतभारवाही राजास्मि किल । मया धर्मेण न्यायेन लोकपरिरक्षणमभ्युपेतमङ्गीकृतम् । वसन्ततिलकं वृत्तम् ॥ ११ ॥ **अधिगतेति** । अधिगतः नृपशब्दः येन तम् । धार्यमाणमातपत्रं यस्मिंस्तम् । विकसित उज्ज्वलः कृतः मौलिः येन तम् । तीर्थतोयैरभिषिक्तम् । अधिगतो लीलाविलासो येन तं जनौघैर्जनसमुदायैर्वन्द्यमानं नवशशिनमिव गुरुमार्यं पश्यतो मे न तृप्तिः । मालिनी छन्दः ॥ १२ ॥ **एतदिति** । आर्याभिषेकेण नष्टकल्मषमेतन्मे कुलं सोमस्योदये जगद् इव पुनः प्रकाशतां याति ॥ १३ ॥

विज्ञापयति । सुग्रीवनीलमैन्दजाम्बवद्धनूमत्प्रमुखाश्चानुगच्छन्तो विज्ञापयन्ति—दिष्ट्या भवान् वर्धत इति ।

रामः—सहायानां प्रसादाद् वर्धत इति कथ्यताम् ।

काञ्चुकीयः—यदाज्ञापयति महाराजः ।

कैकेयी—धन्या खल्वस्मि । इममभ्युदयमयोध्यायां प्रेक्षितुमिच्छामि । (धण्णा क्खु ह्मि । इदं अब्भुदअं अओज्झाअं पेक्खिदुं इच्छामि ।)

रामः—द्रक्ष्यति भवती । (विलोक्य ।) अये प्रभाभिर्वनमिदमखिलं सूर्यवत् प्रतिभाति । (विभाव्य ।) आ ज्ञातम् । सम्प्राप्तं पुष्पकं दिवि रावणस्य विमानम् । कृतसमयमिदं स्मृतमात्रमुपगच्छतीति । तत् सर्वैरारुह्यताम् ।

(सर्वे आरोहन्ति ।)

रामः—

अद्यैव यास्यामि पुरीमयोध्यां
सम्बन्धिमित्रैरनुगम्यमानः ।

लक्ष्मणः—

अद्यैव पश्यन्तु च नागरास्त्वां
चन्द्रं सनक्षत्रमिवोदयस्थम् ॥ १४ ॥

(भरतवाक्यम् ।)

यथा रामश्च जानक्या बन्धुभिश्च समागतः ।
तथा लक्ष्म्या समायुक्तो राजा भूमिं प्रशास्तु नः ॥ १५ ॥

(निष्क्रान्ताः सर्वे ।)

सप्तमोऽङ्कः ।

प्रतिमानाटकं समाप्तम् ।

कृतसमयं कृतसंकेतम् । **अद्यैवेति** । अद्यैव सम्बन्धिमित्रैः अनुगम्यमानः अयोध्यां पुरीं यास्यामि । अद्यैव नागरा उदयस्थं उदयो राज्यप्राप्तिरूपस्तत्र तिष्ठतीति तम् । पक्षे उदयगिरिस्थितम् । सनक्षत्रं चन्द्रमिव पश्यन्तु । इन्द्रवज्रावृत्तम् ॥ १४ ॥ भरतवाक्यं नटवाक्यम् । नाटकाभिनयसमाप्तौ सामाजिकेभ्यो नटेनाशीर्दीयते इत्यर्थः । प्रस्तावनानन्तरं नटवाक्याभावादत्र भरतवाक्यमित्युक्तिः । इति शाकुन्तलटीकायां राघवभट्टः । **यथा रामश्चेति** । स्पष्टार्थं पद्यम् ॥ १५ ॥ इति प्रतिमाटीकायां सप्तमोऽङ्कः ।

एतन्नाटकान्तर्गतानि सुभाषितानि ।

श्लोकानुक्रमणी.

PRATIMA.

TRANSLATION.

ACT I.

(Enter the Sûtradha'ra *immediately after the recitation of the Nándî (invocation).*

Sûtradha'ra—May Ráma, the supporter of the world, protect you (or, us) in life after life : Ráma, who was the source of Sîtá's prosperity, who was pleased with good counsel (or his father's charioteer, Sumantra), who had a beautiful neck, who had Lakshmaṇa for his constant associate, who became the foe of Rávana, but a matchless one, on account of his queen (being carried off by him), and also displayed a fierce nature (or, identified his interest with that of Bibhîshaṇa ! (1)

(Looking towards the tiring room (or curtain). पृ २

Wife, come here at once.

(Entering)

The Actress—Husband, here I am.

Sûtra.—Lady, do sing a song with reference to this autumnal season.

Actress—Noble one, I will. *(Prepares to sing.)*

Sûtra.—In this season,

A female swan, living on the Kâśa-covered bank (of a river, or covered with white wings) and being in high glee, roams about on sandy banks—

(Behind the curtain). पृ ३

Sir ! Sir !

(Listening)

Sûtra.—Well, I have it.

Like the delighted female guardian of the door, in great haste, in the king's palace. (2)

(Exeunt both).

End of the Prelude.

(*Entering*).

A Female Door-keeper—Sir, which of the chamberlains is present here ?

(*Entering*)

पृ. ४ CHAMBERLAIN—-Lady, here I am. What is to be done ?

FEM. DOOR-KEEPER—Noble one, the great king Daśaratha, a Maháratha (or, whose great chairiot is) never repulsed in the wars between the gods and the demons, orders—Let all the materials (required) for the coronation of Ráma, which is to invest him with sovereign power, be brought in at once.

CHAMB—Lady, what was ordered by the great king has been fully got ready. Behold,

The royal umbrella together with the chauries, and the royal throne with the drum announcing the joyous occasion have been well kept ready. Jars of gold filled with sacred water and with flowers and Kus'a grass strewn about are placed in (their proper places). The pleasure-car is kept ready-harnessed. The citizens with the councillors have all arrived in time. And that revered sage Vasishtha, the very cause of auspiciousness of all these, has taken his seat on the Vedî (the dais raised for coronation). (3)

FEM. DOOR-KEEPER— If so, it is all well done.

CHAMBER.—What joy, ho !

Now are the subjects made to gain their wishes by the king, installing the moon, bearing the name of Ráma, as sovereign of the earth ! (4)

FEM. DOOR-KEEPER – Let the noble one hasten, hasten (to his duties).

CHAMBER.—Lady, here I speed away, (*Exit*).

FEM. DOOR-KEEPER—(*Turning round and looking on*) Sambhavaka, noble Sambhavak, please go. You too, with due formalities make the revered priest hasten at the king's bidding. (*Going to another place*) Sárasîká, O Sârasîka, go to the concert-hall and tell the actors there to be ready with a play befitting the occasion. In the meanwhile I will tell the great king that all has been done (according to his directions). (*Exit*).

(*Then enter* AVADA'TIKA' *with a bark garment*).

AVADA'TIKA'—Oh the great misfortune! I felt so much fear when bringing this bark garment for fun; how much पृ. ६
more ought he to feel who robs another of his wealth through avarice. I as if feel inclined to joke; but one cannot, indeed, crack a joke oneself.

(*Then enter* SI'TA' *with her retinue*).

SI'TA'.—Wench, Avalokitá looks like one afraid (of something). What can this be?

MAID.—Mistress, it is, indeed, easy for servants to be in fault. She might have been guilty.

SI'TA'.—No, no; she seems to be desirous of making fun.

AVADA'TIKA'.—(*Approaching*) Prosperity to my lady. Lady, I am not guilty.

SI'TA'.—Who asks you that. But what is this held by you in your left hand?

AVADA'.—My lady, it is a bark garment.

SI'TA'.—Why have you brought the bark garment?

AVADA'.—May my lady hear. The worthy Revá, the keeper of the stage materials, was requested by me to give me a sprout of the Asoka tree after the stage-purpose was served. She did not give it. So thinking that her fault deserves (such treatment) I took away this (bark garment).

SI'TA'.—A sinful deed was done by you. Go, and पृ. ७
restore it (to her).

AVADA'.—My lady, it was, indeed, for the sake of fun that I brought it.

SI'TA'.—Mad girl, in this case the crime becomes worse. Go and return it to her; do return it.

AVADA'.—As my lady commands.

(*Wishes to depart*).

SI'TA'.—Friend, come back just.

AVADA'.—My lady, here I am.

SITA'.—Friend, (I wish to see) if it appears well on my person (when worn by me).

AVADA'—Lady, beauty, indeed, adds grace to every thing. May my lady deck herself with it.

SITA'—Just bring it to me. (*Taking and wearing it.*) Friend, see if it becomes me.

AVADA'TIKA'—It does appear splendid on you. The bark-garment has become golden as it were.

SITA'—You do not say anything, wench !

MAID—No necessity for words. This horripilated hair itself speaks for me.

पृ. ८ SITA'—Maid, just bring a mirror.

MAID—As mistress commands. (*Going and returning with a mirror*). Mistress, here is the mirror.

SITA'—(*Looking at the face of the maid*). Let aside the mirror. You seem to be wishing to say something.

MAID—Mistress, this is what I have heard. Noble Bàlàkì, the chamberlain says—There is coronation, there is coronation.

SI'TA'—Some king, it seems, will be installed on his throne.

(*Another* Maid *entering*).

MAID—Mistress, good news for you, good news for you.

SI'TA'—Having what in your mind are you talking ?

MAID—The Prince (Ráma) it is said, is to be installed.

SI'TA'—Is my father-in-law all well.

MAI'D—He is to be coronated by the great king himself.

SI'TA'—If so, this is the second agreeable thing that I have heard. Widen very much your lap.

पृ. ९ MAID—Mistress, I will. (*Does accordingly*).

SI'TA'—(*Takes off her ornaments and presents them to her*).

MAID—Mistress, something like the sound of a drum.

SI'TA—(Why,) the very same.

MAID—The sound of the drum has ceased as soon as t was struck out.

SI'TA'—What possibly can be the obstacle to the coronation? Or why, royal palaces, as is well known, are full of various incidents.

MAID—Mistress, this is what I heard—

The great king will retire to the forest after having installed the crown prince (on the throne).

SI'TA'—If so, it is not the coronation water (that he will pour on him) but water for washing (the tears from) the face.

(*Then enters* RA'MA).

RA'MA.—Alas! Oh!

When the drum had begun to sound, the elderly person had stood about, the auspicious throne was ascended (by me) and water was about to fall down from the mouth of the jar as it was bent after being raised up to the shoulder, I was called by my name and sent away by the king; and people stood astonished at my fortitude (mental calm): if a son obeys the order of his father, what room, oh, is there for astonishment? (5)

As I was sent away by the king himself saying—' Son, पृ. १०
let the ceremony be stopped for the present,' my mind breathed a sigh of relief, as it were, owing to the load (responsibility of government) being removed (from my head). Fortunately I am the same Ráma (heir-apparent) and the great king the great king (as before). I will just see the princess of Mithilá now.

AVADA'TIKA'.—Lady, the prince, indeed, is coming while the bark garment is not removed.

RA'MA.—Maithili, what are you sitting here for?

SITA'.—Oh, my husband! (*Rising*). Prosperity to my husband.

RA'MA.—Maithili, please sit down. (*He sits down*).

SITA'.—As my husband commands. (*Sits down*).

AVADA'TIKA'.—(*Aside*) Lady, the same (as usual) is the prince's dress. So untrue seems to be this (the news about his coronation).

SÎTA'.—(*Aside*) People of that stamp do not tell a falsehood; or rather, various are the incidents occurring in palaces !

RA'MA.– Maithili, what is this that is being talked about (by you) !

SÎTA'.—It is nothing serious, indeed. This girl was saying-coronàtion, coronation.

पृ. RA'MA.—I understand your curiosity. There was a
११ coronation. Listen. To-day after having placed me on his lap, with which I was familiar in my childhood, and having described in terms of affection my mother's family, the great king addressed me in the presence of the priests, ministers, friendly persons and the citizens, having thereby consolidated the Kosala kingdom, saying 'Son, accept the sovereignty'.

SI'TA'—What did my husband say to that then ?

Ráma—What is your own guess, Maithili ?

SI'TA'—I think my husband, without saying anything, must have heaved a long sigh and fallen at the feet of the great king.

RA'MA—Rightly guessed. Rarely are created couples whose dispositions agree. There I did fall at his feet.

By the tears simultaneously falling—his on me and mine down (on his feet), were rendered wet my head and the feet of my father. (6)

SI'TA'—Then, then ?

RA'MA—Then when I did not accept his solicitations (to accept sovereignty), I was conjured by him by his own life, already smitten by the infirmities of age.

पृ. SI'TA'—And then ?
१२ RA'MA—

Then, at the time when for the coronation the jar was taken up by Śatrughna and Lakshmaṇa, and the royal umbrella was held by the king himself, shedding tears (of joy), something was whispered into the ear of the king by Mantharâ, who came up in haste, and I at once ceased to be the king. (7)

SI'TA'—That is after my heart. The great king is just the great king, while my husband is just as he was before.

RA'MA—Maithilī, why have you taken off your ornaments?

SI'TA'—I have not, indeed; put them on yet.

RA'MA—It cannot be. The ornaments must have been taken down just recently. For,

Your ears have their lobes curved owing to the ornaments being removed in haste; and your hands have the surface of their palms turned reddish white on account of their ornaments being pushed down with force; while these several parts of your body, depressed by the weight of the ornaments, have not at all recovered their evenness. (8)

SI'TA'—My husband has the power to represent even पृ. १३
an untruth as truth.

RA'MA—If so, then put on the ornaments. I will hold the mirror.

(*Doing so and observing closely.*) Wait.

In the mirror they (the garments you have put on) appear like bark garments; or are these the rays of the sun? I know now from your (way of) smiling; is this (mere) fun or a desire to take some vow? (9)

Avadátiká, what means this?

AVADA'TĪKA'—My lord, they were worn by her out of a curiosity to see whether they would become her or not.

RA'MA—Maithili, what is this, that you wear this ornament of the persons of the Ikshváku race in old age? I, too, feel pleasure in wearing (a bark garment); bring me one.

SI'TA'—Not indeed. not indeed, let my husband utter what is inauspicious

RA'MA—Maithili, why do you prevent me?

SI'TA'—It appears as if inauspicious to me in the case of my husband, who has (just) left off the coronation.

पृ. १४ RA'MA—Do not yourself entertain (lit. create) an evil idea, especially in a matter of jest; and when they (bark-garments) have been already worn by you (who form) half of my body. (10)

(*Behind the curtains*).

Alas ! Alas ! The great king—

SI'TA'—Husband, what can this be ?

RA'MA—(*Listening.*)

Since this clamour of women and men is loud beyond limit, it is quite evident, Fate has struck at the very root, thinking itself to be all-powerful. (11)

Quickly let the (cause of the) clamour be ascertained.

(*Entering*)

A CHAMBERLAIN.—May the prince protect ; may the prince protect !

RA'MA.—Noble one, who is to be protected ?

CHAMB.—The great king.

RA'MA.—You say the great king. Noble one, you should rather say the whole earth, compressed into one body, is to be protected. Now from whom has the danger arisen ?

पृ. १५ CHAMB.—From a relative.

RA'MA.—You say from a relative. Then alas ! there is no remedy for it.

An enemy strikes at the body, a relative does so at the heart. To whom does this term 'a relative' belong, that will cause shame to me ? (12)

CHAMB.—To her ladyship, Kaikeyī ?

RA'MA.—What ? To my mother. Then in this case the result will be blissful.

CHAMB.—How possibly ?

RA'MA.—Hear—

What object does she long for, who has a husband that is Indra's peer, and who has a son in *me*, that she may do a reprehensible deed ? (13)

CHAMB.—Prince, you should not attribute your own straightforwardness to the perverse tendencies of a woman's mind. It was in fact at her bidding that your coronation was stopped.

RA'MA.—Noble one, this is, indeed, fraught with advantages.

CHAMB.—How, pray ? पृ. १६

RA'MA.—Listen—

In the first place there is the cessation from retirement to the forest of the king himself ; then I am under my father (have no responsibilities of independence), and my position as a child remains the same. The subjects will have no misgivings about the administration (of the kingdom) by a new king ; and lastly my brothers are not deprived of the enjoyments of pleasures (which they share with me now). (14)

CHAMB.—Moreover, by her who came without being called, Bharata was asked to be installed on the throne. Even in doing this did she display (the virtue of the) absence of avaricce ?

RA'MA.—Noble one, simply through partiality towards us your honour does not see the real thing (take a right view of the matter). For,

If the kingdom, promised as a marriage gift be demanded for her son, there is avarice on her part in acting thus, and none on my part, depriving a brother of his (rightful) kingdom !

CHAMB.—Then again—

RA'MA.—I do not wish to hear any more reproachful talk about my mother. Tell at once the news about the great king.

CHAMB.—Then after that ;

I was sent (to you) by the king with a motion of the hand alone as he was struck dumb through sorrow and it was somewhat desirable that the king fell into a swoon, I think. (16).

RA'MA.—How did he fall into a swoon !

(*Behind the curtain.*)

How do you ask ' How did he fall into a swoon

If you bear not the king's swooning away, touch (take up) your bow ; let no mercy be shown ;—

RA'MA.—(*Hearing the words and looking forth.*)

By whom is thrown into agitation Lakshmaṇa, the ocean of fortitude and incapable of being agitated ? Who provoked, I behold a crowd of hundred (Lakshmaṇas) in front of me. (17).

(*Then enter* LAKSHMAṆA *bow and arrow in hand*).

LAKSHMAṆA.—(*Wrathfully*) How do you ask—'How did he fall into a swoon' ?

If you bear not &c. ; every one who is tender-hearted and conniving at (the acts of) his relatives, is thus insulted. On the other hand, if you like not this, give me leave (to act as I like) ; I have formed my resolution to make the world destitute of young women, since we are defrauded (by a young woman). (18).

पृ. १८ SI'TA'.—Husband, Sumitrá's son has taken up his bow at a time deserving weeping (when he ought to weep).

RA'MA—You who have Sumitrá for your mother, what is this ?

LAKS.—How, how do you ask me ' what is this '?

When the kingdom come by right succession has been snatched away (from you) and the king is lying in a lamentable plight on earth, is there hesitation still (as to how to act); is this forgiveness or absence of self-respect ? (19).

RA'MA —Sumitrá's son, my loss of kingdom incites you to action. Ah ! You are, indeed, without discrimination.

Whether Bharata becomes the king or I, surely it is the same to you. If you boast of your bow-manship, let *that* king be protected. (20)

LAKSH.—I am not able to restrain my anger. Well, well. Here I depart at once. (*Starts to go*).

RA'MA—

Like fate, of fixed operation, this frown of Lakshmaṇa, appearing on the surface of his forehead, is fixed there as if desirous of consuming the three worlds. (21)

Son of Sumitrá, here, for a moment.

LAKSH.—Noble one, here I am.

RA'MA—I spoke this in order to produce calmness in you. Say now—

Shall I bend the bow against father who had regard for truth? Shall I discharge an arrow against mother taking away her own property? Shall I slay my younger brother, Bharata, who was quite guiltless? Which of these three sins commends itself to you for being angry? (22)

LAKSH.—(*With tears*) Alas! pity!

You blame me without knowing me properly—the real cause of my anger—that—

The great hardships (to be caused to you) by which, revolving in my mind I had no desire for a kingdom. (It is this) that you have surely to live for fourteen years in a forest. (23)

RA'MA—On this account his Honour fell into a swoon!

Alas! He has indicated his absence of mastery over himself. Maithili,

Give me for an auspicious purpose the bark-garments given to you by her (this maid): I will perform a religious duty for which an opportunity was never obtained and which was never performed by other kings. (24)

SÍTA'.—May my husband take these!

RA'MA.—Maithilî, what have you undertaken to do?

SÎTA.—Why, I am surely your partner in duties

RA'MA.—But I have, indeed (or, according to my father's order) alone to go.

SÎTA.—For this very reason, indeed, I will follow you.

RA'MA.—You will have to dwell in a forest.

SÎTA.—That, indeed, is a palace to me.

RA'MA.—But you have as well to devote yourself to the service of your mother-in-law and father-in-law.

SITA'.—As regards that I offer my bow to the gods (invoke the gods to keep them safe).

RA'MA.—Lakshmaṇa, keep off (dissuade) her (from following me).

LAKSH.—Noble one, I cannot bring myself to dissuade her at a time deserving praise (for this her resolve).

A star follows the moon even when eclipsed by Ráhu; a creeper comes down to the ground when a forest-tree (its resort) falls down; a female elephant leaves not the lordly elephant though stuck in mud; let her go with you and discharge her duty; for women entirely depend on their husband (lit. have their husband for their protector). (25)

(*Having entered*)

पृ. २१ A MAID:—Prosperity to the mistress! The noble Revá, the keeper of the stage-materials, requests, after having made her obeisance—Avalokitá has taken away by force some bark-garments from the Concert-hall. These are others, not used before. Have your purpose served with these, if any?

RA'MA.—Good girl, bring them here. She has her purpose served. I am in need (of those).

MAID.—May master take them! (*Exit, having handed them over.*)

(Ráma *takes them and puts them on*).

LAKSH.—Please, my noble brother—

Having (until now) given me half of all such things as raiment, ornaments, garlands (and the like) you have alone worn the bark-garments; you are, indeed, jealous as regards the bark-garments. (26).

RA'MA—Mathili, ward him off (from this).

SITA'—Son of Sumitrà, desist from this.

LAKSH.—Noble lady,

You desire alone to serve the feet of my revered
पृ. २२ brother: the right foot you alone will have (for serving), while mine will be the left. (27)

SITA—My husband should, indeed, show pity; Lakshmana is feeling distressed.

RA'MA—Sumitrâ's son, listen to me. Bark-garments are, indeed, (or, serve as)

An armour in the battle of penance, a goad for controlling the elephant of the vows (to be observed); a bridle for checking the horses of the senses; and a charioteer leading to (the discharge of) duty : take them. (28).

LAKSH.—I am favoured. (*Takes and wears them.*)

RA'MA—The high road is closely crowded by the citizens, who have heard of this affair. Let it be cleared, let it be cleared.

LAKSH.—I shall march in the front. Disperse men, disperse.

RA'MA—Maithili, remove your veil.

SÎTA—As my husband commands. (*Does so.*)

RA'MA—O you citizens, hear me, sirs, hear me.

May your honours behold, at will, this my wife with your faces, having the eyes filled (lit. disturbed) with tears; for women may be looked at without (sin) in a sacrifice, at the marriage ceromony, when under calamity and when (living) in a forest. (29)

(*Entering*)

A CHAMBERLAIN—Prince, not indeed, not indeed, should you depart. For here the great king,

Having heard of your departure (resolve to go) to the forest with your wife, wherein Lakshmana is determined to follow you on account of his fraternal affection, has like an old wild-elephant, risen up, with his body besmeared with the dust of the surface of the earth, and is coming hitherwards. (30)

LAKSH.—Noble one,

What is to be seen of us, dressed in tattered barks only (and almost) living in a forest ?

RA'MA—When we shall have departed, let the king see the principal places of our residence. (31)

(*Exeunt Omnes*)

End of Act I.

ACT II.

(*Then enter a* CHAMBERLAIN).

CHAMBERLAIN.—O you that keep guard at the door (door-keepers). Be you careful at your respective posts.

(*Entering*)

A FEMALE-DOOR-KEEPER.—Sir, what is this for?

CHAMB.—This great king here, who was intent on keeping his solemn promise (*lit.* his truthful words), who, unable to dissuade Ráma from going to the forest, and having thereby his heart burnt with the fire of the sorrow of his son's separation, is lying in the *Samudra* house, raving a great deal like one frenzied (where),

Like Meru having its foundation shaking, or like the measureless great ocean beginning to dry up, or like the sun falling down with his orb only visible, at the approach of the end of an Æan (destruction of the world) the king has (the frame of) his body and mind greatly unhinged (*lit.* loosened) owing to sorrow. (1).

FEM. DOOR-KEEPER.—Alas, oh pity! Such has been the great king's plight!

CHAMB.—Lady, go (to attend to your duty).

FEM. D.—Noble one, so I do. (*Exit*).

CHAMB.—(*Looking all round*). Oh, verily from the day of Ráma's departure this Ayodyâ appears to be quite void of interest. For

The lordly elephants show no desire for (to eat) fodder; the horses have their eyes filled with tears and mouths devoid of neighing; and these city folks includ-ing old men, women and children, having given up all talk about taking food (or taking food and merry talks) with faces extremely miserable and loudly crying, are looking in that direction, by which Râma accompanied by his wife and brother has gone. (2)

Now I too shall be by the side of the great king. (*Walking on and looking*) Ah, here is the great king attended upon by the chief queen and Sumitrá, who are composing him, having suppressed the grief although very unbearable, caused by their son's separation. The situation is heart-rending, indeed! This, this great king

Falls down after having risen again and again, repeatedly uttering in a loud voice the words Alas! alas! and looks in the very direction by which the chief of Raghus has departed. (3)

(*Exit*).

Here ends the mixed Viskambhaka.

(*Enter the* KING *as described and the two* QUEENS).

THE KING—Ha! dear child Ráma, the elixir to the eyes of the worlds! Ha, dear boy Lakshmana, with all your limbs having their proper auspicious marks! Ha, chaste Maithilî, the thoughts of whose mind are fixed on your husband! Alas, alas! pity; gone to the forest, indeed, are my children! (4)

This is strange that I long to see Lakshmana, though he has renounced his affection for his father, owing to his love for his brother. Daughter, Vaidehî,

Abandoned even by Ráma and reprehended by Lakshmana, I, an object of infamy in the world, am deserted even by you. (5)

Son Râma, child Lakshmaṇa, daughter Vaidehî, give a reply to me, my suffering children. Oh, it is all vacant here. No one returns a reply to me. Son of Kausalyá, where are you?

O you, true to your promise, with anger conquered, free from jealousy, loved by the world and devoted to the service of the elders, give me a reply. (6)

Ah, where is that Ráma, the joy to the eyes and hearts of all men? Where is he deeply devoted to me? Where is that embodiment of compassion towards those distressed with sorrow? Where is he who despised the splendour of royalty like a blade of grass? Son Ráma, abandoning me, your father, what have you to do with duty, which does not stand to reason (or, not connected with you)? Oh, pity! How painful?

Ráma has departed like the sun; Lakshmaṇa has followed him as day-light does the sun; Sítá is not seen like a shadow at the disappearance of the sun and day-light. (7)

(*Looking up.*) Oh cursed Fate,

Why did you not do these three things—me, sonless, Ráma, the son of another king, and Kaikeyí, a tigress in the forest, (8).

KAUSALYA'.—The great king should not lament very much and make himself helpless. Surely she and the two princes can be seen by the great king at the end of the period fixed.

KING.—Who are you?

KAUSALYA'.—I am, indeed, the mother of an unloving son.

KING.—What! Are you Kausalyá, the mother of Ráma, charming to the eyes and hearts of all people?

KAUSALYA'.—Great king, I am, indeed, the same hapless woman.

KING.—Kausalyá, you are, indeed, possessed of substance. By you, indeed, Ráma was borne in the womb.

For, I, deprived of the power of my senses, am able neither to bear or suppress grief which is extremely unbearable and fire-like. (9)

(*Looking at* SUMITRA') Who is this other lady?

KAUSALYA'.—Great king, dear Lakshmaṇa—

(*At this half uttered*)

KING.—(*Rising up suddenly.*) Where is he, where is that Lakshmaṇa. He is not seen. Oh misery!

(*The* Queens *rise in haste dnd support the* King)

KAUSALYA'.—Great king, I had begun to say—'Dear Lakshmaṇa's mother, Sumitrá.

KING.—O Sumitrá,

Your son alone is a worthy son, since as by him is followed, day and night in the forest, by: his shadow, Ráma, the best of Raghu's race. (10)

(*Entering*)

A CHAMBERLAIN—Victory to the king! Here indeed, comes his honour Sumantra.

KING—(*Rising up suddenlg in joy*) With Ráma?

CHAMB.—Not indeed; with the chariot.

KING—How, how with the chariot alone?

(*Falls down in a swoon*).

THE TWO QUEENS—Great king, take heart, take heart.

(*They pass their palms along his limbs*).

CHAMB.—Oh, it is painful. (The will of) Fate is intransgressible since high personages of his type meet with such a calamity! Sire, take courage, take courage.

KING—(*Recovering a little*) Has Sumantra returned alone, I ask?

CHAMB.—Sire, just so.

KING—A sad thing, oh!

If the chariot has returned empty, my desire is destroyed (the chariot of my mind is shattered); surely it is the chariot sent by the destroyer to take me, Daśaratha, away as it is empty. (11).

If so, usher him in quickly.

CHAMB.—As sire commands. (*Exit*).

KING—Blessed, indeed, are the breezes in the forest that blow along the tanks, as they touch Ráma, moving in the forest at pleasure. (12) पृ. २९

(*Then enter* SUMANTRA).

SUMANTRA—(*Looking in all directions sorrowfully.*)

These servants, who have left off their duties, whose eyes are disturbed (or closely filled) with tears caused by their affection for Rāma, who are miserable-looking owing to sad thoughts and who are burnt by (the fire of) sorrow, are reproaching the loudly-lamenting king. (13)

(*Approaching*) Prosperity to the great king!

KING—Brother Sumantra, where is my eldest—? No, no, I did not say what was proper.

Where is that eldest son of you, O you lover of sons; where is that daughter of the king of the Videha country, whose devotion to her elders is unsurpassed; or where is the son of Sumitrá? Have they sent any message to their wretched father, who is on the point of death and who created a sea of sorrow for all people (to plunge in)? (14)

SUMANTRA—Sire, do not, please do not, utter such inauspicious words. You will behold them before long.

KING—Really I spoke what was improper. This is not a fit question in the case of ascetics. Tell me then—Does the penance of the ascetics go on well? I hope Vaidehí does not feel fatigued while roaming through forests brought under her sway (rendered safe for her) by Ráma.

SUMITRA'—Sumantra, does not she (Sítá) the sharer with her husband in his duties, clad variously in bark garments, and of conduct befitting a grown up woman, though young, say anything (send any message) to us and to the great king?

SUMANTRA—To the king, all of them—

KING—No, not so. Communicate (their message to me, with (a mention of) their very names, the elixirs to my ears and medicines to my distressed heart.

SUMANTRA—As the great king commands. Ráma, of long life—

KING—Ráma, you say; here is Ráma. By my hearing his name he appears to have touched me as it were. What next?

SUMANTRA—The long-lived Lakshmaṇa—

KING—Here is Lakshmaṇa. And further?

SUMANTRA'—The long-lived Síta, daughter of king Janaka—

KING—Here is Vaidehî. Râma, Lakshmaṇa, Vaidehî. This is not the proper order.

SUMANTRA—Then what is the proper order ?

KING—Say—Râma, Vaidehî, Lakshmaṇa.

Let Maithilî stand between Ràma and Lakshmaṇa, even here; the forests abound in perils; she will have protectors. (15)

SUMANTRA—As the great king commands. Ráma, of long life—

KING—Here is Ráma,

SUMANTRA—The long lived daughter of Janaka—

KING—Here is Vaidehî.

SUMANTRA—The long lived Lakshmaṇa.

KING.—Here is Lakshmaṇa. Ráma, Vaidehî, Lakshmaṇa, embrace me, my children.

Once I touch Râma, once I see him again—with this nectar I think I live, as one whose life has ended lives with nectar. (16).

SUMANTRA.—All of them, having alighted from the chariot, stood with their faces turned towards Ayodhyá and having bowed with their heads to the great king, began to think of a message.

Having mused over something for a long time they made a quivering motion of their lips in order to speak ; but their throats being choked up with tears, they departed to the forest just without saying anything. (17)

KING.—How did they depart to the forest without saying a word at all ? (*Doubly faints*).

SUMANTRA.—(*In haste.*) Baláki, say to the ministers—the king is in an irremediable condition.

CHAMB.—So I will. (*Exit*).

THE QUEENS.—Great king, cheer up, cheer up.

KING.—(*Recovering a little*).

Touch my body, O Kausalyá ; I do not see you, with my eye. My mind, gone to Ráma, does not return even yet. (18).

Son Ráma, what I always revolved in my mind, (*viz.*)

Having installed you on the throne and made the subjects happy by their acquisition of a good king, and also having asked you always to raise your brothers to a status equal to yours, I should retire to a penance-grove from here—all that has been, in a moment, entirely undone by this Kaikeyî. (19).

Sumantra, tell Kaikeyî—

Ráma is gone ; may you gain your desired object ! I too am abandoned by my life : let your son be brought (here) quickly, that your sin (evil desire) may have its fruit. (20).

SUMANTRA.—As the great king commands.

KING—(*Looking upwards*) Ah ! the spirits of my ancestors have come to comfort me whose heart is burnt by the hearing of Ráma's account. Who is here ?

CHAMB.—(*Entering*) Victory to the great king !

KING—Just bring me water.

CHAMB.—As the great king commands. (*Going out and entering.*) Victory to the great king ! Here is water.

KING—(*Performing A'chamana and looking.*)

Here is Dilîpa, the friend of the lord of the gods ; this is Raghu, and this is the revered Aja, my father. What is the reason of your coming (here); this is the time for me also to dwell with you there (in heaven). (21)

Ráma, Vaidehî, Lakshmaṇa, I go from here to be by the side of my departed fathers. My forefathers, here I come. (*Is overpowered by swoon*).

(*The* CHAMBERLAIN *spreads over him a shroud.*)

ALL—Alas ! alas ! the great king !

(*Exeunt omnes*).

END OF ACT II.

ACT III.

(Then *enter* SUDHA'KA'RA).

SUDHA'.—(*Having done cleaning of the ground and other things*). Well ; I have done the work to be done here as ordered by the noble Sambhavaka. I will just sleep for a while. (*Sleeps.*)

(*Entering*)

BHATA.—(*Approaching* CHETA *and beating him*). Ah, thou whore's son ! Why dost thou not do thine duty ? (*Beats him*).

SUDHA'.—(*Waking up*) Beat me ; do beat me.

BHATA—When beaten, what wilst thou do ?

SUDHA.—Unfortunate that I am, I have not got a thousand arms like Kártavírya.

BHATA.—What is to be done with a thousand arms ?

SUDHA'.—I will kill you.

BHATA—Come, thou son of a slave. I will let thee off when dead. (*Beats him again*).

SUDHA'—(*Having cried.*) Is it possible now, master, to know my fault ?

BHATA—No fault, no fault surely on thy part ! Why ! Wast thou not told by me that all the ladies of the harem, headed by Kausalyâ, would come here to-day to see the statue-house of king Daśaratha, gone to heaven owing to the affliction caused by prince Ráma's loss of the kingdom? Now what hast thou done with regard to this ?

SUDHA .—May my master see. In the first place the inner shrine has been cleared of the nests of pigeons. The walls have the marks of the five fingers smeared with sandal paste impressed on their chunum-coating. The doors are charming with garlands of flowers suspended from them. And the sands have been scattered about. So, what have I not done in connection with this?

BHATA—If so, go in full confidence (fearlessly). In the meanwhile I, too, will tell the minister that all has been accomplished.

(*Exeunt Both*).

END OF PRAVES'AKA.

(*Then enter* BHARATA *in a chariot with the* CHARIOTEER.)

BHARATA—(*With agony*) Charioteer, owing to my long stay with my maternal uncle I am ignorant of the affairs (at Ayodhyá). I heard that the great king was severely indisposed in body. Tell me then—

What is my father's malady ?

CHARIOTEER—Great mental torment, to be sure.

BHARATA—What do the physicians say to him. (about that) ?

CHARIOTEER—The physicians, indeed, have not the skill to treat that (malady).

BHARATA—Does he eat his food, or sleep ?

CHARIOTEER—He lies on the ground without food.

BHARATA—Can there be any hope (of his living) ?

CHARIOTEER—(It rests with) Destiny.

BHARATA.—My heart palpitates; drive the chariot. (1)

CHARIOTEER.—As the long-lived one commands. (*Drives on the chariot*).

BHARATA.—(*Marking the velocity of the chariot*). How great is the velocity of the chariot ! Here these

Trees seem to run, the spaces between them being shortened by the swift motion of the chariot ; like a river with its water curling up the ground seems to fall (enter) into the cavity of the rim (of the wheels); the spokes have ceased to appear distinctly ; the felly of the wheels stands still as it were through speed ; and the dust kicked up by the horses falls forward but does not follow (the chariot). (2).

CHARIOTEER —Long-lived one, on account of the glossy appearance (or freshness) of the trees, Ayodhyá must be in the vicinity.

BHARATA.—Oh ! how great the impatience of the mind which is eager to see my relatives ! For now,

My head is, as if, fallen at the feet of my father, and I am, as it were, raised up by the king melting with affection ; my brothers have quickly come up to me, and the mothers bathe me as it were with their tears (of joy); I am praised as it were by the servants for pleasing me with expressions like—He is like (his father), he has grown stout and is tall (or well developed by exercise); and I fancy Saumitri there laughing at (the mode of) my dress and my accent (*lit.* my language). (3-4).

CHARIOTEER.—(*To himself*) Oh, pity! That the prince, ignorant of the demise of the great king, will enter Ayodhyá, entertaining a hope which is to prove vain in the end. And no communication can be made by us although knowing (every thing). For,

His father's relinquishment of life; his mother's avarice for royalty, and the exile of his eldest brother—who will give utterance to these three disasters? (5).

(*Entering*)

BHATA.—Prosperity to the Prince!

BHARATA.—Good man, has S'atrugna come up (to receive me).

BHATA.—The prince, indeed, has come up; but the priests send word to your honour—

BHARATA.—What is it, what is it?

BHATA.—The period of the constellation Kṛttiká has (only) one Náḍiká left of it; the prince, therefore, should enter Ayodhyá as soon as Rohiṇí sets in.

BHARATA'.—Very well, I will do so; I have never transgressed the words of my preceptors. You may go.

BHATA.—As the prince commands. (*Exit*).

BHARATA.—Now in what region shall I rest myself? Well, I have seen. I will take rest for a short while in this temple, disclosed by the spaces between the trees. A double object will be gained by this—worship to the deities and rest. Moreover, it is the practice of the good that cities should be entered after sitting on the outskirts. Let the chariot, therefore, be stopped.

CHA.—As the long-lived one commands. (*Stops the chariot*).

BHARATA.—(*Alighting from the chariot*) Charioteer, let the horses rest in a secluded place.

CHARIOTEER.—As the long-lived one commands. (*Exit*).

BHARATA.—(*Going forth a little and seeing.*) Here are offerings, as shown by the flowers and fried grain, well arranged. The walls have marks of five fingers with sandal-paste impressed on them. The doors appear beautiful with the garlands hanging from them. And the sands have been scattered. Is this a special decoration belonging to a *parvan* or a daily performance? To what deity can this place belong? No external sign (of a deity) is seen here, such as a weapon or a flag. Well, I shall know it on entering it. (*Entering in and looking.*) Oh, the attractiveness of the workmanship of (exhibited on) the stones. How wonderful the life-likeness (lit., the expression of inward feelings on the faces) of the images! These statues, though meant to be of deites, convey the conviction that they are human. Can it be that this is a group of four deities? Or let them be whatever they are. There is certainly an ecstasy of joy in my mind (on seeing them).

I allow that it is proper to bend the head just thinking these to be (the statues of) deities; but my salutation will be in the manner of a Vṛshala (Sûdra) wherein a deity is worshipped without (the accompaniment of) *matras*. (6)

(*Entering the* KEEPER *of the temple*).

Oh, while I was taking my food (*lit.* attending to the function of living beings) after having finished my daily duties, who can, indeed, this be, possessing a form almost resembling (*lit.* differing very little from) the statues, that has entered the statue-house? (*Enters.*)

BHARATA—I offer my bow to you.

THE TEMPLE KEEPER—Do not, do not make the bow.

BHARATA—Let not this be, oh!

Is there any thing to be found fault with in us? Or is some one superior (to us) being awaited? To what is this prohibition due?

Is it your power to enforce certain rules (to be observed here)?

THE TEMPLE-KEEPER—It is not for these reasons that I forbid your honour. But I prevent a man of the Bráhmaṇa class from saluting these, mistaking them for deities. For, these honoured ones are Kshatriyas.

BHARATA—Is it so? These are Kshatriya personages. Now who can their honours be?

THE TEMPLE-KEEPER—They are Ikshvâkus.

BHARATA—(*With joy*) You say 'Ikshvákus.' These are those (famous) rulers of Ayodhyâ.

These are those (kings) who march with the gods when they have to destroy the city of the demons; these are (the kings) who go to Indra's world with their subjects by virtue of their good deeds; these are the kings who brought under their sway the whole earth conquered by the prowess of their arms; these are the kings that were long spared (lit. not destroyed) by Death that had to seek their pleasure. (8).

Oh by chance, indeed, did I come across this great object.

Tell me then who (pointing to the first statue) this honoured king is.

THE TEMPLE-KEEPER—This, indeed, is Dilîpa, the first performer of the Vis'vajit sacrifice requiring the best things (or wealth) of all kinds to be collected for it, who kept burning the lamp of righteousness.

BHARATA—My bow to him ever devoted to Dharma (the observation of religious law). Tell who this honoured one is.

TEMPLE-KEEPER—This is, very surely, Raghu, who, when sleeping and being roused from sleep, had the expressions—An auspicious day to you, well betide (long life to) you-addressed to him by several thousands of Bráhmaṇas.

BHARATA—Ah! How powerful is Death that overstepped this protection! My salutation be to him, the fruits of whose sovereignty were enjoyed (*lit.* known) by the Bráhmaṇas. Tell me now-who is this revered king?

TEMP.-KEEPER--This is, indeed, king Aja, who cast off the responsibility of government through grief caused by the loss of his wife, and who had the effects of the quality of foulness washed off from him by his constant ablutions at the conclusion of sacrifices.

BHARATA--My homage to him whose penitence was laudable. (*Looking at the statue of* DAS'ARATHA *and being perturbed*). Oh, I did not comprehend very clearly (what you said) owing to my mind being wholly taken up by the high respect (I felt for these). Now tell me—Who is this personage?

TEM.-KEEPER.—This is Dilîpa.

BHARATA.—The great-grand-father of the great king. The next one?

TEMP.-KEEPER.—His honour, Raghu.

BHARATA.—The grand-father of the great king. And this one?

TEM.-KEEPER.—His honour, Aja.

BHARATA.—The father of my father. What, what did you say?

TEMP.-KEEPER.—This is Dilîpa; this is Raghu and this Aja

BHARATA.—I ask you something. Are the statues of living men set up?

TEM.-KEEPER.—Not at all; only of those that have passed away

BHARATA.—Then I take leave of you.

TEMP.-KEEPER.—Stay.

Why do you not inquire about this statue of Daśaratha, by whom his life and kingdom were given up in satisfaction of the promised gift to his wife at marriage. (9).

BHARATA.—Alas, my father! (*Falls down in a swoon; but coming to consciousness again*)

Heart, be you satisfied now; hear of that death of my father of which you had fears; but take courage. If this base talk about (the demand of) the promised marriage-gift has reference to me, and again it proves true (in the eyes of the people) then (in that case) my body will have to be purified (proved innocent) by an ordeal. (10).

Noble sir,

TEMP.-KEEPER.—'Noble sir' is indeed the way of addressing strangers peculiar to the Ikshváku race. May it be, I ask, that you are Bharata, the son of Kaikeyî!

BHARATA.—Yes, yes. I am the son of Dasaratha, not of Kaikeyî.

TEMP.-KEEPER.—If so, I take leave of you.

BHARATA.—Stay; tell me the remaining part of the story.

TEMP.-KEEPER.—What help! Listen. His Honour Daśaratha is dead. But I do not know the reason of Râma's departure to the forest, together with Sîta and Lakshmaṇa.

BHARATA—How, how is it that my noble brother has gone to the forest;

(*Doubly faints*).

TEMP. KEEPER—Be composed, be composed, prince.

BHARATA—(*Recovering.*)

I am hastening to reach Ayodhya' reduced to a forest, being deserted by my father and brother, like a man oppressed by thirst running after a river with its water dried up. (11)

Noble one, hearing a detailed account will give consolation (*lit.* firmness) to my mind. So tell me the whole, leaving out nothing.

TEMP.-KEEPER—Listen. When prince Râma was being installed on the throne by the revered king, your mother is reported to have said—

BHARATA—Enough.

Having remembered that evil (or condemnable) promise of the marriage-gift she must have said—'Let my son be the king'; encouraged by the confidence produced by that (her demand being granted), she must have said to my revered brother—" Son, go to the forest'; seeing him clad in barks the king must have surely met an unworthy death; and verily merited expressions of reproach are being cast on me by the subjects similar to, and after what have remained of, those (cast on my mother). (12)

(*Falls in a swoon.*)

(*Behind the curtains.*)

Move away, gentlemen, move away.

TEMP.-KEEPER—(*Looking on.*)

The queens, indeed, have come in time when their son has fallen into a swoon; for the touch of the hand of mothers is the very (just like the) handful of water to one in want of water. (13)

पृ. ४३ (*Then enter the* QUEENS *and* SUMANTRA).

SUMANTRA—This way, this way, your ladyships.

This is that house of our king now existing as a statue, possessing height scarcely to be found in a mansion; it is visited without a salutation by travellers unrestrained and entering without being announced by door-keepers. (14)

(*Entering and seeing.*) Madams, you should not, indeed, enter, you should not.

Here has fallen (on the ground) some one resembling the king when in his youth;

TEMP.-KEEPER.—

Enough of your taking him for a stranger; lift him up; for he is Bharata. (15)

(*Exit*).

THE QEENS.—(*Advaning in haste.*) Ah, child Bharata!

BHARATA.—(*Recovering a little*) Noble one,

SUMANTRA.—Victory to the great—(*with this half-uttered, sorrow-fully.*) Oh the resemblance of voice; I thought it was the great king in the image that was speaking.

BHARATA.—Now what is the condition of my mothers?

THE QUEENS.—This is our condition. (*They remove their veils*).

SUMANTRA.—Madams, check your sorrow.

BHARATA.—(*Looking at* SUMANTRA,) Your presence (with the queens) in full observance of decorum suggests to me—

Revered one, "I hope your honour is Sumantra", are you not?

SUMANTRA.—Prince, yes; I am Sumantra.

Pursued by the evils of long life, mocked by ingrati- पृ. ४४
tude, I certainly live, the driver of a vacant chariot,
although the king is dead. (16)

BHARATA.—Alas, father! (*Rising.*) Father, I wish to be advised as regards the order of bowing to my mothers.

SUMANTRA.—Excellent. This is queen Kausalyá, the mother of prince Ráma.

BHARATA.—Mother, I, who am innocent, bow to you.

KAUSALYA'.—Child, be free from mental afflicton.

BHARATA.—I am taunted as it were by this. (*Loudly.*) I am beholden to you. Now next?

SUMANTRA.—This is the mother of his Honour Lakshmaṇa, queen Sumitrâ.

BHARATA.—Mother, I who was deceived by Lakshmaṇa, salute you.

SUMITRA'.—Son, may you obtain renown.

BHARATA.—Mother, I will try to win it. I am obliged. Now next?

SUMANTRA—This is your mother.

BHARATA—(*Rising up in anger.*) Ah, wicked woman!

You do not appear well standing between my mother (Kausalyá) and mother (Sumitrá), like a polluted river let in between the Ganges and the Yamuná. (17)

KAIKEYI'—My son, what have I done?

BHARATA—You say—what have I done?

Why, you have joined (with each other the following)— पृ. ४५
me with infamy, noble brother with bark-garments,
the king with death in the house, the whole of Ayodhyá
with continued weepings, Lakshmana with the deer,
the mothers, who loved their sons, with sorrow, your
daughter-in-law with the fatigue of journey, and yourself
with the fierce condemnation 'Oh fie.' (18)

KAUSALYA'—Son, why do you, who observe all the rules of propriety, not salute your mother?

BHARATA—To my mother, you say. Mother, you alone are my mother. I salute you.

KAUS.—No no, not that. Here is your natural mother.

BHARATA—She *was* before; she is *not* now. Your ladyship should just see.—

When a woman gives up affection (for her sons) owing to the evil effects produced by (her wicked) disposition, sons themselves are surely made strangers (*lit.* not sons); I will establish this binding rule, first of its kind in the world—that a mother on account of her hatred (causing the death) of her husband should be treated as no mother. (19)

KAIKEYI'—Son, I said that way to make the great king keep his truthful promise.

BHARATA—What, what did you say?

KAIKEYI—That my son should be the king.

BHARATA—Well; now what was that noble brother of mine to you?

पृ. Was he not a legitimate son of my father? Was he not
४६ being crowned in the due order of succession? Would
he not have loved his brothers (or, would the brothers
not have been loving towards one another)? Was he not
liked by the subjects? (20)

KAIKEYÎ.—Son, is a woman drawn away by the promise of the marriage-gift to be questioned (like this)?

BHARATA.—

Deprived of royalty, Ráma was ordered by you to go to the forest with his wife, clad in bark garments and walking on foot; was this also promised as part of the bridal gift? (21)

KAIKEYÎ.—Son, I will tell you this at the proper place and time.

BHARATA.—

If you had an eager desire for infamy, where was the use of mentioning my name? Was it a craving for enjoying the fruits (benefits) of royalty? Then would not the king have allowed you these? If again the title

'The mother of a king' was coveted by you, then, madam, tell the truth—was not my noble brother your son? (22)

A woeful deed was done by your ladyship.

By you longing after a kingdom the king was not at all reckoned as regards his life. You sent into exile your eldest son bidding him go to the forest; and that your heart which was not shattered on beholding Janaka's daughter clad in bark-garments, was alas, O lady, created as hard as adamant by the Creator (23).

SUMANTRA.—Prince, these two, Vasishtha and Vámadeva, who have come accompanied by the subjects, (or, ministers) to meet you, with reference to your coronation, respectfully say to you—

As cows without a cowherd meet with destruction being unprotected, so subjects having no king meet with ruin. (24)

BHARATA.—Let the subjects follow me.

SUMANTRA.—Leaving off the coronation? (Then) where will your honour go?

BHARATA.—Coronation you say? Let her ladyship here have it.

SUMANTRA.—Where does your honour mean to go to?

BHARATA.—

Thither will I go where lives he to whom Lakshmaṇa is dear; without him Ayodhyá is no Ayodhyá; that is Ayodhyá wherein dwells Rághava. (25)

(*Exeunt omnes*)

END OF ACT III.

ACT IV.

(*Enter two* Maids)

VIJAYA'.—Friend Nandiniká, tell me, pray, tell me. When to-day all the inmates of the inner apartment went to see the statue-house, headed by Kausalya, it is said they saw prince Bharata there. I, unfortunate that I was, had to watch at the door.

Nandinika'.—Friend, we saw prince Bharata, our curiosity being roused.

Vijaya'.—What did the prince say to our mistress (Kaikeyî)?

Nandi.—'What did he say?' He did not even wish to look at her.

Vijaya'.—Oh the great misfortune! Covetous of royalty and making Ráma lose the kingdom, she brought about her own widowhood and led the people into ruin. Cruel, indeed, is our mistress. A wicked deed was done.

Nandi.—Friend listen. Having sent back the materials of coronation brought by the citizens, the prince has gone to the penance-forest of Râma.

Vîjaya'.—(*With sorrow*): Ah! The prince has thus gone. Nandinikà, come; let us see our mistress.

(*Exeunt*)

पृ. ४९ End of Praves'aka.

(*Then enter* Bharata *in a chariot*, Sumantra *and the* Charioteer.)

Bharata—The lord of men (Daśaratha) having gone to heaven, accompanied by his religious merit, I, followed by the tear-waters of the citizens, am going to see, in the generous penance-forests, the second moon of the world bearing the name of Râma. (1)

Sumantra—This, this Bharata of long life, the son of the king who completely humbled (*lit.* crushed) the pride of the lords of demons, the grandson of the king (Aja) who spent his wealth in the performance of sacrifices, and the brother of Ráma who did what was dear to his father and who is the darling of the world, is going by a path similar to that of (followed by) Ráma. (2)

Bharata—O father.

Sumantra—Prince, here I am.

Bharata—Where is his honour, my noble brother, Ráma? Where is that representative of the great king? Where is that excellent model of those possessed of strength; where is that administerer of rebuke to

Kaikeyî) greedy of a kingdom? Where is that receptacle of fame? Where is that (worthy) son of the king? Where is he devoted to the vow of truth?

I wish to see him, the highest deity to me, who पृ. ५० renounced sovereignty in order to do what was dear to my mother. (3)

SUMANTRA—Prince, in this region of the hermitage.

Here (live) Ráma, Sîta and Lakshmana, of great fame, in whom dwell in a bodily form truthfulness, character and devotion (respectively). (4).

BHARATA—If so, stop the chariot.

CHARIOTEER—As the long-lived one commands. (*Does accordingly*).

BHARATA—(*Alighting from the chariot*) Charioteer, make the horses take rest in a secluded place.

CHARIOTEER—As the long-lived one commands. (*Exit*).

BHARATA—O father, let it be announced, let it be announced.

SUMANTRA—Prince, what is to be announced!

BHARATA—That Bharata, the son of Kaikeyi, hungry after a kingdom, has come.

SUMANTRA—Prince, enough of mentioning the blame attaching to an elderly person.

BHARATA—Well said, it is not proper to speak of another's fault. Then say—Bharata, who is a stain on the Ikshâku race, desires an interview.

SUMANTRA—Prince, I am not able to speak in this way. But again I will say—Bharata has come.

BHARATA—No, no. The mere name mentioned appears to me to be one that has undergone no penitence. What? Are Brâhmana-slayers announced by another? So father should desist. I myself will make the announcement. O you, let it be announced to Rághava, who carried out the behest of his father,

That some one who is cruel, ungrateful, an ordinary man, and a lover of adventure, but full of devotion, has come (to see you). How should he act; should he wait or depart? (5)

पृ. ५१ (*Then enter* R'AMA *with* SÎTA *and* LAKSHMANA).

RAMA—(*Hearing with joy*) Lakshmaṇa, do you hear? O daughter of the king of Videha, do you also hear?

Whose voice is that very closely resembling that of my father, which seems to drown the rumbling of clouds on account of its depth; and which, creating a suspicion in my heart about his being a kinsman and full of affection, has agreeably fallen on my ears? (6)

LAKSHMANA—Noble brother, this consonance of sound begets in me also the high respect due to a relative. For this (voice), deep, clear, grave, melodious and attractive like that of a bull in the flush of youth, sweet in the throat and with the force of its passage unobstructed in the breast, its various syllables being uttered with a distinct vocal effort and having come in contact with their proper organs, seems to be endeavouring to vouchsafe protection to the four castes. (7)

RAMA—By no means it can be the voice of one who is not a relative; it wets my heart, as it were, with affection. Dear Lakshmaṇa, see what it is.

LAKSHMAṆA—As my noble brother orders. (*Walks forth*).

BHARATA—Oh, how is it that no one gives a reply to me? Can it be that I am known—that Bharata, the son of Kaikeyî has come?

पृ. ५२ LAKSHMAṆA—(*Looking*). Oh, this is the revered Ráma! No, no; it is the likeness of form.

His peerless face, charming like the moon, has the beauty of my elder brother's face; his stout chest resembles my father's, scarred with the arrows of the demons; surrounded by splendour, a treasure of lustre and of a sight pleasing to the world, is he a king, or Madhusûdana, the lord of gods, himself? (8)

(*Seeing* SUMANTRA.) Ah, here is father (Sumantra).

SUMANTRA—Ah, prince Lakshmaṇa!

BHARATA—He is thus my elder brother. Noble brother, I bow to you.

LAKSH.—Come, come; be of long life. (*Looking at* SUMANTRA) father, who is his Honour?

SUMANTRA—Prince,

He is fourth (in descent) from Raghu and third from Aja and the second (son) of your renowned father: this is prince Bharata, the younger brother of him, who is the honour of his family and whose younger brother you also are. (9)

LAKSH.—Come, come, prince of the Ikshvâku race; Dear brother, hail to you; be of long life.

May you be in this world the receptacle of brilliant qualities like that renowned king Raghu, whose treasure was exhausted in the performance of sacrifices and whose valour matched with that of the monarchs of his race, who were skilled in fighting with demons, whose bows vied with the thunderbolt (of Indra) and whose strength and prowess were incomparable. (10)

BHARATA—I am thankful to you.

LAKSH.—Prince, wait here. I will inform my elder brother of your coming.

BHARATA—Noble brother, I am impatient to bow to him; inform him quickly then.

LAKSHM.—Very well. (*Approaching*) Victory to my elder brother! Noble brother,

Here is your beloved brother, Bharata, affectionate towards his brother (*i.e.*, you) in whom stands reflected your form as in a mirror. (11)

RA'MA—Dear Lakshmaṇa, has Bharata thus come (then)?

LAKSHM.—Noble brother, just so.

RA'MA—Maithili, dilate your eyes to see Bharata.

SÎTA'—Husband, has Bharata come?

RA'MA—Maithili, he has.

To-day, indeed, I shall know the hard lot suffered by my father-of what sort is a father's affection (for his son): as for a brother's affection, it is of this nature. (12)

LAKSHM.—Noble brother, should the prince enter ?

RA'MA—Dear Lakshmaṇa, do you wish to make even this depend on your intention ? Go quickly ; lead in the prince with due honour shown.

LAKSHM.—As my noble brother commands.

RA'MA—Or, you wait here.

Let this (Sîtá) herself go to honour him, entertaining the same feeling towards him as a mother has for her son, dropping tears of joy like a shower, with her eyes like the petals of a lotus full of dew-drops. (13)

पृ. ५४ SÎTA —As my husband commands.

(*Rising up, walking forth and seeing* Bharata) How being there at that time has my husband come out here now ? Oh no, no. It is the resemblance of form.

SUMANTRA.—Oh, our daughter-in-law !

BHARATA—Ah, this is her ladyship, the daughter of king Janaka.

This is that lustre in a woman's form sprung from the interior of a field struck up by a plough, a worthy proof (*lit.* indicator) of the penance of Janaka, the lord of kings. (14)

Revered lady, I bow to you. I am Bharata.

SÎTA—(*To herself.*) (Not only his form but also the tone of voice is the same (as that of Râma). (*Aloud*) Child, live long.

BHARATA—I am blessed.

SÎTA—Come, child. Gratify the wish of your brother.

SUMANTRA—The prince should enter.

BHARATA—I am blessed.

BHARATA—What will father do now ?

I will enter aftewards ; after the king's departure to heaven this is my first time to see Ráma ; so it should be after Ráma has known the fact. (15)

BHARATA—Let it be so. (*Approaching* RA'MA). Noble brother, I salute you. I am Bharata.

RA'MA—(*With joy*). Come, come, prince of the Ikshváku line. Hail to you ! May you have long life !

Stretch out your chest of the measure of the closed panels of a door ; clasp me with your very extensive arms. Raise your face resembling the moon of autumn. Gladden this my body burnt by calamities. (16) पृ. ५५

BHARATA—I am beholden to you.

SUMANTRA—(*Approaching*) May the long-lived one prosper !

RA'ma—Alas, father !

He, who formerly at the time of an advance (against the enemies) having gone to heaven with his forces borne in aerial vehicles like those of the goods, was often pointed out with the words, there is he, there is he,' in the close fight between the demons and the gods—is that illustrious king, leaving his body without you although loved by him, and affectionate towards him, now abiding in heaven revelling himself in the company of the kings, his own forefathers (or of the kings of his race now existing as Pitris) ! (17)

SUMANTRA—(*Sorrowfully.*)

The king's death, your exile, Bharata's sorrow, and the helpless condition of the family—having thus experiened unbearable (miseries) of more than one kind, my (long) life has, as it were, been guilty in what is an advantage to it. (18)

SI'TA'—Father is making my weeping husband weep again.

RA'MA—Maithili, here I compose myself. Dear Lakshmaṇa, just bring me water.

LAKSHM,—As my noble brother commands.

BHARATA—Noble brother, this is not at all just. I पृ. ५६
will serve you according to the order (of birth). I shall myself go. (*Taking a pot, going out and entering again.*) Here is water.

RA'MA—(*Having performed Âchamana*) Maithili, Lakshmaṇa's business is, indeed, obstructed.

SI'TA—Husband, why ? You are to be served by this (Bharata) also.

RA'MA—It is surely proper that Lakshmaṇa should serve me here; let Bharata, staying there (in Ayodhyá) serve me.

BHARATA—May my noble brother be pleased (to allow this).

Here I will stay in body; there by my work (of administration), The kingdom will be protected (administered) in your name alone.

RA'MA—Dear child, son of Kaikeyi, say not so, say not so.

I came to the forest at the bidding of my father, and not, dear brother, through pride, or fear or through delusion. And our family, I tell you, regards truth as its treasure; how do you take to the path followed by the low? (20)

SUMANTRA—Now where should the water for the coronation lie?

RA'MA—Let it be just there where my mother said it should.

BHARATA.—Be pleased, my noble brother. Noble brother, you should not strike at the wound now.

पृ. O you possessed of excellent virtues, is not your race
५७ my race also? And surely that eminently talented (king) is your father and my father as well. Good man, the fault of a mother does not attach itself to men; O granter of a boon, do look at Bharata who is distressed in the proper light. (21)

SI'TA—Husband, Bharata is speaking very piteously. What is my husband thinking about now?

RAMA.—Maithili,

I am thinking of that king, gone to heaven, by whom this excellent quality (trait of character) of his son (Bharata) was not seen. Oh fie, if fate asserts its power over men when they have got in this world (a son who is) a treasure of virtues of this sort. (22).

Child, son of Kaikeyî,

Truly I am pleased with you; you have a guiltless mind; I am ready to act up to your words, being subdued by your well known (or, praiseworthy) virtues: but here is the king's behest and it does not behove you to make it vain; moreover, having generated a son of your type should your father be the utterer of a falsehood? (23)

Bharata—Until the condition imposed upon you (or your vow) comes to an end—king, at your feet till then I will abide here, O Ráma—

Act not so; let the king attain his goal (in heaven) by his own good deeds. I conjure you with my life if you will not protect your kingdom. (24)

Bharata—Alas, you have spoken in a way which precludes (leaves no room for) a reply; well, I will protect your kingdom on a condition.

Ra'ma—Child, what is that condition?

Bharata—I desire you to take back your kingdom, deposited in my hands, at the end of fourteen years.

Ra'ma—Let it be so.

Bharata—Noble brother (Lakshmana), have you heard this; revered Sítá, have you heard this; father, have you heard this?

All—We all have heard it.

Bharata—Noble brother, I wish to seek another boon also.

Ra'ma—Dear one, what is it that you wish for; what shall I give you; what shall I do for you?

Bharata—

Give these two sandals used for your feet to me, who पृ. ५९
have bowed to you with my head. I will act in obedience to these until you achieve your object. (26)

Ra'ma—(*To himself*) Bless me, oh!

I obtained slight fame after a long time, while Bharata has earned that (eminently) to-day just in a short time. (27)

Síta'—Husband, I hope Bharata's first wish will be granted to him.

Ra'ma—Be it so. Dear boy, take these. (*He gives the sandals*).

BHARATA—I am obliged to you. (*Takes them.*) Noble brother, I wish to have the coronation-water poured on these.

RA'MA—Father, do all that is desired by Bharata.

SUMANTRA—As the long-lived one commands.

BHARATA—(*To himself*) What joy, oh !

I have become one worthy of the confidence of my relatives ; liked by the citizens ; fit to be looked at by the people ; a beloved son of the king living in heaven, being (proved to be) endowed with (noble) character ; highly esteemed by my brothers, conspicuous by their merits ; a mighty abode of renown ; the subject of talk in the conversations of the meritorious and dear to those who have gained their wishes. (27)

पृ. ६० RA'MA—Child, son of Kaikeyî, a kingdom, as you know well, ought not to be neglected even for a short time. Therefore, the prince should return this very day for a prosperous career.

SÎTA'—Ah, will the prince go just to-day ?

RA'MA—Enough of excessive affection. Let the prince &c.

BHARATA—Noble brother, I will go just to-day.

Full of hope, the citizens must have been waiting in the city with a desire to see you. To them I shall bring joy by showing them this your favour (the sandals). (18)

SUMANTRA—Long-lived one, what shall I do now?

RA'MA—Father, protect in every way the prince, as you did the king.

SUMANTRA—If I live I shall endeavour (to do it).

RAM'A—Dear son of Kaikeyî, ascend the chariot in my presence.

Bharata—Just as my noble brother tells me. (*The two ascend the chariot*).

RA'MA—Maithili, just come here. Dear Lakshmane just here. We shall follow Bharata just as far as the door of the hemitage.

(*Execent omnes*).

END OF ACT IV.

ACT V.

(*Then enter* Sîta' *and a* female Ascetic). पृ. ६१

Sîta'—Revered lady, I have swept clean the hermitage scattered over with the (stale) flowers of worship. And the usual worship of the deities (also) has been performed with the materials available in the hermitage; so now, as long as my husband does not come, I will favour these young trees by supplying water to them.

Fem. Asce.—May there be no obstacle (in your way).

(*Then enter* Ra'ma).

Ra'ma—(*Sorrowfully.*)

Leaving that delightful city of Ayodhya', bereft of father and myself and making full preparations for my coronation, Bharata came to me; but that repository of virtues was sent back to the very place for the purpose of protection. Oh pity! Alone he bears the very heavy yoke of the king. (1)

(*Musing.*) Such is this course of things! I will then just see Maithilî, my companion in all the states of life, for beguiling sorrow of this kind. But where, indeed, has the princess of Videha gone? (*Walking on and seeing*). Ah! these fresh-watered roots of trees, do indeed, indicate that Maithilî has not gone far away.

For,

The water lying in the basins of trees is whirling about with foam on it. These birds that have darted down being thirsty do not (yet) drink the water as it is turbid (or are drinking the water without difficulty); the insects, wet owing to their holes being filled with water are getting on elevated places (or, dry land); and the trees have fresh circles (of mud) at their roots on account of the line of water being dried up. (2). पृ. ६२

(*Looking on*) Ah! Here is Maithilî. Oh, alas!

That hand of her, which used to be fatigued even by the holding of a mirror, does not (now) feel exhausted as she is carrying a jar of water; alas! a forest (forest-life) hardens a woman's delicacy along with (as it does) creepers. (3).

(*Approaching.*) Maithilî, are your religious observances going on well?

SÎTA'—Oh, my husband! Prosperity to my husband!

RA'MA—Maithelî, if there will be no obstacle in your devotional work, sit down.

SÎTA'—As my husband comamands. (*Sits down*).

RA'MA—Maithilî, I see you as if eager to have a reply to a question (from me). What may this be?

SÎTA'—The expression of my husband's face is like that of one vacant-minded through sorrow. What is this?

RA'MA.—Maithilî, rightly, indeed, have you evinced your anxiety (or, have I been anxious).

My body being struck by the arrow-head of Death, the wound of my heart is just as (green as) before; and the strokes of the arrows of sorrow having various points fall on the same place over and over again. (4).

SÎTA'—What is the nature of my husband's anxiety?

RA'MA—To-morrow must be performed the annual *S'raddha* of my revered father. And the manes desire that the offering of oblations to them should be done in a special style. How am I to perform that?—this is what I have been thinking of. Or rather,

They will be satisfied with what-so-ever things I shall offer to them. For they themselves know my present state. Still I wish to worship (perform the ceremony) in a style befitting father and Ráma. (5)

SÎTA'—Husband, Bharata will perform the Śráddha in a rich style; my husband should perform it offering fruits, water &c. as suited to his condition.

RA'MA—Maithili,

Seeing the fruits arranged on the *Kusa'* grass with my own hands, father, being reminded of my residence in a forest, will weep even there. (6)

(*Then enter* RA'VANA *in the disguise of a wandering ascetic*).

RA'VANA—Oh, here

have I, with soul uncontrolled, started, having assumed this disguise, with the object of carrying off the daughter of king Janaka, like the stream of an oblation offered (to fire) without the utterance of proper accent and syllables, after having deceived the self-controlled Ráma who has roused my enmity by his slaying of Khara. (7)

(*Walking forth and looking about*). पृ. ६४

Here is the entrance to Ráma's hermitage. I will just alight. (*Alights*). Now I will adopt the course proper for a guest. I am a guest. Who is here, ho?

RA'MA—(*Hearing.*) Welcome to the guest.

RA'VANA—My form (disguise), indeed, is well sustained by my voice.

RA'MA—(*Seeing*) Ah, his reverence! Revered sir, I bow to you.

RA'VANA—My blessing to you.

RA'MA—Holy Sir, here is a seat; do sit down.

RA'VANA—(*To himself*) How now, I am as if ordered by him? (*Aloud*) Very well. (*Sits down*).

RA'MA—Maithili, bring water for his revernce to wash his feet with.

SÍTA'—As my husband commands. (*Going out and coming back*). Here is water.

RA'MA—Wait upon his reverence with it.

SÍTA'—As my husband commands.

RA'VANA—(*Getting agitated at the thought of his disguise being exposed*) Hold, hold.

For, she alone is, on earth, Arundhatí among females, of whom you are mentioned with (due) honour as the husband. (8)

RA'MA—Then bring (the water). I myself will serve him.

RA'VAṆA—O, having avoided the shadow I will not violate (defile) the body. Waiting upon with sweet-words, indeed, constitutes a guest's reception. I am honoured. Please sit down.

पृ. ६५ RA'MA—Very well. (*Sits down.*)

RA'VAṆA—(*To himself.*) Now in the first place I, too, will follow the usual practice of a Brâhmaṇa. (*Aloud*) Oh, I belong to the Kâśyapa race. I have studied the Veda with all its accessory and sub-accessory works, as also the religious code of law of Manu, the Yoga philosophy of Maheśwara, the political scienee by Bṛhaspati, the logic of Medhátithi, and the ritual of the Śráddha by Prachetas.

RA'MA—What? What? Did you say 'The ritual of the Śraddha'?

RA'VAṆA—You have evinced a desire to know about the Śraddha-ritual to the exclusion of the other sciences. How is this?

RA'MA—Venerable sir, since I have lost my father, this is the proper branch of knowledge for me to know now.

RA'VAṆA—Enough of avoiding it (hesitation). You may freely ask (about it).

RA'MA—Venerable one, at the time of presenting oblations (at a Śráddha) with what (materials) should I gratify the manes?

RA'VANA—Anything offered in faith constitues a Śráddha.

RA'MA—Holy sir, if offered without regard (to the things liked) it is rejected. So I ask to know the particular things to be offered.

RA'VAṆA—Hear then. Of things that grow, the Kuśa grass; of herb-productions, sesamum; of vegetables, the *Kalaya*; of fishes the large Śaphara; of birds, Vàdhráṇasa; and of beasts, a cow or a rhinocerous:—these are prescribed in the case of human beings.

request (द्वितीयमपि वरं p. 58). अत्र—Scil. on the pádukás; आवर्जयितुं—supply त्वया. See com.

हन्त भो —Bharata is inwardly satisfied at the manifold objects achieved by him. These he states in the next śl.

Śl. 27. अद्वेय:—Because he acted up to his words in refusing royalty to the very last. दृष्टिक्षमः—For people will no longer look at him with abhorrence, he having done the right thing

P. 60. गुणवतां:—Construe this with संवादेषु. Meritorious men only, who are free from jealousy, will appreciate merits and make mention of him in their conversations. लब्धप्रियाणां.—Here the प्रिय may be taken to refer to Ráma's gaining the throne, which was so much desired by the people. *Cf.* I. 4 Prof. Paránjpe notices the reading लब्धः प्रियाणां &c

विजयाय—Here विजय has the sense of उत्कर्ष a prosperous course of life, successful administration.

Śl. 28. स्थास्यान्ति—स्थिता भवेयुः. प्रीतिं करिष्यामि.—The subjects will be glad to see the sandals, if not Ráma actually, as that would mean Ráma's acceptance of the kingdom after fourteen years at least.

महाराजवत्—may mean (1) as did the great king; or (2) as you protected the great king. तावत्—fully, to the best of my ability (साकल्येन). आरोहतः—*i. e.* Bharata and Sumantra, as there was a separate charioteer this time. ०मात्रं.—Here मात्र shows limit (प्रमाण); this occurs in the Mady. तत्र भवन्तं केशवदासमाश्रमपदद्वारमात्रमपि संभावयिष्यामः । अनुयात्रं.—An Avya-Comp.; see com.

ACT. V.

P. 61. उपहारसु०-may mean (1) the stale flowers offered to the deities; it is usual to remove the flowers offered to the house-hold deities the previous day and to throw them away; or (2) strewn over with flowery presentations. विभव—The wealth consisting of fruits, flowers &c. देवसमुदाचारः—Proper conduct towards the deities, *i. e.* worshipping them by offering fruits, flowers &c. *Cf.* अतिथिसमुदाचार further on p. 64, ब्राह्मणसमुदाचार p. 65. अनुकम्प्—Cau. to show one's sympathy for, hence to favour. अविघ्नं—See com. for comp.; this is an indication of Sîtâ's future abduction by Rávaṅa. Here the sense of the negative particle अ is अभाव 'the absence of'. The negative particle has six senses, *viz.*—तत्सादृश्यमभावश्च तदन्यत्वं तदल्पता । अप्राशस्त्यं विरोधश्च नञर्थाः षट् प्रकीर्तिताः ॥

S'l. 1. रम्यामयोध्यां &c.—For the description of Ayodhyà see Ràmá-Bàl. V. 6-23. It is thus succintly described in the Bhatti-Kávya—महेन्द्रलोकप्रतिमां समृद्धया । अध्यास्त सर्वर्तुसुखामयोध्या-मध्यासितां ब्रह्मभिरिद्धबोधैः ॥ निर्माणदक्षस्य समीहितेषु सीमेव पद्मासनकौशलस्य । उर्ध्वस्फुरद्रत्नगभास्तिभिर्या स्थिताबहस्येव पुरीं मघोनः ॥ सद्रत्नमुक्ताफलवज्रभाञ्जि विचित्रधातूनि सकाननानि । स्त्रीभिर्युतान्यप्सरसामिवोर्धैर्मेरोः शिरांसीव गृहाणि यस्याम् ॥ अन्तर्निविष्टोज्ज्वलरत्नभासो गवाक्षजालैरभिनिष्पतन्त्यः । हिमाद्रिटङ्कादिव भान्ति यस्यां गङ्गाम्बुपातप्रतिमा गृहेभ्यः ॥

धुरं सुमहतीं &c.—*Cf.* Śâk. V. अधिश्रमोयं लोकतन्त्राधिकारः । Sl. 4; also राज्ञां तु चरितार्थता दुःखोत्तरैव । and Sl. 6. And राज्यं हि नाम राजधर्मानुवृत्तिपरस्य नृपतेर्महदप्रीतिस्थानम् । कुतः । परार्थानुष्ठाने &c. S'l. 4. Mudrá. III. समुत्कर्षति—has been bearing. It is natural that this incident should be fresh in Ràma's memory even after a period of nearly thirteen years and that he should feel sympathy for a brother, who had shown such exceptional affection for him, and feel sorry for the very onerous task of government entrusted to him, unexperiencd as he was. See below, note on अनुसंवत्सरः श्राद्धविधिः.

ईदृशमेवे॰—He means-things must take their destined course. अवस्थाकुटुम्बिनी—wife (help-mate) in all conditions, good or bad; सर्वास्ववस्थासु सहायभूता; G. S. *Cf.* विभवानुगता भार्या Mrch. III. 28. But here it is used in the sense of 'a bad or adverse state'; *cf.* further on अवस्थानुरूपं p. 63. Note that the word कुटुम्ब has also the sense of 'a wife' in Maráthi प्रत्यग्र—प्रानिगतं or प्रतिनवमग्रमस्य that which has a fresh point or tip; hence new.

Sl. 2. आवर्तः—आवर्तनमावर्तः from आवृत् and अ (घञ्); what turns round and is, in the first instance, applied to the turning round of water, an eddy (स्यादावर्तोम्भसां भ्रमः Amara.); hence what encircles; here a basin. (आलवाल). नैते क्लिष्टं &c.—may be construed as-एते क्लिष्टं dirty, muddy जलं न पिबन्ति; for क्लिष्ट in the sense of मलिन comp. न क्लिष्टं हि शिरोपधानममलं &c. Svap. V. 4.; क्लिष्टेनोत्तमवाससा Râma. Sund. XV. 21. Or क्लिष्टं adv. क्लिष्टं क्लेशेन with difficulty यथा तथा न पिबन्ति *i.e.* drink without difficulty, being easily available. For birds drinking water in the basins of trees, *cf.* विश्वासाय विहंगानामालवालाम्बुपायिनाम् । Ragh. I. 51.

P. 62. स्थलं—dry land; or raised or elevated ground; *cf. infra* निम्नस्थलोत्पादकः कालः VII. p. 83. नववलयिनः—As the water in the basin sank down being dried up, a circle of soft earth was left round the root.

S'l. 3. कलशं वहन्त्याः—does not give the contrast directly; the sense is कलशवहनेन; so the poet should have better written कलशस्य वाहने corresponding with दर्पणे. कष्टम्.—may be taken separately (it is a pity or painful that); or as an adj. (full of hardships) to वनम्. अपि तपो वर्धते.—Here तपः simply means—duties to be performed in the hermitage. धर्मविघ्नः—*i e.* धर्मक्रियाविघ्नः. प्रतिवचनार्थिनी—This is Bhâsa's peculiar way of introducing a new topic. *Cf. supra* त्वं किमपि वक्तुकामेव p. 8. ०र्थिनी.—seeking or solicitous of a reply; and as a reply cannot be given unless a question is asked, this means 'you seem to be eager to ask me a question'. स्थाने खलु &c—The चिन्ता may be on the part of Sítá-(1) You are rightly anxious; or it may refer to Ráma; I am but properly anxious &c; but in this case we should expect क्रियते instead of कृता.

Śl. 4. कृतान्त—Ill luck. तथैव—as fresh as before; because of the constant fall of arrows. नानाफलाः—(1) Producing various results, affecting me in various ways—Here he refers to the various misfortunes that befell him one after another; *viz.* the loss of kingdom and his exile to the forest; Sítá's having had to leave the palace and live in a forest; his father's death; Bharata's being sent back to Ayodhyá against his wish; and his inability to perform his father's anniversary (S'rádhha) in a fitting way as he himself will declare in his next speech. (2) फल also means an arrow-head; having different heads *i. e.* paining me in various ways.

P. 63. क इव—of what sort or nature? अनुसंवत्सरः—Happening every year; see com.; विधिः—The performance of. The use of the word अनुसंवत्सर here indicates that this was not the first S'ràddha after Das'aratha's death. The reference here seems to be to the last सांवत्सरिक श्राद्ध that Ra'ma performed in the forest. For while Ráma and Sítá are thus sitting discussing the subject of the next day's Śráddha, Ra'vaṇa appears on the scene. And we know from the Padma Puràṇa, that Sítá's abduction by Rávaṇa took place in the thirteenth year after Ràma's exile into the forest—अथ त्रयोदशे वर्षे पञ्चवट्यां महामुने । रामो विरूपयामास शूर्पणखां निशाचरीम् । वने विचरतस्तस्य जानक्या सहितस्य च ।

आगतो राक्षसस्तां वै हर्तुं पापविपाकतः ॥ ततो माघासिताष्टम्यां मुहूर्ते वृन्द-संज्ञके । राघवाभ्यां विना सीतां जहार दशकन्धरः ॥ Pátála Khanda, ch. 36 (as quoted by Prof. Parânjpe).

श्वः—Tomorrow. Now the question is—Which day is meant? We have already shown that Das'aratha died on the 15th day of the bright half of Chaitra; and the annual S'ra'ddha should have fallen on that day. But according to the Pad. P. quoted above this would be the 9th of the dark half of Mágha, as Sîtá was carried away on the 8th. The commentator, Ráma, in his com. called Tilaka, however, says that Sîtá's abduction must have taken place on the 8th day of Phàlguna in the thirteenth year of his forest-life—तस्माद् द्वादशसमाप्त्युत्तरं त्रयोदशे किंचिद्व्यतीते फाल्गुनाष्टम्यां रावणकृतसीतापहारः । Yudh. Kan. ch. 108; see also com. on Aran. ch, 42. sl. 31. Whichever view be correct, Bhása departs from either in making Rávaṇa come as a guest on the day previous to the S'ráddha of Dasáratha. **कल्पविशेषेण**.—With special offerings, a special form of performance. **निवपनक्रिया**.—श्राद्धक्रिया. निवपन is an offering made to the departed ancestors; *cf*. को नः कुले निवपनानि नियच्छतीति S'ak. VI. 25, where Rághavabhatta translates निवपनानि by श्राद्धादीनि । **इत्येतच्चिन्त्यते**.—is a reply to Sîtà's question आर्यपुत्रस्य क इव सन्तापः

Śl. 5. **गच्छन्ति**—has the force of the potential, गच्छेयुः. **एव**-should be construed with जानन्ति, do know. **तां**—We expect एतां; but as it is, it means तां यस्यामहं वर्ते । **सानुरूपा**—रूपस्य योग्यं सदृशं वा अनुरूपं तस्य भावः (भावप्रधानो निर्देशः); अनुरूपेण सहिता सानुरूपा.

फलोदकेन—फलानि च उदकं च एतेषां समाहारः फलोदकं तेन.

Śl. 6 **फलानि दृष्ट्वा**—*Cf*. ऐङ्गुदं बदरैर्मिश्रं पिण्याकं दर्भसंस्तरे । न्यस्य रामः सु दुःखार्तो रुदन्वचनमब्रवीत ॥ इदं भुङ्क्ष्व महाराज प्रीतो यदशना वयम् । यदन्नः पुरुषो भवति तदन्नास्तस्य देवताः ॥ Rámá Ayod CIII. 29-30.

Śl. 7. **नियतमनिय०**—Here a contrast may have been intended between नियतं (self-controlled राम) and अनियतात्मा; but Rávaṇa is not likely to speak disparagingly of himself; we may better take नियतं to mean certainly and अनियतात्मा in the sense of whose mind could not be controlled, who could not forgive the insult offered to me.

खरवध०—Khara was Rāvaṇa's half-brother and the brother of S'ûrpanakhá, to whom she applied for the redress of the

ACT VI.

(*Then enter two old* Hermits.)

BOTH—Help, help; ye (that are here).

FIRST.—

Here is this Sîta, overpoweed and carried away by the lord of night-rangers (Râvana) like a doe by one stalking about at midnight (a tiger) having the complexion of a garland of blue lotuses and with the sheen of his jaws, white and bright like a lotus stalk. (1)

SECOND—Here, indeed, is her ladyship the princess of Videha,

Struggling like a female serpent, and tossed about like a creeper full of flowers, being forcibly carrried away from the penance forest, as though she were the fruition (of the penance of asectics) by the wicked Râvaṇa. (2)

BOTH—(So) save, save, your honours.

FIRST—(*Looking upwards.*) Quite simultaneously with our appeal, Jatâyu has flown up into the sky to discharge his debet of gratitude to Das'aratha, having challenged Rávaṇa with the words—Whither can you go while I am here.'

SECOND—Here has Rávana turned back, with his eyes rolling through wrath.

FIRST—This is Rávana—

SECOND—Here is Jatáyu (facing him).

BOTH—Oh ! A fight is begun in the sky.

FIRST—Kás'yapa, O Kás'yapa, behold the might of the lord of carrion-eaters (vultures).

Assailing (Rávana) with his wings he engaged him in a fierce (lit. valorous) duel ; remaining firm he is trying to seize him in his beak with hard and sharp scartches ; and now is the formidable expanse of his chest torn off with his claws sharp like iron nails, as is the rock of a mountain rugged on account of its being cleft with the points of the thunder bolt. (3)

SECOND—Alas, the lord of vultures is struck on the region of his right shoulder by the enraged Rávaṇa.

BOTH—Oh, fie ! the noble Jatâyu has fallen down.

FIRST—Oh, pity ! Here, indeed, has the noble Jatâyu,

Having made a supreme effort as befitted his valour, disregarding his enemy, as though he were a peacock for sport, and treating with little concern the blazing valour of the lord of demons, perished like a forest tree shattered by a lordly elephant. (4).

BOTH—May he go to heaven !

FIRST—Kaśyapa, come away. We shall communicate this incident to his honour, Rághava.

SECOND—Very well ; a fine idea.

(*Exeunt Both.*)

पृ. ६३ END OF VISKAMBHAKA.

(*Then enter a* CHAMBERLAIN).

CHAMBERLAIN—Who is here, ho, keeping watch at the door of the gold-arched outer-gate ?

(*Entering*).

FEMALE-DOOR-KEEPE—Noble one, I am here, Vijayá. What is to be done ?

CHAMB—Vijayá, do tell prince Bharata.

Here, indeed, has returned his honour Sumantra, who had set out for Janasthàna to see Ráma.

VIJAYA'—Noble one, has father Sumantra returned with his mission accomplished ?

CHAMB—Lady, I don't know.

Just as I saw Sumantra now come back with his face parched by the fire of grief burning in his heart, my mind was filled with anguish. (5).

Fem. Door-Keeper—Noble one, on hearing this my mind is, as it were, perturbed.

CHAMB.—Lady, why do you wait (here). Quickly convey (the message).

FEM.—D.-KEEPER—Noble sir, here I convey it. (*Exit*).

CHAMB.—(*Looking on*)—Ah, here is his honour prince Bharata, clad in bark garments and with his head tawny with the mass of his variously matted hair, coming this very way, his heart being filled with curiosity at the arrival of Sumantra.

He whose numerous excellent virtues are well-known, who is the god of death to his enemies, who is the ornament of the solar race, who is almost equal to the lord of the gods, who, in obedience to the order (of his brother) has taken up the duty of protecting the whole world, who is majestic and whose gait resembles that of a stately young elephant. (6).

(*Then enter* BHARATA *and the* FEMALE DOOR-KEEPER.) पृ. ७४

BHARATA—His honour Sumantra has thus returned then?

Having gone first to see my elder brother after I had returned having obtained his favour and promise, has his honour Sumantra returned after seeing Ráma, charming to the eyes, thoughts and the mind of the subjects? (7).

CHAMB.—(*Having approached.*) Prosperity to the prince!

BHARATA—Now in what part (of the palace) is his honour, Sumantra?

CHAMB.—Here at the entrance to the door of the gold-arche gate.

BHARATA—Then let him be ushered in quickly.

CHAMB—As the prince commands. (*Exeunt Both*).

(*Then enter* SUMANTRA *and the* FEMALE DOOR-KEEPER).

SUMANTRA—(*Sorrowfully*)—Alas, oh, alas!

I witnessed the king's death; I also saw the calamity that overtook the king's son; and now I have heard of the disappearance of the princess of Mithilá: my (long) life has been greatly guilty, as it were, as regards what is its merit. (8).

Fem. Door-Keeper—(*Addressing* Sumantra)—May the noble one come in. Here is our master. Your honour should approach him.

Sumantra—(*Advancing.*) Victory to the prince!

पृ· ७५ Bharata—Father, did you see him who showed to the world what affection for the father was? Did you see virtuous life of Arundhati divided two-fold (Sitá). Did you see fraternal affection that has causelessly accepted a forest-residence (Lakshmaṇa)?

(Sumantra *remains pensive*).

Fem.-Door-keeper—The prince, indeed, is asking you, noble one.

Sumantra—Lady, what? me?

Bharata—(*To himself.*) Great, indeed, is his torment; he is absent-minded through affliction. (*Aloud*) Has your honour returned from the middle of your journey?

Sumantra—Prince, set out for Janasthàna to see Râma at your bidding, how can I come back from the middle of the way?

Bharata'—Was it, indeed, through anger or shame that they did not show themselves to you?

Sumantra—Prince,

How can there be anger on the part of those who are well trained, or shame on the part of those whose resolve is well taken? I, however, saw the penance grove vacant, devoid of them. (9).

Bharata—And where were they heard to have gone?

Sumantra—There is a residence of the forest-dwelling monkeys, called Kishkindhá. And it was heard that they had gone there.

Bharata—Alas! Monkeys, indeed, do not know the difference between men and men (or, how to distinguish eminent men). So they must be living there uncomfortably.

Sumantra—Prince, even lower animals know an obligation conferred (how to be grateful).

नैमिशीयाः—Sages dwelling in the celebrated forest, नैमिश, also written as नैमिष, where Sauti related the Mah. bhâ. (at a sacrifice lasting for 12 years), and so called because in it an army of demons was destroyed in a twinkling. Its derivation is thus given by Nilakantha in his com. on Adi. p. I. वाराहे—एवं कृत्वा ततो देवो मुनिं गौरमुखं तदा। उवाच निमिषेणेदं निहतं दानवं बलम्। अरण्येऽस्मिंस्ततस्त्वेतन्निमिषारण्यसंज्ञितम्॥ नैमिशे इति पाठे तु वायवीये—एतन्मनोमयं चक्रं मया सृष्टं विसृज्यते। यत्रास्य शीर्यते नेमिः स देशस्तपसः शुभः। इत्युक्त्वा सूर्यसंकाशं चक्रं सृष्ट्वा मनोमयम्। प्रणिपत्य महादेवं विससर्ज पितामहः। तेपि हृष्टतरा विप्राः प्रणम्य जगतां प्रभुम्। प्रययुस्तस्य चक्रस्य यत्र नेमिर्व्यशीर्यत। तद्वनं तेन विख्यातं नैमिशं मुनिपूजितम्॥

०विपन्नैः—Dead. The *Ṛshis* have not to kill them; knowing their wish the deer breathe their last of their own accord in order to be of service to them. **अभिवर्धयन्ति**—perform, giving special (अभि) satisfaction to the manes.

Sl. 10. **तैः**—may refer to श्राद्ध or better to मृगैः. **सुतफलं**.—For the sons take care to please them and to enable them to rise to a higher world. **हित्वा जरां**—It is difficult to know what the poet means by जरा; for when the spirit is once free from the body it is free from old age. Probably जरा means the last period of their life as पितृs at the end of which they have to come back to this world. *Cf.* नाकस्य पृष्ठे ते सुकृतेऽनुभूत्वेमं लोकं हीनतरं वा व्रजन्ति। Mund. up. I. 10. **खं**—*i. e.* the world of the gods, where they experience a higher joy. *Cf.* ते ये शतं पितॄणां चिरलोकलोकानामानन्दाः। स एक आजानजानां देवानामानन्दः॥ &c. Tait. up. VIII. **आवर्तिभिः**—Because the Vishayas subject a man to birth and rebirth **विषयैः**—विषिण्वन्ति बध्नन्ति इन्द्रियाणि पुरुषपशुं वा इति विषयाः; fr. सि 9th conj. and aff. अ (अच्).

P. 67. Sl. 11. **आपृच्छ**—ought to be आपृच्छस्व, as प्रच्छ् with आ is Atm.; see com.; but Bhâsa is often indifferent to the rules of Gr.; he has used the Par. again in आपृच्छाम्यत्रभवतीं in Act. VI p. 80. He has, however, used the correct pada twice in the third Act; see p. 41. **पुत्रकृतकान्**.—The comp. may be explained in two ways—कृतः पुत्रः पुत्रकृतः, स एव पुत्रकृतकः taking it as a comp. of the आहिताग्नि class, or of the मयूरव्यंसक class; or पुत्रः कृतः पुत्रकृतः सुप्सुपेति समासः। स एव पुत्रकृतकः. A third way is न पुत्रः अपुत्रः अपुत्रः पुत्रः सम्पद्यमानः कृतः पुत्रीकृतः or पुत्रकृतः, the ई being optionally dropped, as in पूगकृत by the rule श्रेण्यादयः कृतादिभिः। The former two ways are, however, better as the श्रेण्यादि group is not an आकृतिगण. For the two forms comp. श्यामाकमुष्टिपरि-

षर्धितको जहाति सोयं न पुत्रकृतकः पदवीं मृगस्ते। Śak. IV. 14. and अमुं पुरः पश्यसि देवदारुं पुत्रीकृतोसौ वृषभध्वजेन। Ragh. II. 36.

विन्ध्यं वनं—Although Ráma was living in the Dandaka forest at this time, he refers to it here as विन्ध्यवन as it covered a larger tract including the Dandaka. Baṇa in his Kádambari describes दण्डका as part of the Vindyátavî. अस्ति मध्यदेशालंकारभूता विंध्याटवी नाम। तस्यां च दण्डकारण्यान्तःपाति &c. Kád. pp. 40–41. Although the boundaries of the D. forest are differently given it lay between the Narmadà on the North and the Godavarî on the south, the mountain Vindhya forming its northern boundary. वत्स्यामि—It is strange that Ráma should, like an ordinary man, precipitately think of residing in the Himalayan woods blindly believing in the words of the guest. दीप्तैः &c.—The mountain Himalaya is described as possessing herbs that blaze at night; *cf.* भवन्ति यत्रौषधयो रजन्यामतैलपूराः सुरतप्रदीपाः। Kum. I. 10, आसन्नोषधयो नेतुर्नक्तमस्नेहदीपिकाः। Ragh. IV. 75. यस्मिन्नज्वालिषू रात्रौ महौषध्यः सहस्रशः। Bhatti. XV. 106. प्रदीप्तसर्वौषधिसंप्रदीप्तं &c. Rámá. Yudh. 74. 57. औषधिवनैरु०—This epithet has no propriety here. Ráma wished to live in the Himalayan forests because they were inhabited by the golden antelopes; and the poet should have stated that as the reason for Ràma's going to those forests.

Śl. 12. दर्शयिष्यति—Ráma means—If the deer are not visible to human eyes I shall force the mountain Himalaya to show them to me. The mountain Himalaya is described as having two forms—a physical one and another that is divine; *cf.* Kum. I. 1; also जङ्गमं प्रेष्यभावे वः स्थावरं चरणाङ्कितम्। विभक्तानुग्रहं मन्ये द्विरूपमपि मे वपुः॥ *Ibid* VI. 58. The latter form is referred to here; the first in the second half. क्रौञ्चरवं—The mountain Kraucha, the grandson of Himalaya, being the son of Mainàka according to the Harivamsá, was pierced through with an arrow by Kártikeya and Paraśuráma; hence Kártikeya was called क्रौञ्चदारण. Bhása has referred to this incident in his other plays also; *e. g.* क्रौञ्चं यथा शक्तिधरः प्रकृष्टः। Bal. II. 23; and again in III. 9 बालेन हि पुरा क्रौञ्चः स्कंधेन निधनं गतः। गुहशक्तिसमाक्रान्तो यथा क्रौञ्चाचलोत्तमः। Abhi. II. 24. *Cf.* हंसद्वारं भृगुपतियशोवर्त्म यत्क्रौञ्चरन्ध्रम्। Meg. I. 60. वा—In case he refuses my request.

दिशो विलोक्य.—This stage-direction is faulty; there is no reason why Ráma should have looked in the directions. It should have been अकस्मात्प्रकाशं दृष्ट्वा दिशः &c. विद्युत्संपात इव.—

This is meant to introduce Máricha in the form of a golden deer. It was arranged that Máricha should make his appearance near Ráma's hermitage sometime after Rávaṇa's entrance into it. **भगवतो वृद्धिः**—A mere compliment paid to the ascetic by Ràma.

Śl. 13. **अर्हति एषः**—एषः refers to the Kánchanapárshva The word पूजां must be supplied from पूजायां. The animal being divine, as appeared from Rávana's 'न ते मानुषैर्दृश्यन्ते above, Ráma thought that the animal deserved to be received with honour. **पूजायां**.—is वैषयिकसप्तमी पूजाविषये. **लक्ष्मणं ब्रूहि**.—Ask Lakshmaṇa to receive the antelope with honour. That Ráma wanted to have honour shown to the deer is clear from Rávaṇa's words further on--अये अयमर्घ्यमादायोपसर्पति राघवः ।

कुलपति--The chief of the hermits (कुलं a multitude) among whom Ráma dwelt. The term has also a technical meaning. It was applied to a sage who taught ten thousand munis, giving them food &c.; मुनीनां दशसाहस्रं योऽन्नदानादिपोषणात् । अध्यापयति विप्रर्षिरसौ कुलपतिः स्मृतः ॥ The name of the Kulpati is not mentioned. अत्रि, however, was the Kul. there; *cf.* एते ते तापसा देवि दृश्यन्ते तनुमध्यमे । अत्रिः कुलपतिर्यत्र सूर्य वैश्वानरोपमः । Yud. K. Ch. 123. 47, 48.

P. 68. **संदिष्टः सौमित्रिः**—This is a deviation from the Ráma., according to which Sítá herself sent away Lakshmaṇa by addressing harsh words to him when she heard the cry for help uttered by Máricha imitating Ráma's voice when pierced with a deadly arrow by Ráma. See Arany. Ch. 45.

अये अयमर्घ्यमादाय &c.—Believing in the words of the अतिथि. *viz.* 'चिन्तितमात्रोपस्थिताविपन्नैः' Ráma thought that the antelope might come to him and so went forth with an *Arghya* to receive it as is due to a guest. But finding that the animal was running on, not caring for the reception, strung his bow which he always carried with him when going out.

Śl. 14. **बलं**—Mere physical strengh with which Ráma could draw the bow. **वीर्य**—valour. **सत्वं**—inner substance or mettle; firmness of the mind which does not allow a man's courage to flog or fail him. **अक्षरैः**—Since the plural is used by Akshara is meant the letters of the alphabet, the vowels and the consonants. **अल्पैः**—*i e.* covering a small place. **व्याप्तं**--*i. e.* Ráma's prowess was known all over the world. **शरविषयं**—The range of the arrow; *cf.* द्रुमाः क्षीणविषयाः III. 2, कृत्तिकाविषय p. 37; चक्षुर्विषय p. 69.

Śl. 15. **मायया**—By the trick of the deer (मायामृग). **अमन्त्रोक्तां**—See note on स्वरपदपरिगृहीणां हव्यधारां *supra* Śl. 7.

यावदुटजं प्र०—From this it appears that Ráma had come with Sîtá out of his hut to receive the guest.

Śl. 16. **युद्धे येन** &c.—*Cf.* येन वित्रासिता लोकाः सदेवासुरमानुषाः । अहं स रावणो नाम सीते रक्षोगणेश्वरः । A'ran. XLVII. 27. **शूर्पणखा**—शूर्पाणीव नखानि यस्याः सा having finger-nails like a winnowing basket. The fem. ई is not added by the rule नखमुखात्संज्ञायां (Pán. IV. 1. 58) when a comp. ends is नख and मुख and it is a proper name the ई is not added; so गौरमुखा (a name); but ताम्रमुखी कन्या. She was the younger sister of Rávaṇa. Her story is well-known. For it see Rámá., Arany. **भ्रातरौ**—Khara and Dûshaṇa.

P. 69. **दर्पाद् दु०**—Who acts wickedly through vanity (being vainly proud of his power). **अप्रमेयबलिनं**—Whose strengh is not to be counted, *i. e.* reckoned or taken into consideration. It cannot be taken to mean 'of matchless power' here, as Rávaṇa is not likely to praise Râma before Sîtâ. **विलोभ्य छलैः**—is put in to show Râma's credulity. He had not the good sense to see that there cannot be a deer of gold.

Śl. 17. **वित्तनाथः**—The lord of wealth, Kubera, the regent of the north. He was the half brother of Rávaṇa. Râvaṇa had a fight with him, drove him away from Lankâ, and wrested from him his aerial car, Pushpaka. He also forced him to furish him money whenever he wanted it. **सोम**—The moon who was also assailed by Râvaṇa. See Râmâ. Uttar. प्रक्षिप्तसर्ग. ४. श्लो. 29 after ch. 23. G. S. says सोमः ब्रह्मा; but that is not possible, as Râvaṇa owed his power to Brahmâ. See Ráma referred to above, and Ragh X. 42. **धन्या भूमिः** &c.—The contrast is not happily expressed. The reason for the earth being धन्या should have been stated as courage as opposed to timidity and not beauty.

Śl. 18. **कुपुरुष**—Weak or powerless men. **वचोभिः**—appeals for protection.

Śl. 19. **विगणय**—विशेषेण गणय specially regard, consider.

P. 70. **हहह ! अहो पति०**—Rávaṇa says this in the hearing of Sîtá and seems to treat the matter jestingly. दग्धः in Śl. 20 is ironical. Had he been really affected by Sîtâ's words he would not have dared carry her off and boastingly said—बलादेष दशग्रीवः &c. *Cf.* for nearly the same observation Abhi. Act. II—

सीता—शप्तोसि ।

रावणः—हहह । अहो पतिव्रतायास्तेजः ।

देवाः सेन्द्रादयो भग्ना दानवाश्च मया रणे ।
सोहं मोहं गतोस्म्यद्य सीतायास्त्रिभिरक्षरैः ॥ 18 ॥

ACT VII.

(*Then enter a* Hermit.)

HERMIT—Nandilaka, Nandilaka.

(*Entering.*)

NANDILAKA—Revered one, here I am.

HERMIT—Nandilaka, the patriarch says—Here, indeed, having slain Rávana, who had carried away his wife and who was the terror of the three worlds, and installed on the throne Bibhíshaṇa, of conduct opposed to that of the multitude of Rákshasas and adorned with a number of virtues, has arrived His Honour Ráma, charming like the moon of the clear autumal sky, bringing with him her ladyship, Sítá, whose spotless character has been attested to by the gods, the heavenly sages and the Siddhas, and accompanied by the chief bears, demons and monkeys. So to-day in this hermitage let all that be kept ready which can be well desired (for his reception) according to our means.

NANDILAKA—Revered sir, all is got ready; but—

HEMIT—What is this?

NAṆDILAKA—Here are demons accompanying Bibhíshaṇa. For their meals the Kulapati will decide (arrange).

HERMIT—What for?

NANDILAKA—They, indeed, devour (men).

HERMIT—Away, away with your fear. The demons, indeed, are under Bibhíshaṇa's control.

NANDILAKA—A bow to the good demons. (*Exit*).

HERMIT—(*Looking on.*) Oh, here is the noble Rághava. He, who,

The lord of men, has alighted on the surface of the earth from the heavenly car, praised by several delighted sages in the words—"Glory to you, oh best of men: may you conquer another enemy (if there will arise one); and may the earth, marked with one royal umbrella, be subject to your power"! (1)

May you prosper, may you be victorious! (*Exit*).

END OF THE MIXED VISHKAMBHAKA.

(*Then enter* RA'MA.)

RA'MA—Oh,

Having destroyed Rávaṇa, of mighty strength and valour, and recovered Sítá, pure (as proved by the ordeal) and possessed of all virtues in the world, and having carried out the order of my father to its last letter, I have once more returned to my forest-residence among the hermits. (2)

Maithilí, who had entered inside to pay her respects to the ascetic-women is, indeed, tarrying. (*Looking on.*) Ah, here is the princess of Mithilâ,

Daughter of king Janaka, slowly coming on, very affectionately addressed, according to their age, by the hermit-women, as a friend, as Síta, as Janakí and as daughter-in-law. (3)

पृ. ८३ (*Then enter* SÍTA *and a* FEMALE ASCETIC)

TA'PASÍ—Friend. here is your husband; approach him; it is not possible (we do not like) to see you alone.

SÍTA'—Yes. Even to-day it seems as if I cannot believe it (what has happened, or I cannot trust myself as safe). (*Having approached.*) Victory to my husband!

RA'MA—Maithilí, do you know (remember) that Janasthàna was our former residence? Do you recognize the trees here, that were considered as sons?

SÍTA'—I know, I know; those whose tender leaves were seen have now become such as are to be seen with upturned eyes (grown high).

RA'MA—It is just so. Time gives rise to low and high places (makes things small and great). Maithilí, do you call to your mind how the herd of the deer was frightened at the sight of Bharata, clad in white garments, underneath this Saptaparṇa tree?

SÎTA'—Husband, I remember it very well, indeed.

RA'MA—Here is the extensive bank (of the Godavarî), the witness of our austerities. It was while sitting here and thinking of the things to be offered to father at the Śráddha ceremony that the deer callad 'the gold-flanked' was seen by us.

SÎTA'—Ha, husband; do not indeed, do not indeed, mention that. (*Trembles with fear*).

RA'MA—Away, away with fear, Past is this time. (*Looking in the quarters.*) Ah! whence, indeed,

Does this dust, white like the *lodhra* flowers, rise up, and being shaken by the wind pervade the directions? And whence too, does this blast of the conches, augmented by the sounds of the drums and the shouts of the people (or, by the deep peals of the sounds of drums) convert the forest into a town? (4)

(*Entering*)

LAKSHMAṆA—Prosperity to my noble brother! Noble brother,

Here has arrived Bharata, affectionate towards his brothers, with a large army and accompanied by the mothers, eager to see you. (5)

RA'MA—Dear Lakshmaṇa, what? Has Bharata thus come then?

LAKSHMAṆA—Yes, noble brother.

RA'MA—Maithilî, expand your eyes to see Bharata, leading your mothers-in-law.

SÎTA'—Husband, he (Bharata) has come at a desirable time.

(*Then enter* BHARATA *with his* MOTHERS.)

BHARATA—With a gladdened heart and followed by my kinsmen, here have I come to-day, desirous of seeing my elder brother, accompanied by the noble lady, who is freed from calamities grown in magnitude, like the clear moon in the autumn, when freed from clouds. (6)

RA'MA—Mothers, I bow to you.

ALL—Child, may you live long! We congratulate ourselves on seeing you with your wife, all safe and with your vow fulfilled.

RA'MA—I am favoured.

LAKSHMANA.—Mothers, I salute you.

ALL—Child, may you live long.

LAKSHMANA—Mothers, I am beholden to you.

SÍTA'—Noble ladies, I bow to you.

ALL—Dear one, may auspicious fortune long smile on you!

SÍTA'—I am favoured.

BHARATA—Noble brother, I bow unto you. I am Bharata.

RA'MA—Come, come, dear child, prince of the Ikshváku race. My blessing to you. Be of long life!

Expand your bosom, of the expanse of the closed panels of a door; clasp me with your very large pair of arms. Raise this face which resembles the autumnal moon and gladden this (my) body scorched by calamities. (7)

BHARATA—It is a favour upon me. Noble lady, my respects to you. I am Bharata.

SÍTA'—May you be long the companion of my husband!

BHARATA—I am obliged to you. Noble brother, I salute you.

LAKSHMANA—Come, come, dear child; be of long life; embrace me firmly. (*Embraces him*).

BHARATA—I am favoured. Noble brother, receive back the responsibility of the kingdom.

RA'MA—Dear brother, how, possibly?

KAIKEYÍ—Child, this desire has, indeed, been long cherished.

(*The enter* Śatrughna.)

Śatrughna—

My mind hastens to see my elder brother, the destroyer of Râvaṇa, harassed by various calamities, but with merits and spirit unaffected (in tact). (8)

(*Approaching*) Noble brother, I, Śatrughna, bow to you.

Ra'ma—Come, come, child ; my blessing unto you. Be of long life !

Śatrughna—I am beholden to you. Noble lady, I salute you.

S'îta'—Dear child, live long.

S'atrughna—I am favoured. Noble brother, I salute you.

Lakshmana—Hail to you ! May you live long ! Noble brother, here are Vasishtha and Vâmadeva, along with the citizens, desirous of seeing you in connection with your coronation,

Multitudes of sages wish to see your face, bathed beforehand, through your favour, with the holy water brought from various rivers, small and great, by the sages themselves, like a lotus sprinkled over with water. (9)

Kaikeyî—Go child ; enjoy the coronation.

Ra'ma—As mother commands. (*Exit*).

(*Behind the Curtains*).

May Your Honour be victorious ; glory to our master ; victory to the great king ; prosperity to the king ; may the auspicious-faced one conquer ; victory to our noble brother ; happy reign the destroyer of Ravaṇa !!! (10)

Kaikeyî—These priests and chamberlains, adding to the loud exclamations of victory to my child, are honouring him with their blessings.

Sumitra'—Ministers, servants and good men are proclaiming victory to my child.

(*Behind the curtains*).

Oh you ascetics, residents of Janasthána, do you listen, listen.

Having dispelled the unprecedented thick gloom arising from the enemy, as the sun does darkness, by the rays in the form of his valour, and haviug recovered Sîtà, not to be assailed by evils of any kind, Ràma, delightful to all the people, now has the earth under his sway. (10)

KAIKEYÎ—Oh ! the acquisition of sovereignty by my son is being proclaimed.

(*Then enter* RA'MA crowned King, *with the retinue*).

RA'MA—(*Looking up in space.*) Oh father,

Although in heaven (now) rejoice; cast aside your melancholy: here is performed the deed (the ceremony of coronation) desired by you with regard to me. I am now, indeed, the king on earth, bearing the honourable responsibility (of government); I have undertaken the protection of the people in conformity with justice (or, sacred law). (11)

BHARATA—

I am not fully satisfiend as I behold, like the new moon, my noble elder brother, who has acquired the title of 'sovereign', who has the royal umbrella held over him, who has put on a resplendent crown, who is bathed in water from the holy places, who has possessed dignity and who is being saluted by multitudes of people. (12)

S'ATRUGHNA—

This my family having its stain removed by the coronation of my noble brother, has again attained brilliancy like the world at the rise of the moon. (13)

RA'MA—Dear Lakshmaṇa, I have obtained sovereignty.

LAKSHMANA—I congratulate you upon this.

(*Entering*)

A CHAMBERLAIN—Victory to the great king ! Here his Honour Bibhîshana, respectfully says, and so do your followers, Sugrîva, Nîla, Mainda, Jâmbavat, Hanumat and others—"We offer our congratulations to you. '

RA'MA—Tell them that Râma owes this good fortune to the favour of his allies.

CHAMBERLAIN—As the great king commands.

KAIKEYÎ—I am blessed, indeed. I wish to see this grand ceremony performed in Ayodhyâ.

RA'MA—Your ladyship will see it. (*Looking about.*) Oh, all this forest is shining with lustre, like the sun ! (*Reflecting*) Oh, I know it. Pushpaka, Râvaṇa's aerial car, has appeared in the sky. For it presents itself, the moment it is thought of, according to the condition made with it. So all should ascend.

(All *ascend.*)

RA'MA—

To-day I will go to the city of Ayodhyâ, followed by my kinsmen and friends.

LAKSHMANA.—

Let the citizens behold you this very day, like the moon stationed on the rising mountain with the stars. (14)

(*Bharata-Vâkya*).

As Râma is united with Jânakî and his kinsfolk, so may our King, endowed with glory, rule over the earth ! (15)

(*Exeunt omnes*).

END OF ACT VII.

END OF THE PLAY, PRATIMA

NOTES.

ACT I.

P. 1. The name of the play is प्रतिमा or प्रतिमानाटकम्. It is so named from the incident that Bharata came to know quite unexpectedly about the death of his father on seeing his statue (प्रतिमा) in the statue-house, as mentioned in the 3rd Act. The news of his father's death and its cause filled him with grief and anger against his mother and he resolved to go to the forest directly from the statue-house.

It is difficult, however, to know whether the play was so named by the author himself. The name was given to it by M. M. G. Śâstri—अस्य तु नाटकस्य मातृकाग्रन्थान्तदृष्टपाठानुसारात्प्रतिमानाटकमिति संज्ञा। For Bhása does not mention the name of his play in the prelude, as is done by the later play-wrights. If the name be supposed to be given from the use of the word प्रतिमा in अप्रतिम in the introductory Śl., it could as well have been named सीताभवम् also. The name is not formed according to any rule of Páṇini's grammar. It may be explained as प्रतिमा एव अभेदोपचारात्प्रतिमा; but then it ought to be प्रतिमम्; *cf.* मृच्छकटिकं, वेणीसंहारं, मुद्राराक्षसम् &c. So it will be better to read प्रतिमानाटकं as one word; प्रतिमाप्रधानं प्रतिमालक्षणं वा नाटकं प्रतिमानाटकम्.

नान्द्यन्ते ततः प्रविशति सूत्रधारः—नान्दी from नन्द् or नन्दि joy (see com. for definition &c.)-that which gives joy—was the chief element of the Pûrvaranga (Preliminary performance), which is defined as 'What the actors perform before the commencement of the main drama for the removal of the obstacles likely to happen to it. It consisted of songs in praise of deities, invoking good luck &c. and was accompanied by instrumental music. It had several elements, such as प्रत्याहार, &c., among which, how ever, the Nándî was to be used as the special means of removing obstacles. See com. As the drama advanced, the elaborate preliminaries were found to be tiresome and were dispensed with, the नान्दी part only being retained. This नान्दी, it seems was recited in Bhása's time behind the curtain and by the Sûtradhára of the Pûrvaranga, called नान्दीवादिन् or नान्दीकर (see A. K.); he was different from the Sûtradhâra of the Prastávaná or Sthápaná, who commenced the main play. **नान्द्यन्ते**—After the recital of the invocatory stanza or stanzas. **ततः**—Immediately after–allowing no time to intervene; see com. **सूत्रधारः**—

The stage-manager who held, as it were, the threads of the plot in his hands. For definition see com. All the plays of Bhása have this stage-direction. This shows that the Nândî was recited behind the curtain and not on the stage, as in the case of the later plays, and by some other person and not the Sûtrā-dhara.* This peculiarity of Bhása's plays was noticed and has been referred to in his introductiou to the Harshacharita by Bána in the verse—

सूत्रधारकृतारम्भैर्नाटकैर्बहुभूमिकैः ।
सपताकैर्यशो लेभे भासो देवकुलैरिव ॥

Sl. 1. According to the dictum आशीर्नमस्क्रिया &c. (see com.) the poet begins his work with an आशिः or blessing and वस्तुनिर्देश or hinting of the plot. For construction see com. **सीताभवः—** The source of Sîtâ's welfare or prosperity (as her husband); Gen. Tat.; or भवः भद्राप्तिः (see com.) restoration to welfare or happiness by her rescue from Ràvaṇa; Bah. comp. This is perhaps better—it indicates power in Ráma to protect his devotees by rescuing them from calamity. **सुमन्त्रतुष्टः**—(1) Pleased by good counsels (and not दुर्मन्त्रतुष्टः as evinced by his declining to follow Lakshmaṇa's advice to seize the kingdom by force, or to return to Ayodhyá at Bharata's request and so forth. Or (2) pleased by the recital of holy mantras; (3) or, pleased with the minister Sumantra. He was one of the eight ministers of Daśaratha *viz.* धृष्टिर्जयन्तो विजयः सुराष्ट्रो राष्ट्रवर्धनः । अकोपो धर्मपालश्च सुमन्त्रश्चाष्टमोऽर्थवित् ॥ Rám. Bál. VIII. 3. But there is no reason why Ràma should have liked Sûmantra alone above others.

सुग्रीवरामः—There is no special propriety of the epithet सुग्रीव; it is put in simply for *S'lesha*. **सहलक्ष्मणः**—Who had Lak. for his companion; see com.; or who was accompanied by Lakshmaṇa.

रावणार्यप्रतिमश्च:—रावणारिश्चासौ अप्रतिमश्च, should properly be अप्रतिमरावणारिः. This epithet is very significant. Who became the enemy of Râvaṇa, but not an imbecile enemy, but one who proved to be more than a match for him. To be merely an enemy of Rávaṇa signified nothing; Rávaṇa had many enemies; but Ráma was not such. The comp. must be taken as a Gen. Tat; and not as a Bah. (रावणः अरिर्यस्य) as the two words will hang loosely (who had Ràvaṇa for his enemy and who was matchless) and

* According to Bharata, the Nândí, being the chief means of removing obstacles, must be recited by the Sûtradhâra and then another person, called the स्थापक should enter and commence the प्रस्तावना।

the epithet will lose its beauty. अप्रतिम is used to suggest the idea of प्रतिमा which figures prominently in the third Act. वैव्या—should better be taken as Inst. हेत्वर्थे. Ráma became Rávaṇa's enemy because his wife was kidnapped by him. This also accounts for बिभीषणात्मा; see com.; Ràma, as his name signifies, was not बिभीषणात्मा, but became such on account of the insult offered to him by Ràvaṇa (see *infra* VI. 14) and slew the Rákshasas mercilessly. It is not so good to take देव्या as सहार्थे तृतीया; for we have to supply सहवर्तमान:; but this idea we have already got in सहलक्ष्मण:; and a great poet is not likely to repeat ideas in the same Śloka. But if so taken, we may separate देव्या अबिभीषणात्मा;. who by nature is not terrific, (may be so when there is cause for being so); or बिभीषण: आत्मा यस्य who regarded Dibbîshaṇa as his own soul, who identified himself with बि० he being his devotee. *Cf.* अहं भक्तपराधीनोऽस्वतन्त्र इव द्विज । साधुभिर्ग्रस्तहृदय: &c. Bhág. P. IX. 4. 63. भरत:—The nourisher, *i. e.* protector, of the world. Hence able to protect in life after life. M. M. G. S. takes बिभीषणात्मभरत: as one word and explains (see com.) बिभीषणे आत्मभे like, identical with, himself रत: delighting *i. e.* taking interest in. But this is rather far-fetched.

This Sl., it will be seen, serves the same purpose as the Nândî verse of the other writers. It contains a benediction. It also suggests the subject-matter of the play by grouping together the names of the principal characters in it, by means of what is technically called the मुद्रालंकार (for which see com.), *viz.* सीता, सुमन्त्र, सुग्रीव, राम, लक्ष्मण, बिभीषण and भरत. Bhása has adopted this device of introducing the subject matter in his three other plays, स्वप्नवासवदत्त, प्रतिज्ञायौगन्धरायण and पञ्चरात्र. But in all these his attempt at the Mudrálankara has been very clumsy. There is very little poetry in the introductory stanzas of these. Of the characters mentioned above Sugrîva and Bibhîshaṇa do not take an active part in the events of the play; they are dismissed with a mere referrence to them in the 6th and 7th Acts.

P. 2. नपथ्याभिमुखं—नेपथ्य is derived as निन: (to the eye, नि neu.) or ने: नेतु: (नि the leader) पथ्यं what is good for; the form is irregular. It means here the curtain; it may also mean 'the tiring room; see com. For a different sense, see *infra.* p. 6. or 21.

आर्ये—The poets generally make the Sutra. begin the prologue by addressing the नटी and asking her to sing a song connected with some season suited to his business, as in the Śak., or an attendant called पारिपार्श्वक or मारिष as in the Veṇi. the Mál-Mad., &c. Bhása does it here, but does not do it in his Svap. and some other plays.

आर्य—The नटी may address the सूत्र० as आर्य or आर्यपुत्र; but the नटी here addresses him as आर्य (अज्ज) as the poet wants to introduce the character to enter on the stage by making the Sûtra. catch up the word अज्ज uttered by a maid-servant behind the curtain. इमं &c.—This, that has just set in. The Sûtra. at once asks the Natî to sing, without waiting for a question from her as regards his immediate business.

शरत्कालमधिकृत्य—The poet here refers to the antumn as it is a pleasant season, the sky wearing a cheerful aspect and nature displaying freshness and vigour all round after the cessation of the rains. It has nothing to do with the time when the action of the play begins. For Ráma's coronation was to come off in the month of Chaitra, the day fixed for it being the tenth of the bright half of that month. See Ráma. Ayod. III. 4, IV. 21. Other poets select a season which is also the time of action of the events of the succeeding Act. In this respect, *cf.* the prologues of the Śak. and the Veni.

इति गायति—गायति means prepares, or opens her lips to sing. But the Sútra. interrupts her, remarking अस्मिन् खलु काले &c. This is the poet's device to cut short the prelude. Bhása's स्थापनाs are never protracted.

Śl. 2. पुलिनेषु—The sandy spots on the bank of a river. For the use of the pl. *cf.* कालिन्द्याः पुलिनेषु Veṇi. I. 2. काशांशुकवा०—applies both to हंसी and प्रतिहाररक्षी; with the latter it means—wearing a garment white like the Kásá flowers. But as applying to the former the meaning is not very clear. It may be taken to mean living on the river-bank covered with Kása reeds in blossom. See com. Káli. describes शरद् as काशांशुका in Rit. II 1 and again in 26 further on, as विकसितनवकाशश्वेतवासो वसाना. So there is no harm to take the bank also as काशांशुकं. Or अंशुक may be taken by लक्षणा to mean 'the covering wings'. Swans have white wings; *cf.* धवलपक्षविहंगमकूजितैः &c. Sis. VI. 45. M. M. G. S. very ingeniously explains काशां० (see com.) as 'bright like the Káśa flower and living in water'. But this explanation seems to be too subtle even for a Śleṣa. सुसंहृष्टा—Swans are described as cackling sweetly through joy in autumn; *cf.* सोन्मादहंसरवनूपुरनादरम्या (शरद्) Rit. III. 1.

P. 3. नेपथ्ये &c.—Here the Sûtra. is interrupted by a voice behind the curtain. He listens to it and says भवतु । विज्ञातं (I have ascertnined whose utterance it is). We have the same words in the Svap. also. सुदिता &c—The Sûtra. completes the verse by thus adding the 2nd half. सुदिता—Because Ràma, the darling of all, was to be crowned king. शरद् brought joy to the हंसी; Ráma's coronation to the maid. नरेन्द्रभवने—*i. e.* in the palace of king Das'aratha. प्रतिहाररक्षी used for प्रतिहारी for metre; *cf.* Káli. पुंवत्प्रगल्भा प्रतिहाररक्षी Ragh. VI. 20

स्थापना—Lit. that in which the theme of the play is established. It corresponds to the प्रस्तावना or आमुख of the later writers. The प्रस्तावना here is confined to a very short dialogue between the Sûtra. and the नटी. The प्रस्तावना here is of the प्रयोगातिशय kind. See com.

काञ्चुकीयानां--Bhása uses the word काञ्चुकीय instead of कञ्चुकी; कञ्चुकः अस्यास्तीति ; see com. The कञ्चुकी was so called because of the long white robe he wore. He was an attendant in the inner apartments, an old man, a Bràhmaṇa, endowed with many good qualities and a clever man of business. In later plays he is represented as mourning his lot on his entrance on the stage; see Śak. V. 3, Vik. III. 1; Mudra. III. 1. &c. But the Kan. here does nothing of the kind.

P. 4. अप्रातिहतमहारथः—महारथ may better be taken to mean 'a warrior of that class'. Four kinds of Chariot-warriors are mentioned.—अर्धरथ, रथ, महारथ and अतिरथ. For महारथ see com.; Das'aratha was a Mahâratha; see Ragh. IX. 1. (दशरथः प्रशशास महारथः &c.). राज्यप्रभाव०—see com.; the comp. may also be dissolved as राज्यं च प्रभावः (sovereign power) च. आनीयतां—*i. e.* to the place where the coronation ceremony was to take place. They had already been collected and kept in the palace. The chief of these are given in the next S'l. The Rámá. enumerates them thus-सुवर्णादीनि रत्नानि बलीन् (पूजाद्रव्याणि) सर्वौषधीरपि ॥ शुक्लमाल्यानि लाजांश्च पृथक्च मधुसर्पिषी । अहतानि च वासांसि रथं सर्वायुधान्यपि ॥ चतुरङ्गबलं चैव गजं च शुभलक्षणम् । चामरव्यजने चोभे ध्वजं छत्रं च पाण्डुरम् ॥ शतं च शातकुम्भानां कुम्भानामग्निवर्चसाम् । हिरण्यशृङ्गमृषभं समग्रं व्याघ्रचर्म च ॥ यच्चान्यत्किंचिदेष्टव्यं तत्सर्वमुपकल्प्यताम् । उपस्थापयत प्रातरग्न्यगारे महीपतेः ॥ Ráma Ayod. III. 8. 12; see also XV. 4-11.

Śl. 3. सव्यजनं—With fan *i. e.* chauri; *cf.* सज्जं तिष्ठति रामस्य बालव्यजनमुत्तमम् । Ayod. XV. 10. सनन्दि—नन्दि joy;—पटह a drum to be beaten on a joyous occasion, as distingnished from a war drum; a comp. of the शाकपार्थिवादि class. *Cf.* नन्दिघोष, नन्दितूर्य, नान्दिवर्धन. सनन्दि॰भद्रासनं simply means 'the drum with the throne, &c ; there is no connection between the two. **भद्रासनं**—A throne set with gems, a chair of state; also called भद्रपीठ—अभिषेकाय रामस्य द्विजेन्द्रैरुपकल्पितम् । काञ्चना जलकुम्भाश्च भद्रपीठं स्वलंकृतम् ॥ Ayod. XV. 4; Ragh. XVII. 10.

P. 5. **तीर्थाम्बु**—water from holy rivers, also holy ponds seas &c.; *cf. infra* VII. 9; see Ráma Ayod XV. 5, 6. **पुष्यरथः**—A chariot for use on a joyous occasion, a pleasure trip &c.; see com. **हि**—has no special propriety here; it is used पादपूरणे. **वेद्यां**-वेदी a raised square dais or ground in the middle of a pavilion and with four pillars at its corners, prepared for the ceremony See Ragh XVII. 9.

Śl. 4. **कृतकृत्याः**—Because it was the desire of every one of the subjects that Ráma should be crowned king. **शशाङ्क**—the gladdener of all like the moon. For Ráma's comparison again to the moon, see *infra* VI. 12; VII. 6, 14.

सम्भवक—may be the name of another charmberlain. **पुरोहितं**—The पुरोहित was Vasishtha as is clear from the verse संविश्य रामं नृपतिः श्वोभाविन्यभिषेचने । पुरोहितं समाहूय वसिष्ठमिदमब्रवीत् ॥ Ayod. V. 1. But as Vasishtha was already present, the प्रतिहारी may be referring to वामदेव, the other priest; see Bál. VII. 4. **यथोपचारेण**—यथा उपचारः यथोपचारस्तेन.

संगीतशाला—A concert or music hall attached to the palace where a play was enacted on special occasions. See Śak. V. p. 158 It was also called प्रेक्षागृह; see Mál. I. p. 40 Priy III. 2. It was a place where usually music was taught and dancing &c. was performed.

अत्याहितं—अतिशयेन आधीयते स्म मनसि, that which deeply affects—sticks to the mind on account of its atrocity or extreme bad nature; hence causes great fear, a grave calamity. Avadátiká as her name signifies, was a maid of virtuous conduct (the poet has aptly given her the name); and as Sítá's friend and servant she is expected to be such. The little theft (if it could be called theft, for she had taken the Valkala by force with a sudden snatch and run away; see Revá's speech at p. 21) she had committed now greatly upset her and she is shocked at her own deed.

परिहासेनापि—It was done simply for joke; there was nothing serious about it. Revá, the custodian of the music-hall would have easily forgiven her on knowing her object.

P. 6. एक पुन: &c.—Avadátiká wonders what must be the state of mind of one who with a selfish motive deprives another of what rightfully belongs to him. The poet by putting these words in the mouth of Ava. hints at the future interference with Ráma's coronation by Kaikeyî and her demanding the kingdom for her son. हसितुं—To laugh, *i. e.* to enjoy a joke.

परिशङ्कित—See com.; वर्ण colour, hence the expression of the face. परिहसितुमिवेच्छति—Sítá, who knew Ava. better, does not think that she was अपराद्धा. Vide her next speech का त्वां &c. She attributes the change of colour in her face to the desire on her part to play jokse being hindered by her own sudden appearance.

नेपथ्यपालिनी—नेपथ्य dresses, colours to be used by actors, and other articles of decoration. See com. निवृत्त०—This does not mean that the play referred to in her speech by the प्रतिहारी on p. 5 was enacted, as Prof. Paránjpe seems inclined to think. The play was to be represented after Ráma's coronation was over. Revá was asked to decorate the stage and the sprouts of As'oka which blossoms in spring, were used for that purpose, as mango sprounts are used similarly for decorating a Mandapa on such occasions as a marriage ceremony, &c. Some sprouts were left after the stage was decorated and Avadátiká wanted one. Women are described as fond of a sprout of As'oka; *cf,* आदाय कर्णकिसलयमस्मात् *i. e.* अशोकात् &c. Mál. III 16; Rit. VI. 16; Raghu. VIII. 62. अस्माभिः—The use of the plural shows that she was not alone in asking for the sprout but also had her companions with her. Ava. was not likely to speak of herself in the plural in the presence of her mistress. अर्हति अपराधः &c.—for the completion of the sentence see com. G. S. translates अर्हति by निवर्तते but without citing authority (except it be धातुनामनेकार्थता). Or we should read अपराधं (अस्मत्कृतं), the subject being सा.

P. 7. दोषो वर्धते--For she brought it for enjoying fun and had no excuse for doing so.

एहि तावत्—Sítá called Ava. back not because she wanted to keep the bark garment, but after she gave the order for returning it, an idea came into her mind that she should see how she would look if she wore one. This was a foreboding of the forthcoming exile of Ráma and her having to wear bark garments.

सर्वशोभनीयं &c.—*Cf.* अथवा सर्वमलंकारो भवति सुरूपाणाम्। Avi. II. The idea is beautifully worked out by Káli. in the line किमिव

हि मधुराणां मण्डनं नाकृतीनाम्। Śak. I. 18; *cf.* also सर्वास्त्ववस्थासु चारुता शोभां पुष्यति। Mál. II. p 50 and सर्वासु अवस्थासु रमणीयत्वमाकृतिविशेषाणाम्। Śak VI. सौवर्णे—It looked yellowish owing to the golden complexion of Sîtá; *cf.* तप्तकाञ्चनवर्णाभा रक्ततुङ्गनखी शुभा। सीता नाम वरारोहा वैदेही तनुमध्यमा॥ Rámà. Aran. XXXIV 16. and हिरण्मयी साललतेव जङ्गमा &c. Bhatti. II. 47.

P. 8. कोपि भर्ता &c.—This brings out Sītá's nobility of mind; she was not like princesses who would like to be queens at any cost. Nothing was further from her mind than the thought that Ráma would be crowned king while Das'ratha lived So she thought that some tributary prince was to be placed on his throne by Das'aratha in his kingdom (राज्ये not राज्यस्य) he being the imperial king. प्रतीष्य—इष् with प्रति properly means 'to receive, to get something'; *cf.* एष नौ स्वामी पत्रहस्तो राजशासनं प्रतीष्य &c. Śak. VI. p.200; सत्कारः सत्करेण प्रतीष्टः Svap. IV. p. 92 Here it means 'having got information.'

अपि तातः कुशली—The news does not bring unmixed joy to Sîtá. She feels anxious fearing there was something wrong with the king's health and asks this question. यद्येवं &c.—This brings out another trait of Sîtâ's character. She feels rejoiced only on hearing that her father-in-law was in good health. विशालतरं &c.—*Cf. infra* विशालीक्रियतां चक्षुः IV. p. 53.

P. 9. अवमुच्य—Having taken off; mark this meaning of मुच् with अव; with आ it has the opposite sense. It was customary in ancient times to give a present, an ornament or ornaments, to a servant bringing some agreeable news. Sîtá being doubly pleased gives away all her ornaments. Mark the poet's skill in creating dramatic incidents. Here again he makes Sîtá divest herself of her ornaments. This is the second step towards her being already prepared to go into exile.

अवघट्टितनूष्णीकः—अवघट्टितमस्यास्तीति अवघट्टितः like पीता गावः; produced by (the drum) being beaten; see com.; some separate ओघट्टिअ and translate it by अवघट्य; which is bad, for पटहशब्दः अवघट्य is absurd. उद्घातः—Properly a blow or stroke; hence here, obstruction, hindrance. बहुवृत्तान्तानि—occurs again at p. 10. तदभिषेकोदकं—Here the syntax is faulty. There is nothing in the Chetî's speech to which तद् can refer. Sîtà takes the idea of अभिषेकोदकं from अभिषिच्य in the previous speech. मुखोदकं—Water for washing the mouth with. She means—If Daśaratha is to retire to a forest after Ráma's coronation, Ráma is sure to weep (and he did that; see śl. 6 below) at the thought of his father's separation and the water meant for अभिषेक will serve him as water for washing his face with. Here also Sîtâ once more evinces her high regard for Daśaratha. हन्त भोः—This speech of Râma is स्वगत; but there is no stage direction to that effect as he was alone.

Śl. 5. पटहे—पटहताडने. स्कन्धोच्चारण०—उच्चारण lifting up of the pot. Dissolve स्कन्धोच्चारणेन हृतुना नम्य०. प्रच्योति—must be taken to mean 'about to drop down'. आहूय—Trans. Having called me by name; having uttered my name. For the king was there holding the royal umbrella over Râma; see śl. 7. धैर्येण—Because his face did not show the least sign of displeasure. He returned as cheerfully as he had come. *Cf.* सर्वेऽप्यभिजनः श्रीमान् श्रीमतः सत्यवादिनः। नालक्षयत रामस्य कंचिदाकारमानने ॥ Ayod. XIX. 36. स्वः—One's own; not one adopted, &c. भोः—This is redundant, as we have already one भोः at the beginning of the speech.

P. 10. विरम्यतां—Supply अभिषेकेण. This reading is preferable to विश्रम्यतां which means 'you may take rest now'. It is better to make the king indirectly tell Râma to go saying 'let the ceremony stop (for the present). Courtesy requires this. उच्छ्वसितं—Relieved, refreshed. Râma considered the responsibility of kingdom to be a burden. That removed, he breathed a sigh of relief. एवोऽस्मि &c.—The sentiment is echoed again by Sîtâ further on.

नापनीतं—Because it was put on by Sîtâ merely out of a curiosity to see how she would look in a bark dress, and she was expected to remove it before any one saw her. But this would not serve the poet's purpose. He, therefore, suddenly introduces Râma on the scene without allowing Sîtâ time to remove the bark garment. हं—expresses Sîtâ's surprise at the sudden appearance of her husband. This portion of the speech is स्वगत. जयतु आर्यपुत्रः—Sîta must have greeted her husband after standing up, as is clear from Râma's next speech, मैथिलि आस्यताम्. So we expect the stage direction (उत्थाय) before these words.

सः—(*i. e.* which he wore usually) and not a rich and gaudy one suitable for a coronation ceremony. इव—seems like. एतत्—refers to the news about the coronation. This and the following speech of Sîtâ must be considered as जनान्तिक, since Râma does not hear them and asks the question किमिदं कथ्यते. Bhâsa is often careless in giving the proper stage-directions. तादृशः

जन :—A man like the revered chamberlain, Báláki, from whom her maid got the news. See *supra* p. 8.

इयं दारिका—Here the question is—Who is referred to by इयं. The conversation was between Sîtâ and Avadátiká; but the former cannot be expected to refer to the latter by the word दारिका. इयं must, therefore, refer to the Chetî, who brought the news to Sîtá and who was still present on the stage; for we are not told that she had left the stage; so here again we expect the stage-direction चेटीं निर्दिश्य.

P. 11. प्रकृति—is a wider term including ministers, friendly kings, citizen &c.; but as the अमात्यs are separately mentioned, it means here citizens (पौराः)-जन the countryfolks (जानपदाः). एकप्रकार०—in one way; without making distinction. कोसल-राज्यं—*i. e.* the उत्तरकोसलs.

बाल्याभ्यस्तं—बाल्ये अभ्यस्तं, whereon I used to sit in my boyhood. Ráma was a young man now and yet Das'aratha asked him to sit in his lap, thus showing his great affection for him. Ráma was 27 years old now; for he was 15 years old when married to Sîtá and passed 12 years in her company in the palace when the coronation was proposed, as the पद्मपुराण tells us—तत्र द्वादश वर्षाणि राघवः सह सीतया। रमयामास धर्मात्मा नारायण इव श्रिया ॥ तस्मिन्काले महाराजः प्रीतो रामस्य सद्गुणैः । ज्येष्ठं राज्येन संयोक्तुमैच्छत्सर्वनृपाज्ञया ॥ मातुः गोत्रं स्निग्धमा०—Thus-ज्येष्ठायामसि मे पत्न्यां सदृश्यां सदृशः सुतः । उत्पन्नस्त्वं गुणज्येष्ठो मम रामात्मजः प्रियः ॥ Ayod. III. 39-40.

आर्यपुत्रेण किं भणितं—Sîtá wants to know whether Ráma accepted the proposal willingly or showed his reluctance, which she expected him to do. दीर्घं निःश्वस्य--to show his great unwillingness to be the king. तुल्यशीलानि—*i. e.* whose hearts know each other exactly. *Cf.* प्रिया तु सीता रामस्य दाराः पितृकृता इति। तस्याश्च भर्ता द्विगुणं हृदये परिवर्तते ॥ अन्तर्गतमपि व्यक्तमाख्याति हृदयं हृदा। Râmâ. Bâl. LXXVII. 26. 28.

Sl. 6. The second line contains प्रक्रमभङ्ग; for the proper order see. com. तस्य ममोपरि पतता बाष्पेण मे शिरः क्लेदितं &c. The father's tears of course were due to joy.

P. 12. Śl. 7. शत्रुघ्नलक्ष्मण०—The natural way to dissolve the comp. is शत्रुघ्नलक्ष्मणाभ्यां गृहीतः; and M. M. G. S. dissolves the comp. like that. But this is against the Râmá., according to which Bharata had gone to his maternal uncle accompanied by Śatrughna. *Cf* गच्छता मातुलकुलं भरतेन तदानघ । शत्रुघ्नो नित्यशत्रुघ्नो नीतः

प्रीतिपुरस्कृतः ॥ Ayodâ. K. I. 1. So to secure agreement with the Rámà., the comp. may be taken as शत्रुघ्नश्चासौ लक्ष्मणश्च तेन. There is also no reason why two men were required to take the jar. But still this does not appear to be the poet's meaning. He makes Bharata stay at home. Prof. Parânjpe thinks that Bhása himself refers to the return of Śatrughna along with भरत in the question किं शत्रुघ्नो मामभिगतः । in the third Act. But the querry does not support this view. That question was asked to the भट who came from Ayodhyá, and would be reasonable only on the supposition that Śat. was in Ayodhyà; for how was the Bhata to know how far Śat. had advanced when Bharata himself did not know it. Again the use of the plural भ्रातरः in III. 3 points to the conclusion that the three brothers were in Ayodhyà. Gana. S'astri also supports this view when he says शत्रुघ्नस्य पृष्ठतो रथान्तरेणानुगन्तुः (*i. e.* following Bhata) स्वान्तिकप्रापणविषयः प्रश्नः. The poet, for dramatic effect, makes Śat. stay in Ayodhyá. For had Śat. accompanied Bharata and was near at hand he would have certainly overtaken his brother in a short time. But the poet did not want Śat. to be with Bharata. The scene in the statue-house would not have been then so pathetic. Śat. would have tried to console his brother and the pathos would have suffered. **मन्थरया**—The poet first makes Mantharâ come with a message from Kaikeyî and stop the coronation. The two चs in the last line show the simulaneousness of the two actions. **न चास्मि राजा**—I at once ceased to be the king. Ráma knows this much only at this stage, that his coronation was stopped at Kaikeyî's suggestion. The further developments will be revealed to him afterwards.

महाराज एव &c.—Mark the nobility of Sîtá's mind again. She is glad to hear that her father-in-law continues to be the king. *Cf.* this with Ráma's speech at p 10. **न आबध्नामि**—I do not, *i. e.* I have no mind to, wear.

Śl. 8. **पाश**—The lobe of the ear (when used separately; added to कर्ण it means 'beautiful'; *cf.* पाशः—कर्णान्ते शोभनार्थः स्यात्कचान्ते निकरार्थकः । It is difficult to understand how the lobes of the ears could have been curved the pendents being removed in haste, unless they were naturally curved; त्वरा has no propriety then. **गौर** reddish or reddish yellow owing to friction; for this meaning *cf.* कुङ्कुमक्षोदगौरैः Rat I. 10; गोरोचनाक्षेपनितान्तगौरै । Kum. VII. 17.

P. 13. स्थानानि नेव समतां &c.—For a similar observation *cf.* शय्या नावनता तथास्तृतसमा &c. Svap. V. 4.

पारयति &c.—Sītá is not speaking seriously here; she wants to defend herself somehow. She means–I told you the truth; you said I took them off and have represented this as true. G. Śás, however, to give a good turn to Sîtâ's speech, adds पारयति । का कथा तात्त्विकेऽर्थे इत्यभिप्रायः । तेन हि—If so, if you had not put them on, do now wear them

आदर्शे धारयिष्ये—This gallantry is not much in keeping with Ráma's character. निर्वर्ण्य—Having closely observed, *i. e.* Sîtâ's reflection in the mirror. It is strange that Râma who could mark from a distance the depressions on Sîtá's limbs caused by the removal of the ornaments should fail to see the bark garments when standing by her side. Perhaps the explanation is this—The bark garments looking like silk garments owing to Sîtà's bodily complexion were not noticed as such by Râma at first sight. He notices them on closer observation and says तिष्ठ. This is a device of the poet to allow Sītá to remain without ornaments.

Śl. 9 वल्कलानीव—Rámа, knowing that there was no occasion for Sîtá to wear bark garments, hesitates to ask her plainly why she should have worn barks, and so says—what I see in the mirror look like bark gadrments. Are they? Or are they the sun's rays flashing forth? We are already told that the garments looked golden (सौवर्णमिव) on Sītá's person. Hence Ráma's doubt; so the figure here is संदेहालंकार.

हसितेन परिज्ञातं—Observing Sîtâ smile he says—I know from your smile that they are bark garments. क्रीडेयं—These are two questions, वा being understood. Is this done for fun or out of a deire to take up some vow? Or the two may be taken as one sentence. Is this desire for a vow, as appears from the fact that you have worn bark garments, mere sport (or fun)?

Here the question arises-How to account for the sudden use of the word वल्कल in the plural here? The word has hitherto been used in the sing. (see pp. 5, 6, 7, 10); while having once used it in the plural the poet has taken care to use it in the plural hereafter. The only possible explanation is that the sing. has been used in the sense of the pl. by the maxim जातौ एकवचनम्. What अवदानिका snatched away from the Music-hall must have been a bundle of bark-garments as is clear from Revá's speech at p. 21. She handed over the same to Sîtá. The latter wore two of them and had one or two left with her. And these Ráma further on asks for himself. See p. 20. Or the use of the sing in the earlier part may be due to the poet's oversight.

किं नु खलु शोभते &c.—Here again the poet has been careless enough to use the sing. (वल्कलं शोभते) and plural in the same sentence. आबद्धाः—वल्कल is both mas. and neu.; see com.

वृद्धालंकारः—For dissolution see com.; is equivalent to वार्धक्योचितोलंकारः. उज्झित &c.—Your coronation has been obstructed and this your desire to wear barks leads me to apprehend some other evil.

P. 14. Śl. 10. मा उत्पाद्य—The use of मा with the gerund is ungrammatical. Bhàsa, however, often uses it thus on the analogy of अलं which can be used with a gerund. See com. विशेषतः परिहासे—Especially when I do it for joke. Or the construction may be परिहासे विशेषतः स्वयं &c. Prof. Paránjpe takes विशेषतः with the second half in the alternative construction suggested by him. शरीरार्धेन —*Cf.* the Śruti quoted in the com.; and for a similar idea king Henry VIII saying to his queen Katherine—

Arise and take place by us; half your suit

Never name to us; you have half our power.

Shakespear's King Henry VIII. Act. I Scene II.

Ráma means—When you who form half of my body have worn them, what apprehension of evil can you have if I, forming the other half, wear them? Or what affects the half must affect the whole.

Śl. 11. निर्मर्यादः—transcending bounds, excessively loud. यदा—since. प्रभवामि इति—इति at the thought that, thinking that. प्रभवामि—I have power over all; I am all powerful; *i. e.* displaying its power without discrimination. मूले—At the root; he fears that some great evil must have befallen Daśaratha; otherwise there would not be such an unprecedented clamour. ज्ञायतां शब्दः—The order must have been given either to अव० or to the चेटी or to both, as they were at hand.

प्रविश्य का०—The Kanch. comes to call Râma seeing Das'aratha lying unconscious; see *infra* s'l. 16. एकशरीर०—Das'a. was the king of the whole earth; if he is to be protected, the whole earth is to be protected.

Cf. for a similar idea—'How easy dost thou bear whole England up' said by Bastard to Hubert when he lifted up the dead body of Arthur, the rightful king of England. King John, Act IV. Scene III. l. 142.

P. 15. **नास्ति प्रतीकारः**—For प्रतीकार would mean destroying one kinsman to save another. *Cf.* for a similar sentiment अहो बत महत्पापं कर्तुं व्यवसिता वयम् । यद्राज्यसुखलोभेन हन्तुं स्वजनमुद्यताः ॥ Bg. I. 45.

Śl. 12. **कस्य** &c.—Ráma means—I cannot punish such a kinsman; I shall simply feel ashamed to own such a person as *my* relative.

उदर्कः—From अर्क् or ऋच् (उदर्क्यते, उदृच्यते वा इति) and aff. अ (घञ्); the consequence or result of an action (उदर्कः फलमुत्तरं Ak). *Cf.* उदर्कस्तव कल्याणि कल्याणो भविता शुभे। Nalo. XII. 67. **गुणेन**—उदर्कः गुणः भवेत्. The result will be a blessing or advantage *i. e.* will lead to something blissful (गुणवान भवेत्).

Śl. 13. **मया पुत्रवती** &c.—He means—What is there that we two cannot accomplish for her? **अकार्यं**--see com., an evil or despicable deed.

उपहत—Condemned as wicked, croocked (as opposed to ऋजु). **तस्याः वचनात्**—her direction—message, conveyed to the king through Mantharâ; see *Supra* śl. 7. The poet represents the matter in this way, of course against the Ràmáyana. **अत्र**—Here it may be in the sense of the abl. or the locative.

Śl. 14. **वनगमन०**—Mark how, like Sîtá, Ràma, too, attaches the first importance to his father's comfort. **पितृपरवत्ता**—He means.—I have no reponsibility hanging on my shoulders; I shall have to execute the orders of my father only and so I shall not incur blame. **बालभावः**—Had I been the king I should have been the head of the family and so ceased to be a child; again the days of childhood are the happiest, *cf.* Uttar. I. 19. **विमर्शः**—Consideration of a matter, judgment, dispensation of justice. **परिभोग**—परि परितो भोगः परिभोग—full enjoyment, enjoyment of pleasures according to their will which they could not have done, had I been the king, feeling constrained.

अनाहूतोप०—The word अनाहुत is significant. Kanch. means--She was not consulted by the king as to what was to be done next. She came of her own accord.

अत्राप्यलोभः—We expect the Kanch. to ask अत्रापि गुण एव referring to Ráma's remark गुणाः खल्वत्र; but he says अलोभ. The reason is this—Kanch. thought that the gist of Ráma's, speech was that what Kai. did was not done through any selfish motive. So he flings a retort at Ráma, saying अत्रापि even in this demand (to have Bharata crowned king) अलोभ: गुण: किम् ।

Cf. The following verse as an illustration of a poet's wit wherein Kaikeyî is represented as having created a puzzle for Das'aratha-व्याकोचेन्दीवराभं वरनयनयुगं बिभ्रती स्वर्णवर्णा गत्वा राजानमेवं सरभसमवदत्कैकयी साधुमध्ये । राजन्रामाभिषेको विरमतु स कथं निष्कलङ्कं च राज्ये भूजा या यस्य जाया स भवति कथं भूपती रामचंद्रः ॥

Śl. 15. शुल्के—शुल्कार्थे; शुल्क the money or present given to a bride by the bride-groom at the time of marriage, a marriage settlement. Das'a. had promised Kai. to grant any two of her requests, she having carefully tended him when wounded in battle. She made use of these on this occasion. That the kingdom was promised by Das'a. to Kaikeyî's father would appear from the following speech of Ráma addressed to Bharata—पुरा भ्रातः पिता नः स मातरं ते समुद्वहन् । मातामहे समाश्रौषीद्राज्यशुल्कमनुत्तमम् ॥ देवासुरे च संग्रामे जनन्यै तव पार्थिवः । संप्रहृष्टो ददौ राजा वरमाराधितः प्रभुः ॥ &c. Ráma. Ayod. CVII. 3, 4.

अथ—The Kan. wished to cite another instance of Kaikeyi's wicked nature, but Ràma cut short his speech, saying अतःपरं &c. Another instance of Ráma's magnanimity of mind.

P. 17. Śl. 16. अवचनात—किमप्यनुक्त्वा. किमप्यभिमतं &c.—This is somewhat obscure. अभिमतं may be an adj. qualifying मोहं, the const. being किमपि अभिमतं मोहं, यथाहं मन्ये, नृपतिः गतः The king fell into a swoon which was somewhat desirable, as I think. Or किमपि &c. may be taken as a separate sentence-नृपतिः मोहं गतः and this I think was in some way a desirable thing.

कथं कथं मोह०—These are the words uttered in anger by Lakshmaṇa who is behind the curtain. The first कथं means—How do you ask कथं &c.

Śl. 17. येन रुष्टेन—In the first line Ráma says क्षोभितः; and for symmetry he should have used the same root and said येन क्षुब्धेन. शताकीर्णमिव—As पश्यामि has no object we may supply स्थानं; अग्रतः स्थानं शताकीर्णमिव पश्यामि; or कीर्ण may be taken as a noun; a crowd of hundred men. For this use *cf.* न शक्नोमि आकीर्णे जिह्मां रक्षितुम् । Vik. II. p. 82 One enraged Lak. appeared to Ráma like a hundred men; *cf.* for the idea एको दाशरथिः कामं यातुधानाः सहस्रशः । ते तु यावन्त एवाजौ तावांश्च ददृशे स तैः ॥ Ragh. 12. 45

Śl. 18. **मा दया**—We expect दयाम्; but as it is we must explain मा दयास्तु. Or read दयाम्. **स्वजननिभृतः**—स्वजने स्वजनविषये (with regard to) निभृत: sitting silent; patiently bearing the injury done. *Cf.* यो न दर्शयते तेजः क्षत्रियः काल आगते । सर्वभूतानि तं पार्थ सदा परिभवन्त्युत ॥ Mahads. Van. Ch. 27; and भरतस्याथ पक्षो वा यो वास्य हितमिच्छति । सर्वांस्तांश्च वधिष्यामि मृदुर्हि परिभूयते ॥ Rámá. Ayod. XXI. 11.

युवतिरहितं—As the present misfortune was brought about by a young woman, Laks. whets his anger against all young women and wants to destroy them.

P. 18. **रोदितव्ये**—For Daśaratha had fainted and it was time to think of the father instead of the bow. **सुमित्रामातः**—Bhása is very fond of using such matronymics; *cf.* कैकेयीमातः, कौसल्यामातः, गान्धारीमातः, शौरसेनीमातः; यादवीमातः in Bala; Panch. &c.

Śl. 19. **शोच्यासने**—शोच्यं आसनं स्थितिः (position, condition) यस्य whose life has been made miserable. **निर्मनस्विता**—supply या. Absence of मनस्विता chivalrous spirit, sense of self respect.

सुमित्रामातः—Here the epithet is significant; the son of Sumitrá also ought to be a *sumitra*. He must take a sober view of a matter.

Śl. 20. **वयं**—Ràma uses the pl. instead of the sing. अहं to please Laks., who has identified his interest with his (Ráma's). **यदि तेऽस्ति** &c.—This line occurs in Abhi. III 22, an evidence of the common authorship of the plays. **न शक्नोमि**—This sentence also occurs in Abh. and Dut.gh.

Śl. 21. **त्रैलोक्यं**—is derived from त्रिलोक and not a Dwigu, which would give त्रिलोकी. **वधुकामा**—The nasal of the inf. is dropped before काम and मनस्. **नियतीव**—A grammatical inaccuracy. It should be नियतिरिव. So to get the long ई we must have recourse to the grammatical device of adding the fem. aff. ई to नियति; see com. The reading वियतीव is free from any grammatical flaw; but the sense is monstrous. **व्यवस्थिता**—Fixed, never failing in its course; the meaning is—as no body can alter the will of fate so no one can withstand Lak.'s. anger.

P. 19. **स्थैर्ये**—Steadiness, the calming of agitation. **एवं** refers to Râma's previous speech.

Sl. 22. **ताते धनुर्नमयि**—The line is obscurse, and the readings are not settled. Symmetry requires a verb in the Impera. 1st person sing. here; for we have मुञ्चानि and हनानि in the next two lines. And looking to the poet's indifference to grammar he might have used नमयि for नमये cau. of नम् Atm. Hence the reading नमयि is adopted here. The reading नमतु is grammatically faultless, but breaks symmetry. Mm. G. S. reads धनुर्न मयि &c. and explains ताते विषये तातं प्रतीत्यर्थः धनुर्न चापप्रयोगकथैव नास्ति । But this reading is against the fourth line. For if the bow is not to be drawn against the father, then there is no sin in that; and then where is the third sin referred to in the fourth line ? स्वधनं हरन्त्यां—*Cf supra* s'l. 15; mark the sarcastic tone of Ráma in this Śloka.

Śl. 23. The sense of the first line is obscure. महति क्लेशे cannot be taken with राज्ये ; that would require महाक्लेशे. Lak. resents the rebuke administered to him by Râma in the previous Śl. and says—You do not know the real state of my feelings, or the cause that led to them by causing such great affliction to me as removed all desire for a kingdom from my heart. To make this sense clear the line must be amptified thus.—यत्कृते येन कारणेन कृते महति क्लेशे मम मनासि स्थिते मे राज्ये मनोरथः न तत् शृणु । एतत्तत्—चतुर्दश &c. This is an instanse of how Bhâsa often leaves his full sense to be understood by his readers. किल surely ; or as I heard.

P. 20. अत्र—At this demand; at this incident. हन्त &c.—Ráma is sorry that his father should have betrayed the weakness of his mind in that way.

Śl. 24. मङ्गलार्थे—is to be construed with आनय. Râma adds this to allow Sítá no opportunity to refuse his request on the ground of अमङ्गलत्व as was done by her when he first asked for them. अनया—refers to अवदातिका; but the poet has not told us how Râma came to know that they were given by Avadátiká; for he was not present then. So this again is an instance of how the poet often leaves things to the imagination of the reader. Here we are to suppose that Râma guessed it from the words of Avadátiká on p. 13 (भर्तः किन्तु खलु &c.). वृत्तान् वल्कलान् *i. e.* those worn by Sítá on her person.

करोमि &c.—Râma attached the highest importance to the performance of धर्म; *cf.* धर्मो हि परमो लोके धर्मे सत्यं प्रतिष्ठितम् । धर्मसंश्रितमप्येतत्पितुर्वचनमुत्तमम् ॥ Ayod. XXI. 41; and धृतं बाल्ये तदार्येण पुण्यमारण्यकं व्रतम् । Uttar I. 22

गृह्णातु &c.—Now Sítá has no option but to offer the bark garments to Ráma. The poet however wants the bark-garments to remain on Sítá's person. So before she takes them off he makes Ráma interfere saying मैथिलि &c.

सहधर्म०—and so I am bound to follow you in your exile. देवतानां प्रणामः &c.—I will offer prayer to the deities and commit my elders to their care and they will look after them. For a similar idea *cf.* Mud. VII अनुगृह्णन्त्वेनं प्रसन्ना देवताः। P. 346

श्लाघनीये काले—The sense is—at a time when she ought to be praised; or श्लाघनीय may refer to the काल also, at a time which is commendable (welcome) on account of her noble resolve. काले-कार्ये *V. l.* is bad from a grammatical point; वृ cau. will require the abl. with it (श्लाघनीयात्कार्यात्)

Śl. 25. Now the poet cites instances to show how women follow their husbands even in adversity. तारा—The wife of Soma. Here a star that appears to follow the moon. वनवृक्षे—Here the word वन has no special propriety.

P. 21. भर्तृनाथाः—*i. e.* solely dependent on their husbands; a woman must be where her husband is. *Cf.* शशिना सह याति कौमुदी सह मेघेन तडित्प्रलीयते। प्रमदाः पतिवर्त्मगा इति प्रतिपन्नं हि विचेतनैरपि ॥ Kum. IV. 33; and पतिकुले तव दास्यमपि क्षमम्। Sak. V. 27.

आर्यरेवा विज्ञापयति—Revá must have guessed that the bark garments taken away by Avadatiká were wanted by Sîtâ, her mistress, and to please her (Sîtá) now sends more. This is the poet's device to provide Ráma with the required bark garments.

Śl. 26. निर्योगात—This is a word of rare occurrence. G. S'. explains it as वस्त्रकञ्चुकादेराच्छादनात् what is used for covering the body with, such as garments; robes, &c.

P. 22. Śl. 27. तवैव—Hereby Lak. admits that Sîtá, as his wife has the first right to serve Ráma; but he may be also allowed to serve him in a subordinate position. The variant तवैव does not bring out this sense so prominently.

Śl. 28. This is an instance of माला or परंपरित रूपक. तपःसंग्राम०—*i. e.* the bark garments enable a man to practise penance resisting impediments (successfully). खलीनमि०—The senses are compared to horses on account of their unruly nature. *Cf.* इन्द्रियाणि हयानाहुः Kathop. III. 4. If the senses grow unruly the bark garments tell a person that they should not be allowed a free course but ought to be checked. धर्मसारथिः—The idea of रथ to which धर्म is compared is included in सारथि. गृह्यतां—The subject of this being वल्कलानि this should be in the plural.

But the sing. is used to give prominence to the predicates which are in the sing.; वल्कलानि ०कवचं गृह्यतां, &c.

Śl. 29. स्वैरं हि &c.—Ráma, thinking that the citizens, who were in tears and who loved them, might like to have a sight of Sîtá, gives them permission to do so. वदनैः—The inst. is उपलक्षणे. निर्दोषदृश्या—&c. *Cf.* व्यसनेषु न कृच्छ्रेषु न युद्धेषु स्वयंवरे। न क्रतौ नो विवाहे वा दर्शनं दूष्यते स्त्रियाः॥ Rámá Yudh. CXIV. 28.

P. 23. Śl. 30. सौभ्रात्र०—शोभनः भ्राता सुभ्राता तस्य भावः; for comp. see com. उत्थाय—for he had fallen into a swoon. क्षितितल &c.—रूषित covered with; *cf.* अन्तर्गिरि रेणुरूषितः Kir. I. 34. This qualifies also कान्तारद्विरद्. Daśa. is compared to an elephant on account of the hugeness of his form.

Śl. 31. चीरमा०—चीरमेव चीरमात्रं. उत्तरीयाणां—Because it is the upper garment that attracts attention first. वनवासिनां—Lak. angrily says this—we are forest-residents now, and not town-residents. गतेष्वस्मासु Ráma means-we are sure to go; nothing can make us change our resolve. शिरःस्थानानि—Principal abodes. G. S. Or स्थान may mean सादृश्य as Prof. Devadhar takes it; शिरःसादृश्यानि likenesses of our heads, *i. e.* our persons painted in his palace. In his anxiety to finish the Act. the poet makes Ráma guilty of indifference towards his father. According to the Rámá. he goes to see his father with Sumantra before his departure to the forest; see Ayod. ch. 33. 29-31 and ch. 34.

ACT. II

P. 24. प्रतिहारव्यापृताः—Lit. engaged *i. e.* keeping guard at the doors. *Cf. supra* प्रतिहाररक्षी p. 3.

उपावर्तयितुं—To make him turn back from; *cf.* for this sense त्वदुपावर्तनशङ्कि मे मनः; Raghu. VIII. 53. The variant अपा० gives the same sense. This may also mean 'to conciliate, to win over; *cf.* कथं वामशीलां मालतीमुपावर्तये। Mal. Mad. VIII. p. 161. समुद्रगृह &c.—occurs also in Svap V.; it was a pavilion or pleasure house built in the middle of an artificial lake, or surrounded by jets of water (see com.) within the precincts of the palace. Káli. also refers to it in his Mal. IV. p. 132

Śl. 1. Construe युगक्षयसंनिकर्षे चलन् मेरुः इव शोषं व्रजन् अप्रमेयः महोदधिः इव शिथिलदेहमतिः नरेन्द्रः तिष्ठति। मण्डल०—His disc only being observable, all light being lost. There is प्रक्रमभङ्ग in this

Śl. as there are epithets used to qualify महोदधि and सूर्य but none to qualify मेरु.

अहो तु खलु—The usual form of the expression is अहो नु खलु; but तु appears in place of नु in Bhása's plays.

P. 25. Śl. 2 **यवस**—Tender grass. यवसे अभिलाषः तस्माद्विमुखाः; वाजिनः अस्रैः सहिते सास्रे ईक्षणे येषां ते सास्रेक्षणाः हेषाशून्यमुखाः च; हेषा neighing, also ह्रेषा, ह्रेषित &c. जनाः उच्चैः क्रन्दन्तः यया दिशा सदारसहजः रामः याति तां दिशं पश्यन्ति ।

महादेव्या—By Kausalyá. **आत्मानमेव**—goes with महाराजः; महाराजः आत्मानमेव (him alone) संस्थापयन्तीभ्यामन्वास्यमानः.

Śl. 3. Supply च after second उत्थाय. The repetition shows that he rose, sat down again, and so on. **रघूद्वहः**—रघूणामुद्वहः, the chief of Raghus. उद्वहतीत्युद्वहः.

विष्कम्भकः—See com ; विष्क० is one which shows in a few words the connection between the parts of the story past and to follow by means of a conversation between characters other than the chief ones. It is शुद्ध when carried on by one or more minor characters and मिश्र when by characters minor and low. There is a शुद्धवि० at the beginning of the sixth Act.

P. 26. Śl. 4. **तनूजाः**—includes Sítá also; *cf.* पुत्रकाः further on.

क्वासौ सर्वजन०......राज्यैश्वर्यः—In the first and fourth of these four sentences Dasàratha undoubtedly refers to Ráma. In the second and the third he appears to refer to his qualities, and so some might find the fault भग्नप्रक्रमता here. But the absence of the word तस्य shows that in these two also he refers to Ràma. In the second गुर्वनुवृत्ति may be taken as a Bah-Comp. (गुर्वी अनुवृत्तिर्यस्य) and then it will refer to Ráma; while in the third Das'a speaks of Ráma as अनुकम्पा itself, identifying it with Ráma (कृपाकर्तरि कृपातादात्म्यारोपः । G. S.). **असम्बद्धेन**—not standing to reason, inconsistent, since it makes one abandon one's father. Prof. Parànjpe thinks that this is used in contrast with (जनकत्वेन सम्बद्धं पितरं).

Śl. 7. **दिवसः**—is used in the sense of 'day-ligh'. The simile shows the inseparableness of the two.

Śl. 8. **रामः अन्यस्य** &c.—At least Ráma should not have been my son. **वने व्याघ्री**—and not a princess, as she was cruel-hearted like a tigress.

P. 27. **अलमिदानीं** &c.—*Cf.* note on कुमार अलमुपहताासु स्त्रीबुद्धिषु &c. *supra* p. 15. अलं परवशं कर्तुं परवशं मा कुरु इत्यर्थः । As अलं has here the force of the imperative, the word महाराज, the agent of the action prohibited, ought to have been in the Voc. and not in the Nom., like कुमार in the above sentence. G. S., however, reads अलं with a *Ka'ku,* taking it in the sense of 'able', and not as a prohibitive particle, which will then require the Nom.; महाराजः आत्मानं परवशं कर्तुमलं । किं समर्थः किम् न समर्थः should not have the power (should not be so weak-minded as) to yield to sorrow. But this is not satisfactory. **अस्निग्धपुत्र०**—Kau. in her dejection calls राम अस्निग्ध since he put his father's life in danger by his obstinacy in going to the forest. Daśa., however, does not like that and hastens to correct her, saying—No, you are सर्वजन० रामस्य जननी. **त्वया हि खलु** &c.—रामः गर्भे धारितः यः सारवान्. He means सा त्वं सारवती असि न त्वहं (which follows from the next Śl.). *Cf.* the similar remark of Vasudeva—अहो गुरुत्वं बालस्य ।.........अयं बालः गर्भे यया धृतः श्रीमानहो धैर्यं हि योषितः । Bal. I. 12.

Śl. 9. **मुषितेन्द्रियः**—With power of perception of the senses gone; and he was such, as is evinced by his question to Kausalyá कात्वं भो and his next question about सुमित्रा. In the Rámá. also he is thus described-चक्षुषा त्वां न पश्यामि स्मृतिर्मम विलुप्यते । दूता वैवस्वतस्त्वेते कौसल्ये त्वरयन्ति माम् ॥ Ayod. LXV. 65. **नैव शक्नोमि**—*cf.* न च खलु परिभोक्तुं नैव शक्नोमि हातुम् । Śak. V. 15. **वच्छलक्खण** (इत्यर्धोक्ते)-कासौ &c.; *cf.* शकुन्तला-वण्णं पेक्ख । कुत्र वा मम माता । वत्सास्य मृत्तिकामयूरस्य लावण्यं &c. Śak. VII. p. 274

P. 28. Śl. 10. **नक्तंदिवं**—A Dwand. comp. of the particles नक्तं and दिवा irregularly formed. See Sid. Kau. on Pan. V. 4. 77.

पुरुषविशेषाः—विशिष्यते इति विशेषः what is left out as distinguished from others; hence preeminent, of exceptional virtue पुरुषाणां विशेषाः.

विधिरनतिक्रमणीयः—अनतिक्रमणीयो हि विधिः । Svap. IV. p. 90

Śl. 11. **भग्नो मम मनोरथः**—has also a side-meaning—The car of my mind is broken and I cannot live now.

P. 29. Śl. 12. *Cf.* धन्याः खलु वने वाताः कह्लारस्पर्शशीतलाः । राममिन्दीवरश्यामं ये पश्यन्त्यनिवारिताः ॥ quoted in the Sah. D. under X. Káriká 59, 60 whereon the com. says वृक्षारस्थस्योक्तिरियम्.

Śl. 14. **क्व मे ज्येष्ठो रामः**—Daśa. impulsively said मे रामः, but suddenly remembering how cruel and unfatherly his treatment of Râma was thought that he had no right to call him his son, and changed his wording saying ते ज्येष्ठः &c. **प्रियसुत**—Ráma deserves to be called your son, because you are प्रियसुत, I am not. **निरतिशयभक्तिः**—A grammatical anomaly; it should निरतिशयाभक्तिः, as पुंवद्भाव (the becoming *Mas.* of a femi. base forming the first member of a Bah. Comp.) allowed by Pán. VI. 3. 34, is prohibited in the case of the words of the प्रियादि group of which भक्ति is one. So this must be dissolved (after Malli. on दृढभक्तिः Ragh. XII. 19), as a नपुंसकपूर्वपदबहुव्रीहि—निरतिशयं भक्तिरस्य, on the principle सामान्ये नपुंसकं 'when the gender of the first member is अविवक्षित (not meant to be prominent) the neu. gen. may be used; as remarked by the Vṛittikára—दृढभक्तिरित्येवमादिषु स्त्रीपूर्वपदस्याविवक्षितत्वात्। According to Bhojarája the word भक्ति included in the प्रियादि group is derived as भज्यते इति भक्ति, the aff. क्ति being added कर्मणि as in भवानीभक्तिः, while here it should be derived as भजनं भक्तिः, ति being added भावे and so there can be पुंवद्भाव.

मां हतपि०—Construe ते हतपितृकं मां किमप्याहुः किम्। कुत्सितः condemned, censurable हतेपिता हतपितृकः; the aff. क indicates कुत्सा or reproach. **सकलजन०**—is meant to indicate the extreme wickedness of his act; he means-I am not only a हतपिता, but सकल०—न तु स्वजनशोककर; न केवलं शोककरः किंतु शोकार्णवकरः।

P. 30. **अमङ्गलानि**—refers to Dasa.'s calling himself आसन्नमरण in the preceding śl. **सत्यमयुक्तमभिहितं मया**—We expect Das'a. to say अमङ्गलं instead of अयुक्तं in reply to Sumantra's words मा मैवं &c. But Das'a. was not thinking of himself at all. The one uppermost thought in his mind was that about his sons in the forest; and the words न हि न हि। अयुक्तमभिहितं मया were still fresh in his memory; and so without taking notice of what Sumantra said he goes on with his own ideas and says सत्यं न युक्तं &c. **तपस्विनां**—i. *e*. his forest-living sons. **स्वाधीनानि**—completely brought under her sway, by being rendered safe for her to move about, by Ráma and Lakshmaṇa.

सुमित्रा—सुमन्त्र &c. Sumitrá who was hitherto silent seizes this occasion to speak as was natural, and asks as a woman, if Sîta' had sent any message to them.

बहुवल्कला०—Here बहु has no propriety unless it be taken to mean 'in various ways (बहु यथा तथा)'. Or बहु may be taken to mean 'large, comfortable (that can be well worn). **चारित्रा** see com. **सर्व एव महाराजं**—The sentence is incomplete and we expect the stage-direction इत्यर्धोक्ते after this. The king not liking that Sumantra should have referred to his sons generally, as सर्वे एव interrupts him here, saying न न &c. **श्रोत्ररसायनैः**—रसायन is a powerful medicine (so called from रस mercury) that prolongs life and keeps off old age; see com.; hence what gratifies or pleases; *cf.* मनसश्च रसायनानि । Uttar. I. 36. **अयं रामः**—As soon as Sum. uttered the name of Ráma, Dasaratha's fancy placed his image before him.

इयं सीता जनकराजपुत्री—Sumantra adds the epithet जनक० because Sîtá was familiarly addressed by one of her patronimics in the household. We have already seen Ráma addressing her as मैथिली in the first Act. And the king here also says इयं वैदेही. Prof. Paràñjpe, rightly thinks that the word Sîtá should have been dropped for the sake of uniformity from this speech; also as we find Sumantra when repeating the names saying आयुष्मती जनकराजपुत्री alone.

P. 31. **अयमक्रमः** &c.—*cf.* द्रोणः—अयमक्रमः । दुर्योधनः—अथ कः क्रमः । Panch. I.

Śl. 15. **अत्रापि**—Even here (in the order of the names) not to speak of the forest. **बहुदोषाणि**—*cf.* बहुदोषं हि कान्तारं वनमित्यभिधीयते । Ayo. XXVIII. 5. **सनाथैषा भविष्यति**—This was actually done by Ráma when wandering through a forest. *Cf.* अग्रतो गच्छ सौमित्रे सीता त्वामनुगच्छतु । पृष्ठतोनुगमिष्यामि सीतां त्वां चानुपालयन् ॥ Ayod. LII. 95-96.

Śl. 16. **स्पृशामि**—He fancies to do so. **गतायुः**—When taken with Daśa. means whose life is almost at an end. **अमृतेनेव**—Ráma's स्पर्श and दर्शन are compared to nectar.

शृङ्गिवेर—शृङ्गवेर is the name found in the Ràmá.; see Ayod. L. 26. **सर्व एव महाराजं**—Sumantra now completes the sentence begun by him on the last page; but as Daśa. wanted details he now begins with शृङ्गिवेर &c.

Śl. 17. **बाष्पस्तम्भित०**—They were so much over-powered by emotion at the thought of your condition and the grief caused to the elders that they were struck dumb and went away with pitiable looks. This was true of Sītá-*cf.* जानकी तु महाराज निश्वसन्ती तपस्विनी । अदृष्टपूर्वव्यसना नैव मां किंचिदब्रवीत् ॥ Ayod. LVIII. 34-35. But the poet, for dramatic effect, represents Râma and Lak. also as going away without sending any message. For their message, see Ayod. LII. 27-36; LVIII. 15-33.

P. 32. Śl. 18. With this *cf.* the Śl. from the Ràmà. quoted in the com.

Śl. 19. **सन्नरपतेः**—सन् (good, just.) चासौ नरपतिश्च तस्य । **कृतार्थाः** *cf. supra* I. 4.

Śl. 20. **जीवितैः**—used in the pl. like प्राण. **पापं** &c.—The student will mark the sarcastic tone of the message.

यदाज्ञापयति &c.—Sumantra, however, does not leave the king as he is in his last moments, knowing that the message was simply meant as a taunt against Kaikeyī.

आगताः पितरः—Daśa. in his mental aberation fancies to see his dead forefathers come down to console him. Dyii g men have often such visions. But the death-scene here is very pathetic and impressive and is a creation of the poet's fancy. In the Rámâ. Daśa. is represented as dying only thinking of Ráma. Bhása has two other similar scenes. In his अभिषेक I he makes Válî., when about to breathe his last, say:—

परित्यजन्तीव मां प्राणाः । इमा गङ्गाप्रभृतयो महानद्यः । एता उर्वश्यादयोऽप्सरसो मामभिगताः । एष सहस्रहंसप्रयुक्तो वीरवाही विमानः कालेन प्रेषितो मां नेतुमागतः । भवतु । अयमहमागच्छामि ।

While in his ऊरुभङ्ग he makes Duryodhana, when in the last agonies of death, say—परित्यजन्ति मे प्राणाः । इमेऽत्रभवन्तः शन्तनुप्रभृतयो मे पितृपितामहाः । एतत्कर्णमग्रतः कृत्वा समुत्थितं भ्रातृशतम् । इमा उर्वश्यादयः &c.—much the same as in अभिषेक.

P. 33. आपस्तावत्—The water was required for आचमन which is enjoined before a religious or a solemn act. We have the same expression in some six of the poet's plays-once again in the present play Act. IV, twice in Mad. Vyá. twice in Panch. and once in Du., Abh., and Prat. Yaug.

Śl. 21. The order of the names of the ancestors of Das'aratha here is the same as that given by Ka li. in his Raghuvaṁsa. Das'a must have recognised them from the order of precedence in which they appeared before his mind's eye, *viz* Dilîpa, Raghu and Aja. According to the lists of the Ikshva'ku kings given in the Ráma'., Vishnu P. and others, some 16 to 20 kings intervene between Dilîpa and Ra'ma. This S'l is meant as an introduction to the scene in the statue—house in the next Act.

मूर्च्छया परामृष्टः—This stage-direction is not proper as the king was actually dead. So one of the variants, *viz.* स्वर्यातः and स्वर्गं गतः, noticed by Prof. Paránjpe, should be adopted. हा हा महाराओ—This is uttered by the two females Kausalyâ and Sumitra'.

ACT III.

सुधाकारः—The servant whose duty, as his name signifies, was to keep the statue-house clean (white). संमार्जनादीनि—what is meant by आदीनि is stated by the man in his speech at p. 34. पश्यतु भर्ता &c. In the next stage-direction he is called चेट.

P. 34. अह्णो—A particle of address expressing anger. दास्याःपुत्र—One word; also दासीपुत्र when censure is implied.

कार्तवीर्यस्य—Ka'rtavîrya was the son of Kritavîrya and king of the Haihayas. His capital was Ma'hishmatî. He propitiated God Dattátreya and obtained from him several boons, such as the possession of a thousand arms, a golden chariot that went wherever he willed it to go, &c. See Ragh. VI. 39. He was slain by Parashura'ma. He was also called सहस्रार्जुन. एहि दास्याःपुत्र &c.—Here we have a picture of how poor servants were treated by persons in authority. नास्ति किलापराधः—is a sarcastic reply to the servant's शक्यमपराधं ज्ञातुम्.

राज्यविभ्रष्ट &c.—Here विभ्रष्ट (loss of) is used as a noun, like विभ्रंश, the aff. त being added भावे. See com. The same is used again in Act IV. रामस्य राज्यविभ्रष्ट०.—The two should have been compounded; but रामस्य is left out of the comp. as the connection is easily known. So this is a case of सापेक्षसमास. Here Ráma's loss of the kingdom is stated as the cause of Das a.'s. death. It was really Ra'ma's departure to the forest that occasioned his death. So विभ्रष्ट may be translated by 'falling off' *i. e.* departure from the kingdom. प्रतिमागेहं—A house containing the statues or images of departed forefathers. According to Mr. A. K. Pisharoty the custom of setting up images of dead ancestors is prevalent in the Kerala country more than any where else. दशरथस्य प्रतिमागेहं—This is again सापेक्षत्वेपि गमकत्वात्समासः For the intended sense is दशरथस्य प्रतिमायाः गेहं; and so the whole should have been compounded. As the ladies of the inner apartment were to come to see the image of Das'a. that was recently set up there, it is called दशरथप्रतिमागेहं. अन्तःपुरैः—अन्तःपुर pl. means the inmates of the inner apartment; the queens; *cf.* अस्मत्प्रार्थनामन्तःपुरेभ्यः कथयेत्। S'ak. II. p. 62; See also VI. 4 *Ibid.*

संदानक—संदान that by which something is bound (संदीयतेऽनेन); a string, a chain; hence a fabric of strings, a nest, as here.

As the house was rarely visited by men, the pigeons ha built their nests in the inner shrine.

P. 35. सौधवर्णकं—the plaster or coating of chunam. चन्द-नपञ्चाङ्गुला:—Impressions of the five fingers smeared with sandal paste.

प्रकीर्णा वालुका:—Soft sand was spread near the door way to make the ground smooth for the ladies to tread upon. Nearly the same is repeated by Bharata when he approdaches the entrance to the statue-house. See *infra.* p. 38.

प्रवेशक:—See com.; a प्रवे० coming between two Acts indicates future events through the conversation of *low* characters. It can, therefore, never appear at the beginning of the first. Act. चिरं—For a long time *i. e.* 12 years. According to chap. 36 of the पातालखण्ड of the Padma P. (see *supre* note on बाल्यमस्तं p. 11) Ráma's exile to the forest took place twelve years after his marriage. And since all the brothers were married at one and the same time and Bharata was sent to his maternal uncle after his marriage, he must have passed the same number of years in the Kekaya country. मातुलपरिचयात्—परिचय familiarily, hence residence together. मातुल—This was अश्वपति *cf.* मातुलेनाश्वपतिन पुत्रस्नेहेन लालित: । Ramá. Ayod. I. 2. अकल्य—not in good health indisposed. अहो तु &c.—The usual expression is अहो नु &c. but तु is found for नु in Bhása's plays.

Śl. 1. भूमौ निरशन:—is the Sûta's answer to the question किमाहारं भुङ्क्ते शयनमपि and so the proper order is निरशन: भूमौ (शेते)

P. 36. Śl. 2. *Cf.* with this the description of Dûshyanta's chariot pursuing the deer at the beginning of the 1st Act of Śak.; also Vik. I. 4. क्षीणाविषया:—विषय one's province or place of residence; hence here the space between two trees. So quick was the motion of the chariot that the distance between tree and tree seemed narrowed and consequently the trees to follow each other rapidly. नदीवोद्वृत्ताम्बु—उद्वृत्तं flooding, *i. e.* piling up from all sides. As the waters of a swelling river pile up from all sides and fall into its centre so the earth also seemed to sink into the interstices of the spokes of the wheels which whirled up with great rapidity owing to the velocity of the chariot.

अरव्यक्तिर्नष्टा—Bharata looking at the wheels through curiosity could not distinguish the spokes from one another; they seemed to be a connected mass owing to the extreme speed of the car.

रजश्च &c—The dust raised by the horses' hoofs was seen once in front of the chariot; but before it could follow it the chariot had moved far away further and the dust could not follow it. The idea is more charmingly expressed by Kálidasa, as—आत्मोद्धतैरपि रजोभिरलङ्घनीयाः । Śak. I. 8.

सोपस्नेहतया वृक्षाणां—On account of the attractive appearance of the trees, their leaves being glossy and green, it was clear that they were watered and so a city was at hand; so he tells Bharata, that they had approached Ayodhyá, giving this as the reason, although he himself must have known it as he had gone from Ayodhyá to bring Bharata. *Cf.* सोपस्नेहतया वनान्तरस्य अभितः खलु किष्किन्धया भवितव्यम् । Abhi. I; and सोपस्नेहतया गृहाविशिष्ट इवायं भवनविन्यासः । Chám. III. त्वरता for त्वरा is unusual.

Śl. 3 & 4. In these two s'lokas Bharata pictures to his mind how he will be received and treated in the palace on his return to it after a long period of time. स्निह्यता इव— इव goes with उत्थापितः. भ्रातरः—proves conclusively that the three brothers were in Ayodhyá; see *supra*, note on शत्रुघ्नलक्ष्मण &c. I. 7. अश्रुभिः—tears of joy on seeing him after a long absence from home. सदृशः—Bhása represents Bharata as resembling his father, both as regards voice and form; *cf.* Sumantra's speech at p. 43 and IV. 6, 8. He resembled very closely his brother, Ráma, also; see Sîtâ's speech at p. 54 महान्—in bulk; व्यायत in stature. सेवया—in order to please me; for सेवा meaning flattery, *cf.* अलं सेवया मध्यस्थतां गृहीत्वा भण । Mal. III. p. 86

परिहसितं—agrees with वेषं being nearer to it; with भाषां we must have परिहसितां by लिंगविपरिणाम. सौमित्रिणा—Because Ra'ma being the eldest and therefore more serious of the brothers and S'atrughna being his younger brother could not have done it. The two S'lokas are wrongly supposed to be one and the metre a kind of Dandaka, as Dandaka requires at least 27 syllables per line. The metre is उपजाति being a mixture of प्रभा and स्रग्विणी. See com. and Malli. on Sis. XII. 1, which is a combination of इन्द्रवंशा and वंशस्थ. There is यतिभङ्ग in the third quarter of S'l. 4.

P. 37. उदर्के—उदर्क is a result that follows a certain act; here Bharata's entrance into Ayodhya'.

Śl. 5. ऐश्वर्य०—Because the charioteer knew that that would give equal pain to Bharata as the other two. दोषान्—दोष is what causes some disturbance; here of the mind, hence a misfortune, a calamity.

अभिगतः—He expected शत्रुघ्न to come to receive him in his eagerness to see his elder brother.

अभिगतः **खलु** &c.—The Bhata does not want to disappoint him; so he says—He is just on the border of Ayodhya'; near at hand; but you cannot see him. For उपाध्यायाः &c. **नाडिका**—a Ghatika' (24 minutes). **कृत्तिकाविषयः**—विषय the period of duration.

प्रतिपन्नायां रोहिण्यां—When the asterism Rohiṇî begins. Each lunar day has a *Nakshatra* assigned to it, but its period is not exactly 60 ghatikás but is less or more by a few ghatikás. Prof S. M. Paránjpe observes—"According to one of the different classifications of the Nakshatras कृत्तिका is regarded to be a क्रूरनक्षत्र and is known by the name of अग्नि and hence it is not auspicious for a person to make his first entry during the period of Kṛttika''. He has also shown how कृत्तिका was the Nakshatra of the day on which Bharata was to enter अयोध्या. Das'aratha died at midnight on the पूर्णिमा of Chaitra; and generally चित्रा is the Nakshatra of the day. And the messengers that were sent to bring Bharata immediately after the death of Daśaratha reached Kekayapura after seven days according to Kshemendra-प्राप्तेषु केकयपुरं दिनैर्दूतेषु सप्तभिः । Ayod. K. रामायणमञ्जरी. According to Rámayaṇa Bharata required the same number of days to come to Ayodhyá; (तां पुरीं पुरुषव्याघ्रः सप्तरात्रोषितः पथि । अयोध्यामग्रतो दृष्ट्वा सारथिं चेदमब्रवीत् ॥ Ayodh. K. LXXI. 14). And allowing the interval of a day to Bharata's departure from Kekayapura he must have arrived near Ayodhyá about the 16th day after Dasśa.'s death; and कृत्तिका is also the 16th Nakshatra from चित्रा. *Rohinî* is one of the auspiceous Nakśhatras, for entrance into a village &c. for marriage, for beginning the education of a child, &c. *cf.* मघामृगशिरोहस्तस्वाती मूलानुराधयोः । रेवती रोहिणी चैव उत्तरात्रितयं तथा । आवाहे च विवाहे च विद्यासंग्रहणेषु च । वापयेत्सर्वबीजानि गृहं ग्रामं प्रवेशयेत् ॥

विश्रमिष्ये—The Atm. is irregular. **उपोपविश्य**—उप is to be taken separately. उप near (समीपं) उपविश्य; occurs in Rámá. Ayod. XLII. 35. where the Com. says उप शयनसमीपे.

P. 38. **साधुमुक्त**—Well placed, well arranged. **लाजाः**—*m.* pl. fried rice formed part of auspicious offerings; *cf.* आचारलाजैरिव पौरकन्याः; Ragh. II. 20. **पार्वणः**—occurring on a पर्वन् which is the name generally given to the full-moon or new-moon day of a month.

आस्तिक्यं—अस्ति परलोक इति मतिर्यस्यासौ आस्तिक: a believer in God and another world; आस्तिकस्य भाव: आस्तिक्यं Faith, belief in God, piety; hence an act of piety, or one done through faith. **प्रहरणं ध्वजो वा**—He would have known in that case to which deity the temple belonged; see com.; for ध्वज see Kád. p. 334.

क्रियामाधुर्यं—क्रिया here means sculpture, माधुर्य the beautiful way in which the several parts of the statues were carved out and brought into relief. **भावगति:**—The expression of the inner feeligs on the faces of the images. *Cf.* the expression अहो भावोपपन्नता in Duta. used by Duryodhana when describing the painted scene of Draupadî's केशाकर्षण. **मानुषविश्वासता**—A strange comp.; मनुषा इति विश्वास: the belief that they may be human beings; a comp. सुप्सुपा; तस्य भाव:. **अथवा यानि तानि**—Here Bharata expresses a doubt as to the statues being of deities.

Śl. 6. **काम**—is used here अकामानुमतौ: granted that, though I am not sure. **वार्षल:**—such as is performed by a Súdra, who is not authorised to repeat a *mantra*. Bharata, not quite sure that the statutes represented gods and yet thinking that they deserved veneration, wishs to make a bow such as the Vṛs'alas make.

नत्यक—comes from नित्य; duties to be performed every day and which are obligatory (as distiguished from नैमित्तिक and काम्य) such as सन्ध्यावन्दन, देवपूजन &c. **प्राणिधर्म**—the function performed by a living creature, here eating, that being the chief one. This shows that the time must have bee about mid-day. **प्रतिमानामल्पा०**—He at once marked the resemblance between the stranger and the statues. That Bharata resembled Daśaratha will appear further on.

P. 39. Śl. 7. This Śl. is an instance of Bhása's condensed style. **वक्तव्यं**—Something to be said by way of blame, a fault. **नियम०**—means the power you have to enforce the rules for entrance here, to offer homage to the statues, &c. It does not seem to mean 'the arrogance due to the power of penance' as understood by G. S. For Deva. could not have appeared like a great ascetic to Bharata.

ब्राह्मणजनस्य—A man of the Brámaṇa class. Deva. thought Bharata was a Bráhmaṇa.

S'l. 8 **असुरपुरवधे**—The word वध does not fit in well with पुर; so either पुर should be taken by Lakshaṇa to mean 'the residents of the cities,' or वध to mean 'destruction or devastation.

अभिसरी—The act of marching along; is a word peculiar to Bhāsa. It is used as अभिसरि in IV. 17. *cf. infra* IV. 10.

शक्रलोके—should rather be शक्रलोकं. सपुरजनपदाः—पुर a city; जनपद the country. Ràma is described to have taken the people of Ayodhyá with him when returning to heaven; see Ragh. XV. 101, 102. अनवासिताः—not perished, lived. छन्दं मृगयता—This shows that they were इच्छामरणs death could approach them only when they wished to die.

सन्निहित०—It seems that the most precious things of all kinds were to be collected for the Vis'vajit sacrifice. Or it may mean 'in which all jewels-wealth in all its forms in the possession of the king—were to be kept at hand for being given away to the Bráhmaṇas as Dakshiná. विश्वजितः—Of the sacrific called विश्वजित्. विश्वं जयतीति विश्वजित् (fr. जि and aff. क्विप्). That which conquers all *i. e.* surpasses all other sacrifices. This is a sacrifice performed by a king who is a universal conqueror and in which the sacrificer has to give away all his wealth to the officiating priests. 'विश्वजित् सर्वस्वदक्षिणः a S'ruti quoted by Malli. on Ragh. IV. 86. प्रवर्तयिता—The institutor of, who performed for the first time. It is not Dilîpa, however, but Raghu who is mentioned as having performed the Vis'vajit sacrifice; see Raghu. IV. 86 (स विश्वजितमाजह्रे यज्ञं सर्वस्वदक्षिणम् ।) and V. 1. According to the Ràmà. Dilîpa performed many sacrifices (see com.) and to Raghu. (III. 38, 69,) 99 sacrifices. So we do not know what authority Bha'sa had for this statement. प्रज्वलित०—Dilîpa was an unswerving follower of Dharma; *cf.* आत्मकर्मक्षमं देहं क्षात्रो धर्म इवाश्रितः । and तस्य धर्मरतेरासीद्वृद्धत्वं जरसा विना। Ragh. I. 13,23. प्रदीपो दिलीपः—Mark the alliteration.

P. 40. संवेशनो०—संवेशन sleeping; for this sense, *cf.* संवेशाय विशांपतिम् । विससर्जोर्जितश्रियम् । and संविष्टः कुशशयने निशां निनाय। Ragh. I. 93, 95. उत्थापन rousing him from slumber. Bhása describes Raghu as greatly devoted to the Bráhmaṇas. Not songs of bards or minstrels, but the holy repetition of *mantras* by the Bráhmaṇas roused him from sleep. पुण्याहशब्दः—पुण्याहमिति शब्दः, the same as पुण्याहवाचन, in which the Yajamána says मम आशीर्वचनमपेक्षमाणाय अमुकं कर्म करिष्यमाणस्य पुण्याहमिति भवन्तो ब्रुवन्तु, स्वस्ति भवन्तो ब्रुवन्तु—and the Bráhmaṇas say in reply अस्तु पुण्याहम् । आयुष्मते स्वस्ति, &c.

एतां रक्षां—Protection of this kind *i.e.* ensured by the Bráhmaṇas with repetition of the holy *mantras.* ब्राह्मणजन०—विदित known enjoyed. Raghu's devotion to the Bràhmaṇa class is also referred to by Káli.; after his conquest of the world which benefitted the other three classes, he performed the Vis'vajit sacrifice to please the Bráhmaṇas. प्रियावियोगनिर्वेद—This is described by Káli. in his Ragh. Canto 8th. नित्यावभृथ०—This is added by the poet to defend the character of Aja. After the sudden death of his beloved queen, Indumatî, Aja yielded to the influence of the Rajas quality, but it was shaken off by his coustant performance of sacrifices. रजस्—There is a pun on this—(1) dust; (2) influence of the Rajas quality.

श्लाघनीय०—Bharata praises Aja for making amends for his temporary weakness of mind. दशरथस्य प्रतिमां &c.—It was natural for Bharata to get confused on seeing the fourth statue, which resembled his farther. For he believed that Das'a. was not dead and yet his statue was there. So he could not understand how that could be, and asks Devakulika to name the other three again to make sure that they were his ancestors. बहुमान &c.—This is a pretext. The real cause of his confusion was the sight of the statue of Daśaratha. किमिति किमिति—indicates greater confusion and anguish on Bharata's part.

अयं दिलीपः &c.—This order of the ancestors of Ráma given by Bhása is supported by Káli. in his Ragh., and both seem to follow the Pad. P. The genealogy given in the Ràmá. is different; see Ayodh. . 110.

धरमाणानां—From. धृ 6 conj. A. to live, to be alive; *cf.* आर्यपुत्र ध्रिये एषा ध्रिये । Uttar. III. p. 82. ध्रियते यावदेकोऽपि रिपुस्तावत्कुतः सुखम् । Sis. II. 35.

P. 41. विसर्जिताः—Should rather be विसर्जितं as agreeing with the nearest subject राज्यम्. *Cf.* in this respect परिहसितं which is correctly used in III. 3. स्त्रीशुल्कार्थे—for the sake of *i. e.* for keeping his promise about. पृच्छसे—Rather read पृच्छासि.

Śl. 10 हा तात—This speech of Bharata must be considered as स्वगत though there is no stage-direction like that. सकामं—He blames his heart for entestaining such fear. स्पृशति—touches, has reference to. नीचः—Bharata regards the promise taken from his father as a base act; *cf.* शुल्कदोषं in sl. 12, below. शुल्कशब्दः—*i. e.* the calumny in connection with it; if people suspect that Kaikeyî did it with my knowledge (that I was so told before I went to my maternal uncle's house). अथ is equivalent to यदि. सत्यं भवति—the subject is एतत्; this talk of the people, if

I find that people believe it to be such. तच—तर्हि in that case देहो विशोध्यः—I shall have to prove my innocence by the purification of my body. There is no point in saying 'If Kaikeyî wanted me to be crowned king &c.; for she could not have asked the kingdom for herself.

आर्य—This must be considered प्रकाशं, and there should have been a stage-direction to that effect preceding it.

आर्येति—Deva. means—It is a characteristic of the persons of the Ikshváku race to address a stranger as 'आर्य'. The fact that Bharata fainted on hearing of Dasaratha's death and that he addressed him as आर्य lead Deva. to guess that he was Kaikeyî's son. This way of making a character infer the identity of an unknown person is a peculiarity of Bhásá. *Cf. infra* सर्वसमुदारसंनिकर्षस्तु...सुमन्त्रो भवान्ननु । p. 43. दशरथपुत्रः—is made to correspond with Devakulika's कैकेयीपुत्रः; Bharata now likes to be called दशरथपुत्र and not कैकयीपुत्र and so says न कैकेय्याः leaving out the word पुत्रः.

द्विगुणं मोहमुपगतः—as contrasted with मूर्च्छितः पताति when Bharata heard of the death of his father. The news of Ráma's departure to the forest gave him a shock which made the pang of his heart doubly unbearable.

P. 42. Śl. 11. अटवीभूतां—May be a *Chvi.* formation, or a comp. सुप्सुपा अटमी भूता, भूत meaning like (सम); *cf.* śl. 25. क्षीणतोयां नदीमिव—The comparison indicates that the sight of his father and brother Ráma would have been as cooling and refreshing to him, fatigued by the journey, as water to a thirsty man. विस्तर—Mark the derivation विस्तर is derived from स्तृ with वि with the aff. अप् (अ) when it means 'a speech in detail,' while विस्तार is derived from the same root with the aff. घञ् (अ); विस्तारो विग्रहो व्यासः स च शब्दस्य विस्तरः । Amara. There is also a third word विष्टर irregularly derived, from the same root, meaning 'a seat,' &c. वृक्षासनयोर्विष्टरः Pán. VIII. 3. 93.

भरतः—तिष्ठ Mark the poet's skill in making Bharata himself state what his mother might have done and the effects of her action, instead of making Devakulika recount the events that had happened in Ayodhyá on account of Kaikeyî's interference with the coronation. This heightens the stage effect.

Śl. 12. शुल्कदोषं—The improper or unreasonable stipulation or promise about. He blames his mother for demanding the kingdom for him on the strength of the promise given at the marriage time, which was itself unjustifiable, when she knew that Ráma, as the eldest son, was the rightful heir to the throne तद्वैर्येण—Here तत् does not refer to any noun in the previous sentence, but means 'the granting of the request by Daśaratha, which emboldened her to make a further demand. असदृशं—Not worthy of him being brought on by grief. Otherwise he would have retired to a forest and died there. *Cf.* नृपो गृहमृत्युना further on, Śl. 18; and *supra*—वनं गमिष्यति p. 9. सदृशाः—Similar to those cast on Kaikeyî. शेषाः—That remained after they had been heaped on my mother; see *infra*. śl. 18. उत्सरतार्याः—This way of introducing persons of high rank is employed in SV. I. and twice in Pra. Yau.

Sl. 13. अजलस्य—Wanting, in need of, water. Water is required for reviving a man under a swoon. Hence the propriety of the simile.

P. 43. सुमन्त्रः—is the aged charioteer of Dasaratha who was almost a member of the household and not a minister, as supposed by Prof. Paranjpe. In the first place a minister was not likely to accompany the queens. Secondly, Bharata addresses him as तात further on, as he does in the fourth Act; see p. 49.

Śl. 14. प्रतिमानृपस्य—प्रतिमारूपः नृपः प्रतिमानृपः here king Daśa., whose statue the party wanted to visit. समुच्छ्रयो यस्य—is meant to show that it was a building high enough to attract attention from a distance. अयन्त्रितैः—not prevented from entering the house. अप्रतिहारि०—The travellers had free access to the statues; they were not required to be introduced by porters as in the case of living kings. The statue-house is contrasted with a palace which has guards to keep off strangers and porters to announce visitors. विना प्रणामं—Being the statues of human beings and not of deities.

Śl. 15. वयस्थः—Here वयस्थः means a youth, one in youthful age. There was such close resemblance between the stranger and Dasaratha that Sumantra thought him to be Daśaratha in his youth.

आर्य—is addressed to Devakulika with whom Bharata was talking before he fainted. Being unconscious he was not aware of the presence there of the queen-mothers and Sumantra. On coming back to his senses he wished to ask a further question to Devakulika thinking him to be still there. But as soon as he uttered the word आर्य, Sumantra, misled by the voice, took him for king Daśaratha and ejaculated जयतु महा०; but he soon knew his mistake and halted at the half-uttered word महाराजः. This intervening speech of Sumantra has nothing to do with Bharata's question, which is आर्य अथ मातृणामिदानीं काऽवस्था। But Deva. was not there to answer his question, and the poet makes the mothers answer it making the scene very pathetic thereby. **स्वरसादृश्यं**—Not only Bharata's person but his voice also closely resembled that of Daśaratha.

उत्कण्ठा—Painful remembrance of past things, grief. **सर्वसमुदाचार०**—Etiquette of every kind. His presence with the queens even when they had removed their veils, the familiar way in which he asked them to check their grief, and his general bearing led Bharata to infer that he must have been Sumantra. The word समुदार 'the duties or conduct proper for' constantly occurs in this play, as देवसमुदाचार, अतिथिसमुदाचार, &c.

P. 44. **०दोषैः**—The disadvantages or evils of. **कृतघ्नभावेन**—As a trusted and devoted servant of the king he should have died or put an end to his life after his master's death; since he did not do that it was sheer ingratitude on his part, and life was a mockery—a source of shame to him. This is an instance of निर्वेद or disgust with oneself. *Cf.* with this the words of the Kanchukī in Priya.—राज्ञो विपद्बन्धुवियोगदुःखं देशाच्युतिर्दुर्गममार्गखेदः। आस्वाद्यतेऽस्याः कटुनिष्फलायाः फलं मयैतच्चिरजीवितायाः॥ I. 4.

उपदेष्टुमिच्छामि—A grammatical irregularity. As it stands it would mean 'I wish to give advice about,' while the intended sense is 'I wish to be advised as to'; and so the proper sentence would have been भवतोपदिष्टमिच्छामि or rather क्रमोपदेशं भवत इच्छामि. It is strange that Bharata who was young enough when he left for his maternal uncle's house should have failed to recognise his mothers.

अनपराद्धः—is meant to show that he was quite innocent in the matter of the kingdom being asked for him by his mother. **आक्रुष्टः**—आक्रुष्टः blamed, rebuked. **अतिसन्धितः**—अतिसंहितः is the proper form being the p. p. p. of धा with अति and सं which means to deceive. Bhāsa is fond of using such out-of-the way forms. It may be explained as formed from अतिसंधा and the aff. इत. Laks. deceived him inasmuch as he took advantage of his absence and accompanied Ráma to the forest, thus leaving him no opportunity to do it himself. प्रयतिष्ये—He means—I will try to win fame by following Ràma to the forest as was done by Lakshmaṇa. And it will be seen that this expectation of his was fulfilled; *cf.* IV. 26.

सरोषमुत्थाय—We had the stage direction (उत्थाय) above. So it seems that Bharata bowed low before Kausalya and then rising up bowed to Sumitrá also bending. But the stage-direction is given here as he rose up angrily when the name of Kaikeyî was mentioned to him.

Śl 17. मातुश्च मातुश्च—The first refers to Kausalyá, the second to Sumitrá. कुनदीव—The water of which is turbid and unclean. So Kaikeyî being wicked-minded was not worthy to stand between the two.

P. 45. Śl. 18. Herein Bharata enumerates the evil consequences of Kaîkeyî's ill-thought action. वयं and the other nominatives to be construed with योजिताः with the necessary change of gender and number; वयं योजिताः; नृपः योजितः, अयोध्या योजिता, &c. अयशसा—Because people would naturally think that he had instigated his mother when going to his maternal uncle's house to ask the throne for himself. गृहमृत्युना—and not in a penance grove as a Vánaprastha, as the kings of the Ikshváka race were wont to do. See *supra* II. 19. कृत्स्ना अयोध्या—Although Bha. could not have seen the people weeping he knew how dearly they loved Ráma and was sure that they would weeps on his account. अम्बाः—Kau. and Sumitrá are meant. The plural is used out of respect. धिगिति०—*Cf. supra.* पात्यन्ते धिक्प्रलापाः &c Śl 12 above. सर्वसमुदाचार—has occured before; मध्यस्थः standing in the midst of, well-versed in, knowing fully. इयं ते जननी—Kausalyá purposely uses the word जननी instead of माता. The three were his मातृs (two being सापत्नमातृs), but Kaîkeyî was his जननी. जननी is one who gives birth to one; जनयतीति fr. जन् and the aff अन (ल्युट्) with the fem. ई. Although मातृ means a mother, the word जननी more prominently brings out the idea of giving birth to. Here is your mother proper and deserves a bow from you in the first instance.

Śl. 19. शीलसंक्रान्त &c.—This is aimed at his mother, though put in a general form. शील may be her own or that of her servants as understood by G. S. Prof. Devadhar's trans—'Sons are ruthlessly disowned for vices which they catch from bad characters' is not very intelligible. तावत्—In the first place. ननु—Surely; or, I say. अपुत्राः क्रियन्ते—and so she has disowned me also as a son along with Ráma. भर्तृद्रोहादस्तु &c.—When a woman aims at the life of her husband she cannot be regarded as a mother by her son. Hence the rule I lay down is अपूर्व, the first of its kind. So I am not her son; she is not my mother.

सत्यवचनं &c.—She means—I wanted the king to be true to his promise; and great men value truth above their life. *Cf.* आहुः सत्यं हि परमं धर्मं धर्मविदो जनाः । सत्यमाश्रित्य च मया त्वं धर्मं प्रति चोदितः ॥ Ayod. XIV. 3.

P. 46. Śl. 20. Herein Bharata states four हेतुs why she should not have objected to Ráma's coronation. Supply किं after each clause. औरसः—उरसा निर्मितः; fr. उरस्+अ (अण्) by उरसोण् च । Pàn. IV. 4. 94. A legitimate son, as distinguished from कुण्ड, गोळक &c. See Manus. IX. 116. Was he not an औरस son that his claim should be set aside in my favour? क्रमेण—*i. e.* by right of precedence. दयिताः &c.—(1) तस्य दयिताः Would he not have loved his brothers after being crowned a king. (2) Would not the brothers have loved one another still?

शुल्कलुब्धा—Here लुब्धा is used as a noun in the sense of लुब्धता a strong desire to have the gift promised at the time of marriage. She means—It was not I but the शुल्कलुब्धता* so natural with woman that was at fault (शुल्कलुब्धतयात्रापराद्धं न तु मया) or लुब्धा may better be taken in its natural sense 'one attracted by' (in which there is nothing wrong) and the whole treated as a question—शुल्कलुब्धा प्रष्टव्या ननु । (see trans.) न एतादृशं प्रश्नमर्हति ।

Śl. 21. वल्कलैः—उपलक्षितः; or सह wearing. पदातिः—पादाभ्यामतति goes इति पदातिः; fr. पाद् and अत् to go with the affa इ (इण्); पाद् is changed to पद by the rule पादस्य पदाज्यातिगोपहतेषु । Pán. VI. 3 52. so पदाजिः, पद्गः &c. शुल्केप्ये॰—Bharata means—You had some excuse if you asked for the kingdom; but did the marriage condition include this also?

देशकाले—This she does further on; see p. 78.

Śl. 22. अयशसि He means—If you courted infamy why did you bring in my name? See *supra* p. 16. l. 7 and III. 12.

* Prof. Paránjpe thinks that although Kaikeyi admits her शुल्कलुब्धत्व here, still a different explanation maintaining innocence on her part is offered by her in Act VI (see p. 79 जात एतन्निमित्तं &c.) And, therefore, her real meaning perhaps is—'She, who is avaricious about the dowry, may be asked to answer that question; whereas I am not at all ambitious.'

You should have simply said 'I want the kingdom'. नृपफल— नृप is used for नृपत्व, the benefits accruing from royalty. तर्ष:—a strong desire for; is an unusual word, though it occurs in the Purânas, as in निवृत्ततर्षैरुपगीयमानात् &c. Bhâg. P. भवति—Voc. sing. Properly this should be भवती; but the metre does not allow that. So we must supply भवती; see com.

Śl. 23. नृपतिः असुभिः &c.—Supply वियोक्ष्यमाणः; or असुभिः सह you did not care for the king as also for his life. व्रज वनमिति—occurs in Śl. 12 above.

P. 47. भवति—may again be Voc. sing. or verb (सृष्टं भवति).

वसिष्टवामदेवौ—Vâmadeva is often mentioned along with Vasistha in the Râmâ, and seems to be another priest of the Ikshvâku kings. *Cf.* वसिष्ठश्च वामदेवाभिमंत्रितो मेध्योऽश्वः । Uttar. II. p. 53. He is also a Vedic sage being the auther of most of the hymns of the 4th Mandala of the Rigveda. सह प्रकृतिभिः—with the ministers; or the principal citizens. अभिषेकं पुरस्कृत्य—*Cf.* ततः प्रभातसमये दिवसेथ चतुर्दशे । समेत्य राज्जकर्तारो भरतं वाक्यमब्रुवन् । त्वमद्य भव नो राजा राजपुत्र महायशाः ॥ आभिषेचनिकं सर्वमिदमादाय राघव । प्रतीक्षते त्वां स्वजनः श्रेणयश्च नृपात्मज ॥ Râmâ. Ayod. LXXIX. 14.

Śl. 24. गोपहीना &c.—The idea is taken from the Râmâ.; *cf.* अगोपाला यथा गावस्तथा राष्ट्रमराजकम् । Ayodh. LXVII. 29.

अभिषेकं विसृज्य—It is better to split up this sentence into two interrogative sentences, as done by Prof. Paránjpe. Are the subjects to follow you leaving off the coronation (without crowning you)? If so where do you mean to go to? अभिषेकमिति—This is a reply to the first question. You talk about coronation? इहात्रभवत्यै &c.—This is the crowning stroke of rebuke administered to his mother.

Śl 25. लक्ष्मणप्रिय:—is purposely used instead of something like ह्यग्रजो मम. He does not want to give Laksh. any advantage over himself. He wishes Râma to be भरतप्रिय: also.

ACT. IV.

विजया—This name of the portress occurs in other plays also, *viz.* Svap. Prat. Y. and Abh. Here she is introduced as the maid-servant of Kaikeyî.

भण भण—The object of this is महिषी कुमारेण किं भणिता. But before Vijayà finished her sentence, Nandi. interrupted her saying हला दृष्ट: &c. किल—means here 'I heard that, it was said that. भणितं—should rather be भणिता as Nandi. repeats the words of Vijayá. अत्याहितं—see p. 5. विभ्रष्टं—used as a noun like विभ्रंशं. पापकं कृतम्—has occurred before; see p. 9.

P. 49. Śl. 1. सकृतानुयात्रे—अनुयात्रं—अनुयात्रा गमनं यस्य तदनुयात्रं what follows, a follower. See com. सुकृतानुयात्रैः—*v. l.* सुकृतानि अनुयात्राणि तैः सह. *Cf.* for the idea धर्मस्तमनुगच्छति and परलोकमार्गे कर्मानुगो गच्छति जीव एकः । अनुयात्र occurs again at p. 60. and in the Rámá सूत रत्नसुसंपूर्णा चतुर्विधबला चमूः । राघवस्यानुयात्रार्थं क्षिप्रं प्रतिविधीयताम् ॥ Ayod. XXXVI. 2. अकृपणेषु—Not niggardly, generous; giving shelter and providing means of livelihood to all. *Cf.* शय्या शाद्वलमासनं शुचिशिला सद्म द्रुमाणामधः शीतं निर्झरवारि पानमशनं कन्दाः सहाया मृगाः । इत्यप्रार्थितलभ्यसर्वविभवे वने । Nág. IV. 2. Uttar. II. 1. जगतः शशाङ्कं—*Cf. supra.* I. 4.

Śl. 2. मथनः—The destroyer of, fr. मन्थ् and अन added कर्तरि. यज्ञोपयुक्त०—of Aja; see *supra,* नित्यावभृथस्नान &c. p 40. This is rather true of Raghu, as the poet himself says further on, śl. 10. रामसदृशेन पथा—Because like Ráma he was going to do what was just—to restore the kingdom to Ráma that was rightfully his. क्व तत्रभवान् &c—shows Bharata's extreme eagerness to see Ráma and his high regard for him. महाराजस्य प्रतिनिधिः—the representative or image of; or प्रतिनिधि may be taken in the sense of सदृश; *cf.* रघुप्रतिनिधिः Ragh. V. 63, where Malli. says रघुकल्पः । उक्तं च दण्डिना सादृश्यवाचकप्रस्तावे—कल्पदेशीयदेश्यादि प्रख्यप्रतिनिधी अपि । इति । सारवतां—Men who do not allow their courage to flag under any circumstances. सार inward substance, mental calibre. प्रत्यादेशः—the repulser or rebuker of; who indirectly served a rebuke to Kaikeyî by renouncing the kingdom. अनुव्रतः—Acting favourably towards; see com., *cf.* क्षत्रं ब्रह्ममुखं चासीद्वैश्याः क्षत्रमनुव्रताः । Rámá. Bál. VII. 19. सत्यम०—devotedly, firmly, attached to truthfulness. अनु is connected with सत्यं. The word occurs in the Rámá. and Mahá. राममनुव्रता । A'ran. XLVII. 34, 36; नैषधं दमयन्तीव भैमी पतिमनुव्रता ॥ तथाहमिक्ष्वाकुवरं रामं पतिमनुव्रता ॥ Sund. XXIV. 12, 13. भर्ता मां च नित्यमनुव्रतः । Nalop. XIII. 56.

P. 50. Śl. 4. महायशाः—may be construed with all the three. सत्यं &c.—(1) may be taken separately (यथासंख्य) as सत्यं in Ráma, &c.; or (2) collectively. रामस्य पितरि, सीतायाः भर्तरि, लक्ष्मणस्य भ्रातरि रामे, भक्तिः.

अलं अभिधातुं—*Cf. supra* note on अलं स्त्रीबुद्धिषु......उपक्षेप्तुम् I. p. 15. परदोषं—Mark how Bharata uses the word परदोषं although Sumantra had said गुरुजना०, showing thereby that he treats

Kaikeyî no longer as a गुरुजन but परजन. न्यक्भूतः—न्यक्भूतः a comp. सुप्सुपा. न्यङ्क is नीचमङ्ग the lowest part of, from अञ्च् with नि to go down. अकृतप्रायश्चित्तं—The प्रायश्चित्त meant is some epithet showing his penitence at the injustice done to Ráma by his mother. ब्रह्मघ्नानामपि—Bharata now changes his mind and says that as he is a great sinner, like one killing a Bráhmaṇa, it is better that he should announce his own name.

Sl. 5. प्राकृतः—An ordinary or base man; *cf.* Amara विवर्णः पामरो नीचः प्राकृतश्च पृथग्जनः । भक्तिमान् is emphatic; although निर्घृण &c.—still he is full of devotion to you. कथं तिष्ठतु &c.—occurs in Panch.—किमुक्त्वा नापराद्धोहं कथं तिष्ठतु &c. II. 58.

P. 51. Śl. 6. सदृशतरः—Very closely resembling; or more closely resembling (than mine or that of Lakshmaṇa). *Cf. supra.* अहो स्वरसादृश्यम् । मन्ये &c. p. 43. इष्टतः—इष्टत्वेन as one desired.

Śl. 7. समदवृषभ०—The sound of a bull is of the pitch of the second note in music and is therefore स्निग्ध and मधुर. *cf.* Nárada षड्जं रौति मयूरस्तु गावो नर्दन्ति चर्षभम् । अजाविकौ च गान्धारं क्रौञ्चो नदति मध्यमम् ॥ &c.

कण्ठे, वक्षसि यथास्थानं—कण्ठ &c. are the different parts of the body from which sound proceeds. The process of the production of voice is thus described by Páṇini in his Sikshá—आत्मा बुध्या समेत्यार्थान्मनो युङ्क्ते विवक्षया । मनः कायाग्निमाहन्ति स प्रेरयति मारुतम् ॥ मारुतस्तूरसि चरन् मन्द्रं जनयति स्वरम् ॥—कण्ठे माध्यंदिनयुगं मध्यमं त्रैष्टुभानुगम् । सोदीर्णो मूर्ध्न्यभिहतो वक्त्रमापद्य मारुतः । वर्णाञ्जनयते ।......॥ अष्टौ स्थानानि वर्णानां &c. see com. स्थानs or the places of pronunciation are the five parts of the mouth, viz. कण्ठ, तालु, मूर्धन्, दन्त and ओष्ठ. Speech becomes audible when the vocal wind starting from its original place (मूलचक्र) comes to the chest (वक्षस्) and thence reaches the place of articulation, *viz.* कण्ठ and produces different letters or वर्णs as it strikes the five places mentioned above. करण is the vocal effort or यत्न that is required to pronounce each sound. It is of two kinds आभ्यन्तर and बाह्य. See Śid. Kau. on Pán. I. 1. 9.

1 9. वक्षस्यनुप०—For the sound to be clearly produced its passage through the chest must not be obstructed but free and smooth. Says the Sikshhá of Pán. व्याघ्री यथा हरेत्पुत्रान् दंष्ट्राभ्यां न च पीडयेत् । एवं वर्णाः प्रयोक्तव्या नाव्यक्ता न च पीडिताः ।

चतुर्णां वर्णानां—There may also be a reference to the four kinds of speech, *viz.* परा वाग्मूलचक्रस्था पश्यन्ती नाभिसंस्थिता । हृदिस्था मध्यमा ज्ञेया वैखरी कण्ठदेशगा ॥

P. 52. **अये** &c.—Lakshmana at first sight mistakes Bharata for Ráma, owing to the former's great similarity of form to the latter. Sitá also commits a similar mistake on seeing Bharata; see p. 54.

Sl. 8. **आर्यास्याभं**.—आर्यास्यस्येवाभा यस्य. or आर्यास्येन सदृशं a Nitya samása. **शशाङ्क॰**—is self contradiction (वदतो व्याघातः) as he has already said अनुपमं. **सुरारिशरक्षतम्**—An oversight of the poet. The chest of Bharata was not wounded by the shafts of demons. The poet wanted to say-सुरारिक्षतपितृवक्षः समम्.

तेजोराशिः—As द्युतिपरिवृतः has already occurred, तेजः must be taken here to mean प्रभाव might, heroic lustre or prower: तेजाः प्रभावे दीप्तौ च Amara. *Cf.* तेजस्तेजासि शाम्यतु । Uttar. V. 7; महतस्तेजसो बीजं Sak. VII. 15. Bharata defines तेजस् as अधिक्षेपावमानादेः प्रयुक्तस्य परेण यत् । प्राणात्ययेप्यसहनं तत्तेजः समुदाहृतम् ॥ **देवेन्द्रः**—As it is, is connected with मधुसूदनः; or one वा may be supplied, देवेन्द्रो वा मधुसूदनो वा । *Cf.* in this respect इन्द्रो वा शरणं तेस्तु प्रभुर्वा मधुसूदनः । Abhi I. 12.

Śl. 9. **प्रकाशस्य**—must be construed with पितुः, as Sumantra could not have meant it to apply to लक्ष्मण in preference to his father., although we expect पितुः to be in the abl. like अजात्. In this case द्वितीयः must he taken to mean 'a son'. **स्वकुलस्य केतोः**—refers to Ráma.

Śl. 10. **संघृष्ट**—came in hard contact or clashed with, as both, the kings of the solar race and Indra, fought side by side with the demons; or better, emulated, vied with, in killing the demons. *Cf.* for this meaning स प्रयोगनिपुणैः प्रयोक्तृभिः संजघर्ष सह मित्रसंनिधौ । Ragh. XIX. 36. विज्ञानसंघर्षो जातः । Mal. I. p. 30 हरदत्तगणदासयोः अन्योन्यसंघर्षित Ibid p. 64 **बलवीर्य॰**—बल physical strength, वीर्य (वीरे साधुः) martial spirit or valour; उत्साहोध्यवसायः स्यात्स वीर्यमतिशक्तिभाक् । Amara. **रघुरिव** &c.—coustrue सः प्रसिद्धः नरेन्द्रः रघुः इव. **यज्ञविश्रान्त॰**—*Cf.* तमध्वरे विश्वजिति क्षितीशं निःशेषविश्राणितकोशजातम् । Ragh. V. 1.

P. 53. **विशालीक्रियतां**—occurs again in Act VII. p. 84; *cf. supra* विशालतरमुत्संगं कुरु । p. 8.

Śl. 12. **दुष्करं कृतं**—The painful state undergone. What torment he suffered. For this sense *cf.* चक्रवाक्यारटति दुष्करमहं करोमीति । Śak. IV. p. 150 **अयं**—This, as evinced by Bharata. **इदम्**—refers to कुमारप्रवेशनं । (the action implied in प्रविशतु कुमारः).

आत्माभिप्रायं—G. S. explains this as मदभिप्रायानुसारि; but आत्मन् can only refer to the subject of the sentence, *scil.* लक्ष्मण; so this means—depend upon my approval of your intention? You ought to have brought him without referring the matter to me.

S'l. 13. मानहेतो—That special honour should be shown to him. तुषारपूर्णोत्पल—Such a lotus looks beautiful; *cf.* बाष्पवर्षेण नीतं वो जगन्मङ्गलमाननम् । अवश्यायावसिक्तस्य पुण्डरीकस्य चारुताम् । Uttar. VI. 29. आसारं—Like a number of dew drops. Ráma knew that Sîtā's eyes would be filled with tears of joy at the prospect of seeing Bharata.

P. 54. हं—Sîtā, like Lakshmaṇa, also mistakes Bharata for Ráma at first sight, and wonders how the latter could come there before her. ततस्तां वेलां &c. The sentence is elliptical; for its completion see com.

Śl. 14. इदं तत्स्त्रीमयं—*cf.* स्त्रीसंस्थानमप्सरस्तीर्थमाराद्धुत्क्षिप्यैनां ज्योतिरेकं जगाम । Śàk. V. 30. क्षेत्रोदरात् &c.—*Cf.* अथ मे कृषतः क्षेत्रं लाङ्गलादुत्थिता ततः ॥ क्षेत्रं शोधयता लब्धा नाम्ना सीतेति विश्रुता । Ramá. Bàl. K. LXVI. 13, 14. संनिदर्शनं.—*cf.* above सन्निदर्शनं सारवतां p. 49.

प्रविशतु कुमारः—From this Bharata inferred that it was not Sumantra's wish to enter into Ráma's presence together with him and hence his question तात, इदानीं &c.

S'l. 15. अहं पश्चात्प्र०—Sumantra wishes to see Râma after Bharata and he assigns the reason for this in what follows. विदितार्थस्य रा०—must be taken to mean 'when Ráma will have known the incident of Daśa.'s death. It is clear from the play that Ráma did not know as yet that Das'a. had died., For in S'l. 12 above Ráma says that he would know from Bharata what effect his departure to the forest had on Daśa., his father; and his question to Sumantra in S'l. 17 below, if his father had relinquished his body and gone to heaven to revel with his dead ancestors there, also leads to the same conclusion. For construction see com. This stanza is repeated in Act VII.

P. 55. कपाटपुट०—The chest of a well developed Kshatriya youth is compared to the closed panels of a door. *Cf.* कपाटवक्षाः परिणद्धकन्धरः । Ragh. III. 34. शरदिन्दु०—For comp. see com. and *cf.* s'l. 8 above. हा तात—Here तात refers to Sumantra, since राम says भवन्तं विना in the 3rd line of the following Śl.

S'l. 17. अभिसरि०—should rather have been अभिसरसमये०; for अभिसरि, see III. 7. समानैर्विमानैः—*Cf.* तुल्यं सुरैः &c. *infra*, V. 10. Here the aerial cars may have been provided by the gods or their own chariots used as such. The chariot of Raghu is described by Kâlidása as having the power to move through the sky, like a *Vimána*. See Ragh. V. 27. भवन्तं विना स्वर्गस्थ—implies that formerly he had gone there with him (त्वया सह पूर्वं गत्वा). रमयति—used for रमते; or supply आत्मानम्. Mark the alliterations in this Śloka.

Śl. 18. नरपतिनि०—For the sequence of events this should have been तव विवसनं नृपस्य मृत्युं, as the king's death followed the exile of Ràma. दुष्प्रसह्यं—used as a noun in the sense of unbearable calamities. गुणे—Long life is a merit, but since it witnessed so many calamities it was a crime on its part, as it were, to be long. The Śl. occurs again with some variations in VI. *Cf.* III. 15. राध् with अप governs the loc. of the person or thing against whom or which an offence is committed; hence गुणे. *Cf.* with this अहो हि मे बह्वपराद्धमायुषा यदप्रियं वाच्यमिदं मयेदृशम् । त एव धन्याः सुहृदः पराभवं जगत्यदृष्ट्वैव हि ये क्षयं गताः ॥ quoted in Kàv. Pr. X as an instance of अर्थान्तरन्यास. आपस्तावत्—see p. 23.

P. 56. आर्य—refers to Ráma. न्याय्यं—what stands to justice (न्यायादनपेतं not departing from). क्रमेण—In the proper order. Bharata being younger and not elder (as Prof. Paranjpe has it) it was his duty to serve Ráma before Lakshmaṇa. According to the Rámá. and also Pad. p. (अन्येषु· पाञ्चजन्यात्मा कैकेय्यां भरतोऽभवत् । तदन्येद्युः सुमित्रायामनन्तात्मा च लक्ष्मणः ॥ &c.), Bharata was older than Laks. by order of birth; but Bhása treats Lakshmaṇa as older than Bharata. *Cf.* above, Bharata's speech—एवं गुरुरयं p. 52. Káli. also follows Bhása in this. *Cf.* व्युत्क्रम्य लक्ष्मणमुभौ भरतो ववन्दे । Ragh. XIII. 72; also 73 (although Malli. interpretes it in a way to reconcile it with the Rámá). शुश्रूषयिष्ये—is grammatically irregular. The Desid. base of the root श्रु is Atm. (शुश्रूषते) according to ज्ञाश्रुस्मृदृशां सनः । Pán. 1. 3. 57. Bhása, however, treats it as a root of the tenth conj. using it in both Padas; see below लक्ष्मणः शुश्रूषयतु । शुश्रूषय भगवन्तं p. 64.

ननु एतेनापि &c.—Sîtá means—How can Lak.'s duty be interfered with? Bharata being your younger brother has also an equal right to serve you. इह—As Laks. is my companion in the forest, it is proper &c. तत्रस्थः—Living there, in Ayodhyá, as appointed by my father.

Sl. 19. कर्मणा—i.e. the administration of the kingdom by appointing deputies; cf. with this हृदयेनेह तत्राङ्गैर्द्विधाभूतेव गच्छति। Balach. I. 13.

भवतः नाम्ना एव.—In your name alone. Bharata means—I will appoint administrators to manage the state affairs, the kingdom being governed in your name alone.

S'l. 20. पितुर्नियोगात्—Owing to father's command, which cannot be transgressed. दर्पात्—through wounded pride or vanity. विभ्रमात्—i. e. I knew my duty very well. I did not wish to contest my father's behest. नीचपथे—By going against our father's wish and asking me to accept the kingdom. Cf. Rámá. Ayodhya. CVI 33.

अथेदानीं &c—Finding the two brothers undecided as to the acceptance of the kingdom, Sumantra asks this question, especially as the coronation water was brought for crowning Ràma king. यत्र मे मात्रा &c.—Because a mother's word also must be honoured. Bharata, however, felt Ráma's words like a stab given to him and says अलं व्रणे प्र०; the व्रण being the wound inflicted on his mind by Kaikeyî's action.

P. 57. S'l. 21. अपि G. S. takes अपि in the sense of यदि; but there is no necessity to do so. अपि here is प्रश्नार्थे; see com. निभृतधीमान्.—Firm-minded and talented; or rather highly-talented; see com. सुपुरुष—Bharata appeals by this to his brother's noble-mindedness. वरद—is purposely used-you have the power, if you mean, to grant my wish.

आर्यपुत्र &c.—This interference of Sîtá is quite in conformity with a woman's kind and sympathetic heart. She has done so before; see p. 22 (दयतामार्यपुत्रः &c.). She again intercedes on Bharata's behalf further on; see p. 59. (आर्य ननु दीयते &c.).

S'l. 22. चिन्तयामि—Said in reply to Sîtá's question आर्यपुत्रेण चिन्त्यते (though with a difference of meaning). आत्मजवि०—It is not a good way to take the comp. as आत्मजेषु विशिष्टगुणः as Prof. Devadhara does. Ráma is not likely to say this in Lakshmaṇa's hearing. It may be taken as a Gen. Tat; or rather as a Karm.; see com. न दृष्टः—means not *actually seen.* This is more in keeping with the Ramá, according to which Das'a. knew this trait of Bharata's character. *Cf.* न कथंचिदृते रामाद्भरतो राज्यमावसेत्। रामादपि हि तं मन्ये धर्मतो बलवत्तरम्॥ Ayod. XII. 61, 62.

ईदृग्विधं &c—The idea is—a पुरुषोत्तम (one with a supreme stock of religious merit-पुण्य) alone can have a son who is a गुणनिधि (*cf.* हितोपदेश—पुण्यतीर्थे कृतं येन तपः क्वाप्यतिदुष्करं । तस्य पुत्रो भवेद्वश्यः समृद्धो धार्मिकः सुधीः ॥); and if Fate has power over such a man even, then धिक् &c. *Cf. supra.* अहो बलवान् मृत्युः &c. p. 40.

Śl. 23. निष्कल्मषात्मा—This is meant to dispel any misgiving on the part of Bharata as to Ráma's doubt about his innocense, as suggested by the words अलं व्रणे प्रहर्तुम्.

P. 58. तदव्रतं कर्तुं &c—*Cf.* Rámá. भवानपि तथेत्येव &c. quoted below CVII. किंचोत्पाद—has an interrogative force; see com.

Śl. 24. यावद्भवि०—Here as also in यावद्भवानेष्यति in Śl. 26 below the clause introduced by यावत् has a negative force; यावन्न भविष्यति तावत्. *Cf. infra.* यावदार्यपुत्रो नागच्छति तावत् &c. p. 61. If you break the king's order and do not accept the kingdom, the king will be मिथ्याप्रतिज्ञ and will not obtain the full fruit of his good deeds in heaven. *Cf.* भवानपि तथेत्येव पितरं सत्यवादिनम् । कर्तुमर्हसि राजेन्द्र क्षिप्रमेवाभिसिञ्चनात् ॥ ऋणान्मोचय राजानं मत्कृते भरत प्रभुम् । तस्मात्त्राहि नरश्रेष्ठ पितरं नरकात्प्रभो । Ayod. CVII. 9, 10, 14. मे—An instance of Bhása's indifference to grammar. The shorter form is not used at the beginning of a sentence. See Pán. VIII. 1. 18. मे may also be taken in the sanse of the Inst. मया हेतुना. अनुत्तरम्—नास्ति उत्तरं यस्मिन्कर्मणि तद्यथा तथा. Adv. comp. प्रतिग्रहीतुमिच्छामि—A violation of Paṇ.'s rule again. By the rule समानकर्तृकेषु तुमुन् Pán. III. 3. 158, the meaning will be 'I wish to take back the kingdom,' which is absurd. The intended sense is त्वया प्रतिग्राहयितुमिच्छामि I desire you to take back &c; see *supra* note on अभिवादनक्रममुपदेष्टुमिच्छामि । p. 44.

P. 59. पादोपभुक्ते—see com. अनयोर्विधेयः—*i. e.* placing them in your place and being subordinate to them.

Sl. 26. अचिरेणैव कालेन &c.—An instance of how Bhása leaves his sense to be understood by the reader. Here we must supply सुमहत् यशः as the subject of सञ्चितम्; for the contrast is between सुचिरेण कालेन and अचिरेण कालेन and किंचिद्यशः and महद्यशः; or सञ्चितं may be taken in the sense 'of heaped up, a great mass of' and the predicati आर्जितं taken from the first half. भरतेन सञ्चितं यशः अर्जितम्.

प्रथमयाचनं—Here Sítá means by याचन 'the thing asked for for the first time. On Bharata's part it was a second

RA'MA—Venerable sir, from the word 'or' I gather that there is something else too. पृ. ६६

RA'VANA—There is, that can be obtained by special prowess.

RA'MA—Venerable sir, this itself (to obtain) is my resolve.

Both the things (means) are at my command, if these can secure that. If the (power of) penance does not prevail there is the bow; if the bow fails, there is penance. (9).

RA'VANA—There are. They reside on mountain Himálaya.

RA'MA.—On the mountain Himâlaya; well, proceed further.

RA'VANA.—There dwell on the seventh peak of the Himálayas deer, named *Kanchanpârs'vas* (Golden-flanked) that drink the water of the Ganges directly falling from the head of Śiva, that have backs dark-blue like Vaidûrya (*Lapis-lazuli*) and that have the fleetness of the wind; and great sages, such as the Vaikhánasas' Valakhilyas, Naimishiyas and others offer Śraddhas with (the flesh of) these, presenting themselves and dying the moment they are thought of.

Gratified with these the manes acquire the fruit of (begetting) sons; and being free from old age ascend, resplendent, to (a higher) heaven; there they obtain a residence in aereal cars along with the gods and are not forcibly drawn away by the objects of senses leading to birth and rebirth. (10).

RA'MA—Maithili, पृ. ६७

Take leave of these antelopes and trees treated by you as your sons, and of the Vindhya-forest and your dear friends, the creepers. I will dwell in those wild forests of the Snowy-mountain, illumined with woods of herbs burning, as it were, with splendour. (11).

SÎTA'—As my husband commands.

RA'VANA—Son of Kausalyá, away with a high-flown desire. They can not be seen by human beings.

RA'MA—Holy sir, do they dwell on the Snowy mountain ?

RAVANA—Just so.

RA'MA—Then, mark your reverence,

The mountain Himálaya will expose them to my view, or pierced with the force of my shafts will fare like (lit. be reduced to the condition of) Krauncha. (12)

RA'VANA—(*To himself.*) Oh, unbearable, indeed, is his vanity.

RA'MA—(*Looking in the directions*) Oh, it seems there is a flash of lightning.

RA'VANA—Son of Kausalyá, Himalaya honours you just staying here. Here is a Kánchanapârsva.

RA'MA—This good fortune is due to your reverence.

SÎTA'—Fortune smiles on my husband.

RA'MA—No, no.

If he has come spontaneously it is father's good fortune : he deserves to be honoured ; Maithili, tell Lakshmaṇa to look to that. (13).

SÎTA'—Husband, you have, I say, deputed Lakshmaṇa saying—Go to meet the patriarch returning from his visit to sacred places.

RA'MA—If so I will myself go.

SÎTA'—Husband, what shall I do ?

RA'MA—Be in attendance on his holiness.

SÎTA'—As my husband commands.

(*Exit* R'AMA).

RA'VANA—Ah, here is Ráma going forth with an *arghya*. Now is Rághava stringing his bow, seeing the antelope running away disregarding the honour shown to him.

Oh his physical strength, oh his prowess, oh his mettle, oh his speed ? It is but meet that the whole world is pervaded by the two short syllables Râma. (14)

Here has the deer, passing with one bound beyond the range of his arrow, entered the dense forest.

SÍTA'—(*To herself.*) Separated from my husband, I feel afraid here.

RA'VANA—

(Râma being lured away by a ruse I will carry away the young Síta, left alone, as she will weep, from this penance grove, like an oblation (to the fire) offered without the recitation of Mantras. (15)

SÍTA'—I will at once enter the hut. (*Wishes to go in*).

RA'VANA—(*Assuming his proper form*). Sítá, stay, stay.

SÍTA'—(*With trepidation*), Ha, who can this person be now?

RA'VANA—Do you not know?

I am that Rávana, who conquered, in battle, the gods, Indra and others, together with the hosts of demons, and who have come here, on seeing the deformation of Śûrpanakhá, and hearing of the slaughter of my two brothers, with a desire to carry you off, oh large eyed one, after having enticed away with tricks Ráma, who, through pride, has been acting wickedly and considers himself as possessed of measureless strengh. (16) पृ ६९

SÍTA—Oh, Rávaṇa by name!

(*Starts away.*)

RA'VANA—Ha! Whither can you go, come within the range of Râvaṇa's eyes!

SÍTA'—Husband, save me, save me. Saumitrí, protect me, protect me!

RA'VANA—Oh Sítâ, hear my prowess.

Indra was overpowered and the lord of wealth (Kubera) was made to quake (with fear); Soma was dragged and Sûrya's son (Yama) was crushed (by me): Oh fie upon heaven, that is inhabited by the timid gods; blessed is earth where dwells Sítá. (17)

SÍTA'—Protect me, my husband, protect me; help, help, son of Sûmitrá!

RA'VA.—Seek the protection of Rāma or of Lakshmaṇa or of Das'aratha himself, the king now living in heaven; what will avail appeals addressed to weak men? Young ones of the deer cannot brave a tiger. (18)

SĪTA'—Protect me, husband, protect me. Saumitri, protect me, protect me!

RA'VANA—You lament; what is this, oh large-eyed one; regard me as you regard your husband. Although possessed of enormous strength and helped by the multitude of gods, this (your) Ráma is quite unable to fight with me. (19)

पृ· ७० SĪTA'—(*Angrily*) Thou art cursed.

RA'VANA—Ha, ha, ha! Oh the power of a Pativratâ (a woman devoted to her husband).

That I, who was not burnt by the (immense rays of the sun when I flew up into the sky with velocity, am burnt by these her measured words 'Thou art cursed'! (20)

SĪTA'—Husband, save me, save me;

RA'VA.—(*Seizing* SĪTA') Oh you ascetics that dwell in Janasthâna! Hear me, do hear me, your honours.

Here is the ten-necked (Rávaṇa) going away having forcibly taken Sītá with him: if Râma has any regard for the duties of Kshatriyahood, let him display his prowess. (21)

SĪTA'—Husband, help, oh, help!

RA'VA.—(*Seeing, while moving on*). Ah, here is Jatâyu, with his formidable beak rushing towards (me), having thrown into agitation the trees of the forest shaken up with the wind of his wings. Ah! wait there now.

I will despatch you to the abode of Yama, with your limbs wet with profuse blood dropping from the wounds caused by your wings being severed with the sword drawn by my hand. (22)

(*Exeunt Both*)

END OF ACT V.

wrong done to her by Lakshmaṇa. He was the general of Rávaṇa's forces stationed in the Dandakáraṇya. He was slain by Ráma. **स्वरपद॰**—For a Vedic *mantra* accompanying an oblation, if not uttered properly and with the proper accent, does not express its intended sense and cannot convey the oblation to the intended deity. *Cf.* मन्त्रो हीनः स्वरतो वर्णतो वा मिथ्या प्रयुक्तो न तमर्थमाह । स वाग्वज्रो यजमानं हिनास्ति यथेन्द्रशत्रुः स्वरतोपराधात् ॥ Pàṇ's. Śikshà 52. Such offerings are supposed to be carried away by demons. The idea is expressed again further on in Śl. 15.

P. 64. **अतिथिसमुदाचारः**—The conduct proper for a guest; *i. e.* I will act as a guest. **विशेषितं खलु रूपं स्वरेण.**—This sentence may apply to Ráma or to Rávaṇa. If to the former विशेषित will mean 'set off, improved.' But Ráma was inside the hermitage; and it was not possible for Rávaṇa to see his form. So it is better to take this as referring to Rávana Rávaṇa is glad to see that his voice passed for that of a guest and that the fraud was not detected. In this case विशेषितं means 'backed or supported by.' साधु may also be taken separately; excellent, bravo ! Râvaṇa thus compliments himself on his successful imitation of the voice of a guest.

आज्ञप्त इव.—For Ràma did not say something like 'आसनमलं क्रियतां भवता, or अलं करोतु भवान्. **पाद्यं**—पादाभ्यामिदं ; by पादार्घाभ्यां च । Páṇ. V. 4. 24.; पाद्यं पादाय वारिणि । Amara. This is in accordance with the dictum of Manu-संप्राप्ताय त्वतिथये प्रदद्यादासनोदके ? अन्नं चैव यथाशक्ति सत्कृत्य विधिपूर्वकम् । Mânu. III. 99. **मायाप्रकाशन॰**—Rávaṇa fears that his passion might be excited on Sîtá's coming in closer contact with him and it might find its expression on his face and his disguise might be exposed, and so wishes to prevent Sîtâ from serving him.

S'l. 8. **अरुन्धती**.—The well known wife of Vasishtha, here represented as the perfect pattern of womanly virtue (पातिव्रत्य). She was so pious and devoted to religious austerities as to be considered almost as a divine being. Káli. compares her to Sváhá, the wife of Agni; अन्वासितमरुन्धत्या स्वाहयेव हविर्भुजम् । Ragh. I. 56. **कथ्यते.**—So you are reported to be. Rávaṇa purposely uses this word, that Ráma should not suspect the stranger as one who knew Sîtá already.

छायां परिहृत्य &c.—If so much respect is shown to the shadow greater respect ought to be shown to the body, which casts the shadow and is therefore superior to it. वाचानुवृत्तिः—*Cf.* भवतीनां सूनृतयैव गिरा कृतमातिथ्यम् । S'ak. I. p. 27. Manus. वाक्चतुर्थी च सूनृता । III. 10. 1.

P. 65. ब्राह्मणसमु०—Mark the change from अतिथि० to ब्राह्मण०; an अतिथि may be of any caste; now he wants to declare him. self as a Bràhmaṇa. साङ्गोपाङ्ग—The अङ्गs or accessory works necessary for the proper understanding of the Vedas are six; they are शिक्षा कल्पो व्याकरणं निरुक्तं ज्योतिषां गतिः । छन्दोविचितिरित्येतैः षडङ्गो वेद उच्यते ।। The *upângas* are four पुराणन्यायमीमांसाधर्मशास्त्राणि. मानवीयं धर्म०—Mansmṛti. माहेश्वरं—The Yogaśastra was first practised and propounded by God Śiva. He is known as महायोगी in whom is centred the highest perfection of austere penance and abstract meditation. बार्हस्पत्यं—बृहस्पतिना प्रणीतं promulgated by Bṛhaspati. अर्थशास्त्रं—Political science or policy. According to the Mah Bhâ. Śántip., the Nitiśâstra originally propounded by Brahmâ was abridged by Śiva, looking to the short period of human life, and given to Indra. It was in i s turn abridged by Purandara and further abridged by Bṛhaspâti. *Cf.* प्रजानामायुषो ह्रासं विज्ञाय भगवान् शिवः । संचिक्षेप ततः शास्त्रं महार्थं ब्रह्मणा कृतम् ।। वैशालाक्षमिति प्रोक्तं तदिन्द्रः प्रत्यपद्यत । दशाध्यायसहस्राणि सुब्रह्मण्यो महातपाः ।। भगवानपि तच्छास्त्रं संचिक्षेप पुरंदरः । सहस्रैः पञ्चभिस्तात यदुक्तं बाहुदन्तकम् ।। अध्यायानां सहस्रैस्तु त्रिभिरेव बृहस्पतिः । संचिक्षेपेश्वरो बुध्या बार्हस्पत्यं तदुच्यते ।। Ch. 59, 81-84. मेधातिथेः न्याय०—This Medhâtithi can not be the commentator of Manu. In the Śantip. of the Mah. Bhâ. मेधातिथि and गौतम are names of the same person; so the science of logic referred to here must be that ascribted to the sage Gotama. प्राचेतसं—That composed by Prachetas. श्राद्धकल्प—A treatise on the ritual of the Śraddha.

श्रुतीः—श्रुति is here used in the sense of a Śástra. आगम इदानीं—Here आगम may mean (1) शास्त्र; in this case supply इष्यते; I desire to know this Śástra; or (2) 'knowledge;' I wish to know about श्राद्ध; for this sense *cf.* प्रज्ञया सदृशागमः Ragh. I. 15. श्रद्धया दत्तं श्राद्धं.—Here Rávaṇa gives the derivative meaning of श्राद्ध; श्राद्धं तत्कर्म निवापदानं शास्त्रतः– Amara. श्राद्धं is the offering of oblations to the पितृs according to the rules of the S'astra. श्रद्धास्त्यस्मिन्निति श्राद्धं; from श्रद्धा and the affix अ (अण); Pàn V. 2. 101. अनादरतः—Through disregard of or indifference to the provisions of the S'ástra. He means—if we offer anything on the principle सर्वं श्रद्धया दत्तं श्राद्धं and do not try to know what things are particularly mentioned by the S'ástra.

विरूढेषु.—विरूढ seems to the used here in the sense of plants that grow straight without branches-of the grass kind. Kshîraswámî commenting on Amara. II. 136 quotes—मूलपत्रकरीराग्रफलकाण्डविरूढकाः । त्वक्पुष्पं कवकं चेति शाकं दशविधं स्मृतम् ॥ and while explaining the term विरूढ says यं तु क्षेत्रोद्गतस्य फलमूलादेः सेकान्नवोद्भिन्नानङ्कुरान् विरूढान्मन्यामहे । **ओषधीषु.**—ओषः पाकः धीयते अस्यामिति ओषधिः a plant that dies as soon as its seed grows ripe. ओषध्यः फलपाकान्ताः । Amara. **कलायं.**—Generally called काल; कलायः स्यात्काले इति वैजयन्ती (as quoted by Malli, on Sis. XIII. 21); it is mentioned by Manu among the articles that give satisfaction to the Pitris. कालशाकं महाशल्काः खड्गलोहामिषं मधु । आनन्त्यायैव कल्पन्ते मुन्यन्नानि च सर्वशः ॥ Manus. III. 272. The well-known physician Charaka thus describes the properties of this vegetable—कालशाकं तु कटुकं दीपनं गरशोफजित् । लघूष्णं वातुलं रूक्षं कालाख्यं शाकमुच्यते ॥ "The vegetable is known even at the present day in the Konkan district under the name of कवला and is made use of in the श्राद्ध ceremony dinners." Prof. Paránjpe **वाध्रीणसः**—also written as वार्धीणस and वाघ्रिणस, means a rhinoceros, or an old white he-goat; or a bird with a blackneck, red head &c., see com.; and this is the meaning here, as Bhása refers to birds, and खड्ग is separately mentioned. As for the flesh of वार्ध्रीणस comp. Manu III. 271, quoted in the com.

वाशब्देनाव॰—Here वा must be taken in the sense of अनुक्तसमुच्चय as done by G. S (अर्थादनुक्तसमुच्चयार्थेन) *i. e.* as including something not mentioned. वास्याद्विकल्पोपमयोरेवार्थे च समुच्चये । इति विश्वः । Ràma thinks from the use of the particle वा that some other animal also is recommended by the S'ástra. This is the poet's device to introduce Marîcha in the form of a deer of gold on the scene.

एष एव—*i. e.* to please the departed father by offering what is to be procured by prowess. See com.

Śl. 9. Herein Ràma tells the guest that he has the means to achieve his object. **धनुर्वा** &c.—**तपः**—*i. e.* the miraculous power which penance gives to punishe one refusing a request; *cf.* क्रोधस्य ज्वलितुं धगित्यवसरश्चापेन शापेन वा । Uttar. IV. 25.

स्थाणु.—God Śiva; lit. he who stands for all times without change, eternal. नित्यमव्यय एव तिष्ठतीति स्थाणुः । स्थाणुवन्निश्चलस्तिष्ठतीति वा । वृक्ष इव स्तब्धो दिवि तिष्ठत्येकः । Svet. Up. तस्य शिरसः पतितं falling directly from the head of, *i e.* perfectly holy. **वैदूर्य.**—the gem called *lapis lazoits* (विदूरे अद्रौ भवं). See Malli. on Kum. I. 24.

वैखानसाः:--A class of great sages. In the Rámá, Ar. Ch. 6 śl. 2 the Vaikhānasas and the Válakhilyas are mentioned among the great Ṛshis that came to see Ráma, after the sage Śarabhanga had gone to heaven after having offered himself up to the sacred fire in the presence of Ráma. The Com. of the Rámá. describes them as born of the nails and hairs of Prajápati (Brahman) respectively. प्रजापतेर्नखलोमजाः । ये नखास्ते वैखानसा ये बालास्ते वालखिल्याः । इति श्रुतेः । In Chap. 35 of the Aran. they are called आजाः (अजो ब्रह्मा तत्पुत्रैरयोनिजैः प्रसिद्धैः) and माषाः; आजैर्वैखानसैर्माषैर्वालखिल्यैर्मरीचिपैः । sl. 15. But these cannot be referred to here as they have no occasion to perform a Śradha, being the sons of Brahmá. The Vaikhánasas mentioned here are Vánaprasthas in the third stage of life. They are the followers of Vikhanas, an ancient sage, who seems to have written a work on the duties of the Vánaprasthas. Haradatta, commenting on Gotama's sutra III. 2 says—वैखानसो वानप्रस्थः । विखनसा प्रोक्तेन मार्गेण वर्तते इति । तेन हि स आश्रमः प्राधान्येन प्रतिपादितः । A Vaikhánasa appears in Śak. I. also. *Cf*. Uttar. I. 25 l. 2.

बालखिल्या:--These, as generally known, are pigmy sages of the size of the thumb and sixty thousand in number. They are represented as preceding the chariot of the sun—वालखिल्याः सहस्राणि षष्टिर्ब्रह्मर्षयो मताः । पुरतोऽभिमुखं यान्ति स्तुवन्ति स्तुतिभिर्विभुम् ॥ Bhág. P. XII. 2. 9. They originally dwelt on a very large branch (शतयोजनमायता Ar. K. 35. 28) of a रोहिण (वट) tree. But as that branch gave way under the weight of Garuda when he, while going to bring nectar (अमृत), perched upon it in order to eat a huge elephant and a tortoise whom he had seized in his bill, he bore that branch also in his beak, on discovering that these and other sages were hanging from it and, going to the mountain Gandhmádana, saw his father Kashyapa there. Propitiated by Kashyapa the sages left the branch and went to the mountain Himalaya to practise penance there; see Mh. Bhà. Adip. Ch. 30; Rámá. Aran. ch. 35-27-33. But these also, like the Vaikhánasas, do not seem to be referred to here as they have no necessity to perform a Śráddha being produced according to the Rigveda from the hairs of Prajápati (Brahmà). See also note on Vaikhanasa above. The sages, meant here are another class of Vánaprasthas. Four classes of these are mentioned in बृहत्पराशरसंहिता-वानप्रस्थश्चतुर्भेदो वैखानस उदुम्बरः । बालखिल्यो वनेवासी तल्लक्षणमथोच्यते । वनस्थो बालखिल्यो यो वसेद्वल्कलचीवरम् । अग्निकार्यकृदात्मज्ञो दुर्जातसेवितं त्यजेत् ॥

BHARATA—Father, how do you mean?

SUMANTRA—

Sugrîva, who was residing on the mountain, deprived of his kingdom, and bereft of his wife by Váli, his elder brother, was relieved by the similarly-afflicted (Ráma). (10)

BHARATR—Father, how similarly-afflicted you mean?

SUMANTRA—(*To himself*). Woe! I have told the whole. (*Aloud*). Prince, there was nothing, indeed. I meant similarity in the loss of sovereignty.

BHARATA—Father, why do you hide facts from me? I conjure you by the root of the feet of my father that has gone to heaven, if you will not tell the truth.

SUMANTRA—What help! Listen.

For the sake of the hermits he roused the enmity of the mighty demon; thereupon Sîtâ was carried away by Rávana, having recourse to a deceitful trick. (11)

BHARATA.—How " carried away ", he said?

(*Falls into a swoon*).

SUMANTRA.—Take heart, take heart.

BHARATA —(*Recovering consciousness again*) Oh, alas!

Having suffered great hardships in the forest region, after being separated from his father and relatives, my elder brother, having again come to be separated from his wife, has been divested of his splendour like the moon overcast by a cloud. (12)

Oh, what shall I do? Well, I have seen (what to do). Father should follow me.

SUMANTRA.—As the prince commands.

(Both *walk forth*).

SUMANTRA.—Prince, you should not, indeed, enter, you should not. This is the quadrangle of the queens.

BHARATA.—It is here that my business lies. Who is here at the door?

(*Entering*)

THE FEM.-DOOR-KEEPER.—May the prince be victorious! I am, Vijayâ.

BHARATA.—Vijayá, inform her ladyship of my arrival.

FEM.-DOOR-KEEPER.—To which of the queens shall I communicate it.

BHARATA.—To her who wishes me to be the king.

FEM.-DOOR-KEEPER.—(*To herself.*) What can the matter be? (*Aloud.*) Master, so I will. (*Exit*).

(*Then enter* KAIKEYÎ *and the* FEM.-DOOR-KEEPER).

KAIKEYÎ.—Vijayà, has Bharata come to see me?

FEM.-DOOR-KEEPER.—Mistress, he has. Father Sumantra has come from his visit to prince Ráma. And with him the prince wishes to see your ladyship.

KAIKEYÎ.—(*To herself*) In connection with what matter will Bharata taunt me now?

FEM.-DOOR-KEEPER.—Mistress, may the prince enter?

KAIKEYÎ.—Go, usher him in.

FEM.-DOOR-KEEPER.—Mistress, so I will. (*Having walked forth and approached*). Victory to the prince! You may, indeed, enter.

BHARATA—What! Did you inform her?

FEM.-DOOR-KEEPER—Yes.

BHARATA—Let us enter then.

(Both *enter*).

KAIKEYÎ—Child, Vijayâ tells me that Sumantra has come from Ráma's presence.

BHARATA—I will tell you something more agreeable still.

KAIKEYÎ—Child, should Kausalyá and Sumitrá be called?

BHARATA—It ought not, indeed, to be heard by them.

KAIKEYÎ—(*To herself*) Ha, what can it possibly be? (*Aloud*) Say it, child.

BHARATA—Listen—

Sîta, the wife of him who, having renounced his kingdom, went to the forest at your bidding, is carried away; (so) your object has been fully gained. (13)

KAIKEYI'—Hum !

BHARATA—

Alas! Oh, that the high-souled Ikshvákus, endowed with fortitude, should, on getting you for their daughter-in-law, have their daughter-in-law outraged ! (14)

KAIKEYÎ—(*To herself*) Well, this is the time to tell (him the fact). (*Aloud*) Child, you do not know the curse of (under which laboured) the king.

BHARATA—What ! Was the great king cursed ?

KAIKEYÎ—Sumantra, tell him in detail.

SUMANTRA—As your ladyship commands. Prince, listen. Formerly by the king, when he had gone ahunting, a young ascetic, who was the eye of the great sage (his father) that had lost his eyes, was killed while filling a pot at some lake, through the mistake arising out of the sound (of the pot) resembling the grunting of an elephant, with an arrow that could hit the mark by following the sound.

BHARATA—You say 'was killed'. Heaven forbid ; let the sin be averted ! What next ?

SUMANTRA—Then seeing him in that state,

The sage, whose words were infallible, wept and said—O king, as I do now, so you will also die through grief for your son. (15)

BHARATA—Oh, this is, indeed, painful.

KAIKEYÎ—Child, for this reason, having exposed myself to blame, I sent child Ráma to the forest and not, indeed, through greed for the kingdom. The inevitable curse of the great sage demanded (*lit.* could not have operated without) the separation of a son.

BHARATA—Now, when a son's separation was equal, why was *I* not sent to the forest ?

KAIKEYÎ—Dear child, separation from you who were dwelling in your maternal uncle's house had been familiar (to the king).

BHARATA—Now, why were fourteen years desired?

KAIKEYÎ—Child, desirous of saying fourteen days, I, in my perplexity of heart, said fourteen years.

BHARATA—She has the cleverness to explain it well. Now, was this known to the elderly persons?

SUMANTRA—Prince, it was known to, and approved of, by Vasishtha, Vámadeva and others.

BHARATA—I am glad; these (sages), indeed, are the witnesses (have knowledge) of the three worlds. Fortunately her ladyship is free from guilt. Mother, I blamed your ladyship through anger caused by my love for my brother; all that should be forgiven by you. Mother, I salute you.

KAIKEYÎ—Child, what mother will not, indeed, forgive the fault of her son? And where is the fault in this?

BHARATA—I am beholden to you: I take leave of your ladyship. Even to-day I will get ready the whole circle of kings for the assistance of my noble brother Here shall I now,

Make this shore of the sea closely covered with the camps of my numerous troops, dark with my powerful elephant; and then will reduce the sea, equally with Rávaṇa, to a state of languidity by my forces crossing it. (16)

Ah, I hear something like a sound; quickly let the (cause of) the sound be known.

(Entering)

A FEMALE DOOR-KEEPER—Prosperity to the prince! On hearing this news the eldest queen has fallen into a swoon.

KAIKEYI—Ah!

BHARATA—How has mother fallen into a swoon!

KAIKEYÎ—Come away, child; let us console (or bring back to consciousnes) the noble lady.

BHARATA—As mother commands.

(Excent Omnes).

END OF ACT VI.

जनस्थान.—Lit. the abode of the people—name of the part of the Dandaka forest which was inhabited by men, being the seat of many Ṛishis, whom Rávaṇa and his followers dared not molest for fear of being cursed. *Cf.* ततः प्रभृति काकुत्स्थ दण्डकारण्यमुच्यते । तपस्विनः स्थिता यत्र जनस्थानमतोऽभवत् ॥ Rámá. Uttar. K. IXXXI. 20. It is supposed to be near Nàsik. Some think that it was much lower down the course of the Godavari.

Śl. 21. **बलादेष** &c.—*Cf.* for a similar challenge Abhi. III. 22—अभिभूतो मया राम दारापहरणाद्भसि । यदि तेऽस्ति धनुःश्लाघा दीयतां मे रणो महान् ॥

स्वपक्षपवनो०—पवनोत्क्षेप: the whirling up of the wind. **षण्ड—a** clump or multitude of. **जटायुः**—Vulture king, son of Śyeni and Aruṇa and younger brother of Sampáti. He was a great friend of Daśaratha whose life he had saved on one occasion.

Śl. 22. **निस्त्रिंशः**—A long sword, निर्गतः त्रिंशतः अङ्गुलिभ्यः निस्त्रिंश a Prádi Tat. Comp. **यमसादनं**—सादन for सदन a house, abode is rare.

ACT VI.

P. 71. **वृद्धतापसौ**—The old ascetics are introduced as they have to appeal for help to others for rescusing Sîtá. **भवन्तः**—Voc. pl.; the full sentence being भवन्तः सीता परित्रायतां भवद्भिः ।

Śl. 1. **वर्चस्**—Bodily lustre or complexion. **मृणालशुक्लोज्वल** &c.—This is taken to mean 'Laughing in such a way as to expose the white colour of his jaws &c. But as the epithet applies to a tiger as well it is better to take it to mean मृणालवत् शुक्लवदुज्ज्वलः दंष्ट्रयोः हासः (the white sheen of) अस्त्यस्य. **निशार्धचारिणा**.—one moving out at about midnight. निशार्ध does not mean exact midnight (that would require अर्ध to be placed first, अर्धनिशा); but about midnight. See Pán. IV. 2. 2. **परिभूय**—In the case of Sîtá means—having defied her power of पातिव्रत्य. *Cf.* for this sense को हर्तुमिच्छति हरेः परिभूय दंष्ट्राम् । Mud. I. 8.

Śl. 2. **विचेष्टमाना**—*cf.* विचेष्टमानामादाय उत्पपाताथ रावणः । Ráma. Arany. XLIX. 22. **भुजङ्गमाङ्गना**—Here अङ्गना simply means 'a female'. *Cf.* for the idea नागीव यासि पतगेन्द्रभयाभिभूता । Cháru. I. 11. The comparison indicates that Sítá's high-mindedness did not allow her to bear the insult tamely. **विधूयमानेव**—The second comparison shows Sîtà's delicacy and the extreme impropriety of the act; and hence पापेन. **सिद्धिरिव**—indicates the high reverence in which Sîtá was held even by the male ascetics in the penance-grove. They regarded her as the very fruition of their penance. Bhavabhûti pays a similar tribute to Sîtá's high sanctity when he makes Janaka say विद्यां वागिव यामसूत भवती तद्वत्तु या दैवतं, and even Arundhatî further on-शिशुत्वं स्त्रैणं वा भवतु ननु वन्द्यासि जगतः । Uttar. IV. 5. 11.

आनृण्यं—Freedom from debt; अविद्यमानमृणमस्य सोऽनृणः तस्य भावः आनृण्यम् . **अन्तरिक्षं**—usually अन्तरीक्ष; the space between heaven and earth. It is derived as अन्तः द्यावापृथिव्योर्मध्ये ईक्ष्यते इति; fr. ईक्ष् and अ (घञ् added कर्मणि); another way is अन्तः ऋक्षाणि stars यस्य अन्तारिक्षं a comp. of the पृषोदरादि class. According to Yàska अन्तरा इमे द्यावापृथिव्यौ क्षयति इति; irregularly formed.

क्रव्यादीश्वरः—Jatáyu, the lord of vultures. क्रव्यमाममांसमत्ति इति क्रव्यात् । By क्रव्ये च Pán. III. 2. 69, अद् takes the aff. विट् (०) when it has for its object क्रव्य raw flesh. It means a vulture, a demon, &c.; otherwise अद् will take अ (अण्); as अन्नादः. The form क्रव्यादः is grammatically inaccurate.

Śl. 3. **परिभूय**—Scil. रावणं; having despised, treated with contempt. **वीर्यविषयं**—Requiring valour; it was no ordinary fight. Or this might qualify रावणं understood वीर्यविषयं रावणं; Rávaṇa, the object of his might *i. e.* against whom he had to direct his power. **तुण्डाभ्यां**—*i. e.* by the two parts of his beak. **सुनिघृष्ट०**—Hard scratched; may also be taken adverbially सुनिघृष्टं तीक्ष्णं च यथा स्यात्तथा । **संवेष्टनं**—covering up, grasping; governed by चेष्टते (attempts, endeavours). **तीक्ष्णैः** &c—Construe आयसकण्टकैः इव तीक्ष्णैः नखैः &c. This is meant to show that Jatáyu employed all his three weapons, *viz.* his wings, his beak and his talons. **वक्षसः**—must be taken as ab. singular, the const. being वज्राग्रैः दार्यमाणविषमात् शैलात् शिला इव नखैः दार्यमाणविषमात् (looking ghastly) रावणस्य वक्षसः भीमान्तरं पात्यते. Here the broad chest of Rávaṇa is compared to a mountain side. **पात्यते**—There is a प्रक्रमभङ्ग as the construction suddenly becomes passive.

Śl. 4. **क्रीडामयूरः**—A peacock for sport (made of clay or the like), a mere toy, not even a living peacock—shows the utter contempt with which he treated Rávaṇa's valour. **नागेन्द्रभग्न** &c.—*Cf.* for the idea कथमिह गजराजदन्तभग्नस्तरुरिव यास्यसि पुष्पितो विनाशम् । Mv. 24. **प्रथमः कल्पः**—occurs in Bhâsa's Mv. 1. Sv. IV, Panch, Avi. and Bâla.

P. 73. काञ्चनतोरण०—occurs in Sva. VI. and Abhi. III. कृतार्थः—Having gained his object, *viz.* रामदर्शन. सुमन्त्रागमन०—Of which he was informed by the प्रतिहारी. चीरवल्कल०—Ever since his return to Ayodhyá after seeing Ràma in the forest Bharata wore bark garments and matted hair until Ráma's return from Lanká. चित्रजटा—The hair was matted in various ways not being combed for thirteen years by this time.

Śl. 6. तिग्मांशु—The sun; see com. त्रिदश—त्रिदशाः the gods; तृतीया यौवनाख्या दशा येषां ते, यद्वा तिस्रः जन्मसत्ताविनाशाख्या दशा येषां ते; त्रिर्दश वा Bah. Comp. by Pàn. II. 2. 25. Now see com.

P. 74. उदार—Noble-looking. कलभेभ—कलभश्चासौ इभश्च; कलभ is an elephant thirty years old. पञ्चवर्षो गजो बालः पोतस्तु दशवर्षकः । त्रिंशद्वर्षस्तु कलभो विक्को विंशतिवर्षकः ॥ इति वैजयन्ती.

Śl. 7. गत्वा &c.—The construction is अयमत्रभवान् सुमन्त्रः पूर्वमार्यनिरीक्षणार्थं गत्वा आर्यं दृष्ट्वा इह पुनः आगतः किम् । लब्धप्रसादशपथे—प्रसाद (see *supra* IV. 28) was the gift of Sandals (पादुका) by Ráma, and शपथ (which means a condition समय here) was the solemn promise by him to take over the responsibility of government from Bharata after fourteen years. See *supra* p.p. 58, 59 बुद्धिमनो०—बुद्धि from बुध् to know, the faculty of knowing; people admired Ráma after appreciating his merits and not blindly.

निष्क्रान्तौ.—scil. प्रतिहारी and काञ्चुकीय.

Śl. 8. इह—cannot be taken to mean ' here ' as it will refer to नन्दिग्राम where भरत then was, while he had heard it when in Janasthána. So it may mean ' अधुना now, ' or in this very life अस्मिन्नायुषि. गुण इव &c.—is repeated from IV. 18.

P. 75. लोकाविष्कृत &c.—refers to Ráma. The intended sense is Who showed to the people what affection for a parent should be—how a son ought to reckon that above every other thing. द्विधा भूतं &c.—*i. e.* Sîtá. This is more forcible than अरुन्धतीतुल्यचारित्रा; *cf. supra* V. 8. निष्कारण &c.—*i. e.* Lakshmaṇa. अवहित is used in the sense of 'accepted with due thought, resolutely taken upon himself. सचिन्तास्तिष्ठति—Remained lost in pensive thought and did not give a reply to Bharata. मार्गात्—*i. e.* from midway; without going to your destination.

Śl 9. कृतचेतसां.—कृतं well cultured चेतः येषां, and who, therefore, will never do anything of which they will have to be ashamed.

वनौकस्.—वनमोकः यस्य lit one living in a forest. But when used as a noun, this signifies a monkey (a sense established by usage रूढ); *cf.* Amara मर्कटो वानरः कीशो वनौकाः. पुरुषविशेषाः—Eminent men, men of distinction; or विशेष may be taken to mean 'the special qualities or characteristics of men.' उपकृतमवगच्छन्ति.—The poet makes Sumantra reply to Bharata indirectly, that the latter might ask to know of the nature of the obligation that might have been conferred and thereby the incident of Sîtâ's being carried away by Rávaṇa might be introduced.

Śl. 10. सुग्रीवः—Son of the sun. He was dethroned by his brother Válin. His wife's name was Rumá. शैल—The Rshyamûka mountain.

P. 76. कथं तुल्यदुःखेन—Sumantra inadvertently said तुल्यदुःखेन मोचितः. This roused a suspicion in the mind of Bharata. How could Ráma, who had lost his kingdom only, be तुल्यदुःख? Did he lose his wife also? किं गूहसे &c.—*Cf.* for a parallel रावणः—बिभीषण किं गूहसे। मम खलु प्राणैः शापितः स्याः यदि सत्यं न ब्रूयाः, Abhi. III. स्वर्गं गतेन—गत qualifies महाराज alone; so the whole should have been compounded.

Śl. 11. वैरं &c.—see *supra* V. 7.

Śl. 12. जीमूतचन्द्रः—जीमूतेनावृतः चन्द्रः जीमूतचन्द्रः a comp. of the शाकपार्थिवादि class. जीमूत itself is a comp. of the पृषोदरादि class, being formed of जीवन+मूतः (a bag). प्रभया—Sitá, the source of his delight (brightness) in the forest.

किमिदानीं करिष्ये। भवतु दृष्टम्—On hearing of Sîtá's abduction Bharata thought of doing two things, to make his mother feel the sting of rebuke more acutely by telling her about the incident as calculated to bring delight to her wicked mind, and of going to his brother's rescue. He decides to do the first of these first. देवीनां चतुःशालं—It seems it was customary in ancient times to lodge the queens in a चतुःशाल (a quadrangular building with four halls on the four sides); we have a reference to it in Bhása's Sva., Avi and Châru.; in the Mrch. pp. 26, 70, 135; in the Mál. p. 89, in the Veni. I. p. 13; &c.

P. 77. या मां राजानमि०—This reply, instead of the direct one मम जनन्यै, leads the प्रतिहारी to apprehend that something had cropped up afresh and that Bharata wanted once more to taunt his mother in connection with her demand of the kingdam for her son.

उद्घातेन—उद्घात anything that suddenly turns up, a fresh subject or matter for consideration; an incident. For a different sense, see p. 9 *supra*. अतःपरं—that is, more than the arrival of Sumantra.

P. 78. Śl. 13. तस्य भार्या &c.—This crowning stroke of rebuke must have come upon the poor and unsuspecting Kaikeyi like a stroke of thunderbolt. पर्याप्तस्ते मनोरथः—*Cf.* हन्तेदानीं सकामा तु कैकेयी बान्धवैः सह । Rámá. Arany. XCIX. 29. and Sumantra's words कैकेयि कामाः फलितास्तवेति Ragh. XIII. 59, when Ráma and Laks. tied up their matted hair in Śṛngavera.

इदानीं कालः कथयितुं.—*Cf. supra* देशकाले निवेदयामि p. 46. वनगजबृंहित —As हेषा signifies a horse's neighing, so बृंहित is the special term for an elephant's sound (बृंहितं करिगर्जितं Ak.). *Cf.* Rámá. अथान्धकारे त्वश्रौषं जले कुम्भस्य पूर्यतः । अचक्षुर्विषये घोषं वारणस्येव नर्दतः ॥ ततोहं शरमुद्धृत्य दीप्तमाशीविषोपमम् । शब्दं प्रति गजप्रेप्सुरभिलक्ष्यमपातयम् ॥ Ayod. LXIII. 22, 23; and तत्र स द्विरदबृंहितशङ्की शब्दपातिनमिषुं विससर्ज । Ragh. IX. 73.

P. 79. Śl. 15. *Cf.* the śl. from the Rámá. quoted in the com. पुत्रको रामः—Mark the change in the wording-Poor Ráma. अपरिहरणीयो मुनिशापः &c.—This defence of Kaikeyî's conduct at first sight seems to be weak. For the question will be-Why was she so anxious that the curse should be fulfilled ? If the son's separation was to bring about the king's death she should have prolonged it by delaying that separation and allowing the curse to take its course as it may. But if we go deep into the matter we shall see Kaikeyī's point. The wording of the curse was 'पुत्रशोकाद्विपत्स्यते । Now पुत्रशोक would be caused by the son's separation or son's death; and if the curse were allowed its own course by allowing Ráma to sit on the throne and the king to return to the forest, it might occasion the son's death and thereby lead to the king's death as in the case of the sage whose son was killed. Fearing the latter catastrophe Kaikeyî chose the lesser of the two evils, as the king was already old, and sent Ráma into exile. And this was approved of by Vasishtha and others, as we shall see further on.

कथमहम०—Mark Bharata's nobility of mind and also power to harass his mother by such pointed questions. प्रकृतीभूतः—Lit. become one with his nature; he was familiarized with it and would not have felt pain at it. अवेक्षितानि—Looked to, desired; not a good reading; अपेक्षितानि would have been better. पर्याकुलहृदयया

&c.—This her defence is not satisfactory. The question remains—why did she not correct her mistake afterwards on realising what difference it would make to Ráma. There is another reading चतुर्दशदिवसा इति मया उक्तम् । पर्याकुलहृदयया मन्थरया चतुर्दश वर्षाणीत्युक्तम् । This somewhat absolves Kaikeyî from the blame. But where was the reason for Mantharà to be पर्याकुलहृदया. It was she who had deliberately advised Kaikeyi to make the demand. Again how did Kaikeyî know that Mantharà was पर्या० when she was not there with Mantharà. (see *supra* 1. 7). **वसिष्टवाम०**—This is an invention of the poet. There is nothing about this in the Rámáyaṇa. **विचारयितुं**—seems to have been used in its literal Cau sense 'to divert a matter (to the right point), to explain away. Or it may mean 'to think properly,' and then it will refer to her sending away Ràma as stated above.

P. 80. **आपृच्छामि**—should be आपृच्छे; as already remarked.

Śl. 16. **वेलामिमां**—Bharata speaks of the shore of the southern ocean as present before his eyes. This śl. contains the figure of speech called सहोक्ति.

ACT. VII.

P. 81. **कुलपतिः**—see *supra* p. 67. **विज्ञापयति**—is used out of courtesy instead of आज्ञापयति. **त्रैलोक्यविद्रावणं**—This passage is full of alliteraions. **विद्रावणं**—Rávaṇa was so called because of his frightful voice. *Cf.* Rámá. यस्माल्लोकत्रयं चैतद्रावितं भयमागतम् । तस्मात्त्वं रावणो नाम नाम्ना वीरो भविष्यसि ॥ and दिव्यास्त्रः सुरदैत्यदानवचमूविद्रावणं रावणम् । Abhi. II. 10. **देवदेवर्षिसिद्ध०**—for comp. see com.; सिद्ध proved; or a class of demi-gods. पिशाचो गुह्यकः सिद्धो भूतोऽमी देवयोनयः । Amara. **कुलपतिः प्रमाणं**—*i. e.* Kual. should manage to feed them.

P. 82. **बिभीषणवि०**—obedient to, under the control of Bhibháshena; and Bibhî. is against man-eating.

Śl. 1. **जेयः**—जेतुं योग्यः जेयः. **द्वितीयः**—The first being Rávaṇa, the most formidable one, a second can be easily conquered.

एकातपत्रा—Marked with one umbrella of white silk, the badge of universal sovereignty. *Cf.* एकातपत्रं जगतः प्रभुत्वम् । Ragh. II. 47; Svap. VI. 19; Av. I. 1.; Bal. V. 20.

मिश्रवि०.—मिश्र because नन्दिलक is a नीचपात्र as he speaks in Prákrit.

Śl. 2. **समुदित**.—Risen high, great; *cf.* रूपश्रिया समुदितां Svap. V. 2. **गुणसमग्रा**.—समग्र what has a prominet point, and thereby attracts attention; hence distinguished by or conspicuous for. **मुनिजनवनवासं**.—Here evidently Ráma refers to the residence of the hermits in Janasthána, which is therefore, the place of action of this scene. See *infra* मैथिलि अपि जानासि &c. p. 83. This is a departure from the account of Ráma's journey back to Ayodhyá as given in the Rámá, according to which he halted for a day before going to Ayodhyà, in the hermitage of the sage Bharadwája at Prayága, in order to learn how things were going on in Ayodhyà—whether it was in a prosperous condition, being free from epidemics, &c. *Cf.* पूर्णे चतुर्दशे वर्षे पञ्चम्यां लक्ष्मणाग्रजः । भरद्वाजाश्रमं प्राप्य ववन्दे नियतो मुनिम् ॥ सोऽपृच्छदभिवाद्यैनं भरद्वाजं तपोधनम् । शृणोषि कच्चिद्भगवन्सुभिक्षानामयं पुरे ॥ Yudh. ch. 124, 1, 2, &c. True that Ráma referred to Janasthána, Chitrakûta, and other places, but that was while flying through the car Pushpaka.

Śl. 3. **यथावयः**—वयः अनतिक्रम्य यथा तथा according to their ages. **स्निग्धतरं**.—अतिशयेन स्निग्धं very affectionately. Sîtá is addressed in four ways, but the degree of affection is the same in all.

P. 83. **कुटुम्बिकः**—कुटुम्बमतस्यस्य; also कुटुम्बी; a house-holder or a married man; a husband. **पुत्रकृतकाः**—see *supra* V. 11.

०पत्रकाः—पत्रकाणि tender, newly sprung up, leaves; which were saplings. This refers to the first year of their residence in Janasthána. The trees had grown to a great height in 14 years. **निम्नस्थलोत्पादकः**—निम्न depressed or low ground, a pit. स्थल—raised or elevated ground. As a direct remark on Sîtá's speech this means—Time turns a low spot into a high ground; makes small things great. It may, however, be taken as a general observation also. Time gives rise to a high ground where there was a pit and produces depressions where there was high ground; makes small things great and great things small. *Cf.* for a similar use क्षितितल प्रच्छन्ननिम्नस्थलं Avi. IV. 11. The usual expression is निम्नोन्नत (see Śak. IV. 15).

उपलभ्यते.—is used in the sense of 'do you call to memory?' lit. is brought within the reach of memory. **भरतं दृष्ट्वा**.—This is also a deviation from the Rámà.; Bharata came to see Ráma when he was on the mountain Chitrkûta and not in

Janasthána. *Cf.* Ráma, असौ सुतनु शैलेन्द्रश्चित्रकूटः प्रकाशते ॥ ४९ ॥ अत्र मां कैकयीपुत्रः प्रसादयितुमागतः । Yud. Ch. 124. **मा खलु एवं भणितुं**—A grammatical irregularity. मा is treated like अलं; *cf. supra* अलं व्रणे प्रहर्तुं p. 56.

P. 84. **संमूर्छितः**—grown strong, deepened. **नगरीकरोति.**—*Cf.* कोयं भो निभृतं तपोवनमिदं ग्रामीकरोत्याज्ञया । Svap. I. 3, and किमर्थमिदानीं भवान् क्षितितलं देवलोकीकरोति । Avi. IV.

एष्टव्ये काले—*Cf. supra* रोदितव्ये काले I. p. 18, श्लाघनीये काले p. 20.

Śl. 6. **प्रवृद्धविषयैः**—विषय scope, province, प्रवृ° grown in magnitude, *cf.* क्षीणविषयाः *supra* III. 2. **विषम**—what is uneven; hence an adverse state, calamity. **तुष्टहृदयः**—Because Ráma had returned safe and would now take back the kingdom.

P. 85. **आर्यपुत्रेण चिरसंचारी भव**—Mark the blessing which was the fittest on the occasion as Ráma was to stay in Ayodhyà now. **कथमिव**—Ráma asks the question, because although Bharata had made a condition with him to that effect, still it required the sanction of his mother, who was there actually present, and he did not know how she would take it. Kaikeyî understands this and says चिरमभि° &c.

P. 86. **एतौ वसिष्ठ°**—See *supra* p. 47, where the two Ṛshis appear with the same object. **रामः**—निष्क्रान्तः—Ráma goes alone for the coronation because the sages had manifested their desire to see *him* after being crowned.

जयतु भवान् &c.—Such exclamations appear in Abhi. VI. also on a similar occasion.

भो भो जनस्थानवासिनः तपस्विनः &c.—The same sages are addressed here to show to them that Râma had accepted the challenge thrown out to him in their hearing by Rávaṇa when carrying way Sîtà from Janasthána and proved his martial spirit and mettle by the destruction of the demon.

Śl. 10. **तमौघं**—The Sandhi is irregular; it ought to be तम ओघं. The insult offered to Ráma and his kinsmen by Rávaṇa is fitly compared to a mass of तमस् as it had cast a deep gloom on their faces. *Cf. supra* VI. 14.

P. 85. **स्वर्गेपि**—The force of अपि is—even though heaven is full of delight, where nothing is to be wished for. **सत्कृतभारवाही**—(1) सत्कृतं भारं वहतीति—bearing the honourable burden *i. e.* office of the king; (2) सत्कृतानां of the pious or virtuous; or, (सत् कृतं कृत्यं येषां तेषां) honoured ones तेषां भारं the responsibility of protection.

धर्मेण लोक०—For क्षात्रियस्य परो धर्मः प्रजानां परिपालनम् । *Cf.* नृपस्य वर्णाश्रमपालनं यात् स एव धर्मो मनुना प्रणीतः । Ragh. XIV. 67.

Śl. 12. **विकसितकृतमौलि**—विकसित (1) full blown flowers; or (2) bright. **विलसित** *v. l.* विलसितः कृतः धारितः G. S. Both the readings are not satisfactory. **लीला**—dignity or grace (of a king). **नवशशिनं**—The new moon is an object of curiosity and is eagerly looked at by the people. *Cf.* नेत्रैः पपुस्तृप्तिमनाप्नुवद्भिर्नवोदयं नाथमिवौषधीनाम् । Ragh. II. 73. प्रतिपच्चन्द्रमिव प्रजा नृपम् । Kir. II. 11.

Śl. 13. **नष्टकल्मषं**--कल्मष sin, fault or infamy. Had Bharata been installed instead of Ráma, the rightful heir, he would have been like a परिवेत्तृ (the younger brother marrying before the elder brother); *cf.* स हि प्रथमजे तस्मिन्नकृतश्रीपरिग्रहे । परिवेत्तारमात्मानं मेने स्वीकरणाद्भुवः ॥ Ragh. XII. 18. see Ayod. LXXII. 22.

P. 88. **वर्धते**—The subject to this is रामः understood. **सम्प्राप्तं** &c.—For the description of पुष्पक see Rámá. Yud. ch. 121 śl. 23-29. **रावणस्य**--It properly belonged to Kubera. *Cf.* पुष्पकं नाम भद्रं ते विमानं सूर्यसंनिभम् । मम भ्रातुः कुबेरस्य रावणेन बलीयसा ॥ हृतं निर्जित्य संग्रामे कामगं दिव्यमुत्तमम् । Yud. K. ch. 121. 9, 10.

Śl. 14. **चन्द्रं सनक्षत्रमिव**—The stars correspond with the kinsmen and friends. **उदयस्थं**—उदय--(1) rise *i. e.* sovereignty;—seated on the throne; (2) the rising mountain. **भरतवाक्य**—The concluding stanza of a drama, containing a benediction and thus called being pronounced by the Bharatas or actors in their own capacity.

Śl. 15. **राजा भूमिं प्रशास्तु नः**—The king is not named. This line with some variations as राजसिंहः प्रशास्तु नः, भूमिमेकः प्रशास्तु नः occurs in Svap. and several other plays of Bhása.

Correctons &c.

P. 13. l. 5. Alter (कृवा निर्वण्य) read तिष्ठ ।

P. 20. l. 5. read मैथिलि.

P. 24. l. 7. Read सत्यवचनरक्षणपरः .

P. 26. Com. last two lines—Read अनपत्याः किं न कृताः । रामः... पुत्रः किं न कृतः । कैकेयी वने व्याघ्री किं न कृता ।

P. 30. l. 6. Read सुमित्रा for सुमन्त्रा

P. 31. Śl. 17. Read चिरं for चिर

P. 52. l. 2. Read त्वार्यास्याभं

P. 34. l. 15. Read प्रतिमातेहं.

P. 65. l. 10. Read पितुंस्त०

P. 66. l. 24. Com. Read वैखानसाः वानप्रस्थभेदाः । and after ऋषिविशेषाः किं तु तेऽत्र नाभिप्रेताः । अत्र वानप्रस्थविशेषा कवेरभिमताः ।

APPENDICES.

I

Peculiar words and expressions occurring in the Play.

ACT. I.

Word	Page
राज्यप्रभावसंयोग	4
सनन्दिपटह	4
पुष्यरथ	5
प्रह्वषितानि तनूरुहाणि	7
प्रियाख्यानिकं	8
विशालतरमुत्संगं कुरु	8
also विशालीक्रियतां चक्षुः	53, 84.
अवघट्टित	9
उद्घात	9, also 77
स्कन्धोच्चारण	9
एकप्रकारसंक्षिप्त	11, 14
प्रत्यग्रावतारित	12
उपहतासु स्त्रीबुद्धिषु	15
शुल्के विपणितं	16
शताकीर्णं	17
स्वजननिभृत	17
रोदितव्ये काले	18
शाच्यासने नृपे	18
निर्मनस्विता	18
धनुःश्लाघा	18
दोषेषु बाह्यं	19
रोषणाय रुचिरं	19
राहुदोषे	20
निर्योग, मत्सरी	21
अनुयात्र	23, also 60.
शिरःस्थानानि	23

ACT. II.

Word	Page
उपावर्तयितुं	24
अप्रमेय, शिथिलदेहमतिः	24
अरण्यानि स्वाधीनानि	30
बहुवल्कलालंकृतशरीरा	30
हृदयातुरौषधैः	30

ACT. III.

Word	Page
राज्यविभ्रष्ट, कपोतसंदानक	34, 48.
सौधवर्णकदत्तचन्दनपञ्चाङ्गुल	35
मातुलपरिचयात्, अकल्यशरीरः	35
आहारं भुंक्ते	35
उद्धृत्ताम्बु, सोपस्नेहतया	36
त्वरता, व्यायतः, सेवा	36
देवकुल, उपोपविश्य	37
साधुमुक्त, आह्निकमास्तिक्यं	30
क्रियामाधुर्यं; भावगतिः	38
दैवतोद्दिष्टानां, मानुषताविश्वासः	38
स्तोमः, वार्षलः प्रणामः	38
नैत्यक, प्राणिधर्म, अल्पान्तराकृतिः	38
वक्तव्यं, नियमप्रभविष्णुता	39
अभिसरी, अनवासिताः	39
संवेशन, धरमाण	40
शुल्कशब्दः, देहो विशोध्यः	41
शुल्कदोषं, तद्वैर्येण	42
प्रतिमानृप, वयः स्थः, समुदाचार—संनिकर्ष	43
चिरजीवद्दोष, अतिसन्धित	44
समुदाचारमध्यस्थः, शीलसंक्रान्तदोषैः	45
शुल्कलुब्धा, नृपफलतर्षः	46
असुभिर्नैव गणितः	46

IV

VI

VII

II.

Grammatical irregularities, peculiar constructions &c.

I.

नाटकीयानां विज्ञापय 5
मा स्वयं मन्युमुत्पाद्य 14
अलमुपहतासु स्त्रीबुद्धिषु स्वमार्जवमुपनिक्षेप्तुम् 15
नियतीव 18
धनुर्नमयि 19
देवतानां प्रणामः 20

II.

अलमिदानीं महाराजोऽतिमात्रं सन्तप्य परवशमात्मानं कर्तुम् । 27
विश्रमिष्ये 37
पृच्छसे 41
परशङ्कामलं कर्तुं 43
अभिवादनक्रममुपदेष्टुमिच्छामि । 44

IV.

अलं गुरुजनापवादमभिधातुम् 50
इदमपि तावदात्माभिप्रायमनुवर्तयितुमिच्छसि । 53
रमयति 55
शुश्रूषयिष्ये, शुश्रूषयतु 56
राज्यं प्रतिग्रहीतुमिच्छामि । 58

V.

पूजां सानुरूपां 66
आपृच्छ (also VI) पुत्रकान् , अर्हत्येष हि पूजायां 67

VII.

आर्यपुत्र मा खलु एवं भणितुम् । 83
रिपुप्रभवं तमौघम् । 86

III.

The Metres used in the Play, their Definitions and Schemes.

1. Sanskrit verse is regulated by quantity, and not, as in English, by accent. A पद्य (stanza) consists usually of four पाद्s (quarters). A पाद् is regulated either by the number of syllables (अक्षरs), or of syllabic instants (मात्राs). When the पाद्s are all similar, it is called a समवृत्त, to which type most of the metres conform. There are अर्धसमवृत्तs, wherein the first quarter corresponds to the third, and the second to the fourth, called respectively the *odd* (विषम) and *even* (सम) quarters. A third class comprises विषमवृत्तs, but these are very seldom used.

2. The vowels अ, इ, उ, ऋ and ऌ are short, and the rest long. The quantity of a syllable is determined by its vowel. A syllable with a short vowel is called लघु ('light'), and a syllable with a long vowel is called गुरु ('heavy'). But a लघु syllable is considered as गुरु if it is followed by an *anusvára*, or a *visarga*, or a conjunct consonant, or when it comes at the end of a पाद्.[1]

3. A set of three successive syllables is called a गण (foot). Marking a short syllable as ◡ and a long one as —, the different गणs,[2] which are 8 in number, may be exhibited as follows:—य ◡ — —; र — ◡ —; त — — ◡; भ — ◡ ◡; ज ◡ — ◡; स ◡ ◡ —; म — — —; and न ◡ ◡ ◡. In the definitions which are given below, a short syllable is indicated by the letter ल and a long one by ग.

N. B. The यति or caesura (pause) is marked by a comma splitting up the syllables of a metre; *e. g.* शालिनी (4, 7) *syllable, i. e.* the voice may rest on the 4th syll.

This play is richer in verse than the Svap-, there being in it 158 Ślokas in all in 16 different metres. Of these, however, 75 are in the अनुष्टुप् or epic metre alone. Vasantatilaká claims 22.

---

1 सानुस्वारश्च दीर्घश्च विसर्गी च गुरुर्भवेत् ।
वर्णः संयोगपूर्वश्च तथा पादान्तगोऽपि वा ॥

2 आदिमध्यावसानेषु य-र-ता यान्ति लाघवम् ।
भ-ज-सा गौरवं यान्ति म-नौ तु गुरुलाघवम् ॥

अनुष्टुभ् (also called श्लोक)—श्लोके षष्ठं गुरुज्ञेयं सर्वत्र लघुपञ्चमम् । द्विचतुः—पादयोर्ह्रस्वं सप्तमं दीर्घमन्ययोः ॥ This has many varieties but the one defined above is most common. The sixth syllable in each páda must be long and the fifth short. The seventh is short in the second and the fourth padas and long in the first and third. The ślokas in this metre which are 75 in number can be easily distinguished and are not given here.

आर्या—यस्याः पादे प्रथमे द्वादशमात्रास्तथा तृतीयेपि । अष्टादशद्वितीये चतुर्थके पञ्चदश सार्या ॥ The four pádas contain respectively 12, 18, 12 and 15 Mátrás.

I. 2; II. 7.

इन्द्रवज्रा—स्यादिन्द्रवज्रा यदि तौ जगौ गः । 11 (5, 6) syllables; sch. ततज गग.

I. 29; IV. 25, VII. 14.

उपजाति—A mixture (of one or two pádas) of इन्द्रवज्रा and उपेन्द्रवज्रा; उपेन्द्रवज्रा जतजास्ततो गौ । 11 (5, 6) syllables; sch. जतज गग.

I. 1, III. 3, 4, 16; IV. 9, 13; V. 3, 4, 5; VI. 16; VII. 3.

शालिनी—मात्तौ गौ चेच्छालिनी वेदलोकैः । 11 (4, 7) syllables; sch. म त त ग ग.

II. 13; III. 19; V. 17.

वंशस्थ (also called वंशस्थविल) जतौ तु वंशस्थमुदीरितं जरौ । 12 (5, 7) syllables. Sch. जतजर.

III. 14; IV. 20; VI. 1, 2.

पुष्पिताग्रा—अयुजिनयुगरेफतो यकारो युजि च नजौ जरगाश्च पुष्पिताग्रा। 1 and 3rd quarter, 12 syllables; sch. ननरय. 2 & 4th, 13 syllables; sch. न ज ज र ग.

II. 21. IV. 18; V. 19; VI. 8.

प्रहर्षिणी—म्याशाभिर्मनजरगाः प्रहर्षिणीयम् । 13 (3, 10) syllables; sch. मनजरग. ।

I. 30; IV. 6; V. 18.

वसन्ततिलका—उक्ता वसन्ततिलका तभजा जगौ गः । 14 (8,6) syllables; sch. त भ ज ज ग ग.

I, 7, 8, 22; II. 1, 4; IV. I, 2, 16, 22, 24; V. 10, 11; VI. 4, 6, 7. 12; VII. 4, 6, 7, 9, 10, 11.

मालिनी—ननमयययुतेयं मालिनी भोगिलोकैः । 15 (8, 7) syllables; sch. न न म य य.

I. 14, 25; III. 10, 22; IV. 10, 21; V. 7; VII. 1, 2, 12.

शिखरिणी—रसै रुद्रैश्छिन्ना यमनसभला गः शिखरिणी । 17 (6, 11) syllables; sch. य म न स भ ल ग.

II. 14; III. 1, 2, 22; IV. 7.

हरिणी—नसमरसला गः षड्वेदैर्हयैर्हरिणी मता । 17 (6, 4, 7) syllables, sch. न स म र स ल ग.

I. 18, III. 18; IV. 8; V. 2.

शार्दूलविक्रीडितं—सूर्याश्वैर्यदि मः सजौ सततगाः शार्दूलविक्रीडितम् । 19 (12, 7) syllables; sch. म स ज स त त ग.

I. 3, 5; II. 2, 19; IV. 23, 27; V. 1, 16; VI. 3.

सुवदना—ज्ञेया सप्ताश्वषड्भिर्मरभनययुता भ्लौगः सुवदना । 20 (7, 7, 6) syllables; sch. म र भ न य भ ल ग.

III. 8, 12.

स्रग्धरा—म्रभ्नौ यानां त्रयेण त्रिमुनियतियुता स्रग्धरा कीर्तितेयम् । 21 (7, 7, 7) syllables; sch. म र भ न य य य.

IV. 17.

IV
Stanzas attributed to Bhása in the Anthologies.

सदुक्तिकर्णामृते

दग्धे मनोभवतरौ बालाकुचकुम्भसंभृतैरमृतैः ।
त्रिवलीकृतालवाला जाता रोमावली वल्ली ॥
विरहिवनितावक्त्रौपम्यं बिभर्ति निशापति-
र्गलितविभवस्याज्ञेवाद्य द्युतिर्मसृणा रवेः ।
अभिनववधूरोषस्वादुः करीषतनूनपा-
दसरलजनाश्लेषक्रूरस्तुषारसमीरणः ॥
प्रत्यासन्नविवाहमङ्गलविधौ देवार्चनव्यग्रया
दृष्ट्वाग्रे परिणेतुरेव लिखितां गङ्गाधरस्याकृतिम् ।
उन्मादस्मितरोमलज्जितरसैर्गौर्या कथंचिच्चिरा-
द्बद्धः स्त्रीवचनात्प्रिये विनिहितः पुष्पांजलिः पातु वः ॥

शार्ङ्गधरपद्धतौ

पेया सुरा प्रियतमामुखमीक्षणीयं
ग्राह्यः स्वभावललितो विकटश्च वेषः ।
येनेदमीदृशमदृश्यत मोक्षवर्त्म
दीर्घायुरस्तु भगवान् स पिनाकपाणिः ॥
तीक्ष्णं रविस्तपति नीच इवाचिराढ्यः
शृङ्गं रुरुस्त्यजति मित्रमिवाकृतज्ञः ।
तोयं प्रसीदति मुनेरिव चित्तमन्तः
कामी दरिद्र इव शोषमुपैति पङ्कः ॥
कपोले मार्जारः पय इति कराँल्लेढि शशिन-
स्तरुच्छिद्रप्रोतान्बिसमिति करी संकलयति ।
रतान्ते तल्पस्थान् हरति वनिताप्यंशुकमिति
प्रभामत्तश्चन्द्रो जगदिदमहो विप्लवयति ॥
अस्या ललाटे रचिता सखीभिर्विभाव्यते चन्दनपत्रलेखा ।
आपाण्डुरक्षामकपोलभित्तावनङ्गबाणव्रणपङ्क्तिकेव ॥
दयिताबाहुपाशस्य कुतोऽयमपरो विधिः ।
जीवयत्यर्पितः कण्ठे मारयत्यपवर्जितः ॥

सुभाषितावल्याम्

बाला च सा विदितपञ्चशरप्रपञ्चा
तन्वी च सा स्तनभरोपचिताङ्गयष्टिः ।
लज्जां समुद्वहति सा सुरतावसाने
हा कापि सा किमिव किं कथयामि तस्याः ॥

कठिणहृदये मुञ्च क्रोधं सुखप्रतिघातकं
लिखति दिवसं यातं यातं यमः किल मानिनि ।
वयसि तरुणे नैतद्युक्तं चले च समागमे
भवति कलहो यावत्तावद्वरं सुभगे रतम् ॥
कृतककृतकैर्मायासख्यैस्त्वयास्म्यतिवञ्चिता
निभृतनिभृतैः कार्यालापैर्मयाप्युपलक्षितम् ।
भवतु विदितं नेष्टाहं ते वृथा किमु खिद्यसे
ह्यहमसहना त्वं निःस्नेहः समेन समं गतम् ॥
दुःखार्ते मयि दुःखिता भवति या हृष्टे प्रहृष्टा तथा
दीने दैन्यमुपैति रोषपरुषे पथ्यं वचो भाषते ।
कालं वेत्ति कथाः करोति निपुणा मत्संस्तवे रज्यति
भार्या मन्त्रिवरः सखा परिजनः सैका बहुत्वं गता ॥

सूक्तिमुक्तावल्याम्

यदपि विबुधैः सिन्धोरन्तः कथंचिदुपार्जितं
तदपि सकलं चारुस्त्रीणां मुखेषु विलोक्यते ।
सुरसुमनसः श्वासामोदे शशी च कपोलयो-
रमृतमधरे तिर्यग्भूते विषं च विलोचने ॥

The following is added by Kuppuswàmi Shástri M. A., of Presidency College, Madras, as mentioned in the अभिनवभारती of अभिनवगुप्त.

त्रेतायुगं तद्धि न मैथिली सा रामस्य रागपदवी मृदु चास्य चेतः ।
लब्धा जनस्य यदि रावण यस्य कायं प्रोत्कृत्य तन्न तिलशो न वितृप्तिगामी ।

V

Ayodhyà as described in the Ràmáyaṇa.

कोसलो नाम मुदितः स्फीतो जनपदो महान् ।
अयोध्या नाम नगरी तत्रासील्लोकविश्रुता ॥ १ ॥
आयता दश च द्वे च योजनानि महापुरी ।
श्रीमती त्रीणि विस्तीर्णा सुविभक्तमहापथा ॥ २ ॥
राजमार्गेण महता सुविभक्तेन शोभिना ।
मुक्तपुष्पावकीर्णेन जलसिक्तेन नित्यशः ॥ ३ ॥
कपाटतोरणवतीं सुविभक्तान्तरापणाम् ।
सर्वयन्त्रायुधवतीमुषितां सर्वशिल्पिभिः ॥ ४ ॥
सूतमागधसंबाधां श्रीमतीमतुलप्रभाम् ।
उच्चाट्टालध्वजवतीं शतघ्नीशतसंकुलाम् ॥ ५ ॥

---

१ शतघ्न्यो नाम प्राकारसंरक्षणार्थमयोभारानिर्मिताः प्राकारोपरिस्थापिता आयुधविशेषाः ।

वधूनाटकसंघैश्च संयुक्तां सर्वतः पुरीम् ।
उद्यानाम्रवणोपेतां महतीं सालमेखलाम् ॥ ६ ॥
दुर्गगम्भीरपरिखां दुर्गामन्यैर्दुरासदाम् ।
वाजिवारणसम्पूर्णां गोभिरुष्ट्रैः खरैस्तथा ॥ ७ ॥
सामन्तराजसंघैश्च बलिकर्मभिरावृताम् ।
नानादेशनिवासैश्च वणिग्भिरुपशोभिताम् ॥ ८ ॥
प्रासादै रत्नविकृतैः पर्वतैरिव शोभिताम् ।
कूटागारैश्च संपूर्णामिन्द्रस्येवामरावतीम् ॥ ९ ॥
चित्रामष्टापदाकारां वरनारीगणायुताम् ।
सर्वरत्नसमाकीर्णां विमानगृहशोभिताम् ॥ १० ॥
गृहगाढामविच्छिद्रां समभूमौ निवेशिताम् ।
शालितण्डुलसम्पूर्णामिक्षुकाण्डरसोदकाम् ॥ ११ ॥
दुन्दुभीभिर्मृदङ्गैश्च वीणाभिः पणवैस्तथा ।
नादितां भृशमत्यर्थं पृथिव्यां तामनुत्तमाम् ॥ १२ ॥
विमानमिव सिद्धानां तपसाधिगतं दिवि ।
सुनिवेशितवेश्मान्तां नरोत्तमसमावृताम् ॥ १३ ॥
ये च बाणैर्न विध्यन्ति विविक्तमपरापरम् ।
शब्दवेध्यं च विततं लघुहस्ता विशारदाः ॥ १४ ॥
तादृशानां सहस्रैस्तामभिपूर्णां महारथैः ।
पुरीमावासयामास राजा दशरथस्तदा ॥ १५ ॥
तामग्निमद्भिर्गुणवद्भिरावृतां द्विजोत्तमैर्वेदषडङ्गपारगैः ।
सहस्रदैः सत्यरतैर्महात्मभिर्महर्षिकल्पैरृषिभिश्च केवलैः ॥ १६ ॥

Ayodhyá as seen by Sumantra on his return after Ráma's departure to the forest as described by the author of the Udárarághava.

पश्चमेहि विनिवृत्य सुमन्त्रः प्राविशत्पुरमुदश्रुरयोध्याम् ।
रामलक्ष्मणविनिर्गमदूनां द्यामिव द्युमणिचन्द्रविहीनाम् ॥ १ ॥
राजहंसरहितामिव वापीं रत्नदीपरहितामिव शालाम् ।
स्वर्णदीमिव सुरद्विपशून्यां वीतकोकिलशुकामिव वन्याम् ॥ २ ॥
हीनहेषितविषण्णतुरंगामस्तबृंहितसमस्तगजेन्द्राम् ।
लुप्तसर्जरसगुग्गुलधूपां मन्दिरोज्झितमहामणिदीपाम् ॥ ३ ॥
देहलीष्वनिहिताक्षतसूनां शान्तदेवगृहनर्तनगानाम् ।
वीतरागवनिताकरतालत्यक्तनृत्यमदमत्तमयूराम् ॥ ४ ॥ सप्तमः सर्गः ।

---

१ अष्टापदं सुवर्णं तज्जलेन कृत आकारोऽलंकारो यस्याः। इत्येके। द्यूतफलकाकाराम्। इत्यन्ये। विमानगृहं सप्तभूमि गृहम्। रा० टी०.

A glossary of important words occurring in the play.

अंशुक २
अकल्यशरीर ३५
अकार्य १५
अंकुश २२
अतिक्रान्त ४०
अतिमनोरथ ६७
अतिसंधित ४४
अत्याहित ५,४८
अनुकम्पा २६
अनुक्रोशय् ६१
अनुनय ११
अनुयात्र २३,४९,६८
अनुवृत्ति २०,६४
अपवाद ५०
अप्रतिहत ४
अन्तःपुर ३४,४८
अन्वास्यमान ४४
अप्रमेय २४
अपवाद ५०
अभिलष ८६
अभिसरी-रि ३९,५५
अयन्त्रित ४३
अर ३६
अरविन्द ८६
अर्णव २९
अलीक १०,१३
अवगुण्ठन २२
अवघट्टित ८.
अवभृथ ४०
अवसक्त ३५,३८
अवसन्न ७२
अवसान २७,३८
अवसित ३९
अवस्थाकुटुम्बिनी ६१
अवहित ७५
असम्बद्ध २६
आकीर्ण १७
आकुल २२
आगम ६५
आतुर ३०
आनृण्य ७१
आपृच्छ् ४१,६७
आबन्ध् १२,१४
आर्जव १५
आवर्त ६१
आवर्तिन् ६६
आस्तिक्य ३८
आह्निक ३८
उच्चारण ९
उच्छ्वसित १०
उज्झित १३
उत्तमाङ्ग ७३
उत्तरीय २३
उदय ८८
उदर्क १५,३६
उद्घात ९,७७
उद्दिष्ट ३८
उद्वृत्ताम्बु ३६
उपक्रान्त २८
उपरत ४१
उपसृत १६
उपहृत १५,५१ (अनुप०)
उपहार ६१
उपावर्तय् २४
उल्लोकयितव्य ८२
ऋक्ष ८१